PASSION'S AWAKENING

"After all the things Webb has stolen from me, wouldn't it be fitting justice if I stole something from him? Something . . . special?" Cole spoke softly as his hand caressed Christina's cheek.

His fingertip trailed down her chin to her throat. It paused a moment, then moved lower. At that instant she felt nothing but the fingertip and the exact spot where it touched her skin. She looked into Cole's eyes, but his gaze was following the slow progress of his finger as it moved down her slender neck.

Finally, he looked straight into her eyes and whispered, "Damn you." And then he kissed her.

Christina gasped softly when Cole's lips touched her own. She felt dizzily, wildly alive. She pressed against him, not sure if she was kissing him as she should be, only knowing that every nerve in her body was singing with passion. In that instant Christina realized she wasn't a child any longer. Her girlish fantasies of chaste kisses from chivalrous knights had been transformed into a reality she could not deny. Cole Jurrell wasn't a dream, he was a man of flesh and blood . . . and desire . . .

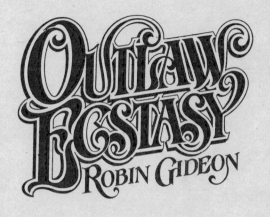

OUTLAW ECSTASY

ROBIN GIDEON

ZEBRA BOOKS
KENSINGTON PUBLISHING CORP.

ZEBRA BOOKS

are published by

Kensington Publishing Corp.
475 Park Avenue South
New York, NY 10016

First printing: April, 1989

Printed in the United States of America

For Shannon and Mary Lou, Mike and Darleen . . .
And for Jennifer, with my love.
rg

Chapter 1

"I want all of us out of there within three minutes," Colton "Cole" Jurrell said, looking at the three men who constituted the infamous, much-feared, and much-written about Jurrell gang. "We start losing odds if we're in there longer than that."

"Yeah, yeah, yeah," Bobby replied in a bored tone, shaking his head. "You've told us that a thousand times."

"It's important." Cole turned cold gray eyes on Bobby. Of the three men in the gang, Bobby was the only one Cole didn't trust completely. Bobby wasn't like the other two, Hans Vogel or Jackie Day. Both of them had lost their family farms to Nicholas Webb. Bobby was driven by different motives, motives that Cole could only speculate about, like Bobby's last name.

Cole continued speaking to all three men, but he looked straight into Bobby's slightly mocking gaze. "We get in there, we get the Webb payroll cash box, and we get out. In and out as quick as possible."

"Just like bad sex," Bobby murmured. He drew soft snickers from Hans and Jackie.

Cole, stony-faced, reined his stallion away from the others. He preferred working alone, but that wasn't always possible on the big jobs. When he worked alone, the only person Cole had to trust was himself. That's the way he liked it.

The train was closer now, and it was beginning to slow

down for the tight curve where the tracks followed the landscape. That's where Cole had positioned himself. Cole studied the big, black, smoke-spewing engine and wondered if this holdup would go as smoothly as the others.

Cole sighed, consciously forcing himself to think about the present and not dwell on potential failure. He pushed such thoughts to the back of his mind. He had more important matters to attend to, like jumping onto a moving train, taking a cash box filled with money, and getting off that train — with the money — without getting killed. All that, with any luck, would happen in the next few minutes.

The train was closer, the speed now no more than four or five miles an hour. Cole could hear the cars pushing together as the lead cars slowed before those later in line. He heard the hiss of steam as dozens of brakes were applied simultaneously, slowing tons of iron, steel, coal, and people.

Cole glanced over his shoulder. The three young men all wore bandannas over their faces, covering them from the bridge of the nose down. Their hats were pulled low over their eyes.

Cole looked at his men and realized once again that he was considered an outlaw, though he never really thought of himself that way. Many people did, of course, but they simply didn't know all the facts, and as long as Nicholas Webb controlled the territory with a dictator's grasp of power, they wouldn't. There were a few small farmers and cattle ranchers who understood why Cole had become an outlaw. Not many, but a few, and to them, Cole was a hero. He had a reason for stealing, and he never stole anything that Nicholas Webb hadn't wrongly taken. And much to Nicholas Webb's annoyance, it was rumored that Cole helped the poor farmers and ranchers with money whenever he could.

The train was very close now. Within fifty yards. Cole felt his stallion, Black Jack, tense beneath him. They had done this before. Cole patted Jack's thickly muscled neck. "Easy, boy," Cole purred, his voice carrying the under-

8

current of finely honed tension of a man about to put his life in jeopardy. "Be patient just a little while longer."

The engine passed below the four outlaws, then the coal car went by. Cole looked back at his men. He saw apprehension in the eyes of Hans and Jackie; in Bobby's eyes, he saw excitement.

"Let's do it," Cole hissed, and the four men rode down the embankment.

Nicholas Webb studied the profile of the young women sitting beside him. Sitting close to Christina Sands made him feel young again. Sleeping with her would charge him like a lightning bolt. He could not ignore the difference in their ages — Nicholas was old enough to be Christina's father — but this only served to make Nicholas's blood boil in his veins. The older he got — the closer to fifty — the more enticing he found young woman.

Christina had a profusion of wavy hair that came tumbling down over her shoulders to a point below her shoulder blades. Precisely defining the color of her hair mystified Nicholas, especially when he wasn't near her, when he thought about her in his restless dreams. The color seemed to change with her moods and surroundings. Sometimes it was a dark golden blond, then a soft honey blond, and if the light struck her silky tresses just right, there were highlights of reddish gold.

Nicholas's attention was continually drawn to Christina's hair because it never seemed to stay where she wanted it to. Christina couldn't know how beguiling she was when she pushed her hair back over her shoulders impatiently. The move — and she'd repeated it serveral times already — caused her breasts to strain against the modestly cut bodice of her dress, making the cleavage tighter. She did not realize that every time she pushed her hair over her shoulders, Nicholas's heart skipped a beat. Sometimes it seemed like his heart stopped altogether.

Nicholas placed his hand lightly over Christina's smaller

9

one, giving it a little squezze. "I'm happy you came to me for advice," Nicholas said. "I want you to know that if you ever need anything else, you only have to ask." He gave her a look of seriousness, like a teacher speaking to a pet pupil. "When you get home, be sure to write down everything you did, the names of everyone you dealt with. Keeping accurate records is vitally important in business."

"Thank you, Mr. Webb," Christina replied. Smiling, her narrow, full-lipped mouth held Nicholas's eyes for a moment, then she gingerly slipped her hand out from beneath his. "You've already done more than I can repay. I don't know how to thank you."

"No thanks are necessary," Nicholas replied. *Not now, my dear. But in time I will show you how to repay me,* he thought wickedly.

The trip to Fargo had not gone exactly as Nicholas had hoped. He had helped Christina with the paperwork necessary to transfer the ownership of the dry goods store and the house on the small plot of land above it over to herself from her deceased father. But when Nicholas suggested they stop and have some dinner, Christina politely but adamantly refused. No amount of coaxing and cajoling on Nicholas's part could change Christina's mind.

She's stubborn, Nicholas had thought at the time, *but I'll win in the end! She'll give herself to me!*

They had boarded the next train bound back to Enderton.

As Christina continued looking out the window, watching the endless, flat grassland roll by, Nicholas let his eyes roam down from her face to her bosom. Christina's body was that of exaggerated femininity. She was barely five feet tall, and though she was only nineteen, she had the body of a woman, with all the sumptuous curves that Nicholas liked in a bed partner. In Christina's critical opinion, her bustline was too full, out of proportion with the rest of her body. Men in Enderton, however, were not of the same opinion. And Nicholas was no exception. To him, Christina's curvy form was the sum and total of what a woman

10

should look like. By comparison, all others were found wanting.

Nicholas knew that eventually he would have Christina. She had been impressed with his wealth all along, and his knowledge of the legal matters involved in transferring titles had made her smile.

All he had to do was wait. He could tell that Christina wasn't the type of woman who could be rushed. He saw in her a stubborn, willful nature. It flared in her blue-green eyes whenever her anger was aroused. Push the issue, and she would shy away or strike back. Patience, Nicholas knew, was the way to get Christina Sands into his bed. Patience, cunning . . . and perhaps deceit and extortion.

She was young, confused, and needing help now that her father was dead and she was left with the responsibility of running the dry goods store in Enderton. Eventually she would need more than just Nicholas's experience in running a business. She would need comfort and emotional support, and that's when Nicholas would smoothly usher her into his bedroom.

That was the way he *hoped* it would happen. If she proved capable of running the store by herself, Nicholas would resort to more drastic measures.

Virgins had always excited Nicholas. Young, innocent virgins made him feel young again. He felt like a stallion and his excitement drove him on to sexual athletics that women closer to his own age couldn't.

"Nobody move!" a hard-edged voice bellowed, obviously several octaves lower than the person's natural tone.

Christina nearly leaped out of her seat as she twisted to look to the back of the car. A man, his hat pulled low with a bandanna covering his face, stood in the doorway of the car, brandishing a short-barreled shotgun. He waved the shotgun frantically, pointing it in turn at everyone in the coach. "The first person who moves gets it! We don't want any dead heroes!"

"Mr. Webb!" Christina hissed, clutching on to the man's arm.

11

Nicholas's blue eyes were flinty. *Damn it, not now!* he thought, looking at the masked outlaw. He turned to Christina, patting her hand, fighting to look more brave than he really felt. "It'll be all right," he whispered. "He won't hurt us as long as we do as we're told."

Nicholas looked into Christina's light blue-green eyes. She was terrified and it showed. A corner of Nicholas's mind whispered, *She'll be so grateful for getting her through this! This will be all it'll take to get her into bed!* Nicholas pushed the thought of bedding Christina deeper into his mind and concentrated on the man brandishing the shotgun. Sometimes it was hard for him to think about anything other than the image of having Christina's petitely curvaceous body writhing in sexual ecstasy beneath his own.

"Get up," the outlaw said, pointing his shotgun at a young boy in dirty clothes. The boy's mother put an arm protectively around her son who hadn't yet reached his teenage years. "I ain't going to hurt him, lady. Not if he does what I tell him to." To the other passengers in the car, the outlaw shouted, "Now listen up, everybody here puts their wallets and valuables in the kid's hat. Hurry! I'll kill the first person who even thinks of pulling a gun!" The outlaw's shotgun backed up his words. Nicholas got the impression that he wanted someone to challenge him so he'd have an excuse to use the shotgun.

The outlaw walked down the aisle, leading the boy, watching as the upturned hat was steadily filled with items. Nicholas Webb kept his face turned down. This was one time he didn't want to be recognized.

Nicholas glanced at Christina. She was squeezing the small purse in her lap, her eyes wide and frightened, watching the outlaw's every move.

"You have nothing worth dying for," Nicholas whispered. He reached into the inside breast pocket of his jacket and extracted a slender wallet fat with paper. He had several hundred dollars in it. A fortune to the outlaw. Not enough for Nicholas to feel any need to defend the cash.

He had plenty more. He dropped the wallet into the boy's hat.

"I'm not giving him my purse," Christina whispered.

Nicholas looked into Christina's eyes and saw fear and indignation there. *Has she lost her mind? Doesn't she know what's happening here?* Nicholas tried to take the purse from her, but Christina's hands held tight.

"He hasn't got the right! It's mine. I worked for it. He can't have it."

"Don't be a fool!" Nicholas hissed. He didn't need Christina drawing attention to herself. He wanted the outlaw to take the money and leave . . . before he was noticed. He pulled harder at Christina's purse, but she still struggled against him. "He'll kill you for it if he has to."

Nicholas heard the distinct click! click! of twin hammers being pulled back. He heard a chuckle of nervous self-satisfaction. Nicholas Webb closed his eyes and thought, *This stupid little girl has gotten me killed!*

"Well, if it ain't Mr. Nicholas Webb himself!" the masked outlaw said. He touched the muzzles of the sawed-off shotgun to the back of Nicholas's head. "What's wrong, Webb? You look white as a ghost." The outlaw pushed the boy out of the way. He never turned the shotgun away from Nicholas.

Nicholas turned his head slowly. The muzzles were big, black holes that looked like railroad tunnels. Nicholas felt like he could walk right into those big tunnels, walk into them and get blown straight to hell. He swallowed dryly, fighting to keep from shaking, feeling the nearness of his own death. He could taste fear on his tongue. It was not a sensation he'd grown used to in the past thirty prosperous years.

The outlaw touched the muzzles to Nicholas's forehead. "I could blow your head clean off your shoulders."

Nicholas watched as the outlaw's eyes went to Christina. The pupils dilated with interest. The physical magnetism of Christina Sands had captured another male soul, and Nicholas groaned inwardly because of it. Christina's extraordinary beauty would prolong the ordeal.

The outlaw looked at the gold locket hanging from Christina's neck, hanging brightly just above the young woman's snug, eye-catching, creamy bosom. At first Nicholas thought the masked man was looking at Christina's breasts, then he realized the man's motivation was avaricious, not—at least for now—lustful.

"Let's have it, little lady," the outlaw said, his voice soft, his words deadly.

Christina looked at the outlaw, her eyes first widening with shock, then narrowing to slits like an angry, threatened feline.

"No," Christina answered. She looked at the outlaw with unqualified contempt blazing in her crystal-blue eyes. Naively believing she could reason with the criminal, she added, "It was my mother's."

Nicholas, seeing the intractability of the woman beside him, sensing the growing impatience of the outlaw who still held the shotgun at his head, was *not* going to die because a strong-willed young woman—no matter how beautiful she was or how much he wanted to sleep with her—refused to give up a family heirloom.

"Give him the damn locket!" Nicholas hissed in a rush of words, panic flowing inside him like floodwaters that soon would rise above his ability to control.

"No," Christina repeated quietly. Her eyes were ablaze with defiance, her chin thrust aggressively forward.

Like a shot, Nicholas's hand flashed out and grabbed the locket. With a hard tug he snapped the small clasp at the back of Christina's neck, pulling the locket from her.

"Here! Take it!" Nicholas hissed angrily.

The outlaw's eyes twinkled with amusement. He took the locket from Nicholas's outstretched hand, dropping it into his pocket. "That's right neighborly of you," the outlaw chuckled. "Now the purse, Webb. Wanna grab that from her, too?"

"Take the money," Nicholas said through tightly clamped teeth. The outlaw was playing with him now, taunting him,

14

trying to humiliate him in front of the other passengers. He jerked the purse from Christina's hands, but instead of giving it to the outlaw, he tossed it to the floor. "If you want it, pick it up off the floor."

"You do too much talking." The outlaw lowered the shotgun to Nicholas's throat. He jabbed Nicholas with the muzzles again and the trapped man sputtered at the pressure against his larynx. "It's not right that you're still alive, Webb. After all the wrong you've done, somebody ought to kill you."

Nicholas locked his flinty eyes with the outlaw. He felt his courage coming back to him. This was not the time for heroics, Nicholas realized, yet he could not allow this small-time hoodlum to humiliate him in front of Christina Sands. In a smooth, steady voice he said, "Go ahead and kill me, if you think that'll prove you're a man. But you're not fooling me. You're not fooling anyone in this car."

A muscle twitched in the corner of the outlaw's eye.

Shut up! the voice of self-preservation screamed inside Nicholas's head, though another part of him was determined to prove his courage to Christina. Nicholas spoke despite his misgivings. "You're just another criminal who thinks that carrying a big gun makes him a big man."

"I'm going to blow you straight to hell!" the outlaw spat, his mask puffing out as he hissed the venomous words.

The car door opened as the outlaw was about to pull the shotgun's trigger. Christina, horrified at the scene being played out beside her, twisted sharply in her seat again, hoping that help had arrived. Advancing from the rear of the car was a tall, slender, long-legged blond man with shocking steel-grey eyes. Even from the distance that separated them, Christina noticed how icy the man's eyes were. On his face was an expression of feral yet controlled rage. Upon seeing the outlaw, the man raised his revolver, holding it steady at his hip as he took long strides up the aisle.

"Put it down!" he said sharply.

"Jurrell, I got Nicholas Webb right where we want him!" the outlaw shot back. He never moved the shotgun from

Nicholas's throat. "You want him dead as much as I do."

The young boy, shocked at the name he'd heard before, dropped his hat. Watches, wallets, purses, and jewelry scattered across the aisle. He looked at the approaching man with openmouthed, wide-eyed awe.

Cole stepped over the assortment of valuables littering the aisle. He kept his pistol trained on the outlaw's ribs. "Put it down now." His voice was calm, yet it carried authority and veiled violence. "This isn't what we're about."

Nicholas spoke up. "Cole Jurrell," he said, affecting a friendly tone. "As I live and breathe!"

"You wouldn't be living or breathing if I had any say in it." Cole spoke to Nicholas, but he didn't let his attention stray far from Bobby. "Someday, Webb, you'll get what you deserve. Someday everyone will know you for the thief and murderer that you are, and then you'll swing from a rope."

"Murderer?" There was a mocking twist to Nicholas Webb's mouth, a sneer on his lips, contempt in his voice. "Murder is your specialty, not mine. That's why there's a bounty on your head, remember?"

Christina was mesmerized by the outlaw Cole Jurrell. She'd heard stories of him, some of them obviously exaggerated, others holding the possibility of truth. All the stories were fascinating. It was said, at least in some of the rumors that circulated among the young women of Enderton, that Cole Jurrell was a sensitive and kind lover who had never hurt anyone. Some stories depicted him as a ruthless, cold-blooded killer, a man capable of such uncontrolled violence that he was wanted for the murder of his own father. Christina questioned now which of those rumors was true. What she could tell was that Nicholas Webb was much more at ease despite the shotgun pointing at his throat now that Cole Jurrell had arrived.

"I said, put the shotgun down," Cole repeated. His pistol never wavered from the masked outlaw.

I'm being held up by Cole Jurrell and his gang! Christina thought. She wasn't sure whether to be relieved that she had been rescued from the masked outlaw's desire for violence or more frightened now that she knew it was Cole Jurrell and his ruthless band of outlaws who was stealing her money.

Christina saw that Cole was, as rumored by the ladies of Enderton, absurdly handsome. He wore blue denim slacks, a denim shirt that had been washed so many times much of the dye was gone from the fabric, and a denim jacket. His shoulders were quite broad, and he carried them squarely. His waist was very trim, slender enough to exaggerate the width of his shoulders.

But of all his considerable assets, it was his eyes — steel gray — that caught Christina off guard. His eyes . . . and something else. But what was that *something else?* Christina thought about it as the three men silently challenged one another.

"Whose side are you on, Cole?" The masked outlaw shoved the barrels of his shotgun harder into Nicholas's throat. "We got Webb right where we want him! Why not let me squeeze the trigger and we're done with him and his thievin' ways forever?"

Cole continued to hold his pistol on Bobby. He thumbed the hammer slowly, sensing Bobby's escalating anger. In the tense, silent rail car, the sound of the hammer being cocked seemed magnified.

"If you kill him, we're no better than he is." When Bobby held steady, Cole raised his pistol and touched the big muzzle to Bobby's head, just behind his ear. "You know my word." There was no compromise in the timbre of Cole's voice. "I'll do it."

Christina watched as the masked outlaw's eyes changed. For one split second, she thought he would pull the trigger of the shotgun. Then she saw that he, too, was afraid for his life. She knew then that Cole Jurrell would, as promised, kill the masked outlaw if he murdered Nicholas Webb. Though her understanding of what was going on was limited, Christina sensed that there was a lot of history between Cole Jurrell and Nicholas Webb. She wondered

17

why Cole didn't wear a mask to hide his identity.

"Let's get out of here," Cole said after a long pause. "We've been here too long already."

The breath hissed from the masked outlaw as he gave up the argument. Christina sighed along with the masked man as the shotgun was turned away from Nicholas.

"Get out of here," Cole whispered to Bobby. "Get out while you still can." Though Cole never actually said as much, everyone in the rail car knew that if the masked outlaw didn't leave immediately, Cole would gun him down where he stood.

Bobby stooped to pick up Christina's purse lying on the floor where it had spilled from the young boy's hat. When he did this, Cole touched his pistol to the back of Bobby's head. "Now!" Cole spat. Bobby straightened slowly, his eyes burning with hatred. He turned and walked slowly down the aisle toward the back of the car, and there was an audible sigh throughout the car as the passengers all breathed deeply in relief.

It wasn't until Bobby had left the car that Cole turned his attention to Webb. But when he did, it was the stunning young woman beside Nicholas who caught his gaze and held it in a grip that Cole could not break. His gaze swept over Christina. His eyes, steel grey, changed instantly from flinty pieces of ice to fire. With a glance he took in Christina, assessing her, his eyes not lingering on her sumptuous curves, but taking them in quickly, greedily. When his eyes met hers, he just looked at her, matching her interest and defiance. Finally, with great effort, Cole jerked his gaze away from Christina's.

"Someday . . ." Cole said, looking straight into Nicholas's eyes. "Someday it'll be just you and me." He eased down the hammer of his Colt. "You and me, then all your money and influence and bribery won't mean a thing."

"How long do you think you can keep running, Cole? Another week? Another month?" Nicholas smiled coldly, cruelly at the standing man. It was a half-smile of triumph, and Christina wondered what had put it there. "Such a big man you think you are, Cole. You don't even wear a mask, so everyone knows who the great outlaw Cole Jurrell is. And what's that—"

"Shut up!" Cole hissed. He put his thumb threateningly on the hammer of his pistol. "You know why I don't wear a mask! You've had me blamed for every crime in this territory! If I don't wear a mask, I won't get blamed for the crimes you commit!"

"Big talk from a criminal." Nicholas's right eyebrow arched, and there was a twinkle of amusement in his eyes. "I'm not the criminal, Cole. I'm a businessman. It's your face on the wanted posters, not mine." Nicholas's smile broadened, and it made Christina shiver a little. "How long can you defy the odds, Cole? Sooner or later your luck is going to change. You can't win every hand."

"Someday . . ." Cole said, leaving the single word hanging threateningly.

Though the pistol was pointed at his face, Nicholas just smiled even more broadly. He said, "You're living on borrowed time."

Cole replied, "You're living on stolen money."

Without another word, Cole turned on his heel and walked quickly from the car.

Christina began shaking uncontrollably. Nicholas put his arm around her shoulders, hugging her securely to his muscular chest.

"It's going to be okay," he whispered, stroking her hair. "They're gone. They can't hurt you now. Don't be afraid, Christina. Nothing is going to happen."

Christina grit her teeth. She didn't want to cry. She felt silly and childish for breaking down. She squeezed her eyes tightly shut, pressing her cheek against Nicholas's shoulder. Christina discovered that despite Nicholas's years and white hair, his arms were like tight leather bands around her shoulders and his chest was a hard wall of flesh and muscle. All his money and nearly fifty years of life hadn't made Nicholas Webb soft and weak. Just the opposite was true.

19

"Shhh," Nicholas whispered, his hand running down Christina's back, his senses cooling down from the danger that had passed and heating up from the soft, exquisite beauty of the young woman he was now able to hold in his arms. He squeezed Christina a bit more firmly against himself, feeling the fullness of her glorious, ample bosom flattening against the side of his chest. He stroked her hair, inhaling the softly feminine fragrance of her. "You're with me," Nicholas purred. "As long as you're with me, nobody can hurt you."

I have got to possess this woman! Nicholas Webb thought.

Chapter 2

Cole reined his black stallion to a stop in front of a small house. In all directions there was nothing but endless prairie. He sighed, exhausted from the ride. It always seemed strange to him that the time when he was most frightened was when he was on the run after a holdup, when he didn't know whether there was a posse after him. All the doubling back, the waiting and listening for the sounds of pounding hooves carried on the night breeze . . . it wore at his nerves in a way that the actual holdup did not. And then, when the adrenaline stopped surging through his blood, he felt totally drained.

This time he had been successful. If only Bobby hadn't gone over the edge!

Cole grit his teeth as he thought about what Bobby had done. Bobby actually intended to steal from the passengers! Cole knew that Bobby wasn't like the others in the gang, but he thought he would stick to their rules. Stealing from a woman, no less!

The locket in Cole's pocket would have to be returned to its rightful owner. Inquiries would have to be discreetly made. He'd find out who the stunning young woman was, and then he'd appear at her home one night to return the locket with his apology.

A smile curled the corners of Cole's mouth. Perhaps if she hadn't been so devilishly alluring, he would be satisfied to simply leave the locket on her doorstep, someplace where she was sure to find it. But she *was* devilishly alluring, and Cole just had to talk to her. The look he had seen in her eyes was burned into his brain, an indelible image of powerful femininity he could not forget.

She was interested in him. He could see that in her eyes. But there was something more about her. She had an internal toughness that wasn't ladylike or feminine, an inner strength that made her even more intriguing and exciting.

Who was she? And why was she with Nicholas Webb? Could she be mixed up in one of his schemes?

Cole tied Jack to the hitching rail. The rickety front door of the house flew open and Angelina exploded onto the porch. Cole turned to her and she leaped into his arms, wrapping her slender brown arms around his neck. She pressed herself against Cole fiercely. "I knew you would come to see me," Angelina whispered into Cole's ear. "I knew you would . . . but still I was afraid that this time you might not."

"You shouldn't worry about me." Cole pushed himself away from Angelina so he could look into her eyes. He flashed her a devil-may-care smile. "I'm unstoppable. Haven't you heard?" He studied Angelina's eyes. She was genuinely worried. Cole kissed her forehead lightly and felt her tremble softly. "Come on, let's go inside."

"Yes," Angelina replied, but she made no move toward the door.

Cole ran his hand from the base of her neck down her back, the contact of her silky jet hair soothing against his palm. He tried to ease out of her grip, but she continued to hold him tightly, possessively.

"I don't know how long I can stay," he said quietly. Cole didn't know why he'd said that. Angelina knew that he was never certain how long he could stay with her.

"Don't think about that now," Angelina whispered in reply. She kissed Cole's cheek and buried her nose in the arch of his neck. "Come in the house. We will talk about your leaving when you must leave."

Cole allowed Angelina to lead him into the house. Everything was the same as it had been the last time he was there. The same small, tidy kitchen area; the same small kitchen table with the two hard, straight-backed chairs; the old mattress on the floor in the corner; the scarred wooden bureau with one drawer missing.

Hanging on a peg in the wall were Angelina's three winter dresses and four summer dresses — all but one a gift from Cole. Beneath the dresses on the floor were the winter boots she'd received from him.

"It's good to see you again." Cole's voice sounded weary. For a reason he did not understand, he exaggerated his exhaustion slightly. "It's always good to see you. It's been a long time."

"Too long," Angelina replied.

She walked barefooted to the cupboard and withdrew the bottle of brandy. Cole noticed that the brandy in the bottle was at the same level as a month earlier. He knew Angelina enjoyed an occasional brandy, but apparently she wouldn't drink *this* brandy without Cole. It made him feel a little guilty, and this emotion made him flinch inwardly. Guilt wasn't one of the emotions Cole was accustomed to, and he didn't like at all the way it tasted in his mouth.

Cole took one of the kitchen chairs and sat on it, leaning back and placing an ankle on the opposite knee. He watched as Angelina brought out two glasses, placing one on the table in front of him.

She really is beautiful, he thought.

Angelina's eyes were as dark as midnight. She had the high cheekbones and tawny skin that was the combination of Mexican and German bloodlines. She drew the eyes and sparked the desire of every man in the county.

Every man, that is, but Cole. Cole was aware of Angelina's exquisite charms, and he knew that she held deep emotions for him. But for Cole, he could not see in one woman friendship and love. Either a woman was his friend, or she was his lover. For Cole Jurrell, no one woman could hold both positions in his soul.

Why don't I really love her? mused Cole. He could speak more freely and openly to Angelina than he could with any lover he'd ever had. Angelina provided a gentle haven for him to rest. She listened to him when he talked, and she made him smile when he didn't feel like smiling. She was all these things to Cole, but he wasn't truly in love with her.

Angelina poured three fingers of brandy into Cole's glass, then did the same for herself. She sat down in the only other chair, her ebony eyes wide, waiting. Cole always told the most fascinating stories when he was finished with a raid, and she was hoping that tonight would be no different. She folded her hands expectantly.

"Thank you," Cole murmured, lifting the glass to his lips. He tasted the Napoleon brandy, sighing softly at the exquisite flavor. Cole smiled. Angelina could never know that the single bottle of brandy had cost more than the home she lived in. It was one more thing he could feel guilty about, and that made Cole wonder why that emotion was suddenly taking up so much of his thinking.

"Did something bad happen this time?" Angelina asked. She kept her eyes trained on Cole's face, looking for something there that wouldn't be in his words. "Did anyone get hurt?"

"No. Of course not." Cole reached across the table, tapping his glass lightly against Angelina's. She hadn't picked her glass up yet. "A toast. I got Webb's payroll and not a shot was fired. What more could I ask for?"

Cole felt Angelina studying him. Something inside him said he should leave. He'd been seeing Angelina off and on for the two years that he'd been a hunted man, since he had collapsed bleeding in her arms and she had nursed him back to health.

Cole had known Angelina prior to that, but they had never really been friends. She had lived in Enderton then, and had gotten involved with a man there. When he turned into the evil monster that everyone had warned her about, Angelina bought her small house and stayed away from

24

everyone.

"Have you thought of moving back?" Cole regretted his question, but felt he had to ask it.

"No."

Something just wasn't right, and Cole could feel it. He wondered if just perhaps Angelina had a gentleman friend. Maybe that's what he sensed in the room. It wouldn't be fair of him to keep seeing Angelina if there was someone else in her life. She would be afraid of hurting Cole's feelings, of not being there if he needed her. Cole doubted any man would understand his friendship with Angelina and believe it was strictly platonic.

Cole promised himself he wouldn't get in the way of Angelina's happiness. She deserved a full-time man, not an outlaw on the run.

"If you want to talk about it," Angelina said, her voice a hushed whisper in the dimly lightly house, "I will listen."

Cole shook his head, hoping she would someday find the happiness he couldn't give her.

All it took was one glance into Angelina's eyes for Cole to know that she didn't have another man lurking around. She loved him in the only way he could be loved — gently, from a distance, without any commitments or expectations.

Everything about the evening impressed Christina. She was at first wary when Nicholas said they would be dining in his private suite at the hotel rather than in the restaurant with the other patrons. Her apprehension vanished, however, when it became clear that Nicholas was a gentleman both publicly and privately. If anything, he seemed to put a bit more distance between them when they were in his suite, as though he could tell she was nervous, as though he was determined to prove by his actions that his intentions were honorable.

After dinner of pheasant, rice, sweet peas, and a delicate white wine (Christina allowed herself one glass and was pleased when Nicholas did not foist more on her, for she had been warned by her father about what happened to women when plied with drink), Nicholas sipped coffee and brandy and smoked a cigar. Christina had tea.

Rather than accepting Nicholas's offer of a ride home in his plush, custom-made carriage, Christina suggested they walk. She was partially aware that she'd suggested the walk to prolong the evening, and this brief moment of courage-once-removed made her blush a little, eliciting a question from Nicholas that Christina pretended she did not hear.

"Thank you for everything," Christina said, standing at the bottom of the stairs that led up to her two-bedroom home above the dry goods store. "It really was a beautiful evening."

Nicholas took half a step closer to Christina. A half-smile tugged at the corners of his mouth, but the smile never quite reached his eyes.

"I'm hoping that this is just the first of many evenings we'll be sharing." His voice was warm and soft as it covered Christina, giving her the impression of fluffy quilts on a winter's evening. "The time I spend with you . . ." Nicholas caught a strand of satiny hair at Christina's temple and twirled it around a finger. He chose his words carefully, for maximum effect. "I cherish our time together."

Christina's cheeks became flushed. She made no move to push Nicholas's hand from her hair, but she wished he wouldn't touch her. She noticed that the warmth of his words was not matched by his eyes. Something in Nicholas Webb's eyes warned Christina not to trust him.

"Are you cold?"

"No. It's actually quite warm." Christina gave Nicholas a puzzled look. "Why do you ask?"

"You shivered." Nicholas released Christina's hair. His fingertips caressed her face lightly at the cheekbone, then traveled slowly downward, over her jaw and her smooth neck. At the embroidered neckline trim of Christina's dress, the fingertips stopped, as though not knowing whether they should move downward to Christina's breast,

26

or over to her shoulder. "I just want you to be comfortable, that's all."

With her hands at her sides, Christina shifted her weight from one foot to the other. She couldn't look into Nicholas's eyes again, afraid to be chilled by the frigid emptiness she sensed in his soul. Was she imagining evil that was not there? She looked instead at a point in space just to the right of Nicholas's face.

"I have something for you," Nicholas continued. His fingertips followed the delicate ridge of the young woman's collarbone. With his free hand he reached into his coat pocket without removing his other hand from Christina. "It's not really much. Just a little something to help you forget Jurrell and his murderous cohorts. Something to chase away those unfortunate memories."

"You don't have to give me anything to do that." Christina fidgeted, not knowing where to look or what to do with her hands. All the easy conversation she'd enjoyed with him during their meal was forgotten. "It wasn't your fault. You were a victim, too."

"Perhaps." Nicholas thumbed open the rectangular box but made no move to show its contents to Christina. "Perhaps that is true. But all they stole from me is money, and I have a great deal of that. They stole from you an heirloom, something irreplaceable from your father, something you loved very much because of the person who gave it to you." Nicholas moved closer. "That locket had memories and meaning for you. It was more than just—" Nicholas bit his tongue to keep the word "cheap" from leaving his mouth "—just a piece of jewelry."

Instantly, hot tears pooled in Christina's eyes. Why did Nicholas have to mention her father? Christina mentally chided herself. Christina knew that her father wouldn't be proud of her if he knew how often she found herself in tears, wishing she could talk with him again.

The combination of Nicholas's thoughtfulness and the still-fresh memories of her father caused two clear teardrops to trickle down Christina's cheeks. She wiped them away quickly and took a step backward, out of Nicholas's reach, away from the hand that always seemed to be touching her.

"A woman with eyes as beautiful as yours should never cry. Never. Nobody has the right to make you cry." Nicholas moved forward, this time taking Christina's small hand in his own. Down low, in his left hand, he held the box. "I cannot replace what was stolen, but I can give you something that I hope will symbolize a new beginning." At last Nicholas presented the contents of the rectangular box to Christina. "This is for you. When you wear it, I want you to think of me . . . of us."

Christina looked in awe at the necklace. It was a gold locket, vaguely similar in size and shape to the one her father had given her. But that is where the similarity ended. This locket was encrusted with jewels — rubies and emeralds, though Christina wasn't sure if the green stones were emeralds or jade — and the chain was shining links of gold.

"Mr. Webb, I . . . I . . ."

"Please, indulge me this one time —"

"— I can't accept that." Christina shook her head slowly, sending her curls dancing flatteringly against her flushed cheeks. "It's got to be worth more money than I've made in my entire life."

"You must accept it." Nicholas edged closer, causing Christina to step backward, moving deeper into the shadows. "It's perfect for you. You, my dear, are the only woman who could do this necklace justice. The locket is beautiful, but its beauty would be diminished worn around the neck of a woman less beautiful than yourself."

Christina looked up from the necklace and instantly regretted it. Nicholas's words had the strange dual effect of calming and exciting her. It was only in his eyes that she sensed all was not as it should be.

"Please, Mr. Webb, you're embarrassing me."

"Nicholas. You promised to call me Nicholas. And now you must also promise to wear this necklace."

Standing very close to the much shorter woman allowed

28

Nicholas a view of Christina's bosom. As she breathed, deeply now with the confusion of the moment, he watched the creamy swells of her breasts rise and fall, pressing against the bodice of her inexpensive gown. Nicholas Webb, despite years of lechery and countless lovers, felt a tightness in his throat and a throbbing in his groin that was hot and fierce, more powerful than anything he'd ever known before. Christina's beauty gripped Nicholas viciously, forcing him to act upon emotions he struggled to keep behind the facade of his gentility.

"Turn around now," Nicholas whispered. "Turn around and I will put this on you."

Christina moved slowly, as though in a deep trance. Things like this just didn't happen to her! Her knight had arrived, swept her off her feet with his charm and manners, his money and gifts . . . it was exactly like Christina's childhood fantasies had said it should be. But still. . . .

The gold was cool against Christina's skin. The sheer weight of the ornate locket against her, nestled between the tightly compressed mounds of her breasts, surprised her. The gold felt unnaturally cool, and Christina inhaled deeply at the shock of it. She closed her eyes and for only a few seconds — as Nicholas worked the clasp of the locket in the dark — the young woman wondered why her father had never approved of Nicholas Webb.

She heard the *snick* of the clasp locking at the back of her neck. Then Nicholas's hand slipped outward and long, slender fingers curled around a small shoulder. Christina's heart was pounding as she turned, half in a trance, half directed by Nicholas's tight grip, until she faced him. His left hand came up to the back of her head and strong fingers pushed into her hair. A silver comb was dislodged from its place in her tresses, falling to the floorboards beneath Christina's dainty feel with a discordant clanging.

Christina grimaced as strands of hair pulled against her scalp. A soft, protesting gasp came from her lips as her head was pulled back on her shoulders, forcing her face to tilt up toward Nicholas's.

29

"So beautiful!" Nicholas whispered, his breath hot against Christina's face. She smelled liquor on his breath and dumbly wondered if it was the alcohol that was making Nicholas behave so brutishly.

His mouth closed harshly over hers. It was not a gentle kiss, not sweetly arousing, not like the kisses of Christina's fantasies. Nicholas kissed her harshly, hurting her mouth with his own, punishing her with the fire of his all-consuming desire to possess her body and soul.

Christina was shocked and revolted by what was happening. The kiss—her first kiss by a man, not a boy—was not the intoxicatingly pleasurable thing she had fantasized. Nicholas had turned into a monster of a man, a caricature of the gentleman he had pretended to be.

Twisting her head sharply, Christina broke the kiss. She pushed against his chest, but his greater weight was too much for her. Christina staggered a single step backward and once again her hair was pulled, causing her head to twist to the side.

"I'm sorry," Nicholas whispered rapidly. He disentangled his fingers from the tumbled mass of satiny hair that had earlier been a beautiful coiffure. "Christina, I swear to you, I'm sorry."

Christina felt trapped but defiant. To her right was the stairway leading up to the security of her home. Her back was against the side of the dry goods store. And directly in front of her, looking contrite yet lustful was Mr. Nicholas Webb, the richest man in Dakota territory, the man Christina thought was a gentleman just a few short moments before.

"Stay . . . stay away from me," Christina hissed in a faltering voice. She cleared her throat and in a tone that seemed much too hard and cold to be coming from her throat, she added, "Don't you ever touch me again. I mean it. Don't you *ever* touch me like that again."

"Christina, you don't understand!" Nicholas was shaking his head and though his eyes pleaded for sympathy, she gave him none. "I didn't mean for this to happen. It's just that—"

"—Don't!" Christina took a step forward, getting her back away from the wall. A fear, new to her, had exploded into her consciousness. She realized, for the first time in her life, that she was vulnerable. Christina knew she could easily be overpowered by Nicholas.

"You've got to listen to me," Nicholas whispered. "It's not like what you think. I'm not that kind of man."

"I don't have to listen to you." Anger blazed in Christina's eyes, replacing the fear that had been there a moment before. "I don't have to do anything I don't want to do." Christina took several quick steps up the stairway, putting more distance between herself and Nicholas. She stopped and turned, her knees shaking but her spirit courageous and unchecked. "I would prefer it if you didn't come to see me again."

Christina's dainty feet stamped on the rickety, unpainted wooden steps as she hurried up to her small, orderly, secure home. She opened the door, then banged it closed quickly behind her. It wasn't until she had thrown the bar over the door that she felt truly safe from Nicholas Webb.

But it was precisely a second later when the hand clamped tightly over her mouth and she was pulled against a hard, masculine body.

"Don't make a sound!" a voice hissed, coming from a mouth so close to her own.

In a split second of time, Christina realized the voice belonged to the outlaw Cole Jurrell. She wondered if Nicholas was still standing at the landing of the stairway, and if he would rescue her if she could somehow get his attention without getting killed.

Chapter 3

Cole pushed himself a bit tighter against Christina. He felt her strike the door and her backward movement stopped. The fullness of her firm breasts pressed warmly against his chest. He kept his left hand held firmly over her mouth, while the heel of his right hand rested threateningly on the smooth-polished butt of his deadly Colt revolver.

Even in the darkness of the small, tidy, home, Cole could see fear glinting in the young woman's shimmering blue eyes. It was that fear, and the realization that he could be hurting her by putting too much pressure against her mouth, that made him relax a bit.

"Don't scream," Cole whispered, his steel-gray eyes boring into the glossy pools of Christina's. "I don't want to hurt you. It's up to you."

Inwardly, Cole cursed himself. It was a monumental mistake on his part to believe that Christina Sands was the innocent victim of Bobby's greed. Though Cole had not been able to hear what Christina and Nicholas had said to each other, the way they had kissed and the sparkling diamond and emerald locket dangling from Christina's neck told Cole that the young woman who had so captured his attention on the train — and then held his mind prisoner afterward — was anything but innocent. Whether by design and intention or completely by accident, Christina had fallen under the influence — financially and probably emotionally, too — of Nicholas Webb. As such, she had to be considered a member of the Webb clan and therefore fair game for Cole and his men.

Cole felt Christina's body relax. He waited, wondering if he could trust her, wondering if his foolish belief that she was a wronged innocent would get him killed this time. He inhaled deeply, then exhaled with a resigned sigh. He caught the scents of shampoo, woman, and perfume. But rather than enjoying the stimulation, he found it strangely offensive. Had Nicholas Webb purchased the shampoo that made Christina's hair smell like lilacs in the spring? Had Nicholas given Christina the perfume she wore? Was Christina bought and paid for, like so many others in the Dakota Territory?

Cole took a full step away from the blue-eyed vixen in the surprisingly inexpensive dress. Two fingertips remained touching her narrow, full-lipped mouth, a reminder that she mustn't speak.

"Easy," Cole purred. His eyes danced from Christina's face down to the enticing swells of her full bosom, then swept upward again to take in the planes of her face. Cole understood full well why Nicholas wanted Christina. She was a bewitching combination of sensuality and feigned innocence. "I haven't come here to hurt you. Don't make any noise and nobody will get hurt. Not you, or me, or lover boy outside."

Cole found it amusing when Christina said with quiet indignation, "Mr. Webb is *not* my lover boy. He's not anything to me at all."

"Right. Who am I to argue with such a virtuous young woman?"

For his sarcasm, Cole was shot with a contemptuous look from Christina's azure eyes. He smiled and a dimple played in one cheek, appearing quickly, then disappearing.

"What do you want?" Christina asked in a voice that carried more confidence that she felt. It enraged her that Cole should find humor in her anger. "What do you want with me?"

This time it was Cole who lashed out with his cold grey

33

gaze. "Don't flatter yourself, Christina. Not every man you see wants you." Cole took another step backward, his gun hand never leaving the butt of his .44 revolver. He found it necessary to put more distance between himself and Christina. Distance was the only thing that could diminish the effect she had on his senses. "Please step away from the door." When she didn't move, Cole added harshly, "Christina, step away from the door *now!*"

Christina did as she was commanded. What choice did she have when trapped with a man wanted for the murder of his own father? But as she moved away from the door, she said in a voice just loud enough for Cole to hear, "This is my house, not yours. Are you always so bossy when you break into a woman's house?"

Cole chuckled. She believed the story of him being a cold-blooded killer. What made him think he could ever possibly change her mind? What made it so necessary for him to try?

Cole reached into the left pocket of his corduroy jacket, feeling the slender links of the gold chain and the small locket attached to it. For a moment he recalled his own pleasure at being able to fix the bent clasp. How happy he had been then, believing he would please the young woman he'd seen so briefly on the train. Now, his eyes roaming over Christina, he questioned whether he had any moral obligation to her.

"How do you know my name?" Christina asked, ending the silence that had fallen over the room like a heavy, cloying shroud.

"I have my ways." Cole caressed the engraved gold locket with his thumb. Knowing that whatever he said to Christina would eventually get back to Nicholas Webb, he added, "I have friends in town. Perhaps not as many as I once had, but enough nevertheless. They keep me informed on who's doing what." In an acid tone he added, "Not everyone in Enderton is bought and paid for by Nicholas Webb."

Cole took easy steps over to the door, his soft-soled

34

moccasins soundless against the wooden floor. He checked the lock and, satisfied, turned slowly to confront the woman who had become the focus of most of his waking thoughts and all of his restless dreams.

Bathed in shadows, Christina was striking, breathtaking. He moved closer to her. With each long-legged stride, he felt the magnetism of her allure become stronger, more insistent, less deniable. "I came here to return something that belongs to you. What happened the other day on the train was a mistake."

"What?" Christina's eyebrows pushed together in confusion. Though she did not trust Cole, she had seen how Nicholas had relaxed when Cole had stepped into the rail car. This made her question the story of Cole being a ruthless killer, a man who would gun down his own father just to gain control of the family fortune.

"This," Cole said calmly, holding the locket in his palm for Christina to see. When her jaw dropped open, Cole could not keep the unaffected smile from spreading across his handsome face.

"My locket? My God, you're giving me back my locket?" Christina reached for the locket. Before she could take it from Cole's palm, his long, strong fingers once again curled around the locket. Christina stared at the fist for a moment, then her eyes went slowly up to Cole's face. "Why? Why are you doing this to me? You must know how important that is to me. If you didn't, you wouldn't be here. Why are you teasing me like this? Are you really that cruel?"

Cole's smile twisted into a half-sneer. "Not usually. I 'm making an exception in your case."

Christina, not used to being treated in such a manner and still reeling from the shock that Nicholas, and now Cole, had put her through, rested her hands on her hips and thrust her chin forward. It was the stance she'd seen her father adopt whenever she challenged his authority. She did not realize that the position caused her breasts to strain mightily against the bodice of her dress. With her

35

shoulders pulled back and held square, she seemed to be inviting Cole's eyes to her bosom.

"Lucky me to get such special treatment from a wanted criminal."

When Christina saw the direction of the tall intruder's intent gaze, she blushed and crossed her arms over her breasts. "Please . . . you're making me uncomfortable."

"That's nice," Cole purred, his smile broadening, but losing its charm and warmth. "Very nice. So believable." He tilted the flat-crowned black hat back on his head, looking at Christina, a little disheartened at the beauty he saw in her. "If I hadn't seen your performance with Webb, I'd get suckered in by it."

Christina scowled. "It wasn't a *performance,*" she snapped. "And what were you doing watching anyway? Are you a thief *and* a Peeping Tom?"

Cole chuckled, turning slightly away from Christina. She studied him, and questions that had first crept into her mind when she saw him on the train returned. Who was this outlaw Cole Jurrell? Killer? He had the look to him. Christina had seen gunmen in Enderton before, and Cole had all the physical makings of a gunfighter. Tall, lean, athletic-looking. And his eyes. They were definitely the eyes of a man who had killed before. His movements were always smooth, fluid, catlike. His revolver was strapped to his thigh, tied down low so that he could draw it quickly.

When Cole sighed, Christina thought he looked tired. Or was he bored? He was acting that way. Like he really didn't want to hear anything more Christina had to say to him. But if that was the case, why was he here? It couldn't be just to return the locket, for wouldn't he have given it to her already? She realized that Cole had taken a risk by coming into Enderton, and the longer he stayed in her home, the more he risked being captured.

Cole rubbed his eyes with his left hand.

He is tired, thought Christina.

She almost suggested that Cole should get some sleep. The words were at her lips before she remembered that this

36

handsome man was holding in his fist the locket that a member of his gang had stolen from her.

"Are you going to give me the locket or not?" Christina asked quietly. Her words seemed to echo in the quiet room. "I don't know why you're here. Why won't you give it to me?" Christina's eyebrows pushed together in thought. "Are you really that heartless? Are you the man everyone says you are?"

"Everyone?" Cole cocked his head and looked sideways at Christina. His eyes, slate gray, were emotionless. "You can believe whatever you want to about me, but I'll tell you this: I didn't kill my father. Nicholas Webb killed him, or had one of his henchmen kill him. And I've never stolen anything in my life." When Christina flashed an unbelieving look his way, Cole added, "Nothing that wasn't Nicholas Webb's, anyway." Cole extended his hand to Christina. He held the locket out to her. "Here. I'm sorry. I didn't mean for this to be taken from you."

Christina looked at the locket in the upraised palm. She wanted it, but she didn't want the hand to close around it again, and wasn't going to let an outlaw like Cole Jurrell, no matter what kind of man he was — criminal or otherwise — tease her and make her feel helpless.

"Take the damn thing!" Cole snapped. Christina could see his tension in the set of his mouth and in the corners of his eyes. His anger seemed to abate slightly as he said, "I'm sorry this had to happen."

Christina took the locket by the chain, raising it slowly from Cole's palm without ever touching him. When she looked at him again, Christina sensed that something had changed. She wasn't frightened of Cole Jurrell. He had scared her by breaking into her home, but once the initial shock had worn off, Christina wasn't frightened.

"I don't . . . I don't understand why you're doing this," Christina whispered. "But, thank you. This is very important to me. It was my mother's. My father gave it to me after she died."

"I thought it was something like that. You're welcome."

Christina looked at Cole thoughtfully, thinking how handsome he would be if he would put on a fine suit instead of the dusty range clothes he now wore, if he shaved off the two-days' growth of stubble on his face.

The silence between them grew.

"Well, I guess that's it," Cole said suddenly, uncomfortable under Christina's guileless gaze. "Please don't shout for help. At least not right away." Cole stepped so close to Christina their bodies nearly touched. "Give me a chance to get away. Call it a favor for returning your necklace."

"I won't say anything."

"Good."

She sensed his indecision. He knew he should leave, but part of him bid him to stay.

Cole raised his left hand and placed his palm lightly against Christina's cheek. She didn't move. She wasn't certain she felt the touch of his hand or the heat of him. As he stroked her cheek his right hand simultaneously curled around the handle of his revolver.

So, she thought, *he's decided he doesn't trust me after all.*

"How does it feel wearing jewelry that's been paid for with stolen money? Do you like that? Does that excite you?"

Christina's heart was pounding. The heat of his palm against her face seemed to burn her flesh. Cole's words confused her, but his pressure — arousingly close — thrilled her in a way that she had never before experienced. Cole Jurrell, the rational part of her mind warned, was a criminal, a man whose face adorned posters throughout the Dakota Territory. And the posters all said: WANTED DEAD OR ALIVE. But it was not the rational part of Christina's mind that was reeling now, spinning under his heady influence. The emotional side of her, the one that had taken such pleasure in youthful fantasies of men and love and other things that her father said would come "in due time" was in the forefront. She was responding to him intuitively, and it thrilled her. *Watch out,* she told herself.

Cole is handsome, obviously virile, and he is dangerous. Very dangerous. Was that what she found so tantalizing?

Cole's hand slipped lightly from Christina's cheek to her neck, sliding under her tumbled coiffure. She felt the clasp of her new necklace come unfastened, and wondered how Cole had managed to do that with just one hand. Nicholas had trouble fastening the clasp using both hands. And he could see what he was doing.

"Is that the kind of woman you are, Christina Sands? The kind that likes laughing at the law?" Cole took the necklace from Christina's throat. His eyes never left hers as he dropped the diamond-and-emerald necklace into his shirt pocket. "You won't be needing this. Since Webb bought it with my father's money, I don't feel bad about stealing it from you." An eyebrow cocked above one eye. "You don't mind, do you?"

A hand, roughened by hard labor yet touching her with caresses so tender they made her shiver, returned to her cheek. A long finger followed the bridge of her nose, then traced the outline of her mouth. It took all of Christina's willpower to keep from kissing the fingertips when it paused at her lips.

"After all the things that Webb has stolen from me, wouldn't it be fitting justice that I steal something from him? Something . . . special."

Deep within her, her heart stopped.

The fingertip trailed down Christina's chin to her throat. It paused a moment, then moved lower. She felt at that instant nothing but the fingertip and the exact spot where it touched her skin. Cole's words were an indistinct buzz in her ears, incoherent sounds that meant nothing to her. She looked into Cole's eyes, but his gaze was following the slow progress of his finger moving down Christina's throat.

"What do you think? Hmmm? Imagine what lover boy would say if he knew."

Though his tone was cool and aloof, Cole's body was burning with need for Christina. He ached to pull her into his arms, to place his hands boldly on her womanly curves and feel her respond to his intimate touch.

Cole struggled to remind himself that Christina was nothing more than the property of Nicholas Webb. Her "services" had been paid for with money stolen from honest, hard-working ranchers—and from his father. Cole wanted Christina to beg him for his kisses. He wanted her to ask for them, and when he was finished with her, he would have stolen something from Nicholas Webb that could never be taken back.

Cole's gaze moved lower. He saw that Christina's nipples had grown taut with desire and the knowledge that she wanted him sparked a passion in him that no amount of hatred for Webb could diminish. He looked straight into Christina's eyes and whispered, "Damn you." And then he kissed her.

Christina gasped softly when Cole's lips made contact with her own. He kissed her softly, nibbling gently at her lips. Christina tilted her head to one side and the kiss deepened. Strong hands slipped down Christina's arms, then wound around her slender waist. Her breasts, trapped in the bodice of her gown, felt confined, overfull, taut with an internal pressure as they pressed warmly against Cole's broad chest. Her arms were trapped at her sides by Cole's hold on her, but Christina did not make any attempt to free them.

The feathery kisses paused a moment. Christina heard herself inhale and realized that she had been holding her breath. She felt dizzy, wildly alive. With her eyes closed, Christina floated, her body seeming airy, unreal. Dimly, faintly, a tiny voice whispered in her foggy mind, *This is what a kiss is supposed to feel like.*

A hand slipped further around Christina's hips, pulling the full length of her body against the hard, lean length of Cole Jurrell. A hand at her shoulder pushed her backward at the same time. The tip of Cole's tongue flashed briefly against Christina's lips, then she heard the unfamiliar sound of her own moan of passion as Cole's right hand slipped between their bodies to cup and squeeze one straining breast. A heat unlike any other passed from Christina's nipple through her body. She felt Cole's tongue at her lips again, but this time Christina opened her mouth to him, inviting further exploration. She danced her tongue against Cole's, not sure if she was kissing as she should be, only knowing that every nerve in her body was singing with passion.

Christina, her arms no longer pinned to her sides, placed her hands on Cole's hips. She wanted to push him away, to free her hips from the contact with his. But her hands would not listen to her better judgment. Instead of pushing Cole away, she pulled him tighter against her body.

She leaned into Cole and felt against her lower stomach the heat of his arousal straining fiercely against his denim slacks. In that instant, Christina realized she wasn't a child any longer. The fantasies of chaste kisses from chivalrous knights had been transformed into a reality she could not deny. Cole Jurrell wasn't a dream, he was a man of flesh and blood . . . and desire.

"Wait! Wait! Please, Cole!" Christina sobbed breathlessly. She put her hands on Cole's chest and pushed, twisting at the same time to work out of his tight embrace.

Though she didn't have a single lamp lit, Christina saw the fire of desire that glowed in the steel gray eyes that surveyed her with suspicion. Frightened by Cole's power over her, confused by the empty ache that throbbed like a hunger within herself, Christina used her azure blue eyes to plead with Cole, asking for but not expecting understanding.

"I'm not like Nicholas Webb," Cole whispered, his hands coming up to Christina's shoulders. "I'm not some old man you can toy with and then walk away from." A cruel twitch pulled at the corner of Cole's mouth, creating a dimple. "What's wrong, Christina? Isn't returning a family heirloom payment enough?"

Under other circumstances, if Christina had been able to think more clearly, she would have been livid with Cole for his accusations. But Christina was not livid. She was

41

shocked that she could feel these deep, hungry emotions for a man. More shocking still was the direction of her newfound amorous desire. Cole Jurrell was an outlaw, a wanted criminal. And he seemed to despise her! Words of protest and passion were caught in her throat.

Christina studied Cole's face, looking at him now as though she had never before seen him. He looked angry, almost viciously so. *Can I stop him?* Christina asked herself. *Do I want to?*

"You're not going to put me off that easily." Cole gripped Christina by the upper arms, squeezing her so tightly she grimaced in pain. She made an effort to back away. "No, Christina. If Nicholas Webb is good enough for you, I damn sure am."

Christina knew now that she could not stop Cole. When she had been kissed by Nicholas only minutes earlier and had seen the lust he had for her in his eyes, Christina knew that she would fight him with every ounce of strength in her body rather than willingly give in to his base desires. But Cole Jurrell was so different. He was so wrong about her relationship with Nicholas Webb, but his kisses felt so right. Would she—could she—try to make Cole stop his amorous advances? She knew she did not want his kisses and caresses to end.

"I may not have you forever," Cole said, his voice a warm timbre of gentle yet insistent desire. "But I'll have you tonight." He took Christina's face lightly in his hand and kissed away her mumbled words of protest. "And after tonight, you'll never look at Nicholas Webb in the same way again." Cole kissed Christina deeply, with an open mouth, and he felt her womanly body go limp. Her fingers splayed out across his chest instinctively to knead experimentally the leathery muscles beneath his shirt. "After tonight, you can go back to Webb, but a part of you will be mine forever."

No! I'm not Nicholas Webb's possession! I don't belong to anyone! Christina's mind screamed. But these words that rang so true and clear in her brain never went past her lips because she was kissing Cole's mouth, feeding off the power that seemed to radiate from every pore in his body. Christina Sands was tasting the forbidden fruit of unleashed desire for the first time in her life, and all she could think about was prolonging this feast of the senses, of finding out what new and delectable course Cole Jurrell would feed her next. She uttered a soft moan of carnal resignation.

The sound of footsteps on the stairs just outside the door stopped Cole and brought him sharply alert.

"Someone's coming!" Cole hissed.

Christina stood on weak and trembling legs. Numbly, she shook herself free of the bonds of passion. She watched him move to the door on catlike feet. The big revolver he had strapped to his hip seemed to materialize in his hand. For the second time, Christina heard the sound of Cole thumbing back the hammer.

"Don't," Christina whispered, surprised at the sound of her voice.

"Quiet!" Cole turned away from Christina, holding the revolver in both hands, waiting impatiently as the sound of the boot heels climbed the stairs.

Chapter 4

There was no sound in the world for Christina except the slowly approaching footsteps. That, and the hammering of her terrified heart.

Christina looked at Cole. His face frightened her. Cold, ruthless determination smoldered like hot ice in his gray eyes. His jaw was clamped tightly shut. A muscle twitched high on his cheekbone. In his hands, as frozen in place as the ice in his eyes, was the big Colt revolver.

"Don't," Christina whispered, and Cole shot her a look that silenced her. He held the revolver pointed toward the door, gripped tightly in both hands, his feet spread to a shoulder's width.

The rasp of leather boot soles against wood continued to get louder, closer. Looking at Cole, Christina could tell he was a man who knew physical danger intimately. Horror-stricken, she knew the man in those boots was coming to her door to die by Cole Jurrell's gun.

The footsteps reached the top landing and paused. Everything in Christina made her want to scream. She should warn Nicholas, let him know that she was not alone, that she was in danger. But if she did that, wouldn't she endanger Nicholas's life? If she remained silent, would she endanger her own life? What about Cole? Did she really want him to fight Nicholas? Cole's predatory aura frightened and fascinated her.

The handle of the door turned slowly. Pressure was

placed against the opposite side of the door. The door moved a fraction of an inch before being stopped by the locking bolt. And then the footsteps began again, moving down the rickety wooden stairs this time, receding into the night.

"Oh, God," Christina sighed, her breath coming out in a soft hiss. "That was just Sheriff Bellows or Deputy Miller. They check my door every night to make sure it's locked. They've been doing that since Papa passed away. Mr. Webb asked them to."

Cole holstered his revolver. He cast a sideways glance at Christina, and she saw the haunted look in his eyes. He was not, as she had first thought, entirely steeled against the potential for violence. It had affected him, too, though he did a better job of hiding his fear than Christina.

"Why in hell didn't you tell me that? For that matter, why didn't you turn me in?" Cole asked. He stepped up to Christina, placing his hands lightly on her shoulders. His eyes, softened now, looked into hers, seeking understanding. "Christina, don't you know who I am? Don't you know anything about me at all?"

Christina searched his face, her mind reeling at the conflicting emotion she was forced to feel when near this enigmatic man. "I couldn't . . . think straight. I was so scared I just didn't remember."

Cole's right hand slipped from Christina's shoulder, the fingers curling softly around the back of her neck. He breathed in deeply, then exhaled slowly, forcing himself to relax. "I thought Nicholas had come back for you."

"So did I."

Cole gave Christina a small smile. "Not that I blame the guy, of course. I can't deny that I would like to be standing in his shoes, now and then."

Cole's fingertips were moving in a circle against the back of Christina's neck, just below her hairline. Warm tingles went through her body, and though she was standing close to a man wanted for the murder of his own father, she closed her eyes and sighed softly, taking glory in the plea-

45

sure of his touch.

Just for a moment, all Christina felt was the hand at her shoulder and the fingers tenderly, teasingly caressing the back of her neck. She felt the presence of Cole Jurrell — strong, masculine, and mysterious — and as never before in her life, Christina Sands felt beautiful and desired. She waited, her head tilted slightly back, for the taste of Cole's warm, searching kisses on her lips. She waited expectantly, wanting the kisses she knew were wrong and sinful.

"They're looking for me everywhere," Cole whispered. "They never stop. There's a bounty on my head."

Don't tell me that now, Christina thought. *Kiss me! Kiss me, even though it's wrong! Teach me how a woman feels when she is held by a man, kissed by a man . . . loved by a man.*

Christina opened her eyes just in time to see Cole's handsome, troubled face come to hers. She sighed softly, a muted sound of pleasure and released denial. The contact of their lips was soft, warm, tender. Christina parted her lips invitingly, but she did not receive the response from Cole she sought.

"I'll be back," Cole whispered, his lips brushing Christina's as he spoke.

"Wait," Christina replied tremulously.

Her knees were shaking. In the core of what she now thought of as her soul — centered at a point somewhere between her hips — she felt a dull, throbbing ache, and emptiness that she had never known before.

She saw in his hawkish, gray eyes that he did not want to leave. And she saw, too, the unending fear of a man who is haunted and hunted by men and memories. It was selfish, Christina realized, to want Cole to stay with her. A tiny voice whispered inside Christina, telling her that she could make Cole kiss her again, touch her again, send her senses spinning dizzily. That voice also whispered that she could not deny her feelings for Cole. Another voice whispered that it was wrong to have Cole stay, wrong, to be alone with a man in her home.

46

"Be careful," Christina heard herself whisper. The voice of reason, she realized after the fact, had won out.

Cole flashed a broad, false smile. "Don't worry," he said, cupping Christina's chin in his palm. "They can't catch me. They never will."

"I don't believe that, and neither do you."

"Damn you!"

Christina's face was in Cole's hands and her lips were feasting on his a moment later. He leaned into her, and Christina did not pull away from the contact. As quickly as the kiss began, it ended, leaving Christina breathless.

He crossed the room and was halfway out the window when he stopped, one leg on either side of the sill. His handsome, boyish face was bathed in moonlight and shadow. The smile he gave her this time had no trace of fear and uncertainty.

"I will be back," he said, then disappeared into the night, leaving Christina alone with her desires and confusion.

The evening air was warm. Cole breathed it deeply, calming himself. He had the sensation of having escaped from some enticing and yet lethal goddess, a siren who, in Greek mythology, sang sweet songs of love to lure sailors to their death.

He listened a moment, knees curled beneath him, crouching in the darkness on the roof of the leathersmith shop adjoining Christina's dry goods store. Fortunately, no lamp had been lit inside her store, or he would have needed precious seconds to let his eyes adjust to the darkness outside.

Cole looked at the rooftops of Enderton's Main Street. As a mischievous child, and later as an even more prankish teenager, he had played hide-and-seek on the rooftops with Zachary Webb, despite their parents — and the shop-keeper's — strenuous objections. He had a momentary image of the childhood games with wooden guns, and a faraway smile played gently with his lips.

His days of superficial pleasure were over. They had gone, but the games he played as a man were much the same as those games of his youth . . . except the games were lethal now. He still played hide-and-seek, but to lose now meant death.

With a smile in his gray eyes and the taste of Christina's kisses still tantalizingly real on his lips, Cole followed the rooftops, moving as silent as the shadows that surrounded him, leaping from one building to the next until he was at the southern edge of Main Street.

Before descending the heavy brick chimney on the side of Mr. Larkin's livery stable, Cole stopped to scan the moonlit surface of the bank's roof on the opposite side of the street. He had seen movement there earlier. Perhaps it was just drifting shadows or the wild imagining of his troubled mind.

Ten seconds passed, then twenty. Then a minute. Cole waited with the forced patience of a man whose life afforded no mistakes.

It was not terribly important to Cole one way or the other if someone was on the bank's rooftop. He had avoided the bank because it was the tallest building in Enderton, and because the building was owned by Nicholas Webb.

A figure appeared at the edge of the bank's flat roof, looking down at Main Street. The figure held the butt of a rifle against his hip, the barrel pointing upward at an angle.

Who? Cole wondered. *Someone who used to be a childhood friend, who now wants the reward Webb has placed on my head?*

With the moon at his back, Cole could not make out his face. There weren't many people in Enderton who he did not know personally. Only a few people in town were total strangers to him—people like Christina Sands, who had moved into town within the past two years, and the ever-increasing number of "hired hands" who worked for Nicholas Webb.

Cole turned away from the bank. What difference did it make, he asked himself, if the man on the bank's rooftop was a friend?

He slipped soundlessly down the chimney, his fingers and moccasin-shod toes finding the gaps in the bricks easily.

When he was on the ground, Cole again checked his surroundings. It was hide-and-seek, just like it had been when Cole was a child. And just like those days of so long ago, Cole Jurrell was the swiftest, stealthiest, the most cunning of those playing this deadly, childhood game.

One night he would be caught. But not *this* night.

Christina sat in the middle of her bed, hugging her knees to her bosom, trying to sort out in her mind all that had happened in this single evening. She had been impressed with Nicholas Webb's charm . . . and his extraordinary wealth. She could not deny that the Webb fortune had played a significant role in her early fascination for Nicholas Webb. Money wasn't *all* Nicholas had going for him, but Christina felt guilty nevertheless that she'd allowed money, and the trappings of wealth, to cloud her judgment.

Her father had informed Christina many times that a man's true nature would always show itself in time. She must never allow herself to be taken in by honeyed words, her father had warned. The words of an evil man can sound like those of an honorable man. Only through time, he had said, would Christina ever be certain of a man's character.

Nicholas Webb had shown Christina his true colors at the close of the evening!

She winced and gritted her teeth at the memory of his transparent attempt to seduce her. How inexperienced did he think she was? She was angry with herself for allowing the absurdly expensive locket to turn her head, even for a moment.

Money and fine clothes can hide the heart and soul of the man who possesses them, but only for a while.

The thought of Nicholas's kisses brought a shudder rippling through Christina's form. Nicholas had forced himself upon Christina, pulling at her hair and defiling her mouth with his lips and tongue.

She huffed, angry with herself again. He almost went too far. She had almost lost control.

In a rush of hurried activity, Christina stripped off her clothes, throwing her finest dress most uncharacteritically on the chair near her bed rather than hanging it up. Then, she found her summerweight nightgown and jerked it over her head. Sleep, she decided, would clear her head.

But her body was not ready to rest. When she put on her nightgown, the soft, often-washed cotton slid over her nipples, and she felt the warmth of the contact pass through her body. She was still sensitive, heightened to the promises of pleasure. Her breasts felt tight, and unfamiliar sensations filled the lush swells. Fighting to ignore the signals of her body, Christina slipped between the sheets and closed her eyes.

The image of Cole Jurrell's hauntingly handsome face sprang into her mind the moment her eyes had closed.

"Stop it!" Christina hissed angrily to herself in the dark. "Just stop it."

But Cole would not leave her mind. Each touch of his hand had branded her flesh. Even now, she could feel the presence of the outlaw. She could feel his lips against hers, feel the power in his broad chest, and feel the burning desire as he pulled her against him. Flashing images, each laced with passion, slithered sensuously across the surface of Christina's mind. She saw the dimple in Cole's cheek when he smiled . . . felt the rough texture of his beard stubble against her cheek when he hugged her close . . . tasted the burnt tobacco on his lips when she explored his mouth with her tongue . . . felt the marrow-deep hunger rise up inside hers when his hands moved intimately over her body.

"Please, please get out of my mind," Christina whispered, her words muffled against the down pillow. There was a desperate quality in her voice as she added, "You're not good for me. You're a criminal. Please, Cole, get out of my heart."

Chapter 5

Nicholas Webb could hardly contain his excitement. He looked at Richard O'Banion, one of the two lawyers he kept on permanent retainer, and allowed his smile to become even more broad.

"You're sure it's all legal?" Nicholas asked rhetorically.

"Mr. Webb, I'm absolutely certain."

Nicholas chuckled hollowly. He laced his fingers together behind his head, leaning back in his swivel chair.

"She suspects nothing?"

O'Banion shook his head. "No, sir. Not a thing. Not the way I wrote the title transfer. Miss Sands would need a lawyer to unravel the legal jargon I wrote. Even then, only a very, very good lawyer would see what she is losing. But, of course, I've told you all this before."

Nicholas had volunteered to buy the mortgage she held with the Bank of Enderton, he had said, so that she wouldn't have to worry about the regulations the bank — which Nicholas owned — placed on its mortgage holders. To Christina, it sounded like a generous thing for Nicholas to do. She never thought that by allowing Nicholas to hold her mortgage note, she in effect transferred a great deal of the authority of running her store over to Nicholas.

Nicholas thought of this and chuckled again. It reminded O'Banion of an icy winter wind blowing through branches that had lost their leaves.

Christina will sing a different tune with me now! Nicho-

52

las thought savagely. *When she finds out I've got the power to throw her pretty little behind into the street, her lips won't be too precious to be kissed by mine!*

"Will there be anything else, sir?" O'Banion rose from his chair. He felt ashamed, even disgusted. Never before had he seen Nicholas Webb so gleeful over a treacherous act. He could see his employer was in another world, a world of avarice and power that he controlled with his immaculately manicured hands.

The bastard, O'Banion thought. He wants the girl. The dry goods store is small change compared to some of his other dirty deeds. But Christina? She's something special.

O'Banion said, "I'll take my leave then, sir, if there's nothing else."

The attorney was almost out of the study when Webb mumbled that he wouldn't need him any more that evening.

It wasn't until O'Banion had ridden to the outskirts of Enderton that he realized where he was going. O'Banion sensed that he should feel some regret over tricking Christina Sands into signing the contract. She thought the contract did nothing more than transfer the title of ownership from her father's name over to her own, and the mortgage from the Bank of Enderton over to Nicholas Webb. But the contract did much more than that. Nicholas had told Christina he could help her keep the dry goods store afloat, that by holding the mortgage in his own hands they were keeping the business "among friends" rather than with a coldly impersonal bank. O'Banion knew that this meant Christina would have to pay Nicholas personally, rather than the bank. She would proudfully come every month to his mansion to pay Webb his tribute. Naturally, Webb would make sure that Christina was late with a payment or two . . . but he would be *so* understanding.

Thinking about Nicholas's seduction and the demise of Christina's virtue left a foul taste in the attorney's mouth. Nicholas had taken the virtue of so many lovely young ladies already, it didn't seem fair to O'Banion that he should have Christina's. She was, as he and Nicholas knew, truly something special.

Riding slowly down Main Street, O'Banion pulled the heavy, gold watch Nicholas had given him out of his vest pocket. It was nearly six o'clock. Almost time for Christina to close up shop. She would be in the store, keeping the shelves orderly and stocked, oblivious of her tenuous future.

O'Banion needed to look into her pretty blue eyes. She'd probably even thank him again for volunteering his legal expertise — on Nicholas Webb's behest — during the past few months. O'Banion wanted to see her smile. He would smile back, secure in his superior knowledge. He would taste bittersweet victory on his tongue.

Why did he do this? When Christina spoke to him in that frisky tone she used with friends, O'Banion would reward her with a smile because she would never know how he had — quite legally — destroyed everything Christina and her father had worked for.

Christina was just stepping up to the front door, reaching to twist the Open sign to read Closed, when O'Banion stepped onto the boardwalk.

"Hi, Mr. O'Banion. What brings you here?" Christina flashed a becoming smile at the young attorney. His boss may be offensive and less than honorable, she thought, but O'Banion was always polite, even nice. Guilt by association wasn't fair. "Is everything all right? Did I forget to sign something?"

"Everything is fine." O'Banion stepped past Christina into the store. "Just thought I'd stop by and see how you were doing."

Christina blushed gently. She always felt slightly uncomfortable whenever people showed concern for her well-being.

"Thanks to your help, Mr. O'Banion, it looks like this store can keep right on operating." Christina cast her eyes down for a moment. She didn't like having to rely on others, and it embarrassed her. "I really don't know how I can ever thank you enough. After Papa passed away, I was poorly prepared. I just didn't know what to do. It was Papa who took care of the legal matters. I just did the bookkeeping."

Christina felt the warmth of tears forming. She blinked them away. Memories of her father were still fresh and comforting, but also heavyhearted.

Ashamed of the emotion she knew showed on her face and in her eyes, Christina turned away from O'Banion.

"Excuse me," she murmured, wiping her eyes and hoping O'Banion couldn't see her.

"No excuse is necessary." When Christina's back was to him, O'Banion flipped the Closed sign in the window. "I don't mind seeing a daughter missing her father. I've never really had much family to speak of. I've never had someone to miss as much as you miss your father."

"That's . . ." Christina said, biting the word "terrible" off before it escaped her lips. She mentally criticized herself for being selfish enough to miss her parents when there were good people like Richard O'Banion who never really knew their parents.

"How was business today?" He began to study some of the tools.

"Fine," Christina answered, glad to change the subject. She moved behind the counter. She needed to clear the till and total the day's receipts. Then Christina intended to go upstairs for a cup of hot milk and cocoa. She was ready to curl up in bed and sleep until morning. The hours she had spent last night tossing and turning as sleep eluded her were taking their toll on her energies today. Tonight, she was certain, she would sleep like an innocent baby.

Christina was counting the money in her hands when O'Banion suddenly stepped up behind her. He reached around her, taking her chin in his hands to turn her face toward his. Shocked by the move, Christina did not protest . . . until his lips were pressed against her own.

Twisting sharply, Christina pulled herself out of the lawyer's grasp. She rubbed the back of her hand over her lips quickly, as though to wipe away something foul that was there.

"Mr. O'Banion! What do you think you're doing?" Christina backed away from him, moving farther into the L-shaped counter. She looked into his eyes, and didn't like what she saw.

"I'm kissing you," O'Banion said. There was a cruel twist to his lips. "If you need to ask, then obviously you need more kisses. Just so you'll know one when you get it."

Christina had never once thought that Richard O'Banion would behave in such a manner, or that he was even capable of expressing sexual desire.

"Come here, Christina," O'Banion said, stepping closer to the golden-haired young woman.

"No!" Christina was still more shocked than angry. In an imperial tone she added, "Stay away from me or I shall inform Mr. Webb that you are not the gentleman he thinks you are."

O'Banion's face twisted into a mask of contempt. "Webb? If you think I'm afraid of him, think again, Christina." O'Banion took another step, keeping Christina trapped behind the counter, closing the distance that separated them. "I can't stand him, you know."

"What?"

"I said I can't stand him." O'Banion reached out and flicked a fingertip across the money Christina held. "How the hell can you make ends meet on this pittance? I spend more than that every day just for my dinner and wine." O'Banion's eyes had an evil glaze as they covetously lingered on Christina's bosom. "Nicholas Webb is a thief. You must know that, don't you? He'll own you, then he'll destroy you."

Christina's fingers unconsciously tightened around the money she held. Not in her most hideous nightmare could she conceive of being "owned" by Nicholas Webb, or any man for that matter.

"Why are you talking this way about Mr. Webb?" Christina asked. "Everyone in Enderton knows you're one of the richest men in Dakota Territory. He's made you rich."

The contemptuous laugh that burst from Richard O'Banion's lips made Christina shiver.

"*He* made *me* rich? Christina, my charming but utterly naive love, you've got that backward. I've made the grand and glorious Nicholas Webb what he is today. If it wasn't for my skill, he'd just be another second-rate hooligan, rich enough and mean enough to bully a few small farmers and ranchers, but without any real power." O'Banion stabbed himself in the chest with a finger. "I've got the brains, Christina. I'm the one who has the *real* power. If you don't believe me, maybe you'd better take another look at the contract you signed the other day."

Christina was scared in a new and horrifying way. Her father's warning of a man's true nature screamed in her mind. Unconsciously, she took another step backward. The glass cabinet stopped her, china tea cups rattling softly inside the case.

"Ah, at last I see the dawn of understanding in your pretty blue eyes, Christina. That's a good sign. Until you understand what power is, and who has that power, you'll just be another beautiful young woman with nothing more going for her than a body that a man wants to touch and a face he wants to see on the pillow beside him at night."

O'Banion saw terror in the young woman's sapphire-blue eyes, and that terror made him feel strong, manly, superior. Christina's fear fanned his desire.

"Stop talking to me that way! You've got to leave right now!"

O'Banion looked at Christina as she stood rigidly erect, hands on her hips, breasts thrust forward, defiance written on her face. He knew that Christina would soon have no choice but to sleep with Nicholas Webb. If she didn't, she would be penniless, and the young miss just was not the type of lady who could adjust to complete impoverishment.

He hated Nicholas Webb and he wanted to have Christina before Nicholas put his hands on her. But if O'Banion didn't act soon, he wouldn't be the first. He wouldn't be the man she would remember for all time.

"I've got the power to destroy Nicholas Webb, Christina. And I've got the power to destroy you, too. Or help you. I can save you. I know which judges Webb's got in his pocket, and the ones he hasn't bribed." O'Banion inched closer to Christina slowly, steadily, an ugly leer spreading across his otherwise handsome face. "I can undo the trap Webb has set for you. I know how to do it and what judge to bring it to."

"What are you talking about?" Christina shrank into the end of the counter. For the second time in two days, she felt trapped. "Mr. O'Banion, you're talking nonsense."

O'Banion laughed at Christina, tossing his head back on his shoulders to issue a short, contemptuous bark of condescension.

"You can't really be that stupid! Did you think a man like Nicholas Webb was going to help you and not expect something in return? Did you imagine *I* would help you without getting my payment for services rendered?"

"Stop this! Stop talking in riddles! You're frightening me!" Christina forced herself to appear more courageous than she felt. She squared her shoulders and stared straight into the lawyer's eyes. "If you have something to say to me, say it and get out of my store. I don't want you here anymore."

On a patronizing tone, Richard O'Banion explained to Christina that she had allowed, for all practical purposes, the controlling power of her store to be transferred into Nicholas Webb's hands. Everything was all quite legal, O'Banion said, and Christina didn't have a prayer of fighting Webb in any court in the land.

"Stop. Wait." The words came from Christina's lips woodenly. The information O'Banion had just given her bounced about in her brain, moving so quickly she couldn't grasp all that she had been told.

Would Nicholas—could Nicholas—be that treacherous? She knew he wanted to sleep with her. But would he destroy her? Would he really want to destroy her future? He had to know that she could never love him if he would even attempt such a thing.

Why? She felt fatigue swirling around her, confusing her. Why was this all happening to her? Since her father's death, Christina had known only problems, tedium, and melancholia. And now this. What O'Banion had told her was the most unsettling of all.

"My father . . . you're not taking this store from me, you're taking it from Papa. Don't you see that? Could you really hate my father that much? He never did anything to hurt a soul in his life."

Richard O'Banion placed his palms lightly on the curve of Christina's hips. He was looking down into her face with power-lust glinting in his eyes.

"I can help you, Christina. But only if you help me. I can invalidate the contract with a word to the right territorial magistrate, or I can bide my time and wait until you're penniless and without a place to live. Then you'll see me as more than just a helpful attorney working for handouts from Nicholas Webb. You'll see me as the man who can feed you and keep a roof over your head. But in order for me to want to take care of you, Christina, you'll have to take care of me. Take care of my every desire, satisfy my every wish."

O'Banion's hands inched upward from Christina's hips. "Either you give it to me now, Christina, or I'll take it from you. One way or the other, I'll have you, Christina. I'll have you every way I want you." His mouth twitched a little with vile desires. "I'm not going to let Nicholas be the first to take you. No, that just won't do. He'll have you eventually, of course, but he won't be the first. Not this time."

Christina exploded into action. She dropped the money as she reached for O'Banion's face with both hands. Her fingers clawed at this eyes, nails gouging paths through tender skin.

An animal howl of pain and rage exploded from Richard O'Banion's throat. He wheeled away from Christina, placing a hand protectively over his eyes. He felt blood, warm and sticky, against his fingers. The treacle smell of blood — his *own* blood — fired O'Banion's rage, as it would a carnivore about to make his kill.

He took his hand away from his eyes. Christina had already twisted away from him.

She's quick! he thought. *But she cannot escape me. Now I'll do more than just rape her. I'll punish her!*

The split second it took for O'Banion to go from protecting himself to attacking Christina did not afford her time to move very far. She was at the end of the counter, headed toward the front door, when O'Banion caught the puffy shoulder of her dress. He gave a savage jerk and Christina's body seemed to twist in midair. The splitting sound of a hand-sewn seam giving way to brute force preceded the young woman's short cry of terror as she stumbled, landing heavily on her knees, her dress tearing again.

O'Banion rushed around Christina, blocking the door with his powerful body, standing with his feet spread, his chest heaving as he gulped in air. Red tracks from Christina's fingernails ran down either side of his face, from his forehead down to the corners of his mouth. He touched a fingertip to his lips to taste his own blood.

"You'll be very sorry you did that," O'Banion said in a calm, even voice as he looked down at Christina. His tone was identical to the one he used in court — aloof, matter of fact, irreproachable. "As God as my witness, I'll make you pay dearly for that."

He touched Christina's exposed knee with the toe of his shoe. "Look at me when I talk to you, wench." Christina turned a tear-stained face up to her tormentor. Even her tears could not diminish her loveliness. The sleeve of her dress was almost completely severed, displaying creamy flesh. And as the shoulder had torn, it had opened several buttons. Christina's tempting, exposed cleavage made O'Banion inhale deeply, the sight of her flawless flesh fueling fires of violent carnal desire.

"Please don't," Christina said. Fresh tears ran down her damp cheeks. "Please . . ."

The small bell affixed to the front door tinkled softly, the sound incongruously light and cheerful. For years, that bell had signified customers for Christina. Now it represented her salvation.

"Get out while you still can," O'Banion said without turning, addressing whoever had entered the dry goods store. He knew there was no law in the territory that would convict him of any wrongdoing. As Nicholas Webb's personal attorney, Richard O'Banion was immune to the laws of the land.

The china tea cups rattled on the glass shelves when the small but lethal derringer leaped into Nicholas Webb's palm, sending a bullet into O'Banion's back.

For an instant, there was a stunned look on the attorney's face, as if he couldn't believe anyone would show the temerity to shoot him in the back. He began to look over one shoulder, but as he twisted, a knee buckled beneath him. He fell heavily to the floor beside Christina, his eyes still open, his face no longer showing any anger or pain.

Nicholas Webb calmly closed the door to Christina's store, crossed the room to where his attorney lay facedown on the floor and fired another bullet into the young man's back.

Christina screamed when she saw the corpse lift off the floor from the impact of lead striking it. She did not stop screaming until Nicholas was kneeling beside her, placing his palm over her mouth while saying that the evil man had been killed and she had nothing to fear now that he was there.

"You k-k-killed him," Christina hissed, unable to look away from the man who had attacked her. She was in Nicholas's arms and he was stroking her satiny hair. "My G-God . . . you killed him."

"You know I had to, my darling," Nicholas said, stroking Christina's tresses, casually removing hair combs. He could feel the warmth of her breath against his cheek, the

61

firmness of her breasts against his chest. As she sobbed softly in his arms, Nicholas found himself imagining the two of them on the floor, locked in a union that would seal them together for all their years. Perhaps he could finish what O'Banion began. Greedy kid. They were both obsessed with Christina, but O'Banion had gotten here first. Now, though, Christina *couldn't* refuse him.

"I'll kill any man who tries to harm you," Nicholas whispered, believing wrongly that the words would calm Christina's fears. "I'll kill any man who even looks at you the wrong way."

Christina pushed weakly against Nicholas's chest. Just now, the magnitude of this man's potential for violence was sinking in. And though he had, in fact, protected her from Richard O'Banion's attempt to rape her, Christina could not allow herself to forget that Nicholas, too, had tried to force himself upon her.

"Don't Nicholas," Christina said, her voice still trembling, but firmer now. She pushed against Nicholas again. "Please, I just want to be left alone."

"No, my darling," Nicholas replied, his tone warm, smooth. "You mustn't be alone tonight. Not after what happened. Don't worry. I'll take care of you. He's dead now and nobody is going to hurt you."

Christina wanted to believe him, and she instinctively clung to him. Her body shook. She had never seen anyone die before, and the shock of seeing death — stark and real — was more than she could take.

"Shh!" Nicholas murmured. "I know you want to be strong. I know you do, my darling. But just this one time, it's okay for you to let someone else take care of you. It's okay for you to just want to be held, Christina. You can be strong and independent later. For now, just feel my arms around you and know that you are safe."

His words were like a salve. Nicholas's arms at that moment, felt like her father's arms, surrounding and protecting her from a hostile world. Christina closed her eyes, fighting against the fear that gripped her like a fist.

Nicholas felt his anger abating. Seeing O'Banion towering over Christina had incited a blind rage in Nicholas, reducing him to behave exactly as he had years ago. Without a moment's hesitation, Nicholas had pulled out the small derringer he kept in his right coat pocket. When he heard O'Banion's self-important tone, it was as though the lawyer had spit in Nicholas's face.

Didn't O'Banion know that he — Nicholas Webb — had claimed Christina Sands as his personal property?

Holding Christina tighter against his chest, pulling against the resistance she put forward, Nicholas looked at O'Banion's corpse.

You damn fool! You could have had anyone else you wanted, and I wouldn't have minded one little bit, but you had to rape my woman.

Nicholas cupped Christina's chin in his palm, forcing her face up so their eyes could meet. Killing O'Banion had brought back old feelings to Nicholas, harkening him back to the days when he had to fight savagely for everything he stole, back to the days when those men who were foolish enough to challenge Nicholas Webb were dealt with at night, with a single, well-placed bullet between the shoulder blades. That was how Nicholas had solved threats to his power long ago, and it pleased him immensely to know that he was still capable of such swift and final action.

"Look at me, Christina. I want you to look into my eyes and know that you are safe, Christina. Safe when you are with me."

Christina looked into Nicholas's eyes. The empty soul she had seen before was still there, vacant and hollow. She tried to turn her face away, but Nicholas firmly led her chin toward him.

"Christina, can't you see how important you are to me? Can't you see how good I am for you? How beautiful I can make your life?" Nicholas felt himself reacting to Christina's closeness. He studied her face, drinking in her youth and beauty. Killing O'Banion had made him feel young again . . . young, potent and virile.

63

"So beautiful," he whispered.

Nicholas's eyes went from Christina's face down to the torn, exposed bodice of her dress. The sight of her breasts enflamed his lust . . . but it did not affect him nearly as strongly as seeing the heirloom locket dangling from Christina's slender throat, the same locket that had been stolen by Cole Jurrell's gang.

"You bitch."

Christina looked at Nicholas, the ice of his words stinging her face.

"You little slut, I trusted you."

"Nicholas . . . what are you . . . why are you . . . ?"

Incredibly, in a moment, his concern was replaced by an ugly, violent scowl.

"You know exactly what I'm talking about!" Nicholas still held Christina's chin between a curved finger and thumb, but now squeezed tightly enough to make the young woman gasp in pain. "And to think I traded O'Banion's life for yours! I killed a skilled attorney—and my friend—to protect the *honor*"—he drawled the word out as though it was his favorite obscenity—"of a whore."

Christina wriggled in Nicholas's arms. His words were frightening her. Worst of all, she had no notion of why Nicholas's mood had changed so fast. When she tried to slide out of his grasp, the silver-haired man's arm tightened around her violently, making it difficult for her to breathe.

"No, no, Christina. I let you stop me once before, but I'll have my fill of you tonight. Your ruse has been discovered, so please don't bother playing coy and virginal with me."

Christina saw the direction of Nicholas's gaze, and in that instant it all became clear to her. Nicholas knew that she had seen Cole Jurrell, and he believed more had transpired between them that just verbal barbs and the return of Christina's locket.

"Oh, my lord, Nicholas, you can't believe . . ." Christina said in a faltering voice.

She knew she could not stop Nicholas this time with a

push against his chest and a cross look. O'Banion had wanted her, and was willing to rape her to get what he desired. Now, to Christina's complete horror, the man she had thought was her rescuer was going to take O'Banion's place—and take her, whether she wanted him to or not.

"Please . . . please, Nicholas, can't you see what I've been through?" Christina whispered, pleading with her eyes as well as her words.

What happened next was a blur for Christina. He began to move, and she sprang into action, clawing at Nicholas's face just as she had O'Banion's. The result was the same, as Christina had known it would be—she got only a temporary reprive from danger when Nicholas released her to protect his scratched and bleeding face.

She seized the moment and rolled away from Nicholas, getting her knees beneath her. He came at her like an enraged animal, and looking into his eyes Christina was reminded of the time she had seen a rabid dog in the throes of its frenzy acting violently, lethally.

Nicholas lunged at Christina, but she was young and quick and darted away from his grasping hands. She stumbled, trying to run in one direction while looking over her shoulder. Again she hit the hardwood floor, pain jarring up her spine from her knees.

Nicholas reached and caught her skirt. He pulled on it, wanting to ensnare the blond girl in his grasp. Instead, he caught the sole of her shoe flush on the face.

"Damn you!" Nicholas howled as blood streamed from his nose. His eyes watered from the blow to his nose, and when his vision had cleared enough to see the blurred image of Christina, he lunged for her again.

Christina brought the flat iron down with all her might. The sharp bottom corner grazed against the side of Nicholas's head, stunning him, continuing downward to smash hard against the flesh and muscle of his shoulder. The silver-haired man dropped to the floor, curling into a ball, clutching onto his left shoulder and rolling away from Christina, trying to protect himself from another blow with his knees.

Christina dropped the iron and rushed to the back room. She was out of the dry goods store in just seconds, her heart thudding in her chest, her young, gentle heart torn apart by the treachery of the men in her life.

Deputy Silas Miller's boots slammed on the boardwalk, drawing Nicholas's attention. He entered the dry goods store with a revolver in his hand.

"Mr. Webb, what . . ." Silas's words trailed off as he saw the body of Richard O'Banion laying facedown on the floor.

"It was Christina," Nicholas said, straightening himself. He placed a hand against his temple and felt the warm stickiness of his own blood. There were also furrowed scratches running down his cheeks.

"She went crazy, Silas. Absolutely crazy. I came here with my attorney to help her with some legal matters. The next thing I knew, she shot Richard." Nicholas groaned expressively, looking at the corpse. "I don't really know what happened next. She hit me . . . from behind. Hit me with something. Then she took off through the back door."

Silas knelt near the body. He touched his fingers against the throat, searching for but not finding a pulse.

"Get a posse together, Silas. I want that woman caught tonight." Nicholas almost smiled at the plan that was forming in his brain. "I want her brought directly to me. Do you understand me, Silas?"

"Sir? If she murdered Mr. O'Banion, then the law says—"

"Don't tell me what the law says!" Nicholas snapped, his voice cold and lethal. "I put you in office, Silas Miller, and I can boot you out just as easily! Now, you get a posse together and you find Christina Sands! And when you've done that, you bring her to my house. Is that understood?"

Silas Miller knew who ran Enderton and the land around it. He knew, too, what happened to people who openly disobeyed an order from Nicholas Webb.

"Yes, sir, Mr. Webb," Silas said after a moment. "I'll get right on it. Right on it this second. Sheriff Bellows is at the saloon. I'll tell him about Miss Sands murdering Mr. O'Banion, and we'll get a posse together."

Nicholas, feeling his power was unchallenged, nodded his approval.

Soon enough he would have Christina Sands in his grasp . . . and in his bed. And if she did not please his every whim and wish, if she didn't satisfy even his most vile desires, he would see her hang for the cold-blooded murder of Richard O'Banion.

Chapter 6

Christina hugged her knees to her chest, pressing her cheek against the rough surface of the old oak rain barrel at the back of her store. She was curled into a ball, and had been that way for some time now. The dull ache in her legs was getting worse by the minute, but she didn't dare move out from behind the barrels until complete darkness enveloped her.

The events of the past ninety minutes were horrifying to recall. There were shouts from Deputy Miller calling for the sheriff, saying Richard O'Banion had been killed. And then, a second before Christina was about to move from her hiding spot to explain the truth, the deputy was explaining to curious onlookers that Christina Sands, with motive unknown, had ruthlessly shot O'Banion in the back. Twice.

A posse was quickly gathered. People who had been steady customers at the dry goods store were anxious to get their hands on the reward money Nicholas Webb offered for the safe return—to him *personally*—of Christina Sands.

With a helpless, sinking feeling of utter doom, Christina stayed huddled between the rain barrels and the solid back wall of her store as men and women she knew gossiped about her, impugned her character, and contemplated whether or not there would be a public hanging in Enderton when the posse caught her.

Christina scanned the shadows of the back street. Slowly, with legs cramped and stiff, she rose to her feet.

She didn't have many options, and she didn't like any of them. If she stayed in Enderton, she would surely be caught. There was a man upstairs in her home at that moment, hoping she would return so he could collect the sizable reward Nicholas Webb had offered. Heavily armed riders were combing the hills outside of town, searching for her tracks. Even if she got to the edge of town under cover of darkness, Christina had to cross paths with torch-bearing riders.

Not liking her choices or her chances of escaping, Christina summoned up all her strength and will. It was best, she decided, to at least try to escape, however horrendous the odds against her success were. It was better to be caught than to simply give up. She had to fight back. She did not know exactly how she would fight against Nicholas Webb. But fight she would, with all her strength and cunning.

Wary of everyone, especially of those people she had hours earlier thought of as her friends, Christina headed into the night, into the unknown.

Cole sat cross-legged in front of the small campfire, staring at the flickering flames of red, yellow, blue, orange, and gold. Between the first and second fingers of his right hand, a cigarette sent a thin trail of smoke spiraling upward into the still night air. Just to Cole's left was a tin cup with coffee steaming in it and a tin plate with the remains of a roasted rabbit.

He should have been content. His belly was full of savory food, and he had even taken the time to leisurely enjoy an after-dinner cigarette and coffee. Near a sharp bend in the Sheyenne River, Cole felt as safe as a man like him could ever feel.

But unwelcome thoughts crowded his leisure time.

Cole Jurrell was not a man given to self-deception. It

was this trait of looking at himself critically, without blinders, that had saved his life countless times. It also made it impossible for Cole to blame his current mental agitation on anyone other than Christina Sands.

She was a mixture of a thousand things that Cole admired and despised. She confused and perplexed him—of that much he was certain. She was stubborn, willful, and seemingly naive. She was radiantly beautiful, kind-hearted, responsible.

It was what he did not know that turned his soul in knots and kept his brain searching for answers even though his better judgment told Cole there were none to be found.

Was Christina Sands the type of woman who was more concerned with what a man had in his wallet than what he held in his heart? That would explain her involvement with Nicholas Webb. Cole had even spied them kissing. The image of Christina and Nicholas standing at the foot of the stairs, kissing deeply, was burned like a scar in Cole's brain.

Stop thinking about her! Cole told himself. *You have duties! You haven't got time for a permanent woman. There's no room in your life for love!*

Cole wanted to have Christina because he hated her relationship with Nicholas Webb. Nicholas represented everything that Cole found reprehensible in this world. He understood how Christina could be attracted to Nicholas, though. He was a handsome man, made more handsome by his wealth. He was charming, Cole supposed, in a deceptive sort of way. And he had possessions—a mansion to live in, employees to tend to his wishes, money to lavish women with gifts.

What Cole could not forget, what he could not forgive, was that Christina apparently didn't care that Nicholas Webb had gotten his money by stealing it from honest, decent folks who asked for nothing more out of life than to have a loving marriage, raise happy, healthy children, and to work their lands for crops to feed and clothe themselves with.

Cole pushed the thoughts of Nicholas from his mind. Thinking about that thief only made him angry. His coffee was cold, and the cigarette had gone out.

Don't dream too much, he warned himself. *This isn't Webb territory, but he's made the reward large enough to make even the most loyal friends turn you in for the bounty.*

Cole relit the cigarette, tossed out the cold coffee, then poured himself a fresh cup. There was no need for him to be too worried here along the banks of the Sheyenne River. He had hunted in this area all his life. There wasn't a deer trail he didn't know about. There wasn't another living person, white man or Indian, who knew the area — the river, or the woods and grassy plains on either side of the Sheyenne — better than he did. If he should be chased here, Cole would lead the hunting party into the forest, and from there he'd tie them in knots, leading them in circles within circles within circles.

Nicholas Webb held the deed for this land, through money and force. But it was Cole Jurrell who owned it. Cole owned the land because he understood it.

These were comforting thoughts to Cole. He felt himself relaxing, the weary, coiled muscles in his back and shoulders releasing the unconscious tension that had kept them tight. When thoughts of Christina crept slowly back into his mind, Cole embraced them this time, no longer frightened that he was letting his guard down.

She is truly something special, he thought. The fleeting moments he'd spent with her in her home had been exhilarating for him. It wasn't just the time when he held her close that came to mind. A mosaic of visual impressions moved sensuously across the surface of his mind.

To Cole, Christina was a mixture of light and shadow, the known and the unknown, the readily conceivable and the unfathomable mystery.

Her kisses were a fire in Cole's soul. He had stolen the kisses from Christina to begin with. Then they had come to him hesitantly, and finally, they had become fierce and

71

hungry, demanding responses from Cole. Searching, fiery kisses of the untutored, clumsily given sometimes, yet in that inexperience, that much more exciting.

Unconsciously, Cole caught his lower lip between his teeth. Thinking about Christina's soft, moist lips pressing against his made it possible for him to practically taste those kisses now. Closing his eyes, Cole could feel every feminine inch of Christina's body pressing firmly against him. He felt the fullness of her breasts flattening against his hard-muscled chest, the warmth of her thighs rubbing against his own as she molded her body against his in their passionate embrace.

The fragrance of her hair and skin came back to him. This last vestige of Christina's presence was more than Cole could take. He bolted to his feet, spilling the coffee that had again gotten cold in the cup.

"I'm losing my mind," he whispered angrily to himself. Black Jack, ground-tied nearby, neighed softly. "Oh, just shut up!" Cole snapped. "I don't need you telling me I'm acting like a lovestruck teenage boy!"

Cole took the coffeepot to the river and filled it, then doused his small fire. After washing the cup, plate, and frying pan and stowing them, he unrolled his blanket and bedded down.

The instant Cole closed his eyes, Christina's face came to mind.

"That damn girl!" he said aloud, shaking his head in self-disgust at what he perceived as a terrible and possibly fatal personal weakness.

Christina was exhausted, hungry, wet, and itched in a dozen different places. She stumbled forward, forcing one foot in front of the next, fighting against an unwilling body that begged for a soothing bath and a soft bed.

The sun would be up soon. And with it, Christina's one great advantage against those who followed her—the cover of darkness—would be gone. She had to find someplace to hide during the day. A place to hide and sleep and regain her strength so she could run again when darkness would conceal her escape.

How much distance had she covered in her night-long run from the posse that Sheriff Bellows and Deputy Miller had gathered? Were they still following her? Had they, in fact, ever really caught her trail? Christina was lost, but had she lost the *posse?*

Huddled behind the rain barrels, she had heard enough to know that the posse split into two groups. Sheriff Bellows had recruited Heinrich Boelke. Boelke's black labrador retrievers were considered the finest dogs in the territory. They were hunting dogs that were also good with cattle. Would they be any good at tracking a woman? It was a question that had haunted Christina throughout the night, spurring her on even when her lungs burned with exertion. On several occasions she had heard the yelp of an excited dog. It was a spine-chilling sound that echoed through the night. Each time she heard the barking, Christina was convinced that her trail had been picked up by one of the dogs. It wouldn't be long, she told herself, until the riders tracked her down and carted her away . . . back to Nicholas Webb, fulfilling whatever vile plans he had for her.

Justice would be looking the other way as he dragged her into his bed.

Christina's dress was wet and heavy, clinging to her calves. She had crossed several streams and on more than one occasion walked in the Sheyenne River for stretches of a hundred yards and more. The dogs, she frantically hoped, couldn't follow her trail through the way. They couldn't, could they?

To her left, the first pink rays of dawn allowed the outline of the trees on the opposite bank to be visible. Seeing the trees now made Christina gasp. It took so little time for the world to go from night to day.

So fast. Everything is happening so fast.

Wearily, she forced herself up the river bank toward the

73

trees. She stumbled into the brush, falling at the feet of the beast she was sure would kill her.

Her breath caught in her throat. Fearfully, she looked up at the largest, most exquisite creature her eyes had ever seen, a big, powerful stallion that could carry her bone-weary body for miles and miles without ever tiring. It was a magnificent creature that would carry her far away from the evil men who hunted her. She nearly wept with relief.

Christina slowly rose, watching. The stallion's nostrils flared. He stood upright, his head held high sniffing the morning breeze. He ambled back into the forest about twenty feet. Then that great beast turned toward her and brown eyes looked straight at her.

Christina held her hands out, palms extended, thinking the gesture would somehow let the horse know that she meant him no harm. Her eyes flashed right and left, searching for the horse's owner. Clearly, this was not a wild horse. Though it was without a saddle, it wore a bridle.

Christina clutched her torn dress tight about her bosom. Was the horse's owner part of the posse that chased her? It didn't seem likely. They had ridden in a pack like wolves, not singly. Then who? Did it matter? Could she reason with the owner of the horse? Not likely. Not with her dress torn in too many places to be modest, her long blond hair all disheveled and countless small scratches on her fore-arms and cheeks from the night-long dash through woods and forests.

The horse eyed her warily.

"Easy, boy," Christina said, her voice a whisper. "Easy now. I'm not going to hurt you. No, I'm not going to hurt you one little bit."

She advanced slowly, fearful the stallion would bolt or charge her.

"Please don't run away from me."

The pleading sound in Christina's voice made her feel

ashamed. She advanced on the stallion, simultaneously trying to watch the horse and look around for its owner. A shiver of fear and frustration worked its way up Christina's spine. Her vision became blurred with tears that she valiantly willed away.

She was close . . . so very close to escaping. With that big stallion carrying her, Christina knew the posse would never catch her. If only he would let her catch his reins . . . if only the owner didn't show up and shoot her for trying to steal his horse . . . if only. . . .

Ten feet separated Christina from the stallion. Ten . . . then five . . . then she slowly reached out and curled her fingers around one dangling rein. She took another step, holding tightly onto the rein with one hand, placing her other palm out for the stallion to smell.

"Easy, boy," Christina said in a soft, soothing voice. "It's just me, boy. It's just Christina."

Christina expected the stallion to bolt, but he never did. She reached around his thickly muscled neck to slide the reins into riding position. As Christina did this, she kept up a steady stream of small talk directed to the big black stallion that was her ticket to freedom.

Once the reins were looped around the stallion's neck, Christina's confidence soared. Now, even if he bolted, she at least had the chance of holding him in check.

"That's my love," Christina said in an affectionate tone. She cupped the stallion's nose in her hand, and he in response, nuzzled her, rubbing his head against her side. "Now just stand nice and still. I'm not going to hurt you. I'm just going to get on your back so you can carry me far away from here."

Since the stallion was very tall and without a saddle, Christina had to leap head-first over the horse to get onto his back. With her head and shoulders hanging over the right side of the horse and her legs hanging over the left, Christina was vulnerable to being bucked off.

The powerful stallion stood rock-still.

Christina had never ridden bareback before. Turning

slowly on the back of the muscular black stallion, she kicked a leg over him, straddling the animal before pushing herself to a sitting position.

"Come on, boy. Let's go," Christina whispered, her concern now centered on the owner of the horse rather than the horse itself. She pulled the reins to turn the stallion.

He didn't move a muscle.

"Come on," she whispered.

Christina nudged the stallion's ribs with her ankles. The animal neighed softly with annoyance. He never took a step.

"Move!"

Christina thumped her heels against the stallion's ribs, hard this time. She expected him to take off like a shot, as most horses would, as any *reasonable* horse would. Instead, this stallion just let out a rumbling sound of protest and turned his big head to one side to take another look at the bothersome young woman who had mounted him.

"Run, you stupid beast!"

Christina hit the stallion's ribs with her heels, using all her might . . . and still he didn't move.

From the woods, hidden by trees, a deep, resonant voice cut through the early morning air. The voice was thickly laced with humor.

"That beast is smart enough to know he doesn't have to take you anywhere."

Christina's heart stopped beating. The pistol appeared from the thin shadows first . . . then Cole Jurrell stepped out. He held the Colt with apparent casualness, but it never wavered from Christina as he approached her. His eyes darted around, looking only briefly at Christina.

"I'm alone," Christina said, sensing the question Cole had yet to ask.

"Sure." Cole stopped when twenty feet separated them. His tone said he didn't believe her. "Try again." Cole eased down the hammer of the Colt, but he didn't turn the muzzle away from Christina. "Around here horse stealing is punishable by hanging."

Christina didn't want to smile. She didn't see any real humor in what was happening, or in the events of the past evening. Still, the whole notion of being tried and convicted for stealing a wanted criminal's horse did have the elements of gallows humor.

"You find this funny?"

Just as Christina had not planned to smile, so, too, she could not keep the smile on her face. The smile faded and all the anger and fear, the unjustice and helplessness . . . it all came out and only Christina's refusal to let Cole see her cry kept the tears from spilling down her cheeks.

"That's very nice." Cole moved until he stood near Jack's head. He patted the stallion's velvet-soft nose. "Almost believable. You really are quite an accomplished actress. With that sorry look on your face and those trembling lips, you look so innocent. Do tell me, Miss Sands, what you're doing here in such a condition."

Cole holstered his revolver and placed his hands around Christina's slim waist as she slipped off Black Jack. He held her suspended in midair a moment before placing her lightly to the ground. Even after Christina had her feet on the grassy riverbank, Cole kept his hands placed lightly on the gentle curve of her hips.

"It'll be more convincing if you turn on the tears." Cole's eyes were hard, his tone softly condescending as he studied Christina. "I don't know what you're trying to convince me of yet, but I'm sure you'll get around to it as soon as you're finished with the theatrics."

To a suspicious audience of one, Christina gave Cole the facts, telling him everything, even how both O'Banion and Webb had tried to rape her. Looking at Cole, Christina couldn't read anything in his expression. No sympathy or sorrow, no understanding. She couldn't read anything at all in the slate gray eyes that looked at her with such icy intensity.

"I've got lousy luck," Cole said after a long pause.

"*You've* got lousy luck?" Christina exclaimed.

"Yeah. I'd hate like hell to get caught by a posse that's

77

chasing after you." Cole shook his head in disgust. "Kid, if this is some sort of trick, I promise you this — you'll never be alive when they get me."

"I'm telling you the truth," Christina replied wearily. She took several steps away from Cole and sat on the banks of the Sheyenne. "Mr. Jurrell, I'm telling you the truth. I don't know what else I can do to convince you."

She no longer felt like crying. She was just tired beyond words and disillusioned beyond hope. Christina put her face in her hands, talking through her fingers. "Go ahead and leave, if that's what you feel you must do. I didn't mean to lead the posse in your direction. I don't even know for sure if they're still chasing me. All I do know is that I'm tired and hungry. I can't keep running. I just . . . I haven't got any strength left."

Cole did not believe all of Christina's story. Nicholas Webb was a thief and murderer, but he hadn't shown any predilection for rape. Hell, he had women throwing themselves at him, hoping for a slice of the Webb fortune.

The torn dress, Cole reasoned, could just be a clever disguise. But the haggard look on Christina's face and the haunted look in her eyes made Cole at least *want* to believe she was telling the truth.

"Where does the truth end? Where do the lies begin?" Cole heard himself ask quietly. The question was for himself, not Christina. He hadn't planned on voicing his doubts.

He glanced to the east. The sun was just rising above the horizon. "I know you want me to believe you, Christina. But I also know you've got something going with Webb. You were kissing him the other night, remember? Why shouldn't I believe you've been sent here to slow me down? Why shouldn't I believe you're just part of some plan to capture me?"

Christina took her face away from her hands. She turned angry, tired eyes up to Cole. "I was trying to steal your horse, if you'll recall. Believe me, you are the last person in the world I wanted to run into."

Christina rose to her feet with a groan. She dusted herself off, then tried to pull her bodice together modestly.

"Believe what you want to believe. I've told you the truth. There isn't any more I can do to make you believe me."

"Oh?" Cole asked, one eyebrow cocked up in false amusement.

"There isn't any more that I'm *willing* to do."

Christina turned away from Cole, walking parallel to the river, pride forcing her to take one step after the other.

Cole Jurrell was the cruelest man alive!

"Where are you going?"

"To find someplace to rest," Christina said over her shoulder, anger adding strength to her words and stride. "I'll wait until darkness, then start up again tonight."

Cole grit his teeth. He didn't need a traveling companion—certainly not one accustomed to sleeping in a bed every night and eating hot meals three times a day. He didn't need a naive, pampered young woman slowing him down. He was fighting a war for the victims of Nicholas Webb.

Cole had promised himself that he wouldn't let anything stand in his way until justice was served, his inheritance was returned—and, most of all, until Nicholas Webb was found guilty for the murder of Cole's father. He'd have to be a damn fool to think he had any time to spend on a silly, spoiled little woman like Christina Sands.

"Wait," he said. "You're dead on your feet. If you wait until I saddle Jack, you can ride with me."

Chapter 7

Cole felt Christina stir against him as she slept. He allowed himself a smile, since she wouldn't be able to see the pleasure he took in cradling her in his arms. Jack didn't seem to mind the extra weight, but cautious of overtaxing his trusted mount's strength, Cole had stopped more often than normal to let his horse drink.

The posse had been able to follow Christina's rambling of the previous evening, but they were still far behind. At least two miles, Cole guessed. Cole had spied the six-man posse through his field glasses several times after crossing a ravine or flat stretch of grassland.

The posse was close enough to concern Cole, but not close enought to worry him greatly.

"No . . . no . . . please don't . . . why?" Christina murmured in her sleep.

She sat side-saddle across Cole's thighs with her head on his shoulder, leaning against him while his strong arms surrounded her.

She's so tired thought Cole. Scared and tired. I know how that feels.

Cole's first instinct was to bring Christina to Angelina's. At Angelina's, Christina could rest in a bed and eat nourishing, hot food. Cole had even started out in Angelina's direction. It wasn't until he caught his first glance of the posse that he changed his mind.

Cole had seen posses before. Plenty of them. He knew

the character of the men compromising a posse gathered under Nicholas Webb's orders. They were a vile, greedy, blood-thirsty bunch, more interested in sating their base desires than seeing that justice was done.

If the posse were able to follow Cole's tracks to Angelina's, he knew she would face the worst of their male compulsions. Angelina was half Mexican, which in the minds of so many of Webb's followers made her only half human. She would be taken by the men in the posse and forced to do unspeakable things.

Cole simply couldn't endanger Angelina that way. Just being her friend put her life in danger.

But there was another reason that Cole had not brought Christina to Angelina's, though he didn't like admitting it to himself. Cole enjoyed having the young woman with him. Even though her dress was dirty and torn, her face smudged with dirt and her hair disheveled, she was exquisitely beautiful to him. And if he could legitimately keep her with him — even for a few extra hours — he would.

"Stay . . . away," Christina mumbled, shifting again in Cole's lap.

"Shhh!"

Cole's left hand held the reins. With his right hand he stroked Christina's mussed, honey blond hair. Her presence, even in sleep, was disquieting, intoxicating. He felt the warmth of her breath against his neck. Whenever he looked down, Cole could not keep his eyes from straying to Christina's bosom. The missing buttons of her dress allowing him to see the fullness of her breasts.

He forced his gaze away, feeling guilty for invading her privacy as she slept. She looked so innocent, so vulnerable. Perhaps she had told him the truth. Perhaps she, too, was a victim of Nicholas Webb.

The sun was high overhead. Cole guessed it would be noon soon. He felt the rumblings of his stomach and wondered if Christina was hungry too. He wished he had something more civilized than his traveling rations to give to her. She clearly was not accustomed to doing without.

For all Cole could gather, until the previous evening she had never known the pangs of real hunger, or the stark terror of feeling like a fox running from the hounds.

Christina stirred again, moaning softly. Her long, dark lashes fluttered against her soft cheeks.

"Wake up gently," Cole whispered. He felt Christina get tense as she realized he was holding her. "There's nothing to worry about."

"What are you . . . ?" Christina pushed herself away from Cole. She studied his face with wide, frightened blue eyes. "Where are we?"

"A long way from where we were, which should please you." Cole flashed a smile at Christina. "With any luck at all, the posse is far behind, and thoroughly lost. They might not even be on our trail by this time."

"Really?"

"Would I lie to you?"

The look Christina gave Cole caused him to laugh heartily. Despite herself, she, too, laughed. Cole didn't know the posse was off the trail, but he didn't see the need in worrying Christina with the truth. Knowing that they were still being followed wouldn't change anything for Christina and would only heighten her anxiety.

"Hungry?"

Christina looked at Cole questioningly. She didn't trust him and said as much with her eyes. In her darkened home, Cole had worked his devilish charm on the beautiful young woman. It still frightened her to remember how her body had reacted to his kisses, to his caresses. It was Cole's ability to make her want him that made him so much more frightening and dangerous than the crudely forward men like Nicholas Webb and Richard O'Banion.

Christina knew, too, that no man gave anything away. Webb and O'Banion had taught her that much. Any good deed done had a price attached to it. A man may not say as much, at least not right away, but Christina knew that sooner or later, inexorably, all men wanted something in return for helping a woman. Christina could guess what that *something* was.

"Well?"

Christina wished Cole wouldn't act so abominably cheerful. It rankled her nerves.

"I don't know."

Cole chuckled softly. "You're hungry. It shouldn't take much thinking. You've been running all night." Cole let his palm rest momentarily on the small of Christina's back. She flinched at the contact. "We'll stop soon and eat. Maybe food can put a smile on your face." Quietly he added, "I sure can't."

It amused Cole enormously to see Christina fidgeting. She was trying to sit across his lap without actually having to touch him. The fact that this was impossible made it all the more amusing for Cole.

Christina sat in stony silence until they stopped beside a natural artesian well. Her body was stiff from head to toe. Her back and neck ached from sleeping while sitting upright leaning against Cole.

Even though the artesian water was brackish and the corn bread was a little stale, Christina ate ravenously.

"I can't believe I'm enjoying this," Christina said. She swallowed a mouthful of corn bread, then washed it down with cool water. "I hate jerky, but this has got to be the most delicious meal I've had in months."

She stripped the beef by pulling it along the grain and chewed it for a long time before it finally broke down enough for her to swallow. Although tough and chewy, it was tasty with natural flavor and the smoke from which it was cured.

"Did you make this yourself?"

Cole shook his head, his cheek puffed out with beef. "No. I bought it from a friend. I used to cure my own, but you need a stable place to call home for that. You can't carry a smokehouse around with you when you've got a reward on your head."

"I suppose not." Christina felt herself blush slightly. "I don't usually ask such stupid questions."

"You're not used to being hunted, that's all." After a pause, Cole added with a tone of sadness. "If what you told me this morning is true, you'll have to start thinking as I do. You're on the run now. You'll learn to never truly trust anyone. Every face you see belongs to a potential enemy."

"Even yours?"

"No. Not mine. But you mustn't trust anyone else."

"Don't," Christina said without looking up.

"Don't what."

"Don't tell me that."

"But it's the truth, Christina. The sooner you accept the way things are now, the sooner you'll get along on your own."

Christina's head snapped up. "You're leaving me?"

"No, not yet. But eventually I'll have to. You don't want to stay too close to me, Christina." There was bitterness in Cole's tone when he said, "I'm not safe to be around."

It was Christina this time who forced a smile on her face and a lightness in her voice as she said, "You've already shown that much to me."

She didn't know how to interpret the look Cole gave her.

Another silence fell over Cole and Christina, shrouding them in an eerie uncomfortableness that didn't fit the bright, sunny day. A thousand questions hounded Christina. She wanted answers, but was leery of alienating Cole by asking more than she should. Though she did not know much about the man, she sensed that he was the brooding type, a man comfortable with silence and solitude.

"Where are we going?" Christina asked as the meal came to a close.

"Fargo. To begin with, anyway."

Christina ached to get answers faster than Cole was giving them to her, but she bit her tongue, waiting for the reticent man to continue. He took tobacco and papers from his pocket and rolled a cigarette. After scratching a match with his thumbnail, he lighted the cigarette and inhaled softly on it.

84

"I've got a place where you can stay a while. You'll be safe there."

"In Fargo?"

Cole shook his head. "No. Another city."

"Why the mystery?"

It chilled Christina when Cole tilted his head up slowly and matched her gaze with his icy gray eyes. "Because I don't trust you." His gaze never left Christina's. "At least not yet. You've got to understand, I've been at this a long time now. You're very beautiful, very . . . desirable. That makes me want to forget who and what I am. I just can't allow that to happen to me.

Cole flicked his cigarette away. He exhaled smoke, shaking his head as though he tasted something foul. "I don't want to die because I've got pleasure on my mind instead of business." He smiled, but there was little warmth in it. "You are very attractive."

"When you say it that way, it almost sounds like an insult, like it's something bad."

Cole was no longer looking at Christina, and it gave her the chance to study him as she hadn't been able to before. *Is he really as cynical as he wants me to be believe?* Christina asked herself. *Will I get like that in time? Is that what happens to people when they're hunted like animals?*

They were unnerving thoughts to Christina, made more disquieting because she knew the answers would not be soon in coming.

"Is there anything I can do to help you?" Christina played with the frayed hem of her dress. Last night, the hem and the rest of her dress were in immaculate condition; now the hem was torn from rushing through prickly brush. "I'm not as good at running as you are, but I'll help you if I can."

"There's nothing you can do."

"I could walk."

"You're too tired." Cole stood up suddenly. "Don't worry about it. If you walked, you'd only exhaust yourself more than you already are. Jack's a big, strong horse. Thoroughbred and quarterhorse. He can carry us both. At least until we get to Fargo. After that, it won't matter."

What does that mean? wondered Christina. She bit her bottom lip between even white teeth to keep from asking the question Cole obviously wasn't inclined to answer.

"Come on. We can make Fargo by tomorrow morning if we push hard."

Cole reached down for Christina's hand, and she placed it in his. For a moment their eyes locked. Cole's long, slender fingers tightened around Christina's small hand, and the faintest hint of a smile played with the left corner of his mouth. In his eyes, as brief as a shooting star, and therefore, as precious as one, Christina saw a gentle, possessive spark of pleasure that touched her soul and warmed her heart.

They stood for a long moment, holding hands, looking into each other's eyes. The heat of Cole's hand surrounding Christina's suffused itself throughout her body. Looking up into his eyes, Christina remembered the dizzying effect of Cole's kisses, how blindingly erotic it had been to have her body molding to Cole's long, powerful frame. Each time he kissed her, he increased her passion until her only reality was her heart's newfound need to feel the passion of the outlaw Cole Jurrell.

And then, just when Christina thought that she would again taste the sweetness of his kisses, when she could once more feel the searing pleasure of his strong, tantalizing caresses—he turned sharply away from her.

"Come on," Cole said, taking long strides to where Jack was ground-tied. "We haven't got time to sit around jabbering like school children."

Marcus Kensington hadn't gotten the word until the following morning, when he showed up at the dry goods store to see how Christina was.

"You can't be telling me the truth," Marcus said. He clenched his hands behind his back to keep Zachary Webb from seeing they were trembling.

"Afraid so, old man." Zachary was leaning against the counter, his left hand toying idly with the few dollars that were still in the till. "She gunned O'Banion down. Shot him in the back twice."

"That sounds more like something you would do. Not Christina."

The laughter Marcus saw in Zachary's eyes made him want to beat the young man senseless. But Marcus knew he was too old for Zachary.

Marcus and Christina's father had been partners, of sorts, in the dry goods store. After the death of his wife, Marcus had been inconsolate. It was only Christina's father who took the time to try to comfort the wealthy recluse, and because of this, Marcus had kept an eye on Christina after she lost her father. It was, to Marcus, only a matter of respect.

"Get the hell out of here," Zachary spat. "Now, old man!"

"No! You get out, you little thief!"

Zachary's black-gloved hand tightened around the handle of his revolver. Marcus looked at the hand, then up at Zachary's dark eyes, and he knew that the young man had killed before. Zachary's reputation as a rich, spoiled, vicious monster, Marcus now decided, was richly deserved.

"Thief?" Zachary laughed softly, his eyes glittering with the potential for violence. "Maybe you've offended my honor."

"You have no honor."

"Outside. And get a gun, you cowardly old man!" The thinly disguised desire for violence Zachary had maintained vanished. "Go on, get a gun!"

It was Marcus's turn to smile. He knew that a gunfight with Zachary Webb was suicide. Zachary's skill was almost legendary. It was said that he was nearly as good as his old childhood friend, Cole Jurrell.

"I wonder if you would be so quick with challenges if you were standing face to face with Cole." Marcus's eyes took on the brightness of humor, though the fear of being gunned down, even though he was unarmed, was starkly real in his breast. He saw a flicker of fear in Zachary's face at the mention of Cole's name. "You talk big with me, Zachary, because you know it's safe. I've never been in a duel in my life."

"And your first fight with me will be your last!"

For just a moment, Marcus thought Zachary would actually draw his gun. He had seen men like Zachary before. Young men who enjoyed violence, who knew what it was like to kill another human being . . . and enjoyed that feeling. The evil of Nicholas Webb had been passed on to his son, and in the exchange, it had become overtly vicious.

"At least your father has a certain amount of sophistication in his thievery," Marcus said quietly. "You must be a terrible disappointment to him."

Hatred oozed from every pore in Zachary's body, pleasing Marcus. Marcus had lived a long, happy life. Now that his wife had passed away, and even Christina was lost to him, death would not be terribly unwelcome. This realization made Marcus feel secure in the knowledge that if he should die now, there would be a better place waiting for him.

"I'm leaving now, Zachary. You can have this store, if that's what you want. You've stolen bigger things before." Marcus took a step closer to the much younger man. He looked straight into Zachary's eyes as he said, "But there's going to come a day when you're face-to-face with Cole. And when that day comes, I'll be there. I'll watch you go for your gun, and I'll watch Cole shoot you down. You'll squirm on the ground like a gut-shot pig before you die, Zachary. And the best part of all will be that there won't be a single person on this earth who will be sad to see you die. Not one sing—"

Marcus staggered backward when the barrel of Zachary's revolver struck his cheek. He felt blood trickling down the side of his face. Calmly, with a smile on his lips, he withdrew a handkerchief and wiped his cheek.

"So much money," Marcus said in a voice just above a whisper. "And so little class."

Zachary was waving his revolver under Marcus's nose. His face was an ugly red mask of primitive rage.

"We'll see who has class! Just wait until the sheriff brings Christina back! Then we'll see who has class! Just wait until that little chit finds out what Dad's got in store for her! Just wait! Then you'll see what she's really like!"

Chapter 8

Cole looked over the prairie to Fargo. It was three miles away, but this section of Dakota was so flat that even the lowest structures were visible. He had put sixty miles between himself and Enderton. The posse that had followed Christina was riding in circles by this time — he hoped. Cole was certain, even with the dogs sniffing at Black Jack's hoofprints, the posse wouldn't be able to follow, at least not without a great deal of time-consuming back-tracking.

He felt Christina begin to slide behind him. Cole slipped an arm around her, hoisting her into position on Jack's back behind him. Christina murmured softly, drifting, as she had most of the day, in the netherworld that was neither sleep nor consciousness. When she sleepily settled into position, Cole felt her cheek against his shoulder. Her arms were loose around his waist. The sleeping periods, Cole could tell, were not restful for Christina. Not only hadn't she slept on a horse before, but each time sleep claimed her, the nightmares returned. Christina murmured fragments of sentences while she slept, the horror of O'Banion, of Webb, of murder happening right in front of her — all coming back to her, undiminished by time.

Cole's sympathy was laced with another sensation. He felt the pressure of Christina's rounded, firm breast against his back as she slept. Though he wanted to see her as just another victim of Nicholas Webb's insatiable greed, Cole couldn't be that single-minded. With Christina's womanly body pressed against him, he could not keep romantic thoughts from entering his mind, no matter how dangerously distracting they were.

Christina tightened her hands instinctively around Cole's lean waist as, once again, she nearly slipped off Jack's back. She blinked her eyes, clearing the sleep from her vision.

"Where are we?" she asked, her voice thick.

"That," Cole said, pointing a finger at the city in the distance, "is Fargo. In just a little while, I'll get you tucked away in a nice hotel where you can take a bath." Cole patted Christina's knee. "You should have let me hold you across my lap, like before. I had to catch you a dozen times to keep you from falling."

If Christina hadn't been so tired and achy, she would have agreed with Cole. It was pride—nothing more or less than stubborn pride—that had made her refuse to sit in front of Cole. Jack's rump turned out to be a poor choice, however.

"I never dreamed a horse could have such a hard back."

Cole's laughter was warm and unaffected. He patted Christina's knee again.

"Even ol' Jack gets pretty uncomfortable after a while, doesn't he?"

Christina pushed on Cole's elbow, forcing his hand off her knee. Cole chuckled again, a boyish, roguish grin dancing across his handsome features.

"Soon, my lady, you'll be rid of me *and* Black Jack."

It bothered Christina that this information didn't make her feel happier.

The bath felt as good as Christina had dreamed it would. No, that wasn't true. It felt better than just good— it was heavenly. Now, if only the woman Cole had quickly introduced as "Missy" would leave the hotel room, Christina could fully enjoy herself.

"I don't think I'll be needing anything else," Christina said. She hoped that would shoo the woman away. Only Christina's head and knees were sticking above the fluffy layer of soap bubbles in the portable bathtub.

"I can't begin to tell you how pleased I am to hear that." Missy's tone didn't match her words. She sat on the edge of the bed, studying Christina from across the room.

At first Christina tried to just ignore Missy. She apparently knew Cole fairly well. Missy had arranged for the room, getting it set for Christina without Christina having to pay or sign anything. Cole and Christina had entered the hotel through the kitchen door in the rear, unnoticed by any of the other guests.

As grateful as she was to Missy, the strange looks Christina had received since she arrived with Cole were beginning to wear on her nerves.

"You don't seem the type," Missy said. She cocked her head to the side, studying Christina from the corner of her eyes.

"What type?" Christina asked.

A warning tingle had started in the pit of Christina's stomach. She instinctively knew it was not in her best interests to prolong a conversation with Missy, yet she couldn't force herself to be so bold and rude as to simply come straight out and ask her to leave.

Missy's mouth pulled up on one side in a smile that wasn't very friendly.

"Cole's type," Missy said after a moment. "You don't seem . . . *knowledgeable* enough for Cole."

Christina almost asked Missy what she was hinting at. The question was at the tip of her tongue when awareness hit her like a fist to the stomach. Anger clenched Christina's insides. Christina had heard that Cole was a womanizer. She knew what his reputation was, and judging from personal experience, it was richly deserved. But to have a woman like Missy saying such things about her riled Christina to the brink of *control*.

The anger displayed on Christina's face brought a

throaty chuckle from Missy.

"You're not really a virgin, are you?" She received a furious look from Christina. Missy fell back on the bed, laughing heartily. When she sat up again, she slapped her knees, looking at Christina as though the woman in the bubble bath was some strange creature that she'd never seen before. "Cole Jurrell saddles up with a virgin? That's just too good to be true! Oh, Lordy! I never thought I'd live to see the day."

"Please leave," Christina said frostily. "I'm very tired. I'd like to be alone."

Missy rose from the bed. The smile never left her face, even though Christina's contempt was undisguised.

"Whatever you want. I promised Cole I'd do what I could to help." Missy headed for the door, stopping midway to look down at Christina. "I can't say I blame you for wanting to be alone with Cole. There are lots of women who want that." Missy's eyes grew hard and cold. In a slow, cruel tone she said, "And a lot of women *have* been alone with Cole."

Christina felt as though Missy had just thrust a jagged knife into her heart. Cole was the man who had rescued her. He had taken her away from the vicious posse that was determined to take her back to Nicholas Webb. She had thought of him as her personal hero. Missy was making it quite clear that Cole belonged to no one.

Never before had Christina felt as though her virginity was something that she should be ashamed of. Yet when Missy spoke her vicious words and cackled her bitter laugh, Christina felt like she should be ashamed of the fact that she hadn't shared her body with a man.

Without another word, Missy left the room. Christina soaked in the tub until the water turned cold. Only then did she get out of the enameled tub and dried herself off with a thin towel that had been washed too many times. Since all of her petticoats were being washed, she didn't have anything to wear. She wrapped the moist towel around her middle, covering herself from midthigh to underarms.

Christina sat down on the bed, folding her hands in her lap. She looked around the spartan hotel room that apparently doubled as a storage area. Christina was bone-weary. Suddenly, a question sprang into her mind.

Where was Cole going to sleep?

Cole made his way quietly down the hallway, his knee-high moccasins making no sound against the wood slat floor.

He had the secure feeling of having planned for and covered himself against every potential problem, leaving him with the sense that an enormous weight had been lifted off his shoulders.

Black Jack was at a livery owned by a man who had been run out of Enderton some years earlier. Cole had paid the man, in advance and quite excessively, to take care of the loyal stallion.

In the pocket of his jacket, Cole had two rail tickets to St. Paul, Minnesota. Cole had paid Missy dearly to purchase the tickets for him. He knew Missy had overcharged him by more than double, but Cole was unconcerned. She might swindle him out of some cash, but she wouldn't turn him over to Webb for the ransom money.

That was about as much loyalty as Cole dared to expect from anyone.

Cole tapped the door softly with his knuckles and entered without waiting for an answer. He froze in his tracks when he saw Christina sitting on the bed, dressed in nothing more than a towel.

"Oh, excuse me," he said. There was a bemused smile on his face, and judging from the look that Christina gave him, she would have liked to rip it off him. "I didn't think you were—"

"You just didn't think!" Christina snapped. She clutched the towel tighter around herself, and squeezed her knees together. Christina felt vulnerable, and she hated that feeling more than any other in the world. In a venomous tone she said, "I'm beginning to understand something about you, Mr. Jurrell."

"Oh? What's that?" Cole was nonchalant as he set down the package he had carried in with him.

"You do whatever you want to do, then apologize for it afterward. But you always do what you want first. You broke into my home and now you just barge right into my room."

Cole shrugged off the words like they were rain. "That's just your opinion, and it isn't a very educated opinion at that. What is it you really know about me? Stop and think about that before you give me an inventory of my faults." A dimple played in his beard-stubbled cheeks. "Besides, this isn't your room, it's *our* room."

"What?" Christina exclaimed. "Oh, no, it's not! If you think—"

Cole wheeled on Christina, pointing an accusing finger at her. "If *you* would just think once in a while, we might not have a posse after us! Now listen to every word I have to tell you and listen carefully because I'm not going to tell you a second time." Cole paused a moment and composed himself, forcing his anger to cool. "We've got men—men who will do just about anything for the right amount of money—after us. They're after you. After me. And we've also got a little problem with money. You see, it costs a lot of money to make sure people don't sell us out to Webb. Missy was good enough to give us—*sell* us—this room. This *one* room." Cole's steel gray eyes bore into Christina. "I'm not any happier about it than you are. So stop crabbing and just live with it. For the time being, that's all we can do."

Christina swallowed and moistened her lips with the tip of her tongue, unaware of how enticing she appeared to Cole Jurrell. She looked at her hands resting in her lap, unable to meet the man's fiery, angry gaze.

"I'm sorry"—she made random, embarrassed gestures with her hands—"I'm just scared. Usually I'm not this . . .

myopic."

Cole's eyes roamed appreciatively over Christina. Her blond hair was a riot of curls and swirls tumbling over her soft, bare shoulders. Christina had pinned her tresses up loosely before taking her bath, and the effect was powerful, gripping. Cole could not keep his anger burning when Christina was the cause of it.

"I brought you something," Cole said after a long pause. He nodded toward the wrapped square box near his feet. "Some things I thought you might need for the trip."

"Thank—" Christina began quietly. Her head snapped up and excitement glowed in her sapphire blue eyes. "Trip? Where are we going?"

Christina's gaze caught Cole's. She saw that his anger had vanished. Now *he* seemed to be the one uncomfortable with the way she was dressed. She knew it was wrong of her to be so scantily attired with a man in the room. Though she did not want him to attack her, it pleased Christina to know that she could affect Cole's masculine senses.

Christina had often felt pretty, but with Cole she felt desirable. It was a subtle and glorious distinction. Knowing that Cole wanted her made her skin tingle all over, like she was simultaneously being touched by a hundred feathers.

"Curious about what's in the box?" Cole cocked an eyebrow above a steel-gray eye.

"Yes," Christina replied.

"Maybe I'm not such a bad man after all."

Christina scowled darkly at Cole. "Mr. Jurrell, the women you know might be irrationally impressed with a pretty gift wrapped in ribbons and bows, but you will find that I am not so easily . . . persuaded."

Cole made a derisive sound deep in his throat. He turned away from Christina, walking slowly over to the bathtub. He could feel Christina's eyes on him as he walked.

"Believe me, my motivation has more to do with my safety than your comfort. We're going to be traveling to-

96

gether. I can't have you seen in public in a dirty, torn dress. You'd just draw attention to yourself, and from this point forward, I want you to understand that any attention you draw to yourself could very likely be fatal."

Cole heard the mattress squeak as Christina's weight was removed from it. He turned slightly and glanced at her over his shoulder. Cole saw long, slender legs with tapering thighs, and breasts that rolled softly beneath the towel with her steps, small, delicate hands and feet, and a profusion of golden hair pinned atop her head with wispy strands falling down her cheeks, curling loosely. He saw a small, straight nose and a narrow mouth with full, generous lips.

Damn, she's all woman, he thought. *She could make a man forget all about his troubles.*

Cole stiffened immediately at the thought. He couldn't allow himself to forget that people were depending on him.

He said, "It's going to make it a lot easier for both of us if you'd stop fighting me every step of the way. In case you haven't noticed it yet, I'm doing my best to help you out of trouble that I'm not personally involved in." *Like hell,* he thought. He forced a hard, uncompromising tone. "I've got plenty of my own problems to worry about. I don't need your troubles heaped onto mine."

"I . . . I'm sorry," Christina said just above a whisper. "This has all been so strange to me. I forget sometimes that I'm not the only person in the world with troubles."

Cole shrugged his shoulders, turning his back on Christina again. "Just don't fight me on everything."

Christina was looking at Cole when he slipped his jacket off and dropped it to the floor. He tested the temperature of the bathwater with a finger.

"Check the box," Cole said. "I think everything will fit, but I want to be sure before tomorrow. I had to guess at your size, and I didn't get the chance to pick them out myself."

Christina grabbed the bed cover and pulled it free from the mattress. She wrapped it around herself protectively. "You're not going to take a bath, are you?" She got back

97

on the bed, leaving the package on the floor near the door.

"Yes. I'm just as dirty as you are—were, rather."

"But . . ."

Christina never bothered to finish the sentence. She spun around on the bed and felt her cheeks get warm with embarrassment. Cole Jurrell knew no shame! Bathing when there was a woman in the room with him!

It was clear to Christina then that he had obviously been naked with many women before. That's why he wasn't in the least bit hesitant about taking off his clothes when she was in the room. Everything that Missy had said—all those lurid little things she hinted at—had to be true!

Christina's sense of hearing seemed heightened. She squeezed her eyes shut, not wanting to know what Cole Jurrell was doing, afraid that she would see Cole even though her back was to him. Nevertheless, she heard his holster, heavy with the revolver and laden with ammunition, get placed carefully on the floor.

Probably within arm's reach, Christina thought caustically. *Outlaws always keep their guns close!*

Christina was quite certain she was committing some kind of sin, even if she did have her back turned to Cole. It just had to be a sin of some sort, though of all her father's teachings, he'd never once warned her about anything like this happening.

"I've got Jack all taken care of," Christina heard Cole say as casually as if they were talking over a dinner table.

She heard a hand splashing in the bathwater, then the sound of a body easing into it. The sharp intake of breath let Christina know how cold the water had become, and she took delight in knowing that Cole wouldn't have the pleasure of a hot bath.

"We're scheduled to be on the train for about thirteen hours," Cole went on. "Missy booked us on a sleeper car, so at least we'll be able to get some decent rest during the ride."

"Sleeper car?"

"Christina, where's the soap?"

"It's right —" Christina started to turn around to face Cole before realizing what she was doing. She spun on the bed again, turning her back to Cole. An angry sound escaped her lips. "It's on the floor to your left, near the back wheel."

"Oh. Thanks." Cole chuckled softly and Christina could picture in her mind his grin. "I really don't mean to embarrass you. I just haven't got any choice, that's all. You must see that."

"Sure," Christina replied, but from her tone it was clear that she didn't want to see *anything*.

The sound of bathing continued, but time did not assuage Christina's discomfort.

After a while, Christina asked, "Doesn't it bother you to wash in cold water?"

"Yes, it does. Whether you want to believe it or not, I am a warm-blooded animal, just like you."

"I doubt we have anything in common," Christina muttered.

Cole soaped up his face, splashing water on himself with cupped hands, then touched the beard stubble — three days growth now — with his fingertips.

"I don't see the need in complaining about the temperature of the water. Why complain if it isn't going to do any good anyway?"

"That's not the point."

Cole chuckled again, but there was very little humor in the sound. To Christina, there seemed to be an underlying sadness in the short laugh, a sadness that confused Christina and made her wonder why it was there.

"That's exactly the point. In time, my dearest and oh-so-naive traveling companion, you, too, will learn to take cold baths and eat cold food for days on end. You will learn to sleep with your hand on a gun and wake with any sound. You'll learn all that and more . . . or you'll learn nothing at all."

Christina shivered. She pulled the towel tighter around her body and pushed an errant strand of hair away from her eye.

"I wish you'd stop talking that way. I don't like to hear things like that." There was an emptiness in her stomach when she thought about how she could never return to Enderton and enjoy the quiet comfort of a small town and a few true friends. "Besides, how could I sleep with my hand on a gun? I've never even shot one before."

"You haven't?" Cole sounded surprised.

"No. Mama and Papa were shopkeepers. Peace-loving. They said nothing good ever came from guns."

"They were right, but that's not the point, either." There was the sound of water dripping into water and Christina realized Cole had stood up. "I'll teach you how to shoot. You won't be very good. That takes a lot of time. But maybe the sound will be enough to scare people away." There was a pause, then Cole asked, "Where's the towel?"

Again Christina blushed, even more crimson that the first time. She still had the towel wrapped around herself. "I've got it," she said softly. "But it's wet. You'll just have to . . ."

"Have to what? You've got the only towel. A damp towel is better than no towel at all."

Christina pulled the blanket completely over her head to hide herself, then angrily loosened the towel from around her body. She tucked her head above the blanket when she was finished, and her embarrassment turned to anger.

"Here!" she hissed, tossing the towel over her shoulder in the general direction of the bathtub. "Doesn't anything bother you?"

Cole stepped out of the tub, dripping water onto the floor. He picked the towel up and began drying himself. He, too, was nervous about being naked with a woman in the room with him — a woman who wasn't his lover, that is.

As he dried himself, the self-control that he prided himself on seemed to slip through his fingers like sand. He didn't need this kind of aggression, not when he had so many people counting on him to put an end to Nicholas Webb and his reign of treachery, thievery, and murder. Not

100

when he had the weight of his murdered father on his shoulders, a weight that could not be removed until justice was served.

"Why don't we just stop talking," Cole said, rubbing the damp towel vigorously over his sinewy chest and taut stomach. "It's not getting us anywhere. Talking with you only makes me angry. I've tried my best to show you the way things are and you fight me every step of the way." Cole threw the towel against the far wall, several feet away from Christina but close enough so that she could see it hit the wall. She couldn't fail to know that Cole really wanted to hit her with it. "It's not my damn fault you're in trouble. You're not my goddamn responsibility!"

A muscle flickered in Cole's jaw as he stared hotly at Christina's back. "Grow up, Christina! The world isn't a pretty place where little girls get to wear pink all their lives! It's a cruel, violent, unjust, ugly place where good people don't just die, they get murdered! Kind, honest people get their land stolen from them! Men who have worked their whole lives to leave a little piece of land for their sons and daughters get hurt, and that's just the way it is! The sooner you accept that, the better it is going to be for you and for me."

Cole made a throaty sound of disgust. "What the hell am I doing trying to talk to you anyway? You'll never learn! You don't want to learn! You just want to live in your childhood dream world where Mommy and Daddy kiss your scratched finger and make everything all better. Then they tuck you into bed at night and your little world is just goddamn perfect!"

Cole stepped into his jeans, pulling them up angrily. He had to put distance between himself and the beautiful woman-child who, he knew, was naked in bed beneath the sheet she had wrapped around herself.

"My damn horse understands more about the world around him than you ever will!"

"Okay . . . okay . . . you've made your point," Christina said, forcing anger in her tone even though all she felt was

101

sad resignation. Hot tears burned at the backs of her eyes. "I'm stupid and naive. There. I've said it. Are you happy now? What else do you want from me?"

Cole voice softened as he said, "I don't want anything from you, Christina. I'm telling you these things for your own good. Can't you see that?"

Christina nodded her head. She was about to speak, but the catch in her throat stopped her. She didn't want Cole to see her cry, or to hear the tears in her voice.

Cole looked at the young woman sitting on the bed. In her disheveled state, she looked soft, innocent, vulnerable . . . and so alluring it tried Cole's willpower. He wanted to hold her gently in his arms and comfort her, to whisper that she had nothing to fear. He wanted to run his hands slightly over her exquisite curves, to caress the satin smoothness of her flesh and kiss those softly shimmering lips. He hungered for her ecstasy, for Christina's passionate response to his touch and caress.

The moment hung in the air, heavy with sudden emotions neither was capable of, nor wanted to, accept.

Needing to distract his thoughts, Cole strode to where he had left the large, wrapped package. He picked it up and brought it to Christina, placing it on the bed beside her.

"Open it up," he said, his tone affecting a lightness that his soul did not feel. "I'm a little curious myself to see what's in there."

"You don't know?"

Cole shrugged his shoulders and in a noncommittal voice that tickled Christina's curiosity, he said, "I can't just walk around the stores of Fargo. I had a . . . ah . . . friend pick them up for me."

Christina undid the ribbons and bows and carefully peeled away the brightly colored wrapper so as to not tear it. She heard Cole sigh with impatience, but her frugal upbringing—prevented her from destroying perfectly good wrapping paper that could be used again.

Christina lifted off the lid and a startled gasp caught in her throat. Inside was a shift, petticoat, pantalets, and dress. She pulled out the contents individually, holding the cloth delicately in her small white hands to inspect the cut and quality of the gifts.

"They're beautiful," Christina whispered. "A little scandalous, but beautiful." She rubbed her thumb against the sheer silk. "I've never bought very nice things for myself. I've sold them to other women, but I've never bought them for myself."

Christina did not see the dimpled smile that crossed Cole's face.

The dress was made of cotton, and though it did not at first glance appear particularly expensive, a closer look at the pale-blue material showed the fine hand stitching and professional craftsmanship that had gone into making it. The dress was trimmed at the sleeves and hemline with white lace.

"Very nice," Cole murmured. He leaned against the foot poster of the bed, his gray eyes warm with pleasure. The dress was neither dowdy nor racy. Strictly functional, the kind of dress a well-to-do woman would travel in. "Just the right look I wanted for you."

The undergarments, however, had a decidedly different look! The petticoat was hand-sewn, and Christina, a merchant who was the daughter of merchants, could tell at a glance the silk was of the finest quality. The pantalets were trimmed with lace and embroidered with small flowers sewn into the waistline beneath the drawstring. And the shift, a silky camisole that came down only to the waist, was made of such fine, light fabric that Christina could hardly feel the weight of it in her hand.

"These look more like they're to be seen rather than worn *under* what's seen," Christina whispered, slightly embarrassed.

"Yes," Cole replied, his tone warm and lazy. "My friend can be a little . . . colorful."

Christina pulled the sheet tighter around herself, bunching it in her fist close to her breast. Though she knew there was nothing really wrong with Cole seeing the garments that she would wear under the dress he'd bought her, she could not ignore her modesty. Especially since she wasn't wearing a single stitch of clothing at the moment.

When Christina looked up, her breath again caught in her chest. Cole was naked from the waist up, and in that single instant, she knew she had never before seen such masculinity. His chest was quite broad, made to look even broader by the leanness of his hips. Her eyes lingered caressingly on his strong chest, its muscles relaxed and yet solid just beneath the surface of the smooth, almost hairless skin.

Christina was surprised to find her eyes drawn to him, surprised to discover such pleasure in seeing the ridge of his ribs and the vertical and diagonal lines of muscles that corded his stomach.

Almost mesmerized, Christina's gaze inched lower. She saw Cole's, large, silver, oval-shaped belt buckle dangling loose from the belt itself. She saw the top button of his jeans and thought in a disconnected sort of way that not many men had flat stomachs.

A fluttery sensation, new to Christina but one she had felt before in Cole's company, went through her.

Blushing crimson and trying valiantly to think of something to say, Christina began folding the gifts and placing them back in the box. She left the petticoat out. She would wear that in place of a nightdress.

The deep, throaty chuckle Christina heard heightened her embarrassment.

What's wrong with me? Christina questioned with silent desperation. *I'm not thinking properly. I'm just not myself.*

"If . . . ah . . ." Christina ran the tip of her tongue over her lips. Quite suddenly, her mouth felt dry as a desert wind. "If you'd be so kind as to turn your back, I'll put on . . ."

"Yes, of course," Cole replied, and Christina hated his amused tone.

He loves it when he's got my mind all muddled! she thought, grasping for anger, which was a much safer and

104

more tangible emotion than those that had turned her otherwise neatly ordered thoughts maddeningly topsy-turvy.

Christina never took her eyes off Cole's back. She was afraid he would suddenly twist about to look at her. She slipped her arms through the petticoat, wondered once again whether he would be dastardly enough to look at her, then whipped the garment over her head. Christina had to wriggle on the bed, rocking from one side to the other to smooth the petticoat down her legs. When she was finished, she pulled the sheet over herself again, clutching it at her throat as she had done before.

"All done?" Cole inquired.

"Yes."

Cole turned slowly. He smiled down at Christina, running a hand through his sandy hair, pushing it back off his forehead.

"If you'll be so kind as to toss me a pillow and let me have one of the blankets, I'll bed down. We both can use some decent shut-eye."

Christina looked at Cole suspiciously. "Where are you sleeping?"

She saw Cole's gaze harden briefly, then soften almost as quickly. With a sigh, as though he was tired of arguing with a child who just couldn't grasp the obvious, he said, "On the floor. You'll be safe and sound and all alone on the bed. Now can I have a pillow and blanket, or won't you even let me have that much?"

"No," Christina said. The look she received was unspeakably malevolent. "You sleep on the bed." Christina, wriggling off the bed with the sheet pressed to the front of her body, decided that she had taken quite enough of Cole's generosity. "I'll sleep on the floor."

"No."

"I've taken too much from you already."

"No, I said." Cole took a single step, moving in front of Christina. When she stood, their bodies were nearly touching. Cole caught Christina by the upper arms, his fingers pressing into her tender flesh painfully hard. "I said no."

Christina looked up into his eyes. "I thought you would be happy to have the bed. Take it," she said quietly. "I'll sleep on the floor."

"No, I said!" snapped Cole.

Christina tried to twist away from Cole so that she wouldn't be pinned between him and the bed. His grip was too strong, too powerful for her to free herself.

"You can't tell me what to do!" Christina hissed defiantly.

"Somebody has to!"

Cole's anger was evident, and it confused Christina. She had thought he would be grateful, at least *hoped* he would be grateful, to sleep in the big bed.

"Don't talk to me that way." Christina tried to free her arms again. Her breasts rolled tautly inside the petticoat and, accidentally, she pressed herself against Cole. The contact of her body, soft and feminine, against Cole's, so hard and masculine, galvanized Christina's resolve, giving her greater strength.

"Let go of me! I said I'll sleep on the floor!"

"And I said you'll sleep on the bed!"

Cole pushed Christina backward. As she toppled, she reached out instinctively to break her fall, catching Cole's wrist. Caught off guard, he tumbled forward, landing atop Christina when she struck the bed.

She felt everything, was cognizant of every minute contact between them. Cole's chest pressed hard against her breasts. His face, cast with an unreadable expression, was close to her own, lips parted slightly, as though anticipating a kiss. She felt the pressure of his thighs against hers, one knee between her own. And when she looked into his eyes, she saw the fire there, the burning hunger he felt deep in his soul.

"Christina," he whispered, his breath touching her face softly, like an invisible caress.

Cole touched Christina's cheek with his palm, the fingers sliding beneath the thick fall of her blond hair. She

106

inhaled deeply and felt the pressure of her breasts against Cole's chest become greater. In a corner of her mind she dimly realized the bodice of the petticoat was too small for her.

"Christina," Cole whispered again, his lips touching her as he spoke the word without actually kissing her.

He spoke her name one more time, and to Christina, the sound was an intoxicating potion that she could not resist. His lips touched hers softly, moving slowly, touching and retreating, then returning again. A thousand sensations went through Christina, and when she felt the warmth of Cole's back against her palm, she realized she had placed her arms around him.

The tip of Cole's tongue traced the outline of Christina's soft lips and she sighed when he caught her bottom lip between his teeth and bit softly on it.

He kissed her again, and this time Christina knew what she wanted, and sought it. She opened her mouth, boldly flicking her tongue against Cole's and felt him momentarily stiffen. His tongue darted with Christina's, and as the kiss deepened, Christina's passion heightened, feeding upon itself, becoming insistent and demanding.

Cole rolled to the side, taking some of his weight off her. Christina, having just discovered the pleasure of Cole's muscular, lean body pressing her curvaceous one into the soft mattress, did not welcome the move. She tugged at Cole's shoulder, twisting on the bed toward him. She felt the sheet being pulled from between their bodies, and then they moved together again.

"Ohhh!" Christina sighed as Cole's lips tantalized the sensitive flesh of her neck, just beneath her ear. She felt the heat of his naked chest against her breast, and her nipples hardened responsively, reacting as though the petticoat did not separate her hungry flesh from Cole's.

He kissed her cheek. Burning with the need to taste his kisses, Christina pushed her fingers into Cole's hair, turning her face toward him. She pulled him to her, pressing her mouth against his, kissing him deeply with an intensity

107

that shocked and aroused them both.

Cole's hand moved from Christina's hip, inching upward with agonizing deliberateness toward the lush mound of one responsive breast. The fingertips traced its lower curve teasingly moving from side to side. Christina, frantic with a desire that never before had gripped her, arched her back, clinging passionately to Cole.

At last the fingers crept upward, touching softly. Christina gasped against Cole's mouth, unwilling to let the kiss end even as she responded to his touch. She leaned into him, forcing her breast into the large, strong, knowing hand that caressed her with such exquisite skill.

"Christina," Cole whispered the name as though it was a prayer.

He caught Christina's nipple between his finger and thumb, pinching softly. Hot waves of pleasure coursed through her, causing her to writhe in ecstasy on the bed.

Cole's hand moved away from Christina's breast, continuing its upward quest. She sighed, fighting against the urge to take Cole's wrist and force his hand back to where it had been. Then she felt the thin strap of her petticoat sliding over a smooth shoulder. A moment later, with a touch as soft as a thief's, Cole's fingertips slipped inside the lace-trimmed edge of her bodice, peeling the cup away from her breast.

"You are . . . everything about you is heavenly," Cole whispered.

He leaned over Christina, planting feathery kisses on her lips and chin, moving upward again to kiss the tip of her nose and eyelids, then nipped at her neck with his teeth. Christina trembled with desire.

The warmth of Cole's tongue and the moisture of it tickled and tantalized her flesh as he followed the line of her collarbone. Slowly, surely, he worked his way downward. As Christina waited, anticipating Cole's intimate kisses and yet frightened of them, she had to force herself to breathe.

Cole's mouth closed over Christina's breast. Her lips, still moist from his kisses, opened in a silent cry of ecstasy. Her fingers tightened in Cole's hair, and she did not realize that she was hugging him tightly, almost painfully, to her breast.

"Easy."

The word seemed to come from far away, and Christina wished the sound would go away. She felt strong fingers tightening around her wrist, and only then did she realize it was Cole talking to her.

"Easy . . . we're in no hurry," Cole said, his breath warm and yet cool against the moist spot where his mouth had been. "Relax, Christina. Just relax, and let me show you."

His tongue circled Christina's nipple, always coming close to the aroused crest of her breast yet avoiding direct contact. When Christina was quite certain she would die if she did not feel his warm, moist lips closing around her nipple again, Cole took her into his mouth. In a distant corner of her mind, she hated Cole a little for being able to play her body with such consummate skill. It was as though he could read her mind and knew precisely what she was thinking and what her body wanted most.

A hand was against Christina's stomach. She felt it moving lower, touching her through the petticoat, branding her flesh with passion. Christina knew where that hand was going, and the dull, throbbing ache deep inside her said that soon, very soon, the dizzying questions that had haunted her would all be answered, and she would know a closeness to a man—to Cole Jurrell—that was infinitely different than anything else in life.

The door opened harshly, swinging around the hinges and banging against the wall.

"Cole, you've got to get out of here!" Missy hissed.

"What the hell are you doing here!"

Christina rolled away from the door, covering her exposed breast. In an instant, unbridled shame took the place of unbridled passion.

"There's a man here," Missy continued. She closed the door, casting a contemptuous look toward Christina before turning her attention back to Cole. "He's looking for your woman. Damn it, Cole! I don't need any trouble here!"

Cole bolted out of the bed, reaching for his guns and his shirt.

"Stall him as long as you can. If there's just one man here, they don't know exactly where she is. Otherwise they would have sent an army." Cole pushed the tails of his shirt into his pants without buttoning it. "Do what you can, Missy. I'll make this up to you someday."

"You're damn right you will! I don't need trouble, Cole! I've told you that before!" Missy hissed, then left the room.

Cole strapped the black holster around his lean hips. "Come on, Christina, get dressed! We'll go out the window. I know of a place we can stay until the train leaves tomorrow morning."

Chapter 9

"Just try to relax," Cole said, leaning close to Christina. "That's the key. Relax and you won't draw attention to yourself."

Christina's hands were shaking so badly she was having difficulty hooking her boots. The hasty exit out the hotel window and down the back stairway had gotten them out of immediate danger. But the question facing them now was how many more men were looking for them? If it was someone from Enderton, Christina would recognize him. But what if Sheriff Bellows had enlisted — as Cole had ominously suggested — local talent?

When she had at last finished with her boots, Christina got to her feet, clutching the box that had held the presents Cole gave her. Those few possessions were all that Christina had now.

"Where can we go?" Christina asked softly.

Cole took Christina's hand and slipped it inside his elbow. "Just follow me," he said, giving her a smile that exuded confidence. He didn't fool Christina. She knew that he was nervous, and that he was putting on a brave exterior for her benefit.

Christina held on to Cole's arm, acting as though he was her beau. When she looked at her, her eyes were fierce, the anger in them thinly concealed.

"Do you really have another place to go?" she whispered.

"I'm thinking, Christina," Cole said through a tight smile. "When I think long enough, I always come up with something brilliant."

"This is hardly a time for your inflated self-esteem to get away from you, Mr. Jurrell," she whispered icily. Her fingers were digging into Cole's biceps as they walked along the boardwalk, passing in front of the shops and stores of Fargo.

Without looking at Christina, Cole replied, "If memory serves me correctly, not all that long ago we were both letting things get away from us, and neither of us were doing much to stop it."

The man has no sense of decency at all! Christina thought.

She grit her teeth in rage, but she kept her feelings to herself.

It rankled her nerves that Cole should make light of her momentary weakness. He knew that she was frightened, confused by the obstacles that life had suddenly and unexpectedly thrown in her path. She was certain he had knowingly used that fear and confusion to satisfy his own base needs. If it hadn't been for Missy's timely entrance into the hotel room, there was no telling what might have happened.

No, that isn't true, thought Christina. She knew exactly what would have happened if Missy hadn't barged into the room when she had.

The closeness of the seduction frightened Christina almost as much as the men who chased her. The difference was that Christina had almost willingly given in to Cole's advances.

Was it "almost"? she asked herself angrily.

At least the posse that chased her didn't put on a friendly face for her benefit. The posse didn't torment her soul and make her want to do things that she otherwise would never even think of doing. The posse wouldn't make her feel all crazy inside and wouldn't cause her to experience sensations in her soul that felt ecstatic at the time, but which Christina knew she would later regret.

The more Christina thought about the things that had happened in the hotel room, the angrier she got. She welcomed the anger because it was familiar and so much safer than any of the other emotions she associated with Cole Jurrell.

He hasn't got the right to make me want him, she thought bitterly. And, to prove her point, she gouged her fingernails into Cole's arm hard enough to make him wince.

"Sorry," Christina said when Cole gave her a questioning look. "I'm a little scared, I guess."

"Yeah, sure."

Christina looked at Cole, gazing at his handsome profile as they walked down the boardwalk.

Her mind whirled in confusion.

You haven't got the right to make me want you, she thought. *All that's happened has gotten me confused, and you're using that confusion to try to make me one of your lovers—one of your* many *lovers. But it won't work, Cole Jurrell! You're really no different than Nicholas Webb or Richard O'Banion. You're just a man, no different than any other man, and I'll never trust you.*

Chapter 10

Sheriff Allen Bellows had been lied to by the best of liars during his years as a sheriff. There had been a time, before Nicholas Webb moved near Enderton and built that huge mansion and bought everything and everyone around him, when Bellows was an honest man.

That experience told Bellows that Missy was lying to him. He had that old feeling, that tickle of the hairs at the back of his neck like he used to get, that said Missy was lying to him through that polite, false smile.

"You're sure it was just your cousin here?" Bellows asked Missy.

He picked up a corner of the bed sheet. The sheets and blankets were completely pulled free of the mattress. Someone had made love on it.

"Yes, sir, Sheriff," Missy replied. Her hands were balled into tight, white-knuckled fists. "My cousin is something of a roustabout. He don't stay anywhere long, and he's never got enough money to put a decent roof over his head or a hot meal in his belly. So when he showed up out of the blue like a lost little lamb, I just had to let him use this room." Missy gave the sheriff a slightly tremulous smile. "You can understand that, can't you, Sheriff? Surely there's enough kindness in your heart for you to understand one cousin helping another in a time of need."

Bellows dipped a finger into the bathwater. It was cold, but there were still some soap bubbles on the surface.

Bellows put a boot on the edge of the tub. He crossed his arms over the upraised knee and turned slowly to look over his shoulder at Missy.

"My dear,"—he spoke in a voice of condescending authority,—"I do believe you're lying to me. Now I can't prove it just yet, but soon enough I suspect I will." Bellows's eyes went up and down over Missy, and she shivered at the unspoken threat in them. "If you're helping Christina Sands, you're guilty of protecting a murderer. That makes you as guilty of murder as she is. An' if that ain't enough trouble, you'll also be keeping me from getting that reward Nicholas Webb has put up."

Bellows moved around the tub until he was behind it. He put his boot on the edge and started pushing, slowly at first since it was very heavy, then with increased pressure. The tub rolled across the room. It struck the wall, and water splashed over the rim, across the floor.

"That little mess there," Bellows said slowly, nodding his head toward the spreading pool of water on the floor, "ain't going to be much of anything compared to the one I'm going to make with you when I find out you're lying to me."

Missy hadn't run a tawdry hotel for four years without knowing how to handle the local law officers. With the others, though, all Missy had to do was have some money change hands, or perhaps have one of her "friends" visit this judge or that sheriff. Something warned her that Sheriff Bellows wouldn't be as easily put off.

From a sheath at his hip, Sheriff Bellows withdrew a razor-sharp, evil-looking knife. He twisted the knife in his hand. An ugly smile twitched at the corners of his mouth.

"Now, Missy, are you going to start telling me the truth, or do I start cutting little pieces of you off?" Bellows began advancing slowly toward Missy as she cowered in a corner of the small, cluttered room. "It's up to you, Missy. How much of you am I going to cut off before you tell me what I want to hear?"

* * *

Nicholas Webb was in a murderous state of mind. When he watched the posse gather, then split into two groups, he was witness to a full display of his power in Enderton. He added the incentive of one thousand dollars to the man or men who returned Christina Sands to him unharmed, and saw greed in the eyes of the posse.

They'll bring her to me before nightfall, he had thought then. *There's no way these men can fail.*

He roamed the corridors of his mansion that night, pacing off his energy, avoiding even a single glass of brandy so his mind and body would be at their sharpest, chain-smoking cigars until his tongue felt raw and burned.

Nicholas knew he looked splendid in his green velvet robe. When Christina was brought to him, kicking and screaming, she would see him for exactly what he was — her salvation. He was handsome, rich, and powerful. Christina would see that the only person separating her from the hangman's noose was none other than Nicholas Webb.

Her display of gratitude would be the single most erotic evening of Nicholas Webb's life.

Now Nicholas looked at the crumpled telegram in his hand, and grit his teeth so hard his jaws hurt.

Damn that Cole Jurrell!

Nicholas didn't know how Cole and Christina had gotten together, but it was clear to him that they had. How else could Christina have escaped an experienced posse with tracking dogs? How else could she have been wearing the locket that Jurrell's gang had stolen from her?

The telegram from Sheriff Bellows said that Christina was in Fargo, or at least had been in Fargo, with a man matching Cole's description. Whoever Bellows was getting his information from had said Christina and her accomplice were headed for Canada, probably Winnepeg.

The door opened and Zachary Webb stepped into his father's study.

"A rider just brought another telegram," Zachary said, hiding his pleasure at his father's agitation.

116

"What's it say?" Nicholas barked.

Nicholas turned his back toward his only child. The sight of Zachary often disturbed him.

Zachary cleared his throat and read: "The woman is headed for St. Louis stop the man to Canada stop sending men to all points in between to have them arrested stop will take custody of prisoners from locals stop Sheriff Bellows."

Zachary looked up from the yellow sheet of paper. Nicholas was staring out the window. "Want me to read that again?"

Nicholas shook his head. He breathed in deeply, puffing out his massive chest trying to calm himself. "They are fools," he said quietly.

"Who?"

"Sheriff Bellows, Deputy Miller—all of them. They're nothing but fools." Nicholas bent his head down and touched his temples, rubbing softly to rid himself of the damnable headache. "Let that be a lesson to you, Zachary. Never forget that most of the men God put on this planet are fools. You are a Webb, so you'll understand when the others won't. You've got my blood running in your veins."

Zachary took a short thin cigar from his pocket. He hated having to sit through his father's lectures, but at least this time he wasn't facing the brunt of his father's wrath.

"I do not know for certain where Christina is headed, but I do know that Cole is not going to Canada," Nicholas said. "Whoever Bellows is following, it isn't Cole. And, most likely, it's not Christina."

"How do you know?" Sometimes his father's brilliance really did amaze Zachary. "Bellows and Miller have tracked a lot of men in their day."

"Not men like Cole. That's why they haven't been able to catch him for two years. You see, if Cole was going to turn tail and run, why would he do it now? We didn't have a clue to where he was. If he's running off with Christina"—the thought of Christina in Cole's arms brought a shiver of revulsion of Nicholas's spine—"why split up? No, Zachary,

117

I'd have to be a fool to think Cole is giving up his fight against us. He won't quit until we kill him. Bellows most likely is following a drunkard dressed up to look like Cole . . . and every minute that passes makes Christina's trail that much colder."

Nicholas turned away from the window and fixed his cold, lethal gaze on Zachary.

"Go to Fargo. Take plenty of money with you. Money will loosen the right tongues. I want you to find out where Christina went, and I want you to bring her back to me."

Zachary plucked the cigar from his mouth and grinned. "Sure thing. You can count on me." The heel of Zachary's palm unconsciously rested on the handle of his revolver. "Hey, we're acting almost like family. The son helping the father and that sort of thing."

Nicholas looked straight into Zachary's eyes. "I know what kind of man you are. I know what happens to the women you see when you're tired of them or if they don't want to play along with your sick games. So hear me, Zachary, and hear me well. If you touch Christina—and you know what I'm talking about—I'll kill you." Nicholas turned back toward the window. "Get out of here now."

"Like father, like son," Zachary muttered as he left the room.

Nicholas closed his eyes and a shudder went through him.

Chapter 11

"It'll be dark soon. That will help." Cole's tone reflected the exhaustion that pressed in tighter from all sides. He looked away from the window to Christina. Her head, resting against the back of the seat, rocked softly against the thin cushion with the rail car's movement. "Soon we'll be out of the Dakota Territory and into Minnesota. Webb won't have as much power there."

The three days had seemed to pile one atop the next for Christina. Sleeping was something she feared, yet all she wanted was a comfortable bed where she could sleep her troubles away. At least she had bathed.

The day had been a nightmare. Though Fargo was a thriving city, with more than three times the population of Enderton, the townsfolk were not immune to the tentacles of Nicholas Webb.

Christina followed Cole through the dirty back alleys of Fargo, occasionally hiding, at other times running from real or imaginary trouble. On two occasions Cole had drawn his gun, and when he did, the heart-stopping memory of seeing firsthand what those instruments of death could do to a human body flashed like lightning across the surface of her mind.

Christina was repelled by Cole's willing acceptance of his role as fox in this real-life game where he was hunted by the

119

hounds. She hated him for accepting his fate, and distrusted him because he was so willing to resort to killing to save himself.

All Christina had to do was look in Cole's eyes when he held that deadly Colt steady in his hand and she knew he had killed before.

And what of her? If Christina became too much of a burden to Cole, would he leave her to the posse just to save himself?

"Christina, are you still awake?"

"Yes," she replied quietly. "I was just resting my eyes for a moment, that's all."

Cole chuckled softly. "Sure you were." He pulled the makings from his shirt pocket and began rolling a cigarette. "It's time for you to get some decent sleep. I'll make one last quick check of the passengers, then be back."

Christina's eyes opened, still a startling brilliant blue, but now red-rimmed from fatigue.

"Do you think the posse is still following us? Are they on the train?"

"Following *you*," Cole corrected lightly. "But no, I think they got fooled in the switch."

Cole stood up in the cramped sleeper car. He spread his feet for better balance as the train picked up speed, moving out of town. He tried to smile for Christina, but it was hard for him and the smile faded.

"Just the same," Cole said, "I'll feel better if I make one last check. While I'm gone you can get in bed and cover up."

Christina gave Cole a wary look, and his smile reappeared.

"Don't worry. I'm as dead tired as you are, Christina."

"I still don't see why Missy had to buy tickets for us as husband and wife."

"She didn't have to do anything for us at all."

Cole lit his cigarette, turning his gaze away from Christina for a moment. Nothing she could do—not blinding

120

fear, confusion, or fatigue—could take away her extraordinary charms.

For the hundredth time, Cole reminded himself that he had pressing responsibilities, and as soon as he had Christina tucked away safe and sound in St. Paul, he had to get back to them. Most of all, Cole knew that he had to separate himself from Christina if he was ever going to stay alive.

"I'll be back later."

Cole closed the door to the private sleeper car behind him, and began to go from one car to the next. Part of him didn't care about the posse and wanted to hurry back to Christina, to surprise her while she undressed. Part of him was helplessly, forever in love with her.

How would she react when he returned? Would she be frightened that he would try to make love to her? Would she put up the stoic facade like she had before? Might she ask him to sleep on the floor?

A woman, perhaps a couple of years older than Christina, with flaming red hair and eyes of emerald green, stood ahead of Cole in the narrow aisle. She was looking at Cole intently, but when their eyes met, she quickly averted her gaze. Cole noticed that she made no move to get out of his way as he approached.

"Ma'am." Cole said politely, touching the wide black brim of his hat. "Excuse me."

Cole started past the woman. She made a soft sound in her throat, pretending to stumble. Her hands went instantly to Cole's chest as he caught her, but she did not push herself away.

"Excuse me, sir," she whispered. She looked straight into Cole's eyes, and this time she didn't break the gaze. "I lost my balance."

Her voice was soft and warm, like a quilt that surrounded Cole from head to foot. He felt her fingers moving against his chest, exploring the steel-hard muscles beneath his shirt.

When Cole had first noticed the woman looking at him, he thought she might have heard about the bounty on his head. Now he realized her interest was not motivated by money.

"These can be bumpy tracks." Cole righted the woman and was pleased when her fingers lingered on his chest before being taken from him.

"Thank you. I might have fallen."

Cole touched the brim of his Stetson again, about to resume his inspection of the train. "Ma'am . . ."

He turned and started down the aisle. He hadn't taken many steps when he felt fingertips on his shoulder. He turned slowly, fixing the striking redhead with his steel-gray eyes.

"The name's Belle," she said, her voice barely above a whisper. "Actually, it's Mabel, but all my friends call me Belle."

Cole looked into Belle's eyes and thought, *She's so beautiful. Why do I want to get away from her? She would provide the kind of comfort I need right now. Why don't I accept what comfort she has to offer?*

"Perhaps we can have lunch together tomorrow," Cole said, having no intention of dining with Belle but knowing that he could make a smooth escape with such words. "Are you going far?"

Belle smiled knowingly, nodded her head, then turned and walked down the aisle with Cole watching every sensuous move.

Christina neatly folded the dress Cole had bought her and tucked it, along with the box containing the other garments, in the compartment above the padded bench seat on the opposite side of the small cabin.

The bed was somewhat larger in size than the bed Christina had at home, but smaller than the one her mother and father had shared for so many years. When she slipped between the cool cotton sheets, Christina sighed and closed her eyes. Had any bed ever felt quite so good to her body? Had any pillow ever cradled her head with such gentle care?

A distant sound in her brain warned Christina that she must not fall asleep. Not until she made sure that Cole returned to her safe and sound. And not until she was assured that Cole Jurrell knew he had to keep his hands to himself, keep his kisses to himself, and keep all that sweet charm and intoxicating caresses to himself.

There is a rhythm to a train that is either soothing or annoying, depending upon one's state of mind. When one is trying to sleep, the click-click of the steel wheels going over the spacers between track sections is like a lullaby and the gentle rocking of the train is as sweet as one's mother gently rocking the cradle.

Christina did not feel these things when she woke shortly after four in the morning. She heard the disquieting sound of metal snapping against metal, and felt the annoying movement of the train as it rolled toward St. Paul.

She did feel the warmth of Cole Jurrell's biceps, which, to her horror, she was using as a pillow.

Christina was awake instantly, but she didn't move a muscle. She was on her side, one knee bent and resting on Cole's thigh. The blanket she had put over herself separated her from Cole.

At first, Christina was shocked to find that Cole had somehow slipped into bed with her while she had slept, but now a soft, sleepy smile tugged at the corners of her mouth.

Cole might be a cad, she thought, but at least, though he had slept in the bed with her, he hadn't gotten under the blankets. It was, to Christina, a small but critical distinction in his favor.

Christina looked at Cole's face, close to her own. She

123

saw him as she had never seen him before. He looked — and this surprised her — peaceful. When he slept, it was as though he didn't have a care in the world. The vitality she always saw in his cold gray eyes was not there, but neither was the hard set of his mouth. The lightning reflexes were dormant, and the sinewy muscles relaxed.

I can see why so many woman have wanted to be alone with him, Christina thought.

And then another thought struck Christina, leaving her with a cold feeling inside. How many women had looked at Cole in exactly the same way she was looking at him now? How many times had one of Cole's lovers studied him as he slept in post-lovemaking exhaustion?

Logic told Christina that she had no right to resent the other women who had slept with Cole. She had no claims on him, and he certainly had no claims on her. That's what logic told Christina. Her emotions played a much different tune.

Cole's arm was looped lightly around Christina's shoulders. For a moment, she closed her eyes and just felt the weight of his arm and the warmth of his flesh against her naked shoulders.

Cuddling, thought Christina dreamily. *This is what cuddling is.*

Christina remembered hearing her mother talking with her aunt one early morning when the relatives were over for Christmas. Christina's mother was whispering to her sister about how much she enjoyed cuddling on cold winter nights. Then, blushing in a way that Christina — then a very young girl — thought was almost childlike, her mother said that Mr. Sands always seemed to want something *more* than just cuddling. The two sisters laughed quietly between themselves, their heads close together and their voices conspiratorially hushed. Christina did not fully understand what they had been talking about then, but she knew what pleasure cuddling was now. She felt as though she now shared something with her mother, and that added to Christina's feelings of warmth, security, and tenderness.

Cole's hair was mussed, and it occurred to Christina that this was one of the few times she'd seen him without his hat. *He shouldn't wear his hat so often,* she thought. *It hides his hair, and he has beautiful hair.*

When Christina inhaled, she caught the scent of Cole. It was man-scent, and new to Christina, though she had certainly been near men before. After a moment, she decided she liked it. There was something primitive and exciting about the scent.

Cole needed a shave. Christina wanted to touch his face. Did his beard still have the texture of wire bristles, or was it softer now that he hadn't shaved in a couple of days? She tried to recall how his stubbled cheeks had felt against her own when they were at the hotel, but she couldn't. Just thinking about what had happened, and almost happened, made her cheeks feel warm, and the heat seemed to pass slowly from her face to her shoulders and bosom.

Christina shifted positions, rolling slightly toward Cole to free her arm. His hand snapped up, catching her wrist with such blazing swiftness it was like the strike of a cat. Steel-gray eyes, wide and searching, drilled her.

For a moment Cole just looked into Christina's eyes. Then, in a hushed voice, he hissed, "Where am I?"

"Shhhh!" Christina touched the side of Cole's face lightly with her palm. "It's all right. We're on a train headed for St. Paul. Remember? We got on last night in Fargo."

Cole's body, which had gone rigid, relaxed again, sinking into the mattress.

"We're safe," Christina continued, not sure why she felt the need to say anything to a man with Cole's experience. "There's nothing for you to worry about."

Cole sighed, breathed in deeply, then exhaled slowly. He rubbed his eyelids with a finger and thumb.

"I hate mornings," Cole said quietly, continuing to rub his eyes.

Christina's first response was to tease Cole for his feelings. She had always loved the morning. To her, it represented a rebirth of sorts, a new beginning. She couldn't understand anyone not loving the morning, with its freshness and unlimited potential.

"Why?" asked Christina softly.

Cole's mouth pulled up in a half-grin as he stared at the ceiling of the sleeper car. "Do you really want to hear this?"

"Yes . . . I think I do."

Cole sighed again, and it was evident to Christina that he was not a man who enjoyed talking about himself. She twisted a little, resting now on her side with her head on Cole's biceps and his arm still around her slender shoulders. She placed her palm lightly on his chest, touching him through his shirt.

"Tell me. I want to know."

"I hate mornings because I hate waking up. I never know where I am. Just for a second, when I wake up, I'm disoriented. I'm always afraid that I've let my guard down. I've got this . . . dream . . . it's more like a nightmare, really, that keeps warning me I'm going to slip up when I'm asleep. In this dream, I wake up just long enough to see who kills me." Cole started to turn his head to look at Christina, then stopped himself. He stared at the ceiling. "I never know where I am when I wake up because I'm never at the same place two nights in a row." He paused for a moment, shaking his head slowly. "That's why I hate sleeping."

"I think I can understand that," Christina whispered. She had learned a little about living like a hunted animal, but being afraid to sleep? It seemed ludicrous to Christina, but the strain was etched plainly on Cole's face. This time he couldn't hide his feelings.

"Maybe it won't always be like this," Cole said quietly. "Someday this will all get straightened out and the world will know what kind of man Nicholas Webb is."

126

And for the first time, Christina realized that she believed Cole's story. She believed that he was unjustly accused of killing his own father. She knew he was not a cold-blooded killer. Yes, he was a thief, but only from the Webbs. He didn't want to see anyone but Nicholas Webb get hurt.

Christina whispered, "I hope so, Cole."

"Someday . . . maybe," Cole continued with a hiss of breath. "Yeah . . . maybe someday the world will believe that I'm telling the truth and know that Webb is lying. But that someday isn't going to be this day, and it isn't likely it's going to be tomorrow, or the next day, either."

At last Cole turned and looked at Christina. His gray eyes were no longer cold. Now they were bright and clear and just a little sad.

"By the way," Cole said, his tone light. "Good morning."

"Good morning," Christina replied, unable to keep the smile of a newly discovered pleasure from spreading across her face.

Cole returned her smile, but only for a moment. He shifted on the too-small bed and Christina raised her head enough for him to slip his arm out from beneath her, then he twisted onto his knees, kneeling on the bed, and raised the curtain above the windowsill enough to peer outside.

"It's still early," Cole said, staring into the blackness, seeing only the moon and the stars. "Four. Maybe five. The sun won't be up for a while yet."

He turned away from the window to look down at Christina bathed in shadows, half concealed and half revealed. The blanket had shifted slightly, and Cole saw the soft, enticing fullness of Christina's breasts straining against the bodice of the petticoat, their fullness too great for the garment's design. A tightness in Cole's chest sent off a warning in his brain, but he could not take his eyes from Christina.

"Tomorrow you'll be safe," Cole said softly, not really knowing why he felt the need to chase away her fears.

"Yes," she sighed and crooked her right arm, resting her head on it. She did not take her eyes off Cole, nor did she realize the effect her beauty was having on him at that moment. She felt warm and sleepy, yet vividly aware of Cole's presence. Closing her eyes for several seconds to savor this moment, she felt the bed move as Cole returned to it, reclining beside her. She could not explain why she reached for him, or why she felt so comfortable with Cole's closeness.

Her hand looped softly around Cole's neck, and as he stretched out on the bed, she pulled his face down to hers, kissing his lips softly, still inexperienced in such matters but learning quickly and eager for knowledge.

The weight of Cole's lean, muscular body felt good against Christina. She rolled toward him, pressing more of herself against him.

"Thank you," she whispered, pulling Cole closer, until their faces were side by side. "Thank you for everything, Cole Jurrell." She inhaled deeply, feeling his warmth and security, feeling, too, the masculinity of the man that seemed to surround her and invade every part of her. "You've been so good to me. I never would have escaped without you. I would have been caught and Nicholas would have—"

"Shhhh!" Cole pulled away from Christina so that he could look into her eyes. He traced the outline of her lips with a fingertip. "Don't think about it. All that's in the past now. And I don't ever want to hear you mention his name again. You're too gentle to ever have the taste of his name on your lips."

He dipped his head down and kissed her. It was a soft kiss, a kiss shared by two people who had lived through difficult and dangerous times together and survived. The kiss was almost friendly . . . at first.

Aware, this time, of what he wanted, she parted her lips and accepted his searching tongue. A low, soft moan escaped from deep in her soul as she tasted the heady wine of

Cole's hungry kiss.

Deeper and deeper he kissed. Christina, warm and secure in this bed that she shared with Cole, felt a thousand different sensations going through her. When Cole put a hand on her shoulder, touching her bare flesh, she sighed again. Somehow, when she was with Cole, every part of her body was attuned to accepting the most glorious feelings. The hand slipped around her, beneath her, pulling her voluptuous body in tighter to his own. When Cole's hand ran down her back, Christina arched toward him.

"Christina," Cole whispered, drawing the name out slowly as he removed the sheet that separated his body from hers.

When he rolled toward Christina again, placing his chest over hers, their bodies molded together as one. Christina felt the pressure of his chest against her breasts, making them feel overfull and taut. And his thigh, pressing against her most private area, created a sweet esthesia that blotted out all fears and doubts.

One kiss passed into the next, and into the one after that. A glow of warmth, like an ember, had started in Christina and was slowly and steadily becoming hotter. When Cole turned his attention away from her mouth and began kissing the smooth arch of her neck, Christina knew where he was headed and welcomed him.

"Ohhhh!" she sighed, turning her face away from Cole, keeping her eyes shut in the dimly lit sleeping car.

She didn't want to see anything, say anything, do anything. All Christina wanted was Cole making her feel all the incredible things only he could make her feel.

He took her hands by the wrists and placed them by her sides. She felt the slender, lace-trimmed straps of her petticoat being drawn over her shoulders and then down her arms. The cups of the petticoat were taken carefully away from her breasts, and for a moment Christina felt as though she was some rare and infinitely precious present that Cole was unwrapping. The sensation made Christina

129

feel differently about herself — unique, coveted, beautiful, and worthy of this enigmatic man's passion.

She heard Cole's sharp intake of breath when her breasts were revealed. With Cole's assistance she slipped her arms out of the petticoat's straps. Still she refused to open her eyes, afraid that something might break the spell of this glorious moment.

"Look at you," Cole whispered hoarsely. "So beautiful and delicate." A fingertip traced a tight circle around one breast. As the hand cupped over the firm mound Cole's tongue traced a similar pattern around the other nipple before he caught the bud between his lips and sucked softly.

Christina shivered and reached blindly for Cole. She found his shoulders, broad and strong, and caressed his body through the rough woven texture of his shirt. Her breasts throbbed as his devastating tongue went from one nipple to the other and his hand slid beneath the petticoat, grazing lightly against the back of her thigh. She stiffened in response and caught his wrist in her hand, twisting toward him on the bed.

"Cole, wait," Christina whispered in a rush of confusion and fear.

"No, darling, don't be afraid." Cole took his hand from Christina's leg and put it against her cheek. "Open your eyes," he whispered in a deep voice, his face close to hers.

She obeyed his soft command and Cole just looked at her for a long, silent moment. "I won't hurt you." He kissed her trembling lips, pushing her slowly but insistently back until she was again lying on the bed and he was above her. "Don't worry, Christina . . . I won't hurt you. I promise you that."

Christina shivered when Cole kissed her. She knew that she could, and should, stop Cole. That was what logic and reason screamed in her head. But logic and reason were less important now than sensuality — new, frightening, exhilarating, compelling — and the unspoken promise of what

130

lay ahead in the dark unknown.

He took Christina's mouth with his own, stealing her breath away, silencing her instinctive protests. Other instincts rose in her as she responded to his kiss, curling her tongue around Cole's, her body trembling in ecstasy within the circle of his strong arms. When she felt the hand once again touching her at the back of the knee, she gave in to the pleasure. She could no longer fight the emotions she had for Cole or the feelings that he elicited from her when he touched her.

The fingertips inched slowly up the back of Christina's thigh, sending shivers through her. She felt her petticoat slowly pushed higher. As she kissed Cole, her tongue searching his mouth boldly, she unconsciously held her breath. Waiting . . . waiting for . . .

Cole's hand slipped around Christina, cupping her buttocks. He pulled her hips to him, hugging her tenderly close as his mouth devoured hers. She trembled softly in his arms, her breasts straining against the hard surface of his chest, the sensation of his shirt against her nipples an unhappy replacement for the contact of his warm flesh against her own.

Back and forth Cole's hand went, the fingertips trailing lightly over the silken smoothness of Christina's thigh. The hand slipped inside her knee, pushing it slightly to the side, then moved down again with deliberate ease.

Though the fire of passion — hotter and more inspiring than anything Cole had known before — spurred him on, he checked his own desire to possess Christina. *Be careful,* a voice inside Cole whispered. *She's not like the other women you've known. Be gentle. Go slow.*

Christina's head was spinning. The sensation of fingertips tracing circles against the smooth flesh of her inner thigh was soul-shattering. She clung tightly to Cole, hugging him close. She kissed him with parted lips, feasting her senses on his masculinity, trusting him to thrill her.

Cole pushed Christina away slightly and looked search-

131

ingly at her. She could feel his gaze upon her, but she did not open her eyes until he stopped his fiercely arousing caresses.

"What?" Christina asked. Her heart was pounding. She did not understand his questioning look. "What's wrong? Have I done something?"

"I don't think you could ever do anything wrong." Cole ran a fingertip over Christina's eyebrow. "I just . . . I'm just not certain that . . ."

Christina touched Cole's face, running her hand lightly down his neck. She struggled with herself, not understanding Cole's words, only knowing what she felt. And then understanding dawned on her, and Cole's loving concern drew tears to her sapphire-blue eyes. Christina willed the tears away, afraid they would shatter the delicate atmosphere that had mysteriously and gloriously blossomed in the sleeping car.

"Don't be afraid for me," Christina whispered. As she looked up at Cole, two tears slipped from her eyes, trickling over her temples into her golden hair. "I'm scared. I've never . . . loved anyone before. But I know I want you, Cole."

Christina's voice was so soft that Cole dipped his head, his ear nearly touching her lips as she spoke. "So much has happened to me in these past few days," Christina continued. "I've known fear and hunger and exhaustion. I've been scared, Cole. Scared to death. But when I'm with you, I feel safe. And when you touch me . . . oh, Cole, when you touch me I feel more alive than I ever have before. I know you're afraid you're going to hurt me," she whispered. Cole's cheek rubbed against hers as he nodded his head. "Don't be afraid, Cole. You won't hurt me. I know you won't."

But Christina's words could not silence the voice of conscience that whispered inside Cole's head. He was guilty of many things, but he had never resorted to taking advantage of a lonely, frightened young girl who was only

132

reaching out for help. He couldn't—he just *couldn't*—take advantage of Christina's gentle, fragile heart that way. Not when he knew that no matter how much he wanted to spend every day and night with Christina, his world wouldn't let him. Christina deserved a home with lovely furnishings, Cole's conscience taunted, not a saddlebag and a life constantly on the run, with nothing but fear and apprehension as her constant companions.

"I . . . can't promise you anything," Cole said finally.

"I don't expect any promises. What promises can we give each other when we don't even know if we'll be alive tomorrow?" Christina stroked Cole's sandy blond hair, moving a little to feel the contact of his beard stubble against her soft cheek. "Before . . . I used to think I needed promises. Now I don't. Not after everything that's happened. All I want is the time we have right now. Nothing lasts forever, Cole. I thought my parents would, but they're gone. Nothing in this world lasts, so please . . . please let me have this one moment. Nobody can take from us what we have right here, right now."

Christina hugged Cole to her bosom again. "Take you shirt off," Christina whispered. "I want to feel you against me. I don't want anything separating us."

Cole eased out of Christina's embrace. He bent to kiss her lips softly, then stood in the center of the sleeping car. Cole took off his shirt as Christina studied him through the thick, hazy curl of her lashes. She saw the powerful muscles in his chest and arms, and she noticed, too, the white, puckered scars on his back—the result of bullet wounds.

"So violent," Christina whispered, almost in awe as she watched Cole removing the rest of his clothes. "You've led such a violent life, but I don't think you wanted it that way."

Cole could find no appropriate words to express all that he felt. He slipped into bed with Christina again. The young woman's ability to see him for exactly what he was

133

shocked and dismayed Cole. He had always thought that he needed a woman with that ability, but confronted with it now, he was not so sure.

"Close to me," Christina purred, her arms going around Cole's lean waist. When she felt the hard warmth of his chest flattening her breasts, she exhaled a blissful sigh. The sensation was even more ecstatic than she had believed it would be. "So warm. Cole, you make me feel so warm and safe."

Cole's arousal brushed against Christina's thigh. The heat of his passion branded Christina and she stiffened at the intimate contact, inwardly praying Cole hadn't noticed her initial, frightened reaction to him.

"I don't want to hurt you," Cole whispered, but as he spoke, his lips brushed intimately against Christina's and he rolled to place more of his weight upon her trembling body.

Christina shivered as the caresses began again in earnest over the length of her satiny body. When Cole's knee pushed between her legs, she hugged him tightly and shed a single tear of joy as she felt herself becoming a part of Cole Jurrell.

Chapter 12

"The sun is coming up," Christina said. She was kneeling on the bed, looking beneath the curtain with eyes that saw the world in a new light. "This is a new day," Christina continued, her voice sounding far away and dreamy. "Dawn. The world is so lovely at this time. I feel like my life is dawning, too."

Cole, on his back and looking up at Christina's naked profile, could not get his mouth to form words.

She looks so sexy and yet so innocent, he thought, studying the side of Christina's face while she watched the sun coming up red and yellow on the eastern horizon. *She was innocent until she met me.*

Cole cringed at the second thought that wormed itself poisonously into his conscience and he struggled to keep guilt pushed to the back of his mind. Misplaced or not, he could sort his feelings out later, after Christina was safely tucked away in St. Paul and he was headed back to the Dakota Territory and the land and legacy that had been stolen from him.

Cole's eyes swept downward. His breath caught in his throat at the rounded curves of Christina's breasts. Though his passion was recently spent, the intoxicating, rejuvenating beauty that Christina presented began to arouse him again. He watched with a strangely possessive sense of fascination as Christina's full bosom swayed slightly with the gentle rocking motion of the rail car. He saw, in the golden glow of the early morning light, a soft pink areola and nipple.

"My God," Cole whispered.

Christina looked over her shoulder, down at Cole. The move did absolutely nothing to dampen the rapidly escalating fires of passion that had been rekindled in Cole's soul.

"You are the most . . ."

Words of love would not come coherently from Cole's passion-addled brain, so he chose to cut off his thought and just look at Christina, a man reacting as though he had never seen a naked woman before.

"Cole, what is it?" Christina asked after a moment.

"Come here." Cole's voice was a hoarse whisper. He reached for Christina, and to his absolute horror, saw that his hand was trembling. "Come to me."

Christina recognized the look in Cole's eyes but now it no longer frightened her. His hunger for her was evident, and Christina welcomed the emotions.

She sat on the edge of the bed, taking Cole's outstretched hand in her own. She brought his hand to her mouth, kissing the palm, then the tips of his fingers.

"Cole . . ." Christina purred, wanting her lover to know how much he meant to her, yet not knowing what words could describe her powerful feelings.

Christina kissed Cole's palm, her blue eyes holding his gray ones. Slowly, she took his hand and placed it over the heated, sensitive rise of her breast.

"I want you . . . again," Cole whispered, pulling Christina's naked body down upon his. He kissed her lips and felt her sigh. "I *need* you again," he whispered, as he rolled onto his side so that he could look at Christina in her naked splendor. "Your body is perfect."

Feeling his eyes upon her, Christina crossed an arm over

her breasts to cover them. Modestly, she placed her other hand lower.

"You make me feel . . . uneasy . . . when you look at me that way," Christina whispered. "Please, Cole, just love me."

The heat of Cole's gaze as his eyes roamed appreciatively over Christina made her feel flushed. She had made love with Cole, but this was different. Now she felt scrutinized, and her self-confidence was not strong enough for her to accept scrutiny without worry.

"Don't be nervous. You're with me." Cole took Christina's wrist and gently lifted her arm away from her breasts. "You don't have to hide with me. You should be proud of the way you look."

Christina turned her face away from Cole. Why did he have to do this to her? Couldn't he just *make* her feel beautiful without talking about it? Couldn't he see how uncomfortable he was making her? All she really wanted was to have his body pressing against her own, feel his strength and power and unspoken love in the magic of his touch. Why must this man, who was so often reticent to a fault, insist on speaking now?

"If only you could see yourself through my eyes," Cole continued, his voice warm and sensual. He began tracing circles on Christina's stomach. His hand moved up slowly until he brushed the crests of her breasts with his fingertips. "If you only knew what you look like, then you wouldn't be so shy with me." Cole sighed, as though perplexed by some great mystery. "It's strange, but women who believe they are irresistible to men are often not very attractive. But you—so lovely—harbor doubts."

The words flowed over Christina and took on a life of their own, touching her body as well as her mind. His fingers played her nipples into erections, then stoked her desire until her breasts pulsed and ached. She kept her face turned away from Cole, but a change had come over her. The tormenting words no longer embarrassed her. Now

137

they caressed her just as gently and erotically as his hands, making her aware of her own sensuality without being frightened by it.

Cole's hand trailed down, past Christina's flattened stomach. She moved her hand, the one she had modestly covered herself with, and felt deliriously shameful for her bold, silent invitation.

"So lovely . . . skin like satin . . . smooth, warm satin," Cole purred, stroking Christina's flesh with consummate skill. She began to squirm on the small bed. "I must . . . explore you."

Cole's mouth closed over Christina's breast. She gasped softly, a tiny cry of pleasure at the warmth and moisture that suffused her senses. Though she felt an urgency to make love to Cole—it was not what he wanted, and Cole was in command.

A tremor went through Christina as Cole's caresses moved lower. His hand played along her trembling thighs, touching and teasing, taunting with the promise of fulfillment, yet always holding back. Sharp teeth nibbled at Christina's stomach and she purred, her whole being feeling every subtle touch, each caress of teeth and lips and tongue. And then Cole was moving lower still, tasting Christina, kissing her with deep intimacy.

Christina inhaled deeply, her mind in a whirl as vague concepts of right and wrong collided headlong with sensations that were exquisite beyond belief. She held her breath until her lungs burned, and still she could not relax enough to exhale. Not until, under Cole's deft ministrations, ecstasy shuddered through her in overwhelming release.

"I can never get enough of you," Cole whispered some minutes later as he eased himself above Christina and kissed her mouth possessively. "Never!"

Christina heard the ticket man calling out the next stop. The sound awoke her, but she refused to open her eyes.

Had it been within her power, she would have forced herself back to sleep and resumed the heavenly dream she'd had of herself and Cole.

"Christina," Cole said quietly and she turned slowly in answer, moving her head from Cole's upper arm to his chest. She pulled a knee up until her thigh rested atop Cole's muscular legs. Her nails scratched sleepily against the smooth, hard, heated surface of his chest.

"Don't say anything yet." Christina sighed in blissful contentment. "Whatever you're going to say can wait."

"But Christina—"

"Shhh!" Christina's hand drifted up Cole's chest until the fingertips pressed softly against his lips to silence him. "Whatever it is can wait."

Cole caressed Christina's shoulder in a desultory manner, and just for a little while she was at peace with a world she no longer understood. Everything, at this single moment, was as it should be for Christina. She was safe and warm in the arms of the man she loved. And though Cole had never said as much, everything he did proved to Christina that he loved her.

If he didn't love her, why risk his life to help her? *Yes*, thought Christina contentedly, *Cole loves me. We're on a train headed away from evil men, going to St. Paul where nobody knows me.*

St. Paul. It sounded magical somehow. Almost holy. Christina could find a new life there, she was convinced. A new life with Cole.

Cole was saying something about getting dressed. The train was pulling into St. Cloud, he was saying.

"How far is St. Cloud from St. Paul?" she asked.

"About seventy miles."

Christina kissed Cole's chest and stretched slowly in feline fashion, rolling toward him to feel the solid warmth of his chest against her breasts. She kissed his chin.

"Seventy miles?" She kissed his mouth, the tip of her tongue making fleeting contact with his lips. "Then I see

139

no reason to get dressed for at least another sixty-five miles."

Cole chuckled and said Christina was terrible, but somehow she didn't believe him.

Chapter 13

The carriage wheels and horse's hooves clacked noisily against the cobblestone streets of St. Paul. Christina, though weary of traveling, felt giddy and lightheaded at being in a new city and having Cole to share the experience with her.

"That's the home of Jerome Borsch, the railroad baron," Cole said, pointing to an enormous marblestone mansion that looked like the European castles Christina had seen in schoolbooks. "He is reported to be the richest man around, but nobody knows for sure. There's also Pillsbury and Hill and a couple of other men in Minneapolis and St. Paul who can give him a run for the money."

"So to speak," Christina said with a laugh and curled her fingers around Cole's arm, giving his biceps a squeeze. She had no idea where Cole was taking her, and she really didn't care. As long as he stayed at her side, Christina was not afraid to confront the world.

Fashions were different here than in Enderton, or even Fargo, Christina noted. The men wore shoes instead of boots, and the woman all seemed to have money for fine, embroidered dresses of tightly woven wool and cotton, or even velvet and silk. St. Paul seemed a city of unimaginable wealth. Wealth and energy exuded from everywhere. Men and women walked here and there, moving from one store to the next, from one business to another. She noticed, too, that the people traveled in carriages instead of riding on horseback.

"St. Paul seems so . . . oh, I don't know the right word for it . . . sophisticated?"

Christina looked at Cole's profile, her eyes caressing and appraising him. She loved what she saw. She was proud of this man for all that he had done, for his struggle against Nicholas Webb, and for simply being the man he was. But Christina couldn't help wondering how Cole would fit into St. Paul society. Two days ago, he needed a shave. Now he *really* needed one. And though he had gone to the bother and expense of purchasing a fine dress and undergarments for her, he hadn't bought any clothes for himself, still wearing the work shirt, black denim pants, and corduroy jacket. And though he had removed his holster, the Colt was tucked inside his waistband at the small of his back.

"Take a right at the next street," Cole told the coachman. "Stop at the third building on the right."

After paying the coachman, Cole took Christina's hand in his. He nearly dragged her along behind him as he took long strides toward the oversized doors of the three-story redbrick building.

Christina didn't have time to admire the foyer or the waiting room as Cole pulled her up the wide, winding stairway. They went past the second floor and up to the third.

Cole pulled a key from the top of the doorsill. He unlocked the door and flung it open with a theatrical flourish.

"For my lady," Cole said, deep dimples appearing in his unshaven cheeks. His gray eyes were bright and sparkling as he bowed low.

Cole's enthusiasm was infectious and Christina didn't try to keep the laughter to herself. She was just about to step through the door when Cole caught her upper arm in his hand.

"I believe carrying you over the threshold is proper etiquette."

Cole swept Christina up in his arms. She slipped her hands around his neck, lacing her fingers together. For a moment they just looked into each other's eyes. Then, with an impish smile tugging at the corners of his mouth, Cole carried her into the apartment.

As he set Christina back on her feet, she looked around and whistled softly, amazed at what she saw. The apartment was breathtaking. Clearly, it belonged to a young bachelor of considerable means. But if Cole used the money he took from Webb to help the displaced farmers and ranchers who had been abused by Webb's thievery, how could he afford this?

"Make yourself comfortable," Cole said, nodding toward the calico sofa near large bay windows that overlooked the street. "It's time I got cleaned up and changed into something a bit more appropriate for city life." He cleared his throat and added in a quieter tone, "My things are in the war room."

"War room?"

"I'll explain later." Cole gave Christina a quick kiss on the cheek. "Just make yourself comfy. It'll take me a while."

Christina didn't know what to say or think. She had believed with all her heart that Cole's struggle against Webb was truly a selfless one. She had been convinced that he sought no personal gain in his battle other than the acquisition of what had been stolen from him. It took only a glance from Christina's experienced merchant's eye to tell her that Cole had profited greatly. The furnishings were of the finest quality, as were the draperies. Even the ashtray on the small table near the sofa was European-cut crystal. Cole took a key resting in the ashtray and stepped to a door along the right-hand wall. He unlocked the door and, before opening it, looked over his shoulder at

Christina. She could not read the expression in his eyes.

"The war room," he murmured, then opened the door and stepped inside, closing it quickly behind him, leaving Christina alone with her doubts and questions and fears.

Christina stepped to the center of the room. She closed her eyes and breathed in deeply. The apartment smelled of stale air, air that had been choked off by windows that hadn't been opened in weeks or months. She pulled open the cream-colored curtains and eased up several windows. Fresh, clean air streamed into the apartment. She sat on the ledge of the bay windows and gazed unseeingly down at the street below and the people walking along it.

Who was this outlaw Cole Jurrell? she asked herself. And why wasn't there dust on the furniture?

Cole closed the door that separated the war room from his "entertaining" apartment. He leaned against the door and sighed. Perhaps it wasn't such a good idea to bring Christina here after all. For years he had carefully guarded his life in St. Paul, going so far as to create a new identity for himself. In St. Paul, he wasn't Colton Jurrell, he was John Colter, banished renegade son of a San Francisco shipping tycoon. He was thought of as a rich, irresponsible womanizer who had money to spend on wine, women, and friends. He came and went without any warning, and nobody expected anything of him other than to be shot someday by a jealous husband.

Cole opened his eyes with hesitation. The war room was dusty. He had a maid clean his apartment once a week while he was gone, and every other day when he was in town. But he never allowed anyone into the war room. It was from here, hunched over the long mahogany table that ran the length of the south wall, that he searched through the blueprints and rail records, looking for a weakness in the Webb chain. He plotted his attacks on the other end of the Webb empire from this room. In here, he was not John Colter, he was the outlaw Cole Jurrell, a man wanted for the murder of his own father.

He kept his real identity a secret from everyone because he knew that his life depended upon that secret.

Cole walked over to the table and unrolled the map of central Dakota. A small pencil mark on the map showed where he and his so-called gang had attacked the last Webb shipment. It was on that train that Cole had first seen Christina, and the memory now brought a fleeting smile to his mouth.

She was good for him, he knew. Good for a soul that had not known honesty in too many months and years. She knew almost everything about him, she believed in him, and she expected very little of him. She was exactly what he had always thought he wanted.

No she's not, his mind teased. *She's gentle and caring and she's falling in love with you, if she hasn't fallen in love already. She trusts you, and even if she doesn't say so, she expects you to stay with her.*

Aloud, he whispered, "This time, Cole, you stole from someone other than Webb. That you did, ol' boy, and you're not going to be able to give it back, like you did the necklace."

Cole scratched his chin, not liking the stubble on his face. It had been itching for two days. A shave, hot bath, and clean clothes were in order. This time, he was not preparing to go out on the town in search of a woman to satisfy his carnal cravings. He was glad he wanted to clean himself for a delicate young woman who was in his apartment, waiting for him. She knew who he was, and if they made love, she wouldn't whisper "John" in his ear.

Knowing that Christina knew all about him and loved him anyway was one of the most disquieting revelations Cole had ever had.

145

Chapter 14

Cole left Christina alone for almost two hours. In that time, she inspected the apartment, curiously looking at the things Cole chose to have in his personal domain.

It surprised Christina that the apartment was pleasantly furnished in a manner not entirely dissimilar to the way she would have furnished it. There was a masculine aura to it, no getting around that. But Cole's tastes were simple, the apartment uncluttered. The calico sofa did seem out of place, not in keeping with the other chairs, which were made of heavy wood and leather. Christina wondered why the sofa was there, and what had prompted Cole to keep it.

A thousand questions went unanswered in Christina's mind. If Cole was a wanted man, how could he keep an apartment in St. Paul, which was hardly more than three hundred miles from Enderton?

Looking at the street below, Christina wondered, too, if she would be living in St. Paul for very long, or if Cole intended on moving her farther away from the clutches of Nicholas Webb. Though Christina wasn't sure, she thought she had heard something about Nicholas having business dealings in the sister city of Minneapolis, across the river—or was it St. Paul? Christina couldn't remember. And though, at present, she felt safe,

146

she doubted that she would ever truly be safe from Nicholas until she lost herself in a city like New York or Santa Fe or San Francisco. Three hundred miles was too little distance for Christina to really feel she had escaped Webb's minions.

She sighed, realizing she was thinking like an outlaw. Was this what she would have to do the rest of her life? She was charged with murder—and the more distance she put between herself and the scene of the crime, the more likely she would never retrace her steps to prove her innocence. She smiled sadly, remembering herself a short week ago.

"Innocence is no longer such a simple thing," she murmured.

On the street below, a young couple was walking together, holding hands. Several steps behind them, an older woman followed. Christina smiled. She'd never had the chance to be courted by Cole in such a civilized manner. She wondered how Cole would have wooed her had the circumstances been different.

Would her feelings for Cole be different if he hadn't been an outlaw? What would he have thought of her father? More importantly, what would Papa have thought of Cole?

Christina wanted to believe that her father would have approved of Cole. Even though her father had passed away, Christina still sought his support, wanted his blessings.

"Oh, Papa . . ." Christina whispered under her breath, watching the young couple until they walked out of sight. "Why did my life have to turn out this way? Why did you have to leave me when I still need you so much?"

When Christina heard a door open behind her, she quickly wiped the mist from her eyes away. It wouldn't do to have Cole see her pining away for a life that, because of Nicholas Webb, she would never have. And it

147

wouldn't do to let him know that she missed being courted by him. Their relationship had taken giant strides forward, and Christina was not unhappy with its extraordinary progress. But there was still a tender spot in her heart that longed for the feeling of stability, for that little-girl giddiness of having a beau and talking about him with her friends.

"Well, do I meet with your approval?" she heard Cole ask. "Can you be seen in public with me without having to pretend you don't know me?"

Christina forced a smile to her lips before turning to face him. When she looked at Cole, her jaw dropped open and her heart skipped a beat.

The transformation was so complete, it shocked Christina beyond words. Cole had, in two hours, gone from an unshaven, dusty outlaw in trailsmen clothes to—at least in appearance—a well-heeled bachelor at home in the city.

"I take it from your silence that you approve of the change," Cole said, amusement shining in his tone.

Christina looked Cole up and down. The gabardine suit was of the highest quality, clearly tapered and tailored to Cole's long, lean physique. A black waistcoat went over a starched white shirt and vest. A gold chain went from one side of the vest to the other, the links heavy and solid looking.

"I wouldn't have believed it unless I saw it with my own eyes." Christina blinked her eyes, giving her head a little shake as though to clear her thoughts. "Cole, I . . . I never thought that you. . ."

"Were a city boy?" He cocked an eyebrow and feigned a look of dissatisfaction at Christina's surprise. "I'll have you know that since I was a wee lad, my dear ol' dad has been sending me to the city." Cole turned in a slow circle for Christina's further inspection. "Dad never did like going into town so he had me training for it almost from the beginning. We planned that I would handle the

148

city end—" Cole spoke the words slowly, imitating his father's voice "—of all our business matters. I dealt with the lawyers, businessmen, buyers, and sellers. Dad was always more comfortable running the day-to-day operations of the ranch."

Cole cleared his throat and turned away from Christina. She guessed that the subject of his father made him uncomfortable, and Christina bit her lip to still the questions she wanted to ask.

"I was thinking that what we should do first is get you the things you'll need to settle down," Cole said after a heavy pause had fallen over the room. "You can't survive with just one dress."

"But, Cole, I haven't got any—"

"Money is no object!" Cole turned a freshly shaven face toward Christina. The dimples were more noticeable in his cheeks without the growth of beard. "We'll dip into my personal fund. Don't worry, the money didn't come from stealing, or from Webb. It's money I've made from investments, securities, that sort of thing."

Cole walked slowly over to where Christina stood near the windows. She held her hands out and he took them in his.

"Cole, I never dreamed that you would ever know anything about securities and investments. From the first time I saw you, I had this image of you in my mind, in my heart. Now I'm seeing how incomplete that image was."

"You'll find I'm not the man the good folks in Enderton think I am," Cole said with bitter sarcasm. "I'm a lot of things to a lot of different people." He shook his head and added softly, "Hell, I'm a lot of different people." He tilted his head up to meet Christina's gaze. "Does that scare you?"

"No, it doesn't scare me. It just surprises me. Every time I think I've got you figured out, you show me something else about yourself, and then I'm all confused

149

about you again."

Cole took Christina's chin between his index finger and thumb, tilting her head back. He gazed into the deep blue pools of her eyes for a moment, smiling almost mockingly at her. He kissed her softly once, twice, three times.

"We'd better get a coach before I change my mind," Cole said quietly, his tone husky. "I want to show you the city, but if we stay here much longer, I'll be inclined to make the city wait for introductions."

Fluttery sensations went through Christina. She half turned, moving away from Cole, wanting his kisses to continue yet feeling that she should avoid them.

"Yes . . . yes, of course," Christina said. "The city. We must see the city."

Christina took Cole's hand as they left the apartment. She knew that if Cole had kissed her one more time, she would be the one to suggest they stay in the apartment and make love.

Zachary had seen his father angry before, but he couldn't remember a time when Nicholas had allowed his temper to run loose like this. Nicholas had been ranting for twenty minutes—since Zachary's empty-handed return from Fargo.

"Hey, it wasn't my fault," Zachary said.

"Don't talk back to me!" Nicholas pointed an accusing finger at his son. "I thought you would be different. I really thought you would be able to find Christina and bring her back to me." Nicholas's face twisted into a scowl of utter contempt. "You're a Webb . . . and yet you failed!"

Zachary wanted to block his father's voice out, but he knew better. If Nicholas should ask him a question then catch him not listening, the wrath he would face would be hell's fury.

"I want her," Nicholas continued. He lit a long, thick cigar and puffed furiously on it, sending a gray cloud rolling across the ceiling of his study. "Don't get confused, Zachary. This isn't like the others. She's not like any of the other women I've wanted. It's not just . . . animal lust." He stared at this son with undisguised contempt. "I want her, and by God, I'm going to have her."

"I know you will," Zachary replied, nodding his head. He hated his father as much as Nicholas hated him, but that didn't prevent Zachary from knowing how to assuage his temper when it was running rampant. "You always get what you want. You've told me that a thousand times."

Zachary chuckled softly. He knew when he did that, he sounded like Nicholas.

Staring at the ceiling, Nicholas nodded his head. "It's been a week," he said. "The trail's gone cold, but it isn't dead. You can still find Christina. This is just the kind of thing that you're good at, Zachary. But I also know that you don't give a damn about me or what I want."

Zachary straightened in his chair. Before he could put forward a denial, he was stopped by Nicholas's motion for silence.

"This isn't a time for lies, Zachary. You hate me, and I hate you. We both know that. It's no secret. I know you're hanging around waiting for me to die. You're my only heir, and you'll get everything I've worked hard to build." Nicholas swiveled his chair so that he could look out the window. It always soothed him to survey his kingdom. "I'll give you one thousand dollars now, plus another four thousand when you return with Christina."

Zachary's face creased into a smile. The working girls at Beth Ann's parlor would be happy to see him with a bankroll like that.

Nicholas pushed himself out of the chair, striding purposefully now that a decision had been made and his mind was set. He pulled a landscape painting aside and spun the dial on his wall safe.

"Mark my words, Zachary. If you don't come back with Christina, you're out of my will. I'll give everything I have," he said, "to a total stranger. I'll give it all away rather than let you have another dime from me . . . unless you bring me Christina."

Nicholas pulled open the heavy metal door. Inside the safe was several thousand dollars, neatly wrapped in bundles and stacked in piles. He removed a thousand-dollar bundle and ran his thumb across the edge of it, fanning the crisp ten-dollar bills for Zachary to see.

"You can be a rich man, or you can die in the gutter," Nicholas said, his voice low, threatening. "It all depends on whether you bring Christina to me or not." He reached out with the money, but pulled the stack of bills away before Zachary could pluck them from his fingers. "If, when you bring her to me, I find out you were with her, I'll kill you. Don't think that I won't." He paused, and his tone softened. "Ever since your mother died when you were small, I've been honest with you about how I need . . . certain women. Your time will come, Zachary. This time *now* is my time with Christina."

Zachary gave his father a crooked smile as he took the money and tucked it into his shirt pocket.

"I know you'll kill me. I've known that for a long time. Ever since you told me you never wanted me to call you 'dad.' And if I had any doubts, you laid them all to rest when you shot Richard O'Banion in the back. You actually liked him." Zachary stood up, his eyes locked onto Nicholas's. "Look, I hate your guts and you hate mine. That's a fact. To me, this is just another one of our business arrangements. I do the things you think your hands are too clean for these days, and you make sure I stay riding high in the saddle."

Zachary turned away from Nicholas, heading for the door. He spoke over his shoulder. "I'll bring her back. It

152

may take a while, but I'll bring her to you." Just before he left Nicholas's study, Zachary said under his breath, just loud enough for his father to hear, "Just don't blame me if you can't satisfy her."

Chapter 15

Christina propped her head and shoulders up, resting on an elbow. The grass was soft beneath her. The sun was warm, almost uncomfortably so, but she didn't mind. The large bonnet protected her hair face from the sun. She hoped freckles wouldn't appear on her cheeks and nose, as they sometimes did when she was exposed to the sun.

In the distance, Cole was tearing apart a fresh loaf of French bread, throwing the small pieces to the ducks that swam in the Minnehaha River, at the foot of the waterfalls. Christina watched him, admiring everything about him, finding it slightly surprising that Cole should take such pleasure in something as inconsequential as feeding ducks.

For three weeks, Christina's life had been a dream come true. It was as though she had never known fear, never had to run from the law, never had a care in the world. For three weeks, she lived with Cole in his grand apartment, going to new restaurants each night for dinner, sometimes taking a picnic lunch. Breakfasts were brought to them by servants. At first modesty dictated that Christina couldn't stay in bed when the servants brought breakfast in on silver trays. But with a little time and a lot of Cole's insistence, Christina learned to accept—even cherish—breakfast in bed.

The young lovers had settled into a morning ritual of sorts, and Christina loved every minute of it. For breakfast Cole ate a thick stack of wheatcakes smothered with honey and butter and washed it down with coffee. Christina had buttered toast, tea, and a glass of orange juice. After breakfast, Cole read two newspapers—one mainly concerned with the news of Minneapolis, another with St. Paul—and muttered about the business forecasts, his personal financial outlook, and politics. Christina's initial reaction to Cole's mutterings was annoyance, but eventually, she learned to take a certain pleasure in them. Watching him from the corner of her eyes as he scanned the newsprint, he looked, with the exception of being too young and handsome, just like any well-to-do businessman.

Their life together, Christina thought with satisfaction, was really quite normal. They certainly did not act like wanted criminals.

The sound of throaty laughter broke Christina's reverie. She looked up and saw that Cole was near the crashing, roaring Minnehaha Falls, shrouded in the mist that billowed around the lower area of the falls, tossing bits of bread into the air for the blackbirds that circled overhead. If the blackbirds didn't catch the bread in midair, the ducks got the bread the moment it landed on the water.

Cole cocked his arm and launched the last of the bread into the air.

I'm glad he's laughing, thought Christina. *Cole doesn't laugh enough. He takes too much too seriously.*

Cole returned to Christina, jogging the distance. His dark navy-blue suit was covered with a fine mist, the water glittering like diamond dust in the sunlight.

"You've gotten yourself all wet," Christina chided.

Cole took off his hat, running his fingers through sandy-blond hair. He smiled at Christina, dropping down

155

on the blanket with the picnic basket between them.

"I'll dry in the sun. No harm done." He grabbed a cold chicken leg and took a hearty bite, munching happily. "Did you figure out what we're going to do tonight? Is it the theater or the orchestra?"

"The theater, I think. It's supposed to be a pretty good comedy."

"That's what the newspaper said."

Cole tilted his head back, turning his face up to the sun. He let out a long, exaggerated sigh of pleasure. "I wish we could do this forever. This is how our lives should be spent."

"We can't. You've got to run out of money eventually." A twinge of guilt went through Christina. "You've already spent a fortune on me."

"Ah, yes. But it was a fortune well spent. Every night I am reminded of how well it has been spent." Cole turned onto his side so that he faced Christina. "Wherever we go, the men all look at you. At first it bothered me, but no more. Those poor beasts will just have to settle for second best, or third best, or whatever rank you want to name. I've caught the brass ring. I'm the lucky one, and I want it to stay that way."

"Brass ring, but not the gold ring." She saw Cole stiffen. Christina's instantly regretted the comment. He turned his eyes away from her. "I'm sorry. I don't mean to spoil the picnic." Christina felt a tightness in her chest. She knew she should stop, but words that could not remain silent continued. "It's just that we're *living* like man and wife. Why shouldn't we *be* man and wife?" Christina swallowed away the tightness in her throat. "I . . . I got used to . . . being with you every night. You know how hard that was for me . . . at first. I mean, that's got to be wrong, a sin."

"You want an apartment of your own?"

"No. I didn't say that. I just said that it was difficult for me at first to . . . live with you. Now I don't know

156

what I would do if I couldn't wake up with you in the morning, go to sleep with you at my side every night."

Christina did not know how deeply her words cut into Cole's soul. She could not know that Cole, too, was living a dream that he thought could never come true. But Cole was aware of the shadows lurking around them, even if Christina wasn't. He knew that soon his duty would weigh upon his shoulders so heavily he could no longer ignore it.

"I love making love to you," Christina said, her voice a whisper. "I know that we can't be like other couples." A sad smile tugged at the corners of Christina's lush mouth. "I'm not *that* naive, despite what you may think. I just don't see why we can't. . . ?"

Cole sat up, folding his long legs beneath him. He rolled a cigarette and lit it. The silence between them was thick. Christina could almost hear the beating of her own heavy heart.

"You want to get married? Fine. That's just fine." There was a hard, bitter edge to Cole's tone. The anger was not directed at Christina. "But you won't be Mrs. Colton Jurrell. You'll be Mrs. John Colter. Think about that, Christina."

"Don't tease me like that."

"I'm not teasing you, I'm telling you the truth. You know that I'm John Colter here. That's the man I pretend to be, but we both know it's not who I really am. I'm an outlaw, a man with a price on his head." Cole exhaled smoke with an expressive sigh, as though he was tired of the world continually intruding upon his happiness. "If I could marry you, I would, Christina. But I can't . . . at least not yet, not now. I can't jeopardize your safety more than I already have."

Words were difficult for Cole. He searched for just the right ones to make Christina understand the complex times they lived in.

"I live . . . so many lies," Cole continued slowly,

"Sometimes it's hard for me to remember where the truth ends and the lies begin. I have to be so many different people. And none of those people are really me. I'm not really who I want to be."

Christina felt like someone was squeezing her around the ribs, making her struggle for breath. Cole had just told her that he would, if he could, marry her. But in the same breath he had let her know that he couldn't marry her. Not now, anyway. Not until his life changed.

And when would that be? When Nicholas Webb was finally destroyed by his own greed? When Nicholas Webb was finally banished from civilized society and sent to jail, where he belonged? When Cole's good name was finally cleared? How long would all that take, if it ever came about at all?

"I never realized," Christina said softly. "You've always seemed so . . ." Her words trailed off. "I didn't know. You always appear as though you can handle anything, like nothing bothers you." She looked at Cole, loving him more than she ever had before. "Isn't there anyone else who can fight Mr. Webb? I don't know much about how you make your money, but it seems you're quite well off. Can't you just be happy with what you have and walk away? Just forget about Mr. Webb completely?"

Cole shook his head. He flicked his cigarette away. "It's not that simple," Cole said. "There are farmers who depend on me to help them. The money I steal from Webb goes to them. Sometimes I feel guilty about having it so nice here, but even if I gave away everything I have, it wouldn't help the families that used to live and farm on my father's land. It wouldn't help them for long, anyway. I've got to keep fighting. People are counting on me to bring Webb to justice."

"I never realized you have so much responsibility."

Cole's mouth curled in a sardonic half-smile. "I'd be lying to you, Christina, if I told you it was just for the ranchers. It's for me, too. And not just because Webb killed my father and should be brought to trial. That's a big part of why I do what I do, but it isn't all of it."

From the basket, Cole withdrew the bottle of delicate French white wine and poured some for himself into a glass. He sipped it before continuing.

"I also keep fighting Webb because it's exciting to me. I guess I had it pretty easy when I was a kid. I grew up rich and bored. I studied hard at the things Dad wanted me to learn, but essentially I didn't have anything really pressing me. Now, when I'm planning to rob a stagecoach or a train where I know Nicholas has his payroll, it's like I'm wired into a telegraph. I feel myself tick inside. I can feel the electricity running through me."

A quiver went through Christina. Looking at Cole, she got the feeling that he was telling her something he had never told anyone. The revelations, she sensed, were as new and freshly realized to Cole as they were to her.

"It's the only time that I'm not bored. It's being on the edge . . . and I like it." Cole smiled, but he wasn't looking at Christina. "A drunk likes his whiskey. And me? I like knowing that whatever decisions I make are important. If I make a mistake, I'm going to pay for it in a big way."

"Danger excites you."

"Yes."

Christina grinned, though she was surprised and a bit dismayed at Cole revelation. "That's why you wanted to make love with me the other night when we were at the theater, alone in the balcony," she said. "It was the danger that maybe someone would see us."

Cole grinned sheepishly. "No. It was you. You just looked so damned beautiful I had to make love to you." He cleared his throat, embarrassed at the recollection. "I can be impatient when I'm with you. I've never wanted to make love with . . ." Cole's words faltered as he pondered telling Christina the truth.

"Yes?" Christina prompted.

"I've never known any woman who excites me the way you do. Maybe the element of danger had something to do with it at first, but it's you, Christina. Nobody else could have made me want to make love so desperately. When you looked at me and smiled the way you did, it was like you were letting me know that you were anxious to get home so that we could make love. And knowing that you—and you looked *so* damn beautiful!—wanted to make love with me was . . . it was more than I could take. I didn't want to wait to be with you. I wanted you right then, right there."

Christina had chastised Cole in the theater when she discovered his intentions. Now she wondered whether she'd made the right decision to turn Cole away.

"Cole, can you have Anders prepare the carriage? I'd like to go home now. I want to take a bath before we go the theater tonight."

Christina watched Cole as he walked away. An indistinct sadness, its origin unknown to Christina, crept into her soul.

Why can't the world just leave us alone, in peace, so we can enjoy our love for each other? she asked herself, knowing that no one could give her the answer.

A soft moan of anticipation escaped Christina's lips as she applied a drop of perfume to the pale flesh between her breasts. She looked at the reflection in the mirror, unable to fully believe the face she saw was her own.

Is that really me? she mused.

Joy surged in her heart. It was her own reflection, and the knowing smile that curled her full, sensuous mouth spoke of things she used to deny. She had changed from the young woman she had been only weeks earlier. Changed, she thought, in ways she had never dreamed possible, ways that thrilled and sometimes frightened her.

160

Such a wanton I am! Making Cole wait and wait like this!

Christina had not known a moment's peace since her picnic that afternoon with Cole. When they went to the theater and she saw that Cole had bought tickets in a private balcony turret, she had thought for sure that at some time during the performance, Cole would reach out for her, wanting to make love. When he did, she would not turn him away. She wouldn't disappoint him, or herself, a second time. But Cole never bridged the space between them. When he reached for her hand and she placed hers in his, she kept expecting to see the playful smile in his eyes. Their eyes met, but his smile was loving, not playfully passionate.

Now that they were home, Christina had waited for Cole's love as long as she possibly could. He had taught her the pleasure of being with a man she loved. She knew now what it was like to be with Cole, and she knew what it was to be without him.

In the adjoining bedroom, Cole waited for her. Christina delayed leaving the dressing room. It wasn't out of fear that she hesitated. She wanted Cole desperate for the sight of her. She wanted him able to think only of her. She wanted to consume all his senses, just as he consumed hers, filling her days and nights with romantic fantasies and beautiful realities.

She had never dreamed it was possible for her to feel this way. Happiness of this nature was for others, Christina had thought. Now she knew differently. Cole had changed all that. Cole, with his piercing gray eyes and the quirky half-smile he reserved only for her. Cole had changed Christina with his fiercely gentle touch that inflamed her senses and swept away her doubts and fears.

It was finally Christina's time — awesomely, frighteningly, beautifully her time.

She forced her mind back to the present. She knew

the intensity of Cole's passion would not allow her to delay much longer. And she knew her own passion, sparked by Cole's, would propel them into a world of ecstasy they could share only with each other.

She took the peignoir from the chair and slipped it over her head. Her fingertips played lightly over the delicate embroidery along the seams and dipping neckline. The ebony nightgown made her blond hair appear even more pale and honey-hued, if that was possible.

The peignoir was a gift from Cole. As Christina smoothed the material down her legs, the memory of their first lovemaking brought a warmth to Christina's cheeks, making her feel flushed from head to toe.

Taking a brush from the nightstand, Christina ran it slowly through her hair, smoothing the shimmering, satiny tresses down over the front of her shoulders.

Returning the brush to the table, she discovered her hand was trembling. Quickly, she folded her hands together, pressing them against her lips. The tiny quiver inside her spoke of her own tenderly passionate need. Christina was filled with a combination of fear and fascination. Cole—this one man—had brought the passion in her to bloom and had taught her pleasures and fulfillment her young mind had never dreamed of yet her young body had instinctively yearned for.

It was knowing that she wanted Cole, that she craved his touch and needed the feel of his great chest pressing down upon her . . . it was these things that more than forced Christina to realize she loved him now and would love him for all time.

Christina's knees felt weak as she rose from the small table. She stepped through the door, into the bedroom. Pressing her back against the doorframe, she struggled to calm her shallow, rapid breathing.

Cole sat in the big, brass, four-poster bed. When he saw Christina, his eyes widened.

"My God, look at you," he whispered, his tone hoarse

with tension.

Christina began crossing the room, but Cole couldn't wait for her. He slipped out of bed, unmindful of his own nakedness. He placed his hands on her shoulders, looking down into Christina's clear blue eyes.

"You are so beautiful," he whispered. His fingertips trailed over Christina's shoulders to lightly play across her lips and cheeks, touching her softly. "Sometimes . . . when I'm looking at you . . . I can't believe you're real. It's like you're a dream, too beautiful to be true."

Christina stood with her hands at her sides, looking up into Cole's face. The fierceness of his gaze and the gentleness of his touch thrilled her. Her breasts rose and fell beneath the soft silk peignoir. Her nipples were now taut with passion and aching for his soft, knowing caresses.

Cole's thumbs passed lightly over her eyebrows, then down to her eyelids. Christina rolled her head back on her shoulders, trembling softly, giving herself freely. She reached for the knotted straps at her throat to untie her robe, but he caught her wrist softly.

"Let me," he whispered, the timbre of his voice speaking more than the mere words.

Christina felt the three lace bows come unfastened. Her fingers caressed the flesh of Cole's hips, but again he caught her wrists, preventing her from exploring, heightening the ache that was building deep within her.

"No, my darling. Just stand there. I just want you to feel. I just want to please you."

"But —" she whispered, silenced when his lips touched tenderly against her own.

The gentle kiss soon became a hungry, searching one. He devoured her, his warm lips pressing ravenously against hers. She felt Cole's lips part and she shivered with joy, accepting his probing tongue. His strong arms wound around her, pulling her voluptuous body against the broad, masculine length of him.

163

Christina trembled as Cole's hands moved around her body. Despite his great strength, he held Christina as though she was some rare, delicate, infinitely precious jewel that might shatter at any moment if not handled with special care.

"Beautiful . . . so beautiful," he whispered, planting feather-soft kisses on her eyelids and brows, ears and cheeks.

Christina thrilled at the myriad of sensations going through her. Cole's touch seared her soul. His fingers set her flesh ablaze as they curled inside the nightgown and slipped it over her shoulders.

"Please," Christina whispered. She wanted to show Cole how much she loved him but he would have none of it . . . yet.

"Just feel" was Cole's husky reply. He lowered the nightgown past her full, rounded breasts. Bending down, he pressed a moist kiss on one taut, pink crest. "Just feel."

Christina gasped as the warmth and moisture of his lips surrounded a nipple, spreading fire through her limbs. She shivered, unconsciously leaning closer to him, pressing more firmly against him.

The nightgown slipped past the sweeping, womanly curve of Christina's hips, then fell in a silky tumble around her ankles. She rolled her head on her shoulders, her body tingling, her mind reeling. Christina was no longer in control of what she thought or felt. Cole had taken control of her senses.

She wasn't certain she could remain standing. Her legs were weak and trembling as the last vestige of her self-control was stripped away by Cole's hands and lips and the powerfully masculine aura that emanated from him.

Strong hands cupped her buttocks, kneading the firm flesh. Hot, moist kisses trailed from one nipple to the other. Christina pushed her fingers through Cole's blond hair, hugging his face to her breast. The tongue circling her nipple intensified a desire that was already blazing uncontrollably, a fire only this man could ignite, a fire only he could quench.

Cole released her breast from his lips' loving embrace. Christina cupped his chin, turning his face up to hers.

"Please . . . I need you now," she whispered.

All she got in return was that half-smile she loved so much and that was reserved only for her.

"You kept me waiting," Cole replied softly, his tone husky with passion yet holding a hint of devilish humor in it. "Now it's my turn to make you wait. Close your eyes, Christina, and feel. Just *feel.*"

Christina did as she was told, trusting Cole, cursing him for making her need him so much. His tongue explored her navel and she moaned. Her stomach sucked in as though trying to avoid the contact, though the opposite was true. The outline of her ribs became more defined as his tongue danced over her navel, then left a moist trail down to the point of her hip.

Christina gripped his shoulders to support herself. The steel knots of corded muscle beneath his flesh rippled smoothly as his hands caressed her buttocks. Her head hung down, her chin nearly touching her chest. The ends of her golden hair tickled the tips of her breasts.

"I love everything about you," Cole murmured. "I love the sight of you, the smell of you . . ." he kissed her stomach above the small mound of her passion ". . . the taste of you . . ."

His words trailed off. His moist tongue followed the juncture of Christina's hip and thigh, and she squirmed, aching for Cole to reach the center of her pleasure.

Cole teased her, his tongue coming close to the center of her need without ever quite touching her there. His hands went from her buttocks to her thighs, and finally to the back of her knees. His searing tongue delved and taunted, establishing a rhythm that carried Christina up and away. A tumultuous floodtide of sensations swept

165

over Christina. She wanted to make this feeling last forever, but then she could do nothing but surrender. She leaned into Cole, arching backward at the same time. Christina pushed fingers into her golden hair. Her scalp felt tingly. She hugged her head between her forearms, feeling that unless she physically held herself together, she would explode.

The moment seemed suspended in time and space for an eternity, an agonizing time of such exquisite, intense pleasure she thought she could not help but cry out. The force of her pleasure was breathtaking.

When reality drifted back into her consciousness, Christina reached for Cole, leaning against him when he stood upright. The length of his manhood was pressed between their bodies, making her tremble. She touched its quivering shaft, feeling its strength and heat. She looked up into Cole's face, and what she saw was unbridled desire.

"I never knew it could be like this," Christina whispered. She tried to moisten her lips, but her tongue felt dry. "Can you ever really know how you make me feel?"

She kissed his chest, slowly making her way toward one nipple. Her fingers curled around the thickness of his masculinity. His hoarse sigh delighted Christina when she flicked her tongue against his nipple. His manhood leaped in her hand, and Christina felt powerful in the knowledge of this man's passion for her.

Cole moved swiftly placing one arm beneath her knees, the other under her arms. He raised her easily and carried her to their bed. Their lips were joined in passionate understanding, moving together, parting, accepting. Christina trembled, feasting her senses, her hands exploring the powerful expanse of his hairless chest and shoulders.

"I cannot wait," Cole whispered, placing Christina lightly on the bed. Though his words were barely audible, they were commanding, speaking from the insatiable

hunger that Christina elicited from him. "Christina . . .
I need you now . . . *forever!*"

Christina could not speak. She, too, could no longer
control herself. Their dalliances and teasing had been
exquisite, but now she needed to feel his great heart
beating with her own, to feel him inside her, consuming
her with his love.

Reaching between their bodies, she caressed him tenderly. A sob of joy caught in Christina's throat as she
kissed his mouth, guiding him with a trembling hand.

He entered her slowly. The searing heat inflamed
Christina's senses. His cheek pressed against Christina's
as she hugged him close.

Christina rolled from the peak of one summit to the
next, tumbling endlessly, joyously, headlong into the
world where only Cole could take her. Joy filled Christina's heart as Cole whispered her name over and over
again . . .

Chapter 16

Loretta Pembrook—*Mrs.* Loretta Pembrook—was a force to be reckoned with. She knew it, everyone knew it, including her husband, president and owner of the second largest bank in St. Paul.

Beautiful and brilliant, Loretta looked at the world without any sociable notions of it being anything other than a hostile, unjust institution. She saw her world as something that beat women down and kept them from achieving their full potential—especially ambitious women, like Loretta.

In her late thirties, she had lost the blush of youth, replacing it without a backward glance, happily and fortuitously, with a sophisticated charm and aristocratic bearing that younger women could only grasp for.

Loretta was—and she wasn't shy about telling anyone who cared to listen—nobody's fool. She had married a bank vice president who was quickly on his way to becoming president and eventual owner of the bank. The fact that Mr. Pembrook was twenty years her senior never caused her a moment's hesitation. Though he lacked the energy to satisfy Loretta's sexual needs, that, too, was only a minor inconvenience.

Sophisticated, cultured, self-possessed, and aloof, Loretta knew she had what men of power wanted. What she wanted was money, and with that, power; what the men wanted was her. Loretta saw it as an equitable exchange.

Loretta leaned back in the seat of the enclosed carriage and drew the curtains. Closing the curtains would stifle the circulation in the rented carriage. That, too, was an inconvenience that Loretta could accept. She couldn't afford to be seen. Not where she was going.

Thoughts danced nervously in Loretta's head, and she gritted her teeth against them. The conclusions she came to were infuriating ones. Still, there must be some explanation, something that she hadn't thought of yet to make sense of it all.

Yes, of course, there had to be . . .

Loretta had gone through a series of lovers during her twenty-year marriage to the honorable Mr. Pembrook. She was always discreet, but she tried men on as another woman would try on a pair of expensive slippers. Loretta had to make sure the fit was comfortable before the purchase.

Though several of her lovers were rather skilled, none of them truly passed the test that Loretta had put them through. None of them, that is, until Loretta was introduced to a young man with a questionable professional life. His name was John Colter.

John had been at a party for local businessmen, and when Loretta asked him questions about what he did for a living—and it was quite obvious that Mr. Colter was well off—he gave her a quick story about living off "profitable ventures." Loretta didn't believe him for a second.

John's good looks and ready smile warmed Loretta's desire. After talking with him, Loretta found he was clever, charming, and had a devilish sense of humor. He knew the difference between naughty and vulgar humor, and he made Loretta laugh more than anyone ever had.

Loretta's instincts told her John was a man of prodigious sexual skill. In bed, he wouldn't disappoint her. Her instincts, she concluded later, were never wrong.

It took Loretta just one night of lovemaking to know that she had met her match. John more than satisfied her, he exhausted her. Loretta was chuckling throatily, bathed in perspiration, when she said, "No more!" on that first night together with John.

Loretta liked to acquire things. She had acquired a rich husband. She acquired a magnificent lover. And Mrs. Loretta Pembrook had no intention in the world of sitting idle while some cheap harlot stole John from her.

It wasn't just that Loretta didn't want to lose John, though that would certainly be bad enough. Loretta didn't like the notion of anyone taking something from her. Especially not if the taking was done by a younger woman.

Time was creeping up on Loretta, and she was sage enough to know that her years as a predator were numbered. Soon she would have to be content with money. She would lose her sexual power over men, no matter how skilled she was.

When Loretta first heard the rumor that John Colter was back in St. Paul, she dismissed the rumor as groundless. If John was back in town, he would find some way of getting together with her, of being alone with her. John wsa a gypsy, and he'd been one since she knew him, but he always made a point of seeing her the moment he got back into the city.

When the rumor about John continued, this time including a blond woman who was on John's arm, Loretta's jealousy could not be contained.

Her first reaction was to rush over to John's apartment and confront him. It was her second thought that saved her. However much she wanted him, Loretta wasn't going to upset the shaky boat of her marriage. Granted, Mr. Pembrook was a colossal bore, and he wasn't at all satisfying in the bedroom, even on the occasional times his thoughts turned amorous. But he was rich, he was powerful, he had rich and powerful friends, who treated Loretta as though she was rich and powerful in her own right.

Being jealous of her lover sleeping with another woman was one thing; being irrational enough to destroy a profitable marriage just because she was losing her favorite toy was quite another.

Loretta tapped on the ceiling of the carriage with the tip of her parasol.

"Driver, can't you hurry? I told you, I'm in a great hurry!"

"Yes, ma'am," the coachman replied.

Loretta gritted her teeth when she did not hear the whip being taken to the horses. She couldn't use her own carriage because the coachman was under her husband's employ. Loretta didn't trust anyone. The rented carriage was slow, but the driver wouldn't tell anyone where he'd taken her.

Loretta closed her eyes for a moment. She was still beautiful, she reminded herself. Very beautiful. And she was certain that John wouldn't cast her aside for a younger woman . . . would he?

Cole looked down at Christina as she slept. Though they had spent many hours the previous evening making love, his passion for her was still strong, always just beneath the surface of his skin. He couldn't get enough of her, it seemed.

It was a little past eight. Cole had slept five hours. Even though he had been rising early every morning since returning to St. Paul, he was still uncomfortable with the hour. He was on an outlaw's clock, sleeping during the daylight hours to avoid detection, moving only at night.

Words Christina had spoken, said only moments be-

171

fore they had made love for the first time, came back to Cole.

She loves the morning, thought Cole. *Me? I'm like an animal afraid of being eaten. I stay in the shadows.*

Cole took a blue silk robe from the foot of the bed and slipped it on. He knotted the sash, kissed Christina lightly on the forehead, then left the bedroom.

He was sipping his second cup of coffee when, faintly, he heard a knock at the door.

Two years of being hunted like an animal prevented Cole from believing that his early-morning visitor was anything but trouble. He crossed the room in several quick strides and removed the small revolver he kept in a drawer of the table near his rocking chair. He thumbed back the hammer. He felt the rapid acceleration of his heart, the quickening of his senses, the tingling along the surface of his skin that told Cole he was at the edge and ready for anything.

Cole stopped at the door.

Christina!

Cole cursed himself for being weak enough to have kept Christina near him instead of giving her a fistful of money and shipping her off to Boston. His weakness now not only put her life in jeopardy, but his as well. With Christina sleeping in the bedroom, Cole couldn't risk getting in a gunfight.

Another knock at the door, slightly louder than the first, sent fresh concern charging through Cole.

Seconds ticked by. Cole's reflexes had saved his life a dozen times over the years. But now, Cole was strangled with indecision. He couldn't run. He couldn't fight. He would spend a month in jail, sit through a preposterous trial, then walk the gallows.

"Yes?" Cole said at last, his voice just a whisper.

"John? John . . . it's me. Open the door."

Damn!

Cole had consciously put Mrs. Loretta Pembrook to

172

the back of his mind when he returned to St. Paul with Christina at his side. A few days and blissful nights with Christina and Cole had completely forgotten about his former lover.

Cole jammed his hand and the small pistol into the pocket of his robe. He took a deep breath, forced himself to relax, then opened the door just a couple of inches, keeping the doorway blocked with his body.

"John, are you going to let me in?" Loretta frowned at Cole, then smiled prettily. There was a time when that smile had had a lot of influence over John. "Come on, silly. Do you want me to wake the neighbors?"

"I'm not dressed."

Loretta made a sound in her throat and rolled her eyes. "John, darling, there isn't a part of you I haven't caressed, let alone seen. I promise not to blush."

Cole could not keep the disappointment in seeing Loretta from appearing on his face. He cursed himself now for ever having spoken to Loretta, for listening to her when she cornered him at that disastrous party, for taking any sympathy on her when she told him of her miserable marriage. And, most of all, Cole cursed himself for ever letting Loretta coax him into bed.

Cole thought of closing the door on Loretta, but he knew she would never be so easily put off.

Loretta's smile disappeared, and her eyes became cold and hard.

"John, have you got a woman in there? Is that why you didn't let me know you were back?"

"Wait a minute, Loretta. Just keep your voice down. I can explain everything." Cole put a finger to his lips, seeking silence. He stepped into the hallway, quietly closing the door behind him. "I've been dying to see you. You're just not going to believe the things that have happened to me."

"I'd better believe them, John," Loretta replied, the malice thick in her voice.

173

Cole looked into Loretta's eyes for a moment. His mind was whirling. Everything inside Cole told him that if he was any kind of man at all he would tell Loretta to go back to her husband and forget about him. But Cole's internal gyroscope warned that a jilted Loretta Pembrook was an enemy he could ill afford.

"You have got a woman in there!" Loretta snapped. Anger stole Loretta's beauty and made the cords stand out in her neck.

"She's my cousin," Cole answered quickly. He put his hands on her shoulders. "I'm not happy about having her here with me, but there isn't anything I can do."

Loretta slapped a hand from her shoulder. "Do you really expect me to believe that? What kind of fool do you think I am?" Loretta looked up and down Cole, pretending to be repulsed by him. The fact was, seeing Cole in his blue silk robe—the one she had given him— was making it difficult for her temper to remain hot.

Loretta noticed that the robe didn't hang on Cole's body quite like it used to. The robe drooped on one side. Inside the pocket, Loretta caught a glimpse of a pistol butt.

"John, what have you gotten yourself into? You're in some kind of trouble, aren't you?" Loretta asked.

Cole closed his eyes, shaking his head in mock anger. He was stalling for time until he could think of a believable lie. Loretta was too intelligent, and too suspicious, to believe anything less than a first-rate story.

"There's a reason for everything." Cole glanced down both directions of the hallway and let his voice dip a notch to add suspense. "I've got the pistol because of my cousin. She . . . she got involved with a man. The guy is evil through and through."

"So why does she have to stay with you?" Loretta's concerns always came first. She didn't like being inconvenienced by someone's little cousin.

"She was supposed to marry this guy. The marriage

date was set and everything." Cole looked into Loretta's eyes and knew that he was running out of time. He still hadn't fully constructed the lie in his mind. "Then the family found out this guy wasn't what he said he was. He was a swindler. Penniless. He didn't have a dime to his name. He was just using my cousin."

"Oh . . ."

"You can imagine the bind she was in. About to marry an impoverished swindler. And he really broke her heart, too."

"The bastard! He ought to have his—"

"Now he's out for revenge. He's promised to do something terrible to my cousin when he finds her. That's why I've got the gun with me now."

"Does he know she's with you?"

"No. Nobody knows." Cole let his voice dip lower. "You're the only person I trust enough to tell."

"Really?"

Loretta was visibly impressed. Cole took his first easy breath since she showed up at his door. But now that he had soothed Loretta's temper, he had to get rid of her. The longer she stayed around, the more likely his story would crumble under the weight of its own mendacity.

"I've been wanting to see you," Cole said.

"But you went to the theater with her," Loretta replied, not listening to Cole. "If you were so afraid for her life, why do that?"

"My cousin understands the risks. She wants to go out so that this guy can find us. With any luck, she'll spot him and I'll be able to get the drop on him. Then the problem will be over once and for all." Cole looked deep into Loretta's eyes. "I couldn't leave her alone, and I couldn't see you without putting you in danger. If anything ever happened to you because of me . . . I couldn't live with myself."

"Now I know the truth, John. You should have come to me right away." Loretta nibbled on her lower lip

175

thoughtfully, wishing she could taste his kisses once again. "When can I see you?"

"I don't know. Soon, hopefully."

"When?" Loretta persisted. Cole's heroism fueled Loretta's desire for him. "I know there's a risk in seeing me. There always has been. But I'm worth that risk. Can't you see that I want you just as much as you want me?"

"Soon."

"When, John?" There was that hardness in Loretta's voice again. She wasn't going to be put off easily, certainly not without a promise of some sort.

"Meet me at the Empress tonight at six. I'll be in a closed carriage. That should be safe enough."

Loretta nodded her head slowly, her dark eyes never leaving Cole's. The corners of her mouth turned up in a smile that was somehow carnivorous.

"Don't bring your little cousin along," Loretta said in a silky purr. "I don't like sharing."

Chapter 17

The words Cole had spoken rang in Christina's ears. She stepped away from the door, her body numb with shock.

I shouldn't have been eavesdropping, thought Christina. *If I had stayed in bed and minded my own business, I wouldn't have known about Cole's deception. Then I could still love him. If only . . .*

Christina staggered back to the bedroom. She leaned against the bedroom door, pushing herself against it as though she was certain he would try to break in. She didn't want to be near Cole when he returned to the bedroom. She didn't want to hear his voice or see his smile. She had trusted Cole's smile, but he had used it and his looks and charm to conceal a false heart.

But had he deceived Christina? Cole had never once promised himself exclusively to her. And, in the sleeper car of the train before they made love, it was Christina who had said they had no commitment to each other. She had even said she didn't expect any promises. It had been her choice to live for the moment, to accept pleasure whenever they could.

But Christina had believed there was more in Cole's kisses than just his passion. His caresses, his sweet love-making, were an extension of something greater, something emotional. Certainly his lovemaking was an expression of a love that was too dear to put into words . . . or so Christina wanted to believe.

She waited for Cole to return to the bedroom. He didn't. He stayed at the kitchen table, sipping his morning coffee.

What is he thinking about? taunted Christina's mind cruelly. *About making love to that woman? Is that what occupies his mind now?*

Christina hated to believe Cole could be such a cad that he would sleep with another woman while she, Christina, was living under his roof and sleeping in his bed. But before she would set Cole free—and if he was sharing his passion with another woman, that's what Christina would have to do—she had to be sure of Cole's infidelity. There couldn't be any mistake about something as important as this.

Tonight . . . six o'clock . . . in front of the Empress . . .

The rest of the day was a quiet horror for Christina. She tried to put up a false front for Cole. She painted on a friendly face, but Cole soon saw through the facade. He questioned her sadness, and Christina evaded the questions. When they continued, she said she was homesick, missing the friends she had left behind in Enderton.

They stayed together but separate in the big, silent apartment. Christina curled up on the calico sofa with a novel, but she couldn't concentrate on the printed words. The only words that played in Christina's mind were those that she had heard Cole speak to the woman in the hallway.

"Did you want to do anything tonight?"

Christina looked up from the book in her lap. It seemed impossible that Cole would ask such a preposterous thing.

Do you really think so little of me? Christina thought.

"Honey, did you want to do anything tonight?" Cole asked again.

Christina shook her head. "No," she said after a moment. "Actually, if you wouldn't mind, I'd like some time alone." *That would make it easy for you to see your lover, Cole. Your other lover.*

Cole sat on the padded arm of the sofa. He smiled at Christina and put his arm around her shoulders and pulled her against him. Through his white silk shirt, she felt his ribs against her cheek. For the first time in the past three weeks — for the first time since she had willingly and lovingly given her virginity to Cole — Christina cringed at his touch.

"I know its hard for you, being away from all your friends and all the people you love," Cole said. He patted Christina's shoulder. She found it a condescending gesture rather than a comforting one. "It won't always be like this. Men like Webb . . . eventually, their lies catch up with them."

"I suppose," Christina replied. *When will your lies catch up with you, Cole?* she thought.

"You're sure you want to be alone?"

"Yes. That's what I told you, isn't it?"

"It's just as well, I suppose. I've got some things to do. I've postponed my responsibilities longer than I should have." Cole put his fingers under Christina's chin, tilting her head back, forcing her to look up into his gray eyes. Christina now believed they were eyes that hid an empty heart. "It shouldn't take me too long. I'll leave now. Lock the door behind me and don't let anyone in. I shouldn't be too late."

Cole kissed Christina softly on the mouth, and she hated him then, hated him because her heart still trembled when he kissed her, even though his lips would soon be pleasuring another woman's mouth. She hated Cole with all her heart and soul because she knew that no matter how much the outlaw deceived her, he could still make her body respond with his smooth charm and his warm, tempting kisses.

When Cole closed the door behind him, leaving Christina alone in his apartment, she felt as though all the air in the room had suddenly been sucked out. She now realized this man always left a vacuum in his wake. Wherever he went, all the attention was directed toward him. It was Cole who always took the center stage. And when he left, he left behind him a void in the lives of everyone who had been near him, who had been under the influence of his magnetism.

Christina breathed the rarefied air, steeling her nerves, summoning strength and courage from a wellspring she had not known existed. She had to find out if her suspicions of Cole's faithlessness had any foundation.

From the coat tree, Christina pulled down the green velvet robe. Cole had bought it for her just a week earlier, to shield her from the rain that had caught them by surprise. She put the robe around her shoulders and clasped the gold chain at her throat.

"Mr. Kjellgaard," Christina called out as she descended the wide stairway. The white-haired doorman gave Christina a strange smile. Christina wondered what it meant. "Mr. Kjellgaard, can you please get a carriage for me? I'm in a terrible hurry."

The old man nodded his head slowly. His eyes held a hint of sadness. He did not miss the tension that showed in Christina's blue eyes, in the set of her mouth, in her quick movements, or in the tone of her voice.

"Yes, ma'am, right away." Mr. Kjellgaard stopped halfway through the double doors, turning to look quizzically at Christina. "You won't be returning, will you, miss?"

"Of course, I—"

The words froze on Christina's tongue. Mr. Kjellgaard had stood at the door for many years. He'd seen many women come and go from Cole's apartment. Now, with nonjudgmental wisdom and innocence, he wanted to know if Christina's time with Cole was over.

"I'm sorry, ma'am. I just thought that—"

"Stop thinking that, Mr. Kjellgaard!" It unnerved Christina to know what he had assumed. "I've already told you I'm in a hurry. Now please call a carriage for me immediately."

"Yes, ma'am. I'm terribly sorry."

Mr. Kjellgaard shuffled off hurriedly. Christina felt guilt well up inside her bosom. It was unfair of her to be cruel to Mr. Kjellgaard. It was not his fault that he had seen a score of women leave alone from Cole's apartment.

Christina was filled with anger and doubt, and because of this, she was being rude to a man who had always given her a smile when he saw her, had always been polite and helpful.

Mr. Kjellgaard returned shortly to the foyer where Christina waited impatiently.

"Your carriage is here, ma'am."

"Thank you." Christina stepped up to the wise old man whose eyes had seen so much and yet continued to look at the world without criticism or judgment. "I'm very sorry. I didn't mean to be rude to you. Forgive me?"

In all his years, Mr. Kjellgaard had never received an apology from a resident, no matter how unjustly he was treated. He was unsure of how to politely receive an apology.

Christina, anxious to beat Cole to the Empress, raised up on her tiptoes and kissed Mr. Kjellgaard's forehead.

"You're a sweet man," she said, then left Mr. Kjellgaard, who was openmouthed with surprise.

A five-dollar bill palmed into the coachman's hand got Christina the desired results. With a crack of the whip, the carriage bolted down the cobblestone streets of St. Paul. Cole had a lead of three or four minutes, by Christina's estimate. The driver promised to have her at the Empress by five-fifty.

At five minutes to six, the carriage came to a rattling

halt a hundred feet from the entrance of the Empress. Christina mentally added the carriage horses and several unnamed pedestrians to her growing list of those to whom an apology was due.

"Papa would be so ashamed of me," Christina mumbled under her breath, leaning back in the carriage.

"Eh? Didn't I tell ya you'd get here in plenty o' time?" the coachman asked. He turned in the seat and gave Christina a crooked grin. His eyes slithered over her, his gaze touching her. "Who is 'e? Brother or husband?"

Christina shot the coachman a malevolent glare. She wasn't in the mood for insipid conversation when the man she loved was about to fulfill his end of a lover's tryst.

"I'll give you an extra dollar if you don't ask me any more questions," Christina said icily, looking straight into the coachman's eyes.

"Suit yerself." The coachman turned his back to Christina, mumbling under his breath, "Actin' pretty high an' mighty for a girl o' yer ilk."

Christina pulled the collar of her robe up against her cheeks. The collar, combined with the bonnet, kept her face hidden from the men and women who walked along the crowded city streets.

She searched for Cole's carriage, but didn't see it. In front of the Empress, under the overhanging eaves, were several couples and some individual men and women. Everyone was smiling, having a good time. Christina envied the people.

What kind of woman would Cole be attracted to? Christina asked herself. *A woman like me* was her ready answer, though she realized it was a self-serving response.

A brunette woman with the bearing of someone who had lived with the luxury of great wealth all her life, spectacularly dressed in an evening gown of black-and-gold velvet, gave the appearance of waiting expectantly for someone.

Not her, Christina thought. *She's too old for Cole.*

Christina saw the woman's handsome features light up in a broad smile. Whoever she was waiting for had arrived.

Christina's gaze followed that of the woman's. When she saw Anders at this spot in the seat of the carriage that Christina had spent so many wonderful nights in, the young woman's heart skipped a beat.

Anders rented out to someone else. It's not Cole inside that carriage.

Christina's futile hopes were dashed when the door opened. As the woman was getting into the carriage, Christina saw a long arm extend out to help the woman in. She saw Cole's face, saw his smile . . . and she knew that her lover was also another woman's lover.

Chapter 18

"John, I couldn't wait to see you." In a single move Loretta closed the carriage door and slipped her arms around Cole's neck, sitting intimately close to him. She kissed his mouth hard, sealing her lips to his. When he didn't respond with the passion she'd expected, Loretta pulled her head back, staring fiercely into Cole's gray eyes, searching for answers.

"It's not what you're thinking," Cole said. He took Loretta's wrist in his hand, pulling her hands apart so her arms were no longer looped around his neck. "Like I told you before, a lot has happened to me since the last time we had a chance to talk."

A shiver of suspicion worked its way up Loretta's spine but pushed it away with effort. After all, she had already talked with John, and she knew that the rumors she'd heard were no more than silly gossip.

"Do we have to talk now?" Loretta raised her eyebrows, her eyes shining with mischief. She was looking for proof from John that she was the one he wanted. "Is that all you want to do, talk after more than two months of being apart?"

Loretta leaned into Cole, forcing her breasts to press against his chest. She snaked her arm around his neck, pulling Cole toward her even as he pushed away. When she

184

kissed him a second time, Loretta knew that it was more than just being in a carriage that was preventing her lover from treating her to the kisses she wanted—it was something else. . . maybe some*one* else.

"Listen to me, Loretta," Cole began. He pushed himself into a corner of the carriage and forced Loretta to sit at his side. He tapped on the roof of the carriage with his knuckles and Anders headed the team down the street. "There's something very important that I've got to tell you."

Loretta searched Cole's face, trying to see something in his eyes that hadn't been there the last time she saw him.

"It's that tramp, isn't it? She's not really your cousin."

"No. She's not my cousin." Cole took tobacco and papers from an inside jacket pocket and quickly rolled himself a cigarette. He lit it before continuing, feeling Loretta's eyes on him every second. "That's what I've got to talk to you about. I didn't want to lie to you this morning, but I didn't see that I had any choice. It wouldn't do either of us any good to make a scene."

Loretta's first instinct was to scratch Cole's eyes out. She did not, however, follow her instincts but slid across the seat, putting some distance between herself and the man she still considered her lover.

"Then you've been sleeping with her?" The words were hardly out of Loretta's mouth when she issued a short, humorless laugh. "What a silly question? Of *course* you've slept with her. You sleep with every woman you want to. That's just the man you are. I've always known that."

Cole turned his head and sent a stream of smoke out the window. Once again, Loretta was taken by his handsome, strong profile, the virility that seemed to hover about him like an aura. It infuriated her that he had slept with another woman. But could she expect him to remain celibate for two months? Him? Not even Loretta's vaunted opinion of her own sexual skills could make her believe that John Colter would do without just because he

185

couldn't have the best.

In a voice that was sharp and polished, like the blade of a stiletto knife, Loretta said, "I don't like you sleeping with other women. I'm possessive that way. Call it selfishness, if you will. But I'll forgive you this time." As though it explained everything, Loretta added, "You were gone quite a while." Loretta gave Cole a smile and patted his cheek with a white-gloved hand. "Sleeping with that girl must have been very disappointing for you. Very . . . unfulfilling. You've got to stop taking on charity cases."

Loretta expected him to agree with her . . . but he didn't. In fact, when he turned his face toward her, she didn't see any of the repentance she was expecting. And could that really be derision showing in his eyes?

"It's over, Loretta."

Loretta Pembrook took great pride in her ability to never lose her composure. Not under any circumstances. When she heard the coldly spoken words, she simply smiled and shook her head.

"No, no, no," she said, smiling and patting the blond man's thickly muscled thigh. "Don't be silly. You've made a mistake, a ridiculous error in judgment. But I forgive you for that, don't you see? You've hurt me, John. You've hurt me grievously. But that doesn't mean our . . . *arrangement* has to end. Just tell this little tramp to be on her way. Her day in the sun is over. Now she can go back to wherever she belongs and you and I can be together once again. Just you and me."

"You're rather conveniently forgetting about your husband, aren't you?"

Loretta's eyes hardened, turning cold and angry. She looked at the man seated next to her in disbelief. Was he really casting her aside for another woman? Could that really happen to her, Loretta Pembrook?

Through the haze of disbelief came another emotion, one that Loretta was unaccustomed to. Fear. She was losing someone who belonged to her. No, it wasn't just

186

losing someone, she was having that special someone *stolen* from her.

"Don't be a fool," Loretta whispered. She heard the slight pleading quality in her voice. She hated the sound of it. "I've told you I've forgiven you. Now let's just stop all this nonsense. You can't really expect me to believe you would rather be with some tawdry little trollop than with me. I can't believe that, John."

Loretta leaned across the seat, placing her hand again on Cole's thigh, much higher this time. "No woman can please you the way I can."

Loretta's hand moved higher and he caught it in his, preventing it from moving higher.

"Come on, John, you've been waiting for me to . . . well, you know, for a long time." Her tone was filled with desperation as she added, "Let me show you how good I can be, how good *it* can be."

Loretta was shocked at her words. The voice was hers, but the words didn't—they just couldn't!—belong to her. She had never before concerned herself with a man's pleasure. Just being with her was pleasure enough for any man, she had always believed. Her amorous companionship was more pleasure than any mere man deserved.

"No." The single word came from Cole's lips, cold and emotionless. "Never again, Loretta. I've found someone special. She's changing me, and I like the changes."

"I know the kind of man you are, John. You'll never change."

"You know the kind of man I *was*. You knew me so well only because you are exactly like me—like the way I was."

Cole looked into Loretta's eyes. There was defiance and triumph showing in his handsome countenance, a refutation not only of Loretta, but of his own weaknesses.

"It's over. Let it die peacefully." Cole said. He gave Loretta an odd little smile. It was an expression she'd never seen before, and instinctively she didn't like it. "I'm in love with her. I truly am. And do you know what, Loretta? For

187

the first time in my life I like being with someone after we make love. Not just before we make love, or when we make love, but *after* we make love. She makes me feel so . . . good about *myself.* I've never felt that way before. If someone like" — Cole stopped himself before he spoke Christina's name — "her can love someone like me, then maybe I'm not such a bad fellow after all."

"You're leaving me. My God, you're actually leaving *me.*" Loretta's scowl held unbridled contempt. It lasted only a moment before her composure returned with a vengeance. "So this is my fond farewell, I suppose. Well, let me tell you something, John Colter. You needn't have gone to such trouble. I wouldn't make a scene. Not for you. What? Did you think I couldn't live without you? Was that it? Did you think — my God, did you really *believe* — that I was getting serious about you?" Loretta tossed her head back and laughed hollowly, the sound coming from a bitter soul and venomous heart. "You were nothing more than entertainment for me. A little diversion. That's all. If you want to believe you were more than that, you're only fooling yourself."

"I'm sorry." Cole sighed. He hated confrontations, especially with a woman like Loretta. "I don't mean to hurt you."

Loretta's facade started to crumble. It went slowly at first. But then, like a dam breaking, the disintegration went swiftly. The mask of Loretta's sophistication and civility was taken off and Cole was allowed for the first time to see the real person that she had kept hidden behind money and looks.

"Don't for a single second think you can get away with this."

Cole looked at Loretta, wondering how he could have ever allowed his lust to blind him so completely. What he saw in Loretta's eyes was barely human.

"Nobody makes a fool of me, do you hear me? Nobody!" Loretta shouted for Anders to stop the carriage,

188

then wheeled back on Cole. "You bastard! I'll make you sorry for this! I'll make you sorry you were ever born!"

Cole, completely unruffled by Loretta's outburst, opened the carriage door for her. In a voice that held only sadness in it, he said, "Loretta, you've made me sorry that I met you. Isn't that enough to satisfy your desire for revenge?"

Zachary Webb pulled the heavy gold watch from his vest pocket. He pressed the stem and the watch face flipped open. It was a couple of minutes to six. Very soon, if the information he had paid for turned out to be a worthwhile investment, he would find out where Cole Jurrell was hiding.

He leaned against the back wall of the saloon, idly listening to the chatter coming from inside. He could smell the acrid scent of smoke and stale alcohol.

Zachary felt at ease with himself, sure of his abilities and his surroundings. He had spent much of his life in loud saloons, flirting with bar girls, playing—and cheating—at keno and draw poker. Though Zachary's personal fortune could have distanced him from such rowdy surroundings, he still retreated to the dank regions of his world when he sought entertainment. Bar girls and barroom brawls were in his blood.

A couple of minutes passed before the rear door of the saloon opened. Zachary looked at the young man who stepped into the shadows. He gave the traitor a smile.

"I was wondering if you would turn yellow," Zachary said. His smile remained intact.

"I don't run from anyone of the Webb's henchmen," Bobby replied. He eyed Zachary warily, his right hand never leaving the pearl-handled revolver at his hip. "Let's talk business."

"Fine with me." Zachary rolled a wooden match from one side of his mouth to the other. "I take it you got the

189

word on what I'm willing to pay."

"Yeah. Five hundred for the whereabouts of Cole Jurrell." Bobby grinned humorlessly. His body was tensed from hat to boots. Zachary continued to lean backward, his shoulders against the saloon. "I've got what you want. Let's see the cash."

Zachary reached inside his jacket. The five hundred dollars was in five-dollar bills. The stack was thick, bound with a leather thong. Zachary waved the money and locked his gaze with Bobby's.

"The information better be good. I'm not a man who takes getting cheated lightly."

Bobby spit in the dirt between them. "I rode with Cole for a long time. I learned a lot."

Bobby accepted the money from Zachary, counting the bills while keeping an eye on him. When he finished, his shoulders dropped slightly as he relaxed.

"I like a man who understands business," Zachary said. "You've been looking for Cole in all the wrong places. Cole doesn't have a hideout in the Black Hills, like you've been thinking. And he doesn't have a hideout in the Badlands."

Bobby grinned at Zachary. He was enjoying himself and his pleasure was wearing on Zachary's patience.

"Okay. So we both know he hasn't been where my men have been looking. Where is Cole Jurrell *now?*"

"I can't tell you for sure. Cole doesn't talk much, especially about himself. I went through his saddlebag once and found a rail ticket to St. Paul. It was after we made that raid on your payroll near Jamestown. Remember that?"

Zachary bit back his own comments. He remembered his father's rage as he relayed how the wages for a crew of men were stolen. The Webbs had lost some of their most lethal strongmen when they didn't get paid on time.

"St. Paul, huh? You can't get more specific than that? Doesn't really seem like five hundred worth of information to me."

Bobby's smile broadened. "That's business, my friend."

"What about the other two? Where are they?"

Bobby was surprised that Zachary was interested in Hans and Jackie. Though he'd ridden with the two men for over a year, that didn't mean he wouldn't sell them out. With no reservation, he told Zachary where they stayed when separated from their leader, Cole Jurrell.

"Let's step inside," Zachary said. "You can buy me a drink with all that money you got."

At the long, scarred bar, Bobby ordered whiskey.

"To men who understand business," Zachary said as a toast, raising a glass in his left hand.

Bobby felt rich with five hundred dollars in his pocket, and safe inside the saloon. He raised a glass with his gun hand. He clinked his glass against Zachary's and it was almost to his lips when Zachary went for his gun.

Bobby had time to realize he'd been duped and that he wouldn't get his own gun cleared. The heavy lead bullet hit him in the chest, tossing him backward. Bobby died before he hit the sawdust-strewn floor.

Zachary ordered another rye. Men and bar girls looked at him, keeping their distance. Zachary silently raised his glass in a toast to the dead man, then swallowed the rye in a single gulp.

"Get the sheriff," he told the bartender. He said it as a command. "That man's got a reward on his head. Dead or alive."

The bartender leaned over the bar to inspect the corpse on the floor. He said, "Well, mister, he's dead. He surely is."

Cole took a leisurely ride home. He hadn't wanted a bloody row with Loretta, and all things taken into account, it hadn't been as bad as it could have.

His worst fear had been that Loretta would be emotionally shattered by his leaving, but in retrospect, Cole realized that fear was based on his own ego. Cole had been afraid of breaking Loretta's heart. Now he knew she had no heart.

Cole had been shocked at the hatred he'd seen in Loretta's eyes. He had always sensed a whirlwind of selfish ambition hidden beneath the tailored gowns that clothed Loretta Pembrook. He had witnessed more than just the momentary fury of a woman scorned. It was a deep-seated lethal rage.

If Loretta had spoken any truth, it was that she had never cared for Cole at all. She might have wanted him to love her, but she desired love from others but lacked the capacity to love anyone, even herself.

Beside him on the seat were a dozen long-stemmed roses — six white and six red. Cole patted the roses and closed his eyes. He let his mind drift to Christina and a faint, dreamy smile toyed with his sensuous mouth.

Talking with Loretta had, if nothing else, forced him to fully comprehend the depth of his love for Christina. He knew that Christina was special to him, that she wasn't like any woman he'd known before. But it wasn't until he had really looked at Loretta that he realized how lucky he was to have Christina waiting at home for him.

Tonight he would open a bottle of his best wine and leisurely make love to Christina for hours, binding her soul to his, her heart to his.

Cole was so anxious to be with Christina that he never noticed the worried look Mr. Kjellgaard gave him. Cole's long legs took him up the stairway two at a time. As Cole moved down the hallway, he peeled back the paper on the roses, exposing the flowers in full bloom.

The suitcases were lined up, neat and orderly, at the door. Christina, attired in the plain dress that she had traveled in from Fargo to St. Paul, stood beside the suitcases. Her face showed little emotion.

"What the hell is going on?" Cole demanded, his brows

FREE

B O O K   C E R T I F I C A T E

ZEBRA HOME SUBSCRIPTION SERVICE, INC.

YES! Please start my subscription to Zebra Historical Romances and send me my free Zebra Novel along with my first month's Romances. I understand that I may preview these four new Zebra Historical Romances for 10 days. If I'm not satisfied with them I may return the four books within 10 days and owe nothing. Otherwise I will pay just $3.50 each, a total of $14.00 (a $15.80 value—I save $1.80). Then each month I will receive the 4 newest titles as soon as they come off the press for the same 10 day Free preview and low price. I may return any shipment and I may cancel this arrangement at any time. There is no minimum number of books to buy and there are no shipping, handling or postage charges. Regardless of what I do, the FREE book is mine to keep.

Name _____

(Please Print)

Address _____ Apt. # _____

City _____ State _____ Zip _____

Telephone (____) _____

Signature _____

(if under 18, parent or guardian must sign)

Terms and offer subject to change without notice.

4-89

MAIL IN THE COUPON BELOW TODAY

To get your Free ZEBRA HISTORICAL ROMANCE fill out the coupon below and send it in today. As soon as we receive the coupon, we'll send your first month's books to preview Free for 10 days along with your FREE NOVEL.

GET
FREE
GIFT

ACCEPT YOUR FREE GIFT
AND EXPERIENCE MORE OF
THE PASSION AND ADVENTURE
YOU LIKE IN A
HISTORICAL ROMANCE

Zebra Romances are the finest novels of their kind and are written with the adult woman in mind. All of our books are written by authors who really know how to weave tales of romantic adventure in the historical settings you love.

Because our readers tell us these books sell out very fast in the stores, Zebra has made arrangements for you to receive at home the four newest titles published each month. You'll never miss a title and home delivery is so convenient. With your first shipment we'll even send you a FREE Zebra Historical Romance as our gift just for trying our home subscription service. No obligation.

BIG SAVINGS
AND FREE HOME DELIVERY

Each month, the Zebra Home Subscription Service will send you the four newest titles as soon as they are published. (We ship these books to our subscribers even before we send them to the stores.) You may preview them *Free for 10 days.* If you like them as much as we think you will, you'll pay just $3.50 each and save $1.80 each month off the cover price. *AND you'll also get FREE HOME DELIVERY.* There is never a charge for shipping, handling or postage and there is no minimum you must buy. If you decide not to keep any shipment, simply return it within 10 days, no questions asked, and owe nothing.

pushed together in confusion.

Christina looked at the roses and rolled her eyes heavenward. "What are those supposed to do? Make me forgive you? I'm a little naive, Cole. I won't deny that. But do you really think roses are all it will take to make me forgive you?"

"Forgive me? Forgive me for *what?*"

Her strong exterior began to crack, and tears glistened in her eyes, but she was determined to not break down in front of Cole. She wouldn't let him see the pain he had caused.

"Let me guess. You're innocent, right?" Christina said. Cole appeared confused, and Christina shot him a look of absolute disgust. "Can't you ever be honest? Ever? About anything?"

Christina saw the transformation on Cole's features. She had unmasked his treachery, and he wasn't a skilled enough actor to hide his emotions from her. She waited a moment, expecting an apology, or perhaps an explanation. As she looked at Cole, she saw in her mind's eye a foggy image, as though conjuring a vision through a layer of smoke of the dark-haired woman he had helped into his carriage.

"Nothing to say, Cole? How very unlike you." Christina was searching for anger. It felt better to be angry at Cole than to be hurt by him. "I thought you had a quick, glib answer for everything."

"I'm not entirely certain what you're talking about." Cole kicked the door closed. He put his hands on his trim hips, pushing his jacket back. He looked, to Christina's eyes, as handsome as ever. She hated him for it. "Did you hear something that you should let me know about?"

Christina's eyes narrowed with contempt. Cole's tone was accusatory, as though *she* was the one who had done something wrong.

"You're really quite a man, aren't you, Colton Jurrell, or John Colter, or whatever your name is. You really are something special. You sleep with me in the morning and with that brunette at night."

Christina's heart felt like it would burst in her chest. She wanted to cry, but she refused to let the tears spill from her eyes. She struggled valiantly to keep her anger fiery, but it was so hard when she looked at Cole and remembered the beautiful moments they had shared together.

"Did you follow me tonight?" Cole took a couple of steps, closing the distance between himself and Christina. His gray eyes were cold and yet fierce. "You followed me? Like one of the posse? What's next, Christina? Maybe a telegraph message to Webb to let him know where my apartment is? That should net you a good sum of money. You could set yourself up just fine with what Webb's willing to pay to have my head on a silver platter."

"Stop it! Just stop it!" Christina shouted. "I hate it when you're like this! Can't you ever apologize for anything? Just once in your life, can't you take a step backward for someone? Can't you just stop fighting?" Emotion cut off Christina's words. When she spoke again, her tone had softened. "I trusted you. Cole, I loved you."

A sob caught in Christina's throat. She turned away from Cole, pressing the edge of her fist against her lips. In a quiet voice, she continued. "You never admit when you've done something wrong. It's the only thing that I don't like about you. And it's such an important thing to me that I'm going to leave you because of it."

"What? Have you lost your mind?" Cole turned and punched the wall, his fist connecting so solidly with the wood that Christina could feel the impact through the floor. "Not only are you overreacting, you're making a hell of a mistake in the process. You saw Loretta get into the carriage. I can assume that much. But what did you really see, Christina? What? Are you that willing to accuse me of sleeping with another woman?"

"Let's just say that your reputation precedes you."

"Damn it, I didn't do anything with her. *Nothing!* She

194

hates the sight of me now. She hates me because I told her all about us. I told her I—" Cole bit his tongue to keep the word "love" from passing between his lips. He was still shocked that he'd let his protective instincts become dulled enough to not notice he had been followed. It didn't matter that it was Christina who had followed him. If she—an amateur!—could make him drop his guard, then an experienced, deadly enemy could as well.

"What did you tell her, Cole? That you've got a new mistress?" Christina turned her back on Cole. She walked to the big bay windows and looked down at the street. Under the circumstances, she felt surprisingly calm and lucid. "It must be terrible being someone's ex-mistress. To know that you're only in someone's life for a little while. To know that sooner or later you'll be replaced by another woman."

Outside, the sun was just setting. The strolling couples were making their nightly rounds. Christina recognized some of the regulars. A dull, empty ache in her soul made Christina hug her arms around her middle.

"When I asked Mr. Kjellgaard to get a carriage for me, he asked if I'd be returning." Christina looked out the window, oblivious to the gaiety to be found there. Her mind drifted. She felt numb inside. "He thought my time was up. Is it, Cole? Am I making some terrible breach of etiquette by saying I want to leave you? Are you supposed to be the one to do that?"

"Stop talking nonsense. Nobody's leaving anybody." Cole stepped up behind Christina. He put his hands on her arms and was a little surprised that she didn't move away from him. "Our time together isn't over. For God's sake, Christina, you must realize that."

Christina's mouth turned up on one side in a mirthless smile. "I'm getting stronger, Cole. There was a time when I never thought I could live without you. But I think I can now. I'm going to try, anyway. Because, you see, being without you has got to be better than not knowing who

195

you're sleeping with whenever you're not with me. It's the doubts about you that would kill me."

Christina turned slowly. Though her voice sounded very calm, her scalp tingled and her vision was fuzzy, as though she was on the verge of going into a trance.

"You've taught me a lot of things, Cole. One of them is to never trust anyone. Not even you. You said so yourself. You can't be trusted . . . but I'm the trusting kind. I like having friends. I like being able to trust them."

Christina stared into Cole's eyes, then turned away. She couldn't look at his handsome face if she was going to say the things that needed to be said.

"For what it's worth, I don't really blame you," she said. "For a while, I thought you could change. I thought I could make you change. Now I see how naive I was. We are what we are. A person doesn't really change all that much."

"Christina, I didn't sleep with her."

"Then why couldn't you tell her that you . . . ?" Christina shook her head sadly. "Cole, let's just drop it. Whether you did or didn't sleep with—what's her name? Loretta?—isn't the point right now."

"Then what *is* the point?" Cole exclaimed. "You're not making any sense at all!"

"The point, Cole, is that you would have slept with her eventually. Maybe you didn't have time tonight. We both know you would have slept with her sometime soon. It's just the way you are, Cole. Womanizing is in your blood. You swept me right off my feet. I took one look at you and my life hasn't been the same since."

Christina turned to face Cole again. There was a quirky light shining in her eyes.

"See how strong I've become?" she asked. Christina was almost smiling. "I thought I would fall to pieces, but I'm strong enough to take this now. I'm strong because of you, Cole. For that, I thank you."

"Christina, I don't get this. I told you I didn't sleep with

196

Loretta, and apparently you believe me. But you want to leave me anyway? Why? For God's sake, *why?*"

"I've already explained that," Christina replied, her soft, odd smile still in place. "Now tell me, where do you think I should go? I want to find a city where Webb will never find me, someplace where he won't even think of looking."

Cole's face hardened, his lips drawing together in a tight line. A muscle in his jaw twitched.

"You're not going anywhere. I'm the one who has to leave, Christina. I've stayed here too long as it is. I've deluded myself into thinking that I could have a normal life. That was a mistake. I've got responsibilities. I've got people counting on me." Cole waved a hand toward the neatly arranged suitcases. "Unpack them. You'll stay here. Webb won't find you. I'll leave in the morning."

"Very well."

Cole looked at Christina as though he'd never seen her before. She had transformed into the woman he had told her she was . . . and Cole Jurrell hated the change.

"I'd better get to work." Cole went to the side door of the apartment, the one leading into the room he hadn't allowed Christina to see. "I'll sleep in the war room tonight."

Christina watched as Cole stepped through the door. She heard the tumblers click as he locked the door behind him. Then the full magnitude of what had happened hit her, and the fragile hold on her self-control evaporated. The tears came freely, and Christina didn't try to stop them. She walked numbly into the bedroom, undressed, and crawled between the blankets.

I love him, Christina told herself. *But he'll destroy me if I stay with him. He can't be faithful to me or anyone else. All he'll ever be faithful to is his cause. His great, worthy cause that gives him such a wonderful excuse for not committing himself to anyone.*

The nightmares came that night. In them, Christina was searching for something she had lost. She was trapped in a mass of people, shouting for Cole to help her. But Cole wasn't there for her. The faces, all unrecognizable, were threatening. Only the face of Nicholas Webb was clear in Christina's nightmare, and his was the most frightening countenance of all. He was reaching for her, pulling at her clothes, trying to draw her into the circle of his arms. Saliva glistened on his lips and his eyes glowed red as a branding iron. And still Christina shouted for Cole to rescue her, but he wasn't there to hear her shouts.

In Christina's nightmare, she had lost everyone she ever loved . . . including Cole.

Chapter 19

The sofa in the war room looked anything but inviting. The past three weeks had been the most peaceful, romantic, exciting time of Cole's life. Now Cole wanted those days back, to cherish each and every minute of every day he had spent with Christina.

Dear God, a voice whispered, those had been glorious days! Days and nights filled with an honesty and love Cole had thought he would never experience.

But another voice inside Cole whispered that he had become complacent. Complacency, the inner voice whispered, is the result of weakness. And weakness, the voice continued, is reprehensible . . . and always fatal.

He had come to understand the satisfaction and quiet comfort that comes with spending every night with one woman—one woman who he loved with all his heart and soul. Though Cole was unlikely to admit it, he sought the thrill of seducing many women only because no single woman had ever satisfied all his needs. And then he had met Christina Sands . . .

He marveled at the differences between Christina and Loretta. Had he ever really loved anyone before he loved Christina? Was he really so shallow that Loretta had once seemed desirable?

"No good deed goes unpunished," Cole mumbled,

thinking back to how he had refused Loretta.

Cole suddenly realized he was staring at the sofa. He cursed himself obscenely. He took several steps toward the bottle of Napoleon brandy he kept on the long desk where his maps and charts of Nicholas Webb's criminal enterprises waited his inspection.

Cole again stopped himself. He had to push Christina out of his mind, but he couldn't use liquor to do it. That would just be another act of weakness. He'd violated his personal code of strength too many times already.

Cole unrolled a detailed map of the central section of the Dakota Territory. He stood hunched over the map, staring at it but not seeing it. He could have drawn the map himself from memory. He had memorized every hill and valley, every game trail and telegraph pole. He knew where every inch of railroad track was, and how often wagon trails were used, and when. He saw instead the suitcases lined up at the door, and the look in Christina's eyes when she said she was leaving him.

I'm innocent, he cried inwardly.

He had not made love to Loretta in the carriage. He had no desire to see her again. But none of that apparently made any difference to Christina. By her logic, Cole was guilty of infidelity because of his past transgressions— because of the man he had been *before* Christina tied his heartstrings in knots and turned his world inside out. He was guilty of infidelity because she was certain he would someday be unfaithful.

Cold, he thought. *She was calm and cold and let me know that for all she cares, I can go straight to hell.*

He shook his head. Cole knew the only way he could ever get Christina out of his mind was to begin working again on a plan to destroy Nicholas Webb and topple his empire. If he had that, then maybe—just maybe—he could forget that he had just lost the only thing that was more precious to him than his land, his legacy, or even his reputation.

200

* * *

Black Jack looked fit and well cared for but restless. When Cole picked him up at the livery stable, the black stallion pranced around the corral like a colt, as though he was trying to prove to his master that he was ready for the trail again.

When Cole went to the hotel to see Missy, he was not as gladly received. Only Missy knew Cole's true identity at the hotel, and she wasn't there. And nobody was saying where she was. Not until ten dollars was slipped into a maid's apron and Cole had promised repeatedly that he meant Missy no harm did he find out where she was now living.

It was a decaying farmstead outside of Fargo. Cole counted one milking holstein, three scrawny goats, and a handful of laying hens. The house was badly weathered, thirsty for a heavy coat of paint. Even from a distance, Cole could see that the shake-shingled roof leaked like a sieve.

Cole dismounted from Jack and looped the reins over the hitching rail. A tattered curtain moved, even though there wasn't even a breath of breeze. Cole stopped before stepping onto the porch.

"Easy," Cole said. He raised his hands to shoulder level, palms outward to show his hands were empty. "I'm not looking for trouble."

"Whether you're lookin' for it or you ain't, you found it, sonny boy!"

It was a voice that belonged to a spry, elderly man. The curtain moved again. Cole now could see the twin muzzles of a shotgun. The deadly weapon was aimed squarely at his chest. From this distance, the weapon would cut him in two.

"I just want to talk to Missy."

Cole heard the unmistakable metallic clicks of two hammers being cocked. He wondered if Missy had betrayed him to Webb.

From inside the shack Cole heard another voice. At first the voice was very faint. Then he heard Missy ask, "Grandaddy, what's going on? What are you doing?"

"You just never mind none. There ain't no problem here that I can't take care of."

"Grandaddy, who is out there?"

The walls must be thin as paper, Cole thought.

"State your name, boy, an' say it loud and clear." Missy's grandfather said to Cole. "My hearing ain't what it was. I don't wanna shoot you clean through 'less I have to."

Cole moistened his lips. His mouth felt dry. What had happened to Missy?

"Colton Jurrell," he said. Then, louder, "Cole Jurrell."

Ten seconds ticked by. Each second seemed like a minute. He thought about Missy and the times they had shared. He wondered whether she would be the one responsible for his death. He thought of Christina and remembered the tough set of her jaw and the pain that showed in her sapphire-blue eyes when he left her to resume his fight against Nicholas Webb.

He looked down the barrels of the unwavering shotgun and thought at least it would be quick.

The door opened on creaking hinges. Missy stepped onto the porch. She said, "Hello, Cole," and Cole had to clamp his teeth together to keep from screaming.

Missy's once-beautiful hair was gone, apparently hacked off with a knife. An attempt had been made by a beautician to even out the length of what hair was left. There were patches where Missy's scalp was visible.

Even worse was the look in her eyes. Missy had always been full of life, ready to tell a bawdy tale, ready to accept happiness wherever she could find it. And though she could be coarse and sometimes downright crude, Cole had seen past her rough exterior to the gentle, caring person inside.

The luster was gone from Missy's eyes. There was no

shine in them as she looked at Cole. The lifelight had gone out in her eyes, and Cole knew that he had somehow been responsible for extinguishing that light.

She patted what was left of her hair and smiled weakly.

"I suppose I should have put a bonnet on first. Wouldn't want to scare you to death."

"Missy, what happened? Who did this to you?"

Her lips quivered for a moment, then the tears came. Cole put out his hands and Missy rushed off the porch, running into his open arms. Cole held her close, whispering soothing words while Missy sobbed uncontrollably, dampening his shirt with her tears.

When the tears subsided, Missy pushed herself away from Cole. She turned to the window where the shotgun had appeared.

"It's all right, Grandaddy. He's a friend."

"I figgered that much," Grandaddy growled. "I'm hard o' hearin', I ain't blind!"

"Friendly fellow, your grandfather," Cole said out of the corner of his mouth.

Missy slipped her arm around Cole's lean waist. He draped a long arm around her shoulders. Together they walked into the rickety, ramshackle house.

Cole took a chair at the kitchen table. The chair rocked slightly when he sat on it and he felt the legs bow under his weight. Like everything in the run-down one-room house, Cole knew it would break before too long.

While Missy busied herself with pouring coffee, Cole tried to not stare at her. Grandaddy sat on his small straw mattress bed in a corner. He continued to hold the shotgun across his lap. Whatever had happened to Missy wasn't going to happen again if Grandaddy had anything to say about it.

Missy sat down opposite Cole at the table. She smiled, and for a moment Cole thought he saw a flash of the old Missy in her eyes.

"Tell me what happened." Cole said quietly. He sipped

203

his coffee and didn't look up.

"A sheriff came to the hotel," Missy began. "He asked questions and waved a knife around."

"Sheriff . . . ?"

"Sheriff Bellows," Missy answered. "At first I thought he was really going to cut me up bad. He talked big and tough, like he was a real man and all." Her voice dipped low enough so that Grandaddy, across the room, could not hear what she said next. "But he turned out to be no worse than the Fargo officers. He said he wanted to know all about you and your lady, but what he really wanted was me. When that was over, the lion turned into a kitty cat."

Cole almost asked, *Did he hurt you?* But before the question escaped his lips he answered himself, *Of course he hurt you. But you're strong, Missy. Stronger than Sheriff Bellows will ever be. Someday I'll see that he pays for what he's done to you.*

"A while later another man came to the hotel. His name was Zachary Webb. At first I thought it would be the same with him . . . but it wasn't." Missy's throat constricted as the memories came back to her. She turned eyes that pleaded for sympathy and understanding up to Cole. "He was . . . he's a sick, sick man, Cole. Maybe I never really believed that you didn't do what everybody says you did. But after seeing that . . . that . . . devil . . . I know that if a man like him is after you, then you couldn't have done anything wrong."

Cole looked at Missy and tried to relax the muscles in his face. He was responsible for what had happened to her. He had caused yet another life to fill with pain. This time, Zachary had gone too far.

Missy put on a brave face for Cole, mustering her courage.

"He kept asking me where you'd gone. I was going to tell him, Cole. I really was. I didn't tell him right away 'cause I thought maybe he'd offer to pay. But then, when I saw how evil he was, I knew I couldn't. You and me haven't been that close all the time, but I couldn't let him get you." Missy cleared her throat and glanced in Grandaddy's direction as she continued. "Maybe I haven't been the most God-fearing woman in the world, and maybe God will send me straight to hell when my time comes. But he won't send me there on account of me letting Webb know you went to St. Paul."

Cole was not by nature a particularly religious man, but he said with honesty and gratitude, "God will have a place for you in heaven. Right next to Him at His side, Missy. You're a good woman."

Tears glistened in Missy's eyes, and she smiled.

"It's strange, Cole, The worse Zachary got, the sicker he got, the more I knew I couldn't give in to him. Not even when he started cutting off my hair. I just couldn't give in to him."

"For once, Missy, I'm glad you're as stubborn as you are."

They laughed softly together. Cole reached across the table and placed his hand over Missy's. She squeezed it tightly, holding him like she was afraid he would leave if she let go.

"So you didn't tell him anything about the tickets?"

"I told him you gave me money to get tickets for St. Louis."

Cole sighed inwardly. Christina was still safe then.

Cole looked at Missy, seeing the raggedness of her cropped hair and the dullness in her eyes. Guilt and hatred exploded in his breast. He wanted to rush from the tiny, decrepit house. A bullet to the brain was better than Zachary deserved.

"I'll make all of this up to you," Cole whispered. "I can't take away . . . I can't make you forget the things that happened to you. With all my heart and soul—I'm sorry."

Cole paused and looked out across the barren yard. "It's time someone gave you a hand—if he'll let me," he said, cocking his head toward the old man in the corner.

"He's pretty stubborn, too."

Cole glanced over at Grandaddy. The old man watched with hawkish eyes and ears that could not hear what was spoken.

"You'll live in style, Missy. You'll have pretty dresses and beautiful furniture. You can bring your grandfather with you. He'll look after you."

Tears trickled down Missy's pale cheeks. Very slowly, not looking at Cole as she spoke, she told him everything that Zachary had done to her. She told him of the rape, of the vile things he had called her, and of how he had slashed away at her hair with his knife. Zachary had promised to cut her face, to scar her so that no man would ever look at her again and feel anything but disgust. Missy told Cole of how Zachary had enjoyed her torment. When he was above her, she said, she looked into his eyes and she was able to see the sickness that lurked in his soul. "Zachary Webb is not a man, he is the devil incarnate," Missy whispered.

When Missy had finished with her story, when she had lifted that terrible burden from her soul, Cole felt sick inside. His war with the Webbs had claimed another casualty. He had to end this, and end it soon.

The cozy warmth had gone out of the apartment now that Cole didn't share it. Christina felt caged, and her inactivity made her irritable.

She had enough money to live. In fact, Cole had left her sufficient funds to live in affluence. But now that he was no longer with her, Christina could find no enjoyment in fine restaurants or the theater. Those activities were only diversions for her, and when she went, she was painfully reminded that Cole was no longer with her.

She developed a friendship with Mr. Kjellgaard. Sometimes, when his workday was finished, he would come up to the apartment and Christina would make him tea. She occasionally asked him questions about Cole's past, about what he was like before she had moved into the apartment, but Mr. Kjellgaard was the soul of discretion. He revealed nothing, and though Christina respected him for his integrity, he piqued her interest. Somehow, she needed to know what Cole was really like. She knew there was more to him than what he had allowed her to see.

Once Christina forgot about Cole's dual identity and referred to him by his first name. She had to lie to Mr. Kjellgaard, and did it poorly. She said that "Cole" was the nickname she had given John Colter. He smiled and nodded his head, but Mr. Kjellgaard's wise old eyes grew narrow with suspicion.

Cole had been gone two weeks when Christina heard the knock at the door. It was noon, and Mr. Kjellgaard usually didn't call on her this early in the day. When Christina opened the door, she regretted it instantly.

Loretta Pembrook did not lose her composure, but it was clear that she had not expected to see Christina at John Colter's door.

Her eyes went up and down over Christina, critically inspecting her competition. Loretta shrugged her shoulders, then walked past Christina into the apartment.

"John! John, darling, are you here?" Loretta pulled off one lace glove, then the other. She walked into the sitting area, ignoring Christina, who was close at her heels. "John, darling, it's Loretta! Come out, come out, wherever you are!"

Christina was speechless. This was the woman who had met Cole at the Empress. This was Cole's other lover!

"He's not here," Christina heard herself say.

Loretta turned bored, condescending eyes on Christina. "Oh? Then what are you doing here? Are you the new cleaning girl? When will he be back?"

"I live here. I don't know when he'll be back." Christina took a step backward, away from Loretta. "And I don't have to answer your questions."

Loretta made a clucking sound in her throat as she looked Christina over. "Just because he's not here is no excuse to let his home become sloppy, my dear."

"I want you out of here." Christina was just now regaining her senses. "Get out now!" Christina snapped, pointing toward the door.

Loretta's mouth pulled up in something that appeared to be a smile.

"Keep a civil tongue in your empty head, dearie. And don't even think of ordering me around. I'm the one who give the orders around here. And as far as anyone leaving, I'm sure you'll find that as soon as John returns, he'll show you where the door is."

Christina couldn't believe that Cole — *her* Cole — could ever have gotten romantically involved with this woman. What could have been going through his head? Why would Cole even want to *know* someone like her?

"Get some tea for me, dearie." Loretta went to the calico sofa and sat down. "Or maybe some wine. I know it's early, but John always keeps a good vintage on ice for me." Looking up at Christina, Loretta's eyes twinkled with malice. "You see, I know what pleases John, and he knows what pleases me. That's why we're so good together."

Cole did keep wine on ice. It bothered Christina to know that he'd done that for a woman other than herself.

"I want you to leave," Christina said. Her voice was barely above a whisper. She could feel her anger rising with each passing second. Loretta's calm exterior added fuel to the fire of Christina's hatred of her. "I want you out of this apartment this minute, or I'll call Mr. Kjellgaard and have you thrown out of here."

"Mr. Kjellgaard? That old fool?" Loretta laughed softly. The sound of her laughter bit into Christina's reserves of self-control. "No, dearie, I think it best that I wait until John returns. Then you'll find out how much I mean to him, and how little regard he has for you."

208

Loretta nibbled on a fingertip, eyeing Christina as a potential buyer would a thoroughbred mare. "I can see why John might be attracted to you. You are pretty, in a common sort of way."

"Get out of here!" Christina shouted. "Cole isn't here, and I don't know when he's coming back! Why don't you just leave? Leave me and Cole alone!"

"Cole? Is that your pet name for him?"

"Get out of here!"

Loretta, at last feeling awkward, let the veneer of her civility drop. She gazed at Christina with undisguised contempt. Never before had she begged to be with anyone, but she had never had a lover like John Colter. Without him, her life would fade again to a pale and passionless color. She admitted to herself that she would do anything to win him back. Now, facing this younger woman, virulent hatred pooled inside her breast. Loretta's hatred fed upon itself, spilling out suddenly.

"You cheap slut!" Loretta hissed, rising quickly from the sofa. "You may think you've won John, but you haven't! You were a frivolous diversion while I was away, nothing more. Go back to wherever whores like you sleep when you don't have a man to live off of!"

The older woman's anger had a settling effect on Christina. She stepped away from Loretta, instinctively sensing that she was in the company of a violent woman. She put her hands on her hips and smiled softly.

"I'll destroy you!" Loretta screamed. "Do you hear me? You cheap tramp! I'll crucify you!"

"I don't think so," Christina replied calmly.

Loretta's eyes were black and fiery as she continued. "Just because you're young and pretty John falls all over himself. He's such a little boy that way." Loretta was sputtering she was so angry. "But that won't last long, dearie! It won't! And when John comes begging to me, crawling back on his hands and knees, I'll spit on him! Do you hear me?" Loretta Pembrook was nearly hysterical.

209

"I'll spit in his face and I'll spit in yours! You're not going to make a fool of me! Do you hear me? Nobody makes a fool of me!"

Very slowly, a grin of victory playing with the corners of her mouth, Christina replied, "Nobody makes a fool of you, Loretta . . . except yourself."

Loretta slammed the apartment door on her way out.

Alone again, Christina felt a sense of victory. She had defeated Loretta . . . but the victory was hollow, because she still did not know where Cole was. She did not know if he was safe. She did not even know if he would ever return to her.

Christina heard her own words again in her mind. Cruel, heartless words that told Cole she couldn't love him, couldn't live her life with him. She had cut him out of her life before he could hurt her. So why did she hurt so much inside now?

As the walls of the apartment began closing in on Christina, she wondered if she would ever have the chance to tell Cole how much she loved him. Would he ever hear her words? And if she told him that she loved him and would always love him, no matter what he had done . . . would he come back to her? Could he forgive Christina for not forgiving him?

That night, as sleep eluded Christina, she lay in bed, remembering how they had met and missing the warmth of his body beside her own. And then, like a lightning bolt that illuminates an ebony sky so that the landscape is visible, an idea came to Christina.

If she found Cole once near the Sheyenne River, she could find him again!

Chapter 20

Loretta had long suspected John Colter had something to hide. His mysterious absences suggested many possibilities, but everything Loretta needed to know about him was within her reach when they were under the goose down comforter together. Their arrangement suited Loretta just fine. She was too well known to maintain a full-time affair, and even if John had been available around the clock, she would not have been free enough of her church and club activities to see him any more frequently. At least, that's what she had told herself.

Only once in all the time that they had been lovers had Loretta — and jokingly at that, in deference to her marital status — suggested she spend the night at John's. His reply was an emphatic and decidedly unromantic "no."

Loretta thought about Christina and John and gritted her teeth. This Christina girl had not only spent an entire night with John, she had moved into his apartment!

Christina's lack of discretion appalled Loretta. Any woman so brazen as to live in sin with a man — openly, for polite society to see — was clearly the lowest form of tramp. Christina had no self-respect at all! None! If she did, Loretta reasoned, Christina couldn't have allowed John to treat her with so little regard for her social standing.

Until now, Loretta was content to think of John Colter as a man of mystery with needs and passions similar to her own. But she had changed her mind. It was now extremely important to find out exactly with whom she was involved.

Soon Loretta would find out what John's dark secrets were. She would throw open his closet door and find the dead bodies he had hidden away. Men had been employed, on the sly so Mr. Pembrook wouldn't become suspicious, to find out what they could of John Colter. The promise of an extravagant reward would keep the men working and searching like hungry wolves.

For the first time in Loretta's life, she was driven by a desire for something other than power and wealth. Loretta Pembrook was consumed with a blood-lust for vengenance. She was enjoying the hunt for the secrets of John Colter. When she had those secrets, the taste of vengeance—vengeance on John, who had defied her, and on Christina, the tramp he had defied her for—would be sweet on her tongue.

Loretta sensed in him power, ruthlessness, and cunning. She could feel it emanating from Zachary Webb the moment she was near him, just the same as she had felt it in John Colter.

"My man said you had something to tell me." Loretta looked directly in Zachary's eyes. "What is it?"

Zachary pulled a chair away from the table and sat without being invited to do so. His gaze locked with Loretta's.

She's used to intimidating people, Zachary thought.

"I said I *may* have something for you. It all depends on several factors."

"No riddles, Mr. Webb. Please, let's get down to business or end this conversation."

From an inside jacket pocket, Zachary removed a

212

creased page, unfolded it, and placed it on the table. It was a printed picture of Cole, obviously torn from a larger piece of paper. Anxiety suddenly seized Loretta somewhere below her starched whalebone corset.

"Is this John Colter, the man you're looking for?" Zachary turned the paper toward Loretta, keeping it out of her reach. She nodded. "I thought so," Zachary said. "His name's not John Colter. And this picture used to be a 'Wanted: Dead or Alive' poster."

Loretta stifled a gasp. She was both appalled and excited by the revelation. Was her lover a murderer?

"What is his real name?" Loretta asked in a calm voice that hid her turmoil. "What has he done? Why do you have a picture of him?"

Zachary glanced around the Minneapolis restaurant. He did not like having to sit with his back to the door. He also suspected Mrs. Pembrook had minions watching him, protecting her. He couldn't tell which men were legitimate patrons of the restaurant and which were bodyguards.

"We were friends a long time ago." Zachary glanced around again. He didn't want to play his winning cards too soon. "Before I tell you more, tell me why you're looking for him. What do you intend to do once you find him?"

"Humiliate him." Loretta suppressed her smile, though she was relieved to see pleasure spread across Zachary's face. "Mr. Webb, you seem to be a worldly man, so I'll speak with absolute candor. I expect that whatever is said between us stays sub rosa."

"Beneath the roses," Zachary translated. "Kept in total secrecy."

"Very good. A man of learning. Perhaps you can be of service to me after all."

Loretta's instincts told her the best way to fight a man like John—or whatever his real name was—was with a man very much *like* John.

Loretta gave Zachary a hint of a smile and decided she would sleep with him if it was necessary.

"John—"

"His name's Cole."

" 'Cole' and I had an understanding that did not include my husband. We were, you might say, intimately close." Loretta saw in Zachary's eyes understanding without criticism . . . and just a hint of envy. It made her wonder what he would be like in bed. "Our understanding was mutually rewarding, quite agreeable on both sides. Then he met this girl—a young blond tramp."

Zachary's eyes narrowed with interest. He leaned closer to Loretta, his elbows on the table.

"He used me," Loretta continued, searching for just the right amount of heartfelt pain in her tone. "He used me and then he threw me away. He shouldn't be allowed to do that! You see, I'm only trying to protect other women from him. Why, he could have destroyed my marriage!"

"Yes, yes," Zachary replied softly. "I can see that. Cole must be stopped so he can't abuse women like you, Mrs. Pembrook."

For two hours they talked, each giving up a little information and trying to take more. In the end, the charade had been played out. Loretta and Zachary agreed that Cole had to be stopped, and that he should pay dearly for all that he had done. Loretta was not certain, but she suspected Zachary's idea of justice meant Cole's death. With Zachary at her side, she had a hint of the ultimate power—the power over life and death. The notion that she had the ability to put a death sentence on Cole made Loretta's flesh tingle with anticipation.

Loretta Pembrook was getting her first lesson in what having *real* power could do.

"Don't move," Zachary said quietly. The gun in his hand was steady. His voice was calm. "Take two steps backward, Christina. And please believe me when I say I'll kill you if you try anything foolish."

For one second, Christina thought she would faint. She felt light-headed and the apartment spun around her. She stared at the revolver in Zachary's hand, then into his eyes. She did not know which frightened her more.

Zachary stepped through the door. He put a hand to Christina's shoulder, shoving her backward. She stumbled, very nearly falling to he floor before regaining her balance.

"No. . ." she whispered. "No. It's not really you. You can't be here. You just can't."

Zachary was chuckling softly as he kicked the door closed, then threw the bolt to lock it.

"Afraid so, Christina," he said as his eyes flicked around the apartment. He moved to the bedroom, making sure that he was alone with his captive. He tucked the gun into a shoulder holster. "Welcome to the end of the trail. You've gone as far as you're going to go."

Christina's knees shook. The past had caught up with her. It had burst into her lonely world and frightened her to the depths of her soul. Walking on weak legs, she tripped against the coffee table and landed heavily on the calico sofa.

"Please," Christina whispered. It was the only word she could force from her constricted throat.

"Please *what?*" Zachary's hungry gaze was a lustful, defiling thing that touched Christina and made her feel unclean. "Please *what,* Christina? I won't know what you want unless you tell me." He moved closer and Christina saw the evil in his dark eyes. "Or maybe you don't have to tell me what you want. Maybe you just want what all women *really* want, even if they are too shy to ask for it."

"I don't want anything from you." Christina followed Zachary with her eyes as he casually paced the apartment. "I only want you to leave."

"Sorry. Can't do that." Zachary shrugged his shoulders noncommittally. "No, I just can't let you go. I've spent too much time and money tracking you down to get soft-

215

hearted now."

Zachary walked to the window. His back was to Christina, and she glanced at the closed and locked door.

"You'll never make it," Zachary said, reading Christina's mind. He didn't have to look at her to know what she was thinking. "If you try to run, I'll stop you. But I don't think you'll even try. Do you want to know why I think that?"

Christina said nothing at first. She refused to play Zachary's cruel game.

Zachary turned toward Christina and he looked down at her sitting on the sofa.

"Remember your old friend, your father's friend, Marcus Kensington? Well, my men are watching him twenty-four hours a day." Zachary's smile broadened when fear registered in Christina's clear blue eyes. "With a message from me, Marcus is a dead man. Even if you snould somehow escape, you'll never be able to free the old coot. One mistake from you and Marcus Kensington is a dead man."

"You wouldn't!"

"You must know me better than that," Zachary replied, his face twisting a little in scorn. "His death means nothing to me. Absolutely nothing! So if you want to make sure your dear ol' Marcus lives a long and dreary life back at that miserable store of your father's, I suggest you be a good little girl and do everything you're told."

Zachary's mouth tightened into a harsh, thin line. "Make one mistake . . . cause me one little bit of trouble . . . and I'll have that pathetic old man killed. Believe me, Christina, I'll do it."

Christina cleared her throat and said as forcefully as she could, "I know you will. I won't try to escape. I'll do whatever you say. Just don't hurt Marcus."

Zachary looked into Christina's eyes. "You know, I'm almost sorry to hear you say that."

It was four hours of horror for Christina. Her greatest fear was that Zachary would rape her. Could she fight him, knowing it would mean Marcus's death? Zachary was cut from the same bolt of cloth as his father, after all. Christina waited, barely breathing, for Zachary to attack her. He didn't even touch her, though, at least not physically. But he *did* do everything in his power to break her will and shatter her defiant spirit. For one thing, he demanded Christina cook him steak and eggs. Immediately upon receiving his meal, he tossed the place against the wall, declaring the food unfit for civilized palates. Then he ordered Christina to clean up the mess and had her cook yet another plate of steak and eggs. Christina could do nothing but comply.

I can use her as bait, Zachary thought, munching on a piece of steak. His gaze roamed over Christina's curvaceous figure as she stood near the table, ready to receive his next command. *Sooner or later, wherever Cole is, he'll hear that Christina is with me. He'll return for her. Then I'll gun him down like a dog and he'll be out of my life forever. I want her badly, right now. But Dad will kill me if I rape her. All I have to do is bide my time. Sooner or later, I'll kill Dad. First Cole, then Dad. Then I'll have Christina to myself. All to myself . . . forever!*

Zachary was smiling at the wanton thoughts that danced in his mind. Seeing the dissolute, lustful look in his eyes made Christina shudder with revulsion.

"You can't mean that!" Christina exclaimed, wide-eyed and awe-struck by Zachary's latest — and most outrageous — demand.

"I mean everything I say, Christina. Now hurry along. Making me angry will cause dear old Marcus to have an unexpected accident. A *fatal* accident."

Zachary laughed softly and he touched Christina's cheek with his knuckles. She turned away, repulsed by the man.

"I want you to wear something real pretty. The whole

city is going to see you at my side, and I want you looking your best." Zachary's eyes took on a hard, cruel edge, though his tone remained casually friendly. "Right at my side is where you belong, Christina. I know you don't believe that now, but in time you will. I'll show you I'm right. I'll show you I'm always right."

Christina went to her dressing room, closing the door behind her. She sat on the bench stool before the bureau. She looked at her reflection in the mirror, then buried her face in her hands and cried silently, not wanting Zachary to hear her, refusing to give him the satisfaction of knowing how deeply he was hurting her.

There was nothing she could do to fight him. Even if she had an opportunity to escape him, she would still be Zachary's captive. Unless his nightly coded message was telegraphed and received by his men in Enderton, something terrible would happen to Marcus.

Christina was, in effect, bound to Zachary by her love for Marcus Kensington, the dear, sweet old friend of her father who had always been such a rock of strength and support whenever Christina needed help.

And where was Cole when Christina needed him most? He was fighting the Webb dynasty in Dakota when he should be fighting the Webbs in St. Paul!

A vision of Cole's face flashed in Christina's mind. It was not the vision of him that she saw most often, not the smiling Cole with the dimples he tried to hide. It was a grim-faced Cole, sad and stern. It was the Cole Christina had seen just before he left to return to Dakota and his damnable *duty*.

"I don't know how long I'll be gone," Cole had said, standing in the doorway. "You should be okay here. There's plenty of money and Anders can take you wherever you want to go."

"Yes. Thank you" was Christina's wooden reply.

She had wanted then to rush into Cole's arms, to tell him he had to stay, that she would be lost and lonely

218

without him. She wanted to say that he was all she had left in this world, and that she would do anything to save their love. But she couldn't beg Cole to stay because she knew — with greater conviction than she had ever believed anything before — that Cole had been unfaithful to her. Even if he hadn't had sex with Loretta Pembrook in the carriage, as he vehemently claimed, then surely it was only a matter of time before Loretta and Cole would be reunited in their carnal cravings.

Christina loved Cole too much — and knew herself too well — to share him with another woman. Either she would have all of Cole's love, or she would accept none of it.

She selected a gown of black muslin. As Christina took the gown from its hanger, she remembered the first night she had worn it, and the appreciation she'd seen on Cole's ruggedly handsome face when he looked at her. Black, Cole had said more than once, complemented Christina's blond hair and fair skin.

Christina closed her eyes. The memory of Cole's gaze upon her made a warmth spread slowly through her body.

Christina now wore black as a symbol. The beautiful black gown, trimmed in white lace along the throat and cuffs, was Christina's way of showing she was in mourning.

For the next week, Zachary and Christina ate every meal out. They went to the finest restaurants in Minneapolis and St. Paul. When Zachary's funds began suffering from the high life-style, he delved freely into Christina's finances rather than cable to his father for more money.

Zachary and Christina were the latest most-gossiped-about couple in St. Paul. They galivanted here and there, always showing up at the most popular social events.

The talk behind Christina's back was less than charitable. She had, after all, recently been seen on the arm of John Colter, the enigmatic entrepreneur who had captivated the hearts of so many of the single women in St. Paul. John Colter had taken Minneapolis and St. Paul by storm a half dozen years earlier. To outside observers, it looked like Zachary Webb was taking Cole's position.

When John Colter returns, Zachary Webb and Christina Whatever-her-name-is will have some fast explaining to do, the whispered conversations went.

Nobody seemed to take much notice that Christina did not smile as much as she had when she was with John Colter. She did not, in fact, smile at all—at least not freely. On occasion, Zachary would squeeze Christina's arm painfully hard, doing it on the sly so no one could see, demanding that Christina smile . . . or else!

If the days and nights were a living nightmare for Christina, they were a dream come true for Zachary Webb. Men looked at Christina with desire, then looked upon Zachary with envy. He was the man with the most beautiful woman in all of Minnesota on his arm. And judging by her recent change in alliances, the men reasoned, Christina was not the type of woman who was afraid to bestow her physical charms upon a generous suitor.

At night, Christina slept on the calico sofa, and Zachary slept in Cole's bed. He left the invitation open to Christina to join him whenever she tired of the sofa. Christina, her blue eyes smoldering with unchecked contempt, said she could never again sleep in that bed. It had been defiled, contaminated by Zachary. He just laughed at her comments.

Christina had been held captive over two weeks when Loretta Pembrook arrived at the apartment.

"Hello, dearie," Loretta said, her smile dripping with triumph. "You've been making quite a name for yourself around town."

Christina stood in stony silence. Was there no end to the humiliation? Would this living nightmare never end?

"I must admit, though, I have been helping matters along." Loretta walked past Christina. She sat in the rocking chair, the one Cole used to read in. "You see, dearie, whenever anyone has any questions about you, I'm always more than willing to fill in any little details of your life that are missing."

"How can you do that? You don't know anything about me."

"A trivial point, dearie. What I don't know, I simply make up." Loretta offered Christina a smile of pure malevolence. "Once I make something up, it becomes fact."

Loretta crossed her legs at the knee, smoothing her immaculate dress over her thighs. She turned her smile on Zachary for a moment, then let it slide back to the ashen-faced Christina.

"I wonder if you might confirm a rumor I've heard," Loretta continued. "It has been said that Cole found you in a tawdry San Francisco bordello. You were plying the trade of the world's oldest profession when Cole saw your real potential and decided he could turn a profit by teaching you some culture, putting you in fine dresses, and making your profession a little less obvious."

"You bitch!" Christina hissed through her teeth. It shocked her that she could say such a word.

Loretta was unflustered. She cleared her throat, placing a palm demurely to her bosom. "My, all this talking has made my throat dry. Run along, dearie, and fetch me something cool to drink. Lemonade would be nice."

"You go to hell," Christina whispered.

Zachary snapped his fingers, drawing Christina's attention.

"Get it," Zachary commanded sharply. "And bring me a glass as well."

When Christina returned with the lemonade, it took all her self-control to keep from tossing the glass in Loretta's face. Only her conviction that any overt act of defiance on her part could result in Marcus Kensington's death kept Christina from saying what she really thought of Zachary and Loretta. Christina could not retaliate against them in any way, and her frustration made her feel utterly helpless.

"Would you like to hear the rest of your story?" Loretta

asked. She sipped the lemonade, then studied Christina over the rim of the glass. Her eyes twinkled, dark and evil.

"Save your breath. I'm not interested."

"It seems Cole was taking your profits and you fought with him — perhaps even killed him. It wasn't until you met Zachary that you finally retired from that dreadful profession."

Christina could not believe Loretta could be so hateful, so vicious and cruel.

Loretta rose slowly from the rocker. She walked to where Zachary sat on the sofa, she bent at the waist, and took Zachary's face lightly in her hands.

"Don't you think it's time you and I became better acquainted?" Loretta kissed Zachary's mouth. Like a dog watching his mistress with adoring eyes, he rose to follow. She straightened, taking his hand in hers, leading Zachary to the bedroom. To Christina, she said, "And do be quiet, dearie. It makes me terribly angry when my concentration is disturbed."

Christina thought she would get ill as she watched Loretta close the bedroom door.

Chapter 21

Cole felt it in the dull, hollow ache in his stomach. His instincts told him something was desperately wrong. He had not been able to find Zachary. Not at Beth Ann's bordello, not at the saloon.

Where the hell is he? Cole asked himself.

For several days, Cole had remained on the perimeter of the Webb compound, waiting for a sign of Zachary. He spent two nights waiting at Beth Ann's bordello, figuring that Zachary would show up there eventually.

It was an idea born out of anger and a desire for justice that placed him near Nicholas Webb's grand mansion on the outskirts of Enderton in the middle of the night. The plan, as carefully thought out as facts would allow, was the most outlandish and foolhardy one Cole had ever devised. It also had the potential to jeopardize his inside source of information on Nicholas. Cole did not like risking anyone else's safety, but this time he felt he had no choice.

Zachary was nowhere to be seen. Cole had been hunting him, trying to pick up his trail. Once he found that trail, he would figure out some way of getting Zachary alone. Then he would challenge him, and Zachary's pride would overcome his cowardice. He would draw on Cole, and

Cole would settle a debt that had been on his shoulders for two years.

Cole leaned back against a tree, taking his hat off and placing it on the ground. A hundred yards off was the Webb compound, a collection of buildings that showed class distinction. The ornate ranch house was a mansion for the rulers of the compound, Nicholas and Zachary Webb. The smaller buildings were the bunkhouses for the hired hands who worked the cattle and the hired guns who kept all opposition to Webb's rule to a minimum.

Cole studied the buildings in his memory, because it was far too dark to see them now. He needed information, and the place to find it was *inside* Nicholas Webb's home, not outside it. That's why, with the moon half concealed by clouds, he sat waiting anxiously, dressed in black from head to toe. He wore the knee-high moccasins. Moccasins did not leave footprints in grass, like boot heels did. Cole's footwear was silent as the night against a wooden floor.

There were guards posted at the compound. Cole thought, with wry humor, that Webb lived in a fortress, not a home. Nicholas Webb lived every day knowing there were many people who wanted him dead. All his wealth and all his power had to be protected. The cost of his treachery was a life that was lived at the edge of fear.

Behind him, Black Jack neighed softly. Cole got to his feet and walked to the stallion. He patted Jack's mane and let the animal rub his forehead against Cole's chest.

"Pretty stupid plan, isn't it, old boy?" Jack dipped his head to continue feeding on the rich, sweet grass. "Figure this one will kill me? Who'll take care of you if I get shot, huh?"

Cole turned away from the stallion.

It was time to find whatever secrets were inside Nicholas Webb's home.

Cole knew where the guards were positioned, he knew of their bad habits and which ones were lazy. He knew their weaknesses from watching them the past few nights

. . . and he knew he could slip through the security to gain entry.

Flat on his belly, a scant twenty yards from the first sentry posts, he waited and watched. Bushy Moustache, the one who kept a small bottle of liquor with him at all times, moved away from his position near the boulder and masonry wall. He was on his way to speak with Floppy Hat. After that, he would go to the outhouse and spend at least ten minutes there.

The burning inside Cole's stomach grew hotter. He was ready.

Bushy Moustache moved through the halo of light caused by the kerosene lantern fixed atop a pole. When he had disappeared into the night, Cole rose and moved swiftly, crouched over.

At the three-foot-high boulder wall, he stopped. Cole peered over the top. He searched for Bushy Moustache and finally caught his outline in the darkness. Cole leaped over the wall, landing silently.

Now he was inside.

He drew his revolver and cocked it as he ran for the southwest corner of Webb's mansion. His long legs ate up the ground. His heart thudded against his ribs. The area between the wall and the house was the most dangerous, even with the cover of darkness. If his presence was discovered, he had nothing but his guns to protect him against his enemies.

Cole made it to the house. He knelt, his ears keen for any alarm. He waited, forcing himself to be patient, to remain vigilant and cautious. Only when he was certain that his invasion was undetected did he rise and move swiftly toward the rear of the mansion.

The first three windows were open, but Cole moved past them. Vague memories of years gone by warned Cole that the windows led to rooms for the downstairs servants.

The memories were old, bringing Cole back to a time when he was still friends with Zachary, and Cole's father

225

was a fifty-fifty business partner of Nicholas Webb. It was before Nicholas had a stranglehold on the territory, before anyone realized how ruthless and diabolical Nicholas's highblown dreams were.

The fourth window led to the kitchen. The window was open. Cole looked inside, and saw the outline of tables and copper kettles. The kitchen was deserted at this hour. Cole gave a sigh, thinking that not all childhood memories were bad ones. It was through the kitchen window, as children, he and Zachary had been able to sneak in and out of the mansion undetected.

Cole crawled through the window, landing silently on moccasin-shod feet. The floor was hand-polished hardwood, trim and tight. There wouldn't be any creaking floorboards in this ranch house.

Cole's spy told him there were no guards posted inside the house. Only the master of the house and his servants were allowed inside.

Cole moved down the hallway, through the dining area and past the library. He stopped at every door to check for people awake. At the foot of the stairway, leading to the second floor where the master bedroom was, Cole held his breath, listening for movement in the house.

Attached to the low-slung holster belt around his trim hips at the small of his back was a sheath and a long-bladed knife. Cole drew the knife with his left hand. He saw the blade, catching what little light shone in the mansion, gleaming evilly. He hated the thought of carrying the knife. The weapon itself was crude, and the people who used such a weapon generally seemed to enjoy personally inflicting pain on others. It wasn't like a gun, that bucked and roared and did its damage from a distance. It was Zachary's style to use a knife, not Cole's. But if he was discovered by Nicholas, he'd use it.

He ascended the stairway slowly. Cole reached the second floor landing and tried to remember what the house had been like years earlier.

What if Zachary didn't use the same room he had as a child? What if he was discovered by a servant? Could he kill an innocent person just to protect himself?

The door to the master bedroom was closed. For a few seconds, Cole paused at the door. He could enter Nicholas's bedroom and kill him in his sleep. That would put an end to Nicholas Webb and free the citizens of Enderton from his tyrannical rule. But Cole was not a murderer, despite the charges against him. He could not resort to tactics that Webb himself would—and, if Cole's guess was correct, —*had* used. That's not what this fight was about.

Zachary's bedroom door was unlocked. Cole stepped inside, then closed the door behind him. He took a match from his shirt pocket and scratched the sulfur head with his thumbnail.

Everything had changed, yet nothing was different since Cole had last been in it. He moved slowly, holding the match in front of him to light the way. Near the bed was a lamp. Cole lit it, turning the flame down very low.

He paused a moment to look around the room. The proof of Zachary's extended absence was there for the trained eye to see. The bed hadn't been slept in for at least several days. The ashtray was clean, and the washbasin was dry.

Cole went to the bureau and opened the drawers one at a time, not sure what he was looking for. He reached under the neatly folded clothes to feel the bottom of the drawer. Nothing was hidden there.

Cole went to the bed, getting down on his knees beside it. He reached under the bed and smiled when he touched something familiar. Very slowly, he lifted the wooden box, taking it out from beneath the bed. The box was for Zachary's mementos and other tidbits of life. He had had the box since he was a child. It was a Christmas present to Zachary from Cole's father.

Inside the box, Cole found a letter from Marianne Huelmann, a girl who had grown up with Cole and Zachary. She had disappeared rather suddenly from the area. Cole had heard a story that she had fallen in love with a cattleman from St. Louis.

The letter proved that the rumor was false. Marianne had gotten pregnant by Zachary and when she told him of this he apparently was unwilling to accept any of the responsibility.

Cole wondered if Zachary had shown the minimal decency of giving Marianne some money before he ran her out of town, or if he just sent her packing.

Cole's powerful shoulder muscles tightened in anger. How could he ever have been so blind to the kind of man Zachary would become? How could he ever have thought of Zachary Webb as a friend?

Cole found a slingshot that Zachary had made as a very young boy and a small leather pouch holding glass marbles. The items seemed so small and trivial now. A silver pipe tool caught Cole's attention. He wasn't sure at first why the pipe tool, used by pipe smokers to tap down tobacco or scrape it out of the bowl, registered a discordant note in his mind.

Cole picked up the pipe tool, rolling it between his fingers. The tool was not expensive by any means. It wasn't even made of silver, as Cole had first thought. So what was wrong with it, and why had Zachary kept it? Both Zachary and Nicholas smoked cigars.

A chill rippled up Cole's spine when a comment Christina had made once in passing echoed in his mind. As Cole was rolling a cigarette, she had said that she wished he smoked a pipe rather than cigarettes. Her father had smoked a pipe, and one of the things she missed was the sweet aroma of his tobacco after they'd finished their evening meal.

Cole tucked the pipe tool into his shirt pocket and issued a silent prayer in hopes that it did not belong to Christina's father.

The next item that caught Cole's eye brought tears to

them. He remained motionless, kneeling on the floor, looking into the box as tears flowed freely from his eyes.

Cole did not have to pick up the gold watch to know who it had belonged to. He didn't have to open the engraved face of it to read the inscription inside. "To Dad, for giving me so much and asking so little — Cole."

Cole had given it to his father upon graduating from college. It was Cole's way of thanking his father for making life as easy as possible for him, so that he could spend his time studying — and playing — instead of worrying about how he would pay for his education. As real as a dream, Cole could see his father. Cole saw the pride in his father's eyes when he opened the watch and read the inscription.

Cole closed his eyes, fighting against the memories. Now was not the time to get sentimental.

Cole put the watch into his pocket, tilted his head back on his shoulders, and breathed in deeply several times. He must act logically, think clearly.

Zachary had quite probably killed Christina's father. He had certainly killed Cole's father. With each murder, he took something from the corpse, a small memento so he could savor at his leisure his foul crime.

Cole again thought of going into Nicholas's bedroom and killing him in his sleep. Only the logical side of his mind, insisting that he could not prove Nicholas was behind the murders, kept Cole from killing Nicholas.

Cole wiped warm tears from his eyes. He couldn't remember the last time he'd cried, but he did not feel ashamed for his tears. He wanted to stop the tears, but they continued, blurring his vision.

Cole felt, quite suddenly, like a child, helpless against the mysterious forces of the world. Only this time, his father wasn't around to chase his fears away. Cole's father wasn't here to put light into a world that was dark and foreboding.

Cole put the watch into his pocket. Slowly, he rose to his

feet. He felt old and tired, despite the adrenaline charging through him.

Would this war with the Webbs ever end? It seemed as though Cole had been fighting them all his life, though it was only two years since his father was killed and Cole was ambushed and left for dead.

Seconds passed and memories were pushed back. Cole closed his eyes and rolled his head on his shoulders, then shook his arms. He forced his muscles to relax. When he opened his eyes, every nerve was again alert to danger, every muscle ready for action.

Unless Cole concentrated on the present dangers, he would be reunited with his father much sooner than he ever intended.

Briefly, Cole wondered if he should return the pipe tool and pocket watch to Zachary's memento box. The items could be evidence in court, valuable evidence that would convict Zachary of murder.

"It'll take more than what I've got," Cole whispered aloud. He needed solid evidence, something that couldn't possibly be denied by Nicholas's battery of lawyers in a court of law.

Cole left the mansion the same way he entered it. He alerted no one on his way in, and his exit was equally successful . . . until he dropped out of the kitchen window and landed beside Bushy Moustache, who was relieving himself against the side wall of Nicholas Webb's extravagantly expensive ranch house.

"What the—" Bushy Moustache exclaimed.

There wasn't time to use either his knife or revolver, so Cole attacked with his bare hands. His right hand shot out, fingers pointing straight up. The heel of his palm connected solidly with Bushy Moustache's forehead, snapping his head back on his shoulders.

The gunman staggered, one hand continuing to hold himself, the other groping for his holstered revolver.

A looping left fist, followed immediately by a right fist

230

that landed on the point of Bushy Moustache's nose, sent him sprawling. He landed on his back, arms and legs outstretched, his fly unbuttoned, bleeding from the mouth and nose. He was unconscious, and would be for some time.

Cole ran to the corner of the mansion. He drew his revolver and thumbed back the hammer. Though he was in serious danger, a smile curled the corners of his mouth. Somehow it seemed fitting that Nicholas Webb's gunmen urinated on the side of the mansion.

Cole had challenged the Fates again and managed to keep his skin. He hoped his luck would continue.

Cole searched the darkness, knowing there were sentries in the shadows, men who would shoot him on sight. Cole was sure Webb's security men were unaware that he had moved easily through their defenses. Bushy Moustache, however alcoholic and incompetent, had responsibilities. He would be missed before very long.

Cole hit the open area at full stride, not even bothering to crouch low. He had already stretched his luck beyond the limits, stayed on the inside too long . . . and the clock was ticking.

"Hey!" It was Floppy Hat shouting. In the darkness, he couldn't tell if it was Bushy Moustache he saw. It took a moment to realize that Bushy Moustache could never run that fast, and Floppy Hat shouted, "Stop!"

The sentry's bullet whined off the low wall that surrounded the Webb's estate, striking an inch from Cole's foot as he used the top of the wall to leap into the darkness beyond.

Cole sprinted fifty yards, arms and legs pumping. Shots echoed through the night. Five shots, evenly spaced, as Floppy Hat emptied his revolver. Then a volley of rapid fire from several carbines.

It was blind shooting, and Cole knew it. He had put far too much distance between himself and those who wished him dead for the sentries to see their moving target.

A feeling of power, of invincibility, swept over Cole. A half-smile played teasingly on Cole's lips as he mounted Jack. He had made it, and soon would be many miles away.

Chapter 22

"They're looking for you everywhere," Angelina said. She refilled Cole's coffee cup, eyeing him suspiciously. "Old Man Webb has upped the bounty on your head to five thousand dollars."

Cole smiled, a cigarette tucked into the corner of his mouth. He laced his fingers together behind his head, leaning back in the chair.

"Five thousand on my head, eh? I must be doing something right."

Angelina had spent the past hour trying to explain to Cole how foolhardy and downright suicidal his actions were. Seeing his grinning face with those boyish dimples that a man his age shouldn't have pushed her patience beyond her control. Angelina's benevolence snapped like a brittle twig.

"Damn it, Cole Jurrell! You may not care whether you live or die, but there are those of us who do care about you! I don't want to see you get hurt again! I can't . . ." Angelina's outburst of anger ebbed to one of sorrow. "I can't go through that again, Cole." Her voice dipped to a whisper when she said, "There's been so much killing. I don't know what I'd do if you ever got . . ."

"Killed?" Cole had lost his smile. He leaned forward in his chair and snuffed out his cigarette. "I admit that going

233

inside Webb's home was risky, but it was a calculated risk. Believe me, I don't have any desire to find out in the near future if there is or isn't a heaven. There's a reason why I do what I do."

Angelina sat in her chair. She poured a small amount of Napoleon brandy into a coffee cup and sipped the liqueur. Cole's heart went out to this beautiful, lonely woman, and he wished there was some way he could do the things he felt needed to be done without worrying her so.

"Will it help any if I promise to be more careful?" Cole asked with a boyish smile.

Angelina's dark eyes flashed with fire. She glared angrily at Cole, who returned her look with one of doleful innocence.

"Someday, Mr. Jurrell . . ." Angelina hissed, shaking an accusing finger under his nose. But her anger was fading quickly, and it showed in her soft brown eyes. "Oh! Someday I'm going to worry you just as much as you worry me. *Then* we'll see how long that silly grin stays on your face!"

Cole knew there was much truth in what Angelina said. He had challenged the long odds a hundred times, and had always won. His luck couldn't hold forever.

Cole reached over the table, placing his hand over Angelina's as he had so many times in the past. Holding hands was the only physical intimacy they shared, so it took on great importance to them.

For long moments they sat in silence, hands locked, each lost in separate thoughts, individual fears.

Angelina poured more brandy for herself.

"You might just as well say it," Cole said quietly, breaking the silence. "The brandy won't help. I've tried escaping into a bottle myself. Believe me, it doesn't solve anything."

"It's different this time."

Angelina sipped the brandy, hoping it would give her the courage to say what she knew she must.

Cole said, "The problems are the same as they've always been—for the last two years, anyway."

Angelina would rather she felt pain and heartache herself than to cause it in Cole. She had nursed him back to health, stolen him from the clutches of death. Partly because she felt responsible for his life and partly because he was the only man ever to have offered her his friendship without insisting on sleeping with her as payment for that friendship, Angelina wanted desperately to keep him away from harm and sorrow.

"Please, Angelina, tell me what you have to say." Cole gave her small brown hand a reassuring squeeze. "Nothing you have to say can change the way I feel about you."

"I always knew that someday you would . . ." Angelina took a swallow of brandy. She grimaced as the liqueur burned down her throat. "That you would find a woman. A special woman who would share your heart *and* your body. I've known that woman couldn't be me. That bothered me at first, I suppose. But then I realized I have your friendship, and you don't give that to the women you sleep with, so that's something really special, very precious to me."

Cole felt fear tingling inside him. Angelina was a strong woman. She had faced many obstacles in her life and never once bowed her head. Now something was scaring her, and that worried Cole immensely.

"I've heard about what happened to Miss Sands and what she was supposed to have done."

"She didn't kill O'Banion," Cole said quickly, eager to defend Christina. "Nicholas shot him in the back, not Christina."

"I guessed as much. It's not what Miss Sands did or didn't do two months ago that worries me, it's what she's doing now."

"Now?"

"Everyone in Enderton has heard that you helped Miss Sands escape from the posse. I heard that she was living with you."

"She was," Cole said in a whisper. "I love her. I never

235

planned for it to happen. It just did. I love her so much. It's crazy . . . she's all I think about."

Angelina raised her eyes to Cole's. Sorrow was etched across her lovely oval face. "Then you haven't heard?"

"Heard what? Has something happened to Christina?"

"She's in St. Paul," Angelina blurted, forcing the words from her throat. "She's with Zachary Webb. I guess they've been seen everywhere, going to all the high society functions together."

Cole felt like someone had kicked him in the stomach. He couldn't breathe. He wished Angelina would stop talking, but her words continued on in a rush, flowing over Cole, inundating his senses until he felt dizzy.

"I know you love her, Cole, and I hate to have to be the one to say this—"

"I've got to get to St. Paul." Cole pulled his hand away from Angelina's. He rose swiftly from his chair, already reaching for his jacket hooked on a peg near the door. "She needs me."

"No, she doesn't!" Angelina ran around the table, positioning herself between Cole and the door. Now that she had found the courage to start, she wouldn't stop until she had told Cole everything. It was, she believed, strong medicine that was for his own good. "She doesn't need you! She doesn't want you!"

"You don't know what you're talking about." Cole buckled his holster belt, turning his back to Angelina. "You don't know her the way I do. You don't know her at all."

"She's with Zachary! Cole, don't be blind! She's *with*"— Angelina hissed the word, making confusion impossible— "Zachary Webb! Everyone has heard about it! It's not a secret to anyone but you!"

Angelina took Cole by the arm. She forcibly turned him around and pushed him back to the table. Cole dropped heavily into the chair. His eyes were open, but they saw nothing.

236

"You're wrong," Cole said quietly. "You've *got* to be wrong . . . Christina loves me. She told me so. She wouldn't lie to me about something like that."

Angelina stood behind Cole. She gently massaged the tension-knotted muscles in his shoulders and neck.

"I didn't want to tell you." Angelina kissed the top of Cole's head. "I couldn't let you get hurt worse than you already have been. I'm sorry. You deserve better than her."

Cole sat in stunned silence. Christina with Zachary Webb? It couldn't be! No matter how badly Christina wanted her life to return to normal, no matter how much she wanted to return to Enderton so she could run her little dry goods store, Cole would never believe that she had struck a bargain with Zachary to gain her freedom. Christina just wouldn't sell her soul to the devil . . . would she?

Would she go to Zachary for money? Experience had taught Cole that every man—and woman—has a price. Cole had seen too many of his so-called friends end up working for Nicholas Webb to underestimate the attraction of money.

"Why don't you have a little more brandy?" Angelina said, just loud enough for Cole to hear.

"No . . . no, thank you. I need to think."

"What you need to do is stop thinking, Cole. It's thinking in circles that'll drive you crazy."

Cole knew that Angelina was right. If he had a lick of sense in him, he'd crawl into a bottle for the evening. In the morning, he would wake up with a massive hangover and, with any luck at all, he would have Christina out of his mind and banished from his heart.

"I can't stop thinking about her." Cole heard the words and it took a moment to realize that he'd actually spoken them. "I know it's foolish, Angelina, but I've got to find out for myself if Christina really has gone over to the other side."

"And if she has . . .?"

"Then I'll be back here as quickly as possible." Cole said. He knotted the thong around his thigh, tying his holster down for a fast draw. He looked down at Angelina, studying her face, looking into her eyes. "I've got to be sure," he said softly. "You must understand that, don't you?"

Angelina nodded her head. Her arms slipped around Cole's waist and she hugged him loosely, her cheek against his chest.

"Be careful," she whispered. "Be careful for my benefit, okay? Every time you leave, I'm afraid that I'll never see you again."

Cole stroked Angelina's long dark hair. "Don't even think that way. I'll be back. I'll even bring Christina back with me. Then you'll be able to see for yourself that she's perfect for me."

"I hope so, Cole. I really do."

Chapter 23

It was lost to Cole now. Six years of a double life was gone, and nothing Cole could do would bring the peaceful, irresponsible John Colter back to life.

Cole had created John Colter, at least initially, as a lark. It wasn't until after John's creation that Cole realized how he had sought an escape from his own identity. In his early years, Cole sometimes felt as though he had no life of his own, no identity that was uniquely, distinctly his. He was either an executive for the Flying J Ranch or he was his father's son and had to shoulder the responsibilities of being the sole heir to a dynasty.

So Colton Jurrell created John Colter, an irresponsible, devil-may-care young man of wealth, as a way of being himself. Cole never really thought it was terribly odd that he had to pretend to be someone else to be himself. It was just the way it was, and he accepted it.

But that carefree existence was gone now, and Cole mourned the death of John Colter as he would a death in the family.

He spotted Mr. Kjellgaard at his post . . . and three security men. One gunman was at the doorway, much to Mr. Kjellgaard's apparent dismay. One man was on the roof of the apartment building. The third was across the street from Cole's apartment.

A few moments later, he spied two more security men in

rover positions. Their job was to circle the apartment building and walk up and down the street. In theory, their mobility was to make them look just like any other pedestrian, but Cole recognized the hard, cold set to their faces. He saw the way their eyes darted about.

Gunmen, Cole thought miserably. *Zachary's acting like he's still in Enderton. He's got no class at all . . . but he's got Christina.*

Cole crossed his legs at the knee and rubbed his eyebrows against the grain with a finger and thumb. The direct ride from Dakota to St. Paul had been one of his more foolhardy acts in the past two years. He hadn't once done a single thing to cover his tracks. Fortunately, he hadn't seen any of Webb's hired guns along the way.

On the window ledge were the field glasses that Cole had been staring through for three hours. His eyes ached now from strain. The curtain windows were drawn on his apartment, and they hadn't opened once.

Picking the lock on the apartment door was easy. Cole had only flimsy excuses, a barely plausible story to offer if the residents of the apartment he was in returned home. He'd made a few discreet inquiries and discovered the young couple was away on vacation. How long that vacation was to last, Cole had no idea. He couldn't ask too many questions without drawing attention to himself.

Cole scratched his chin and grimaced. He needed a shave and a bath. He would get neither in the near future. Cole could not rest until he saw Christina. He had to find out if she really was with Zachary Webb. Once he had that answer, he had to ask himself whether or not Christina was with Zachary willingly. It was a question, Cole suspected, that would have no easy answer.

A window curtain moved and Cole grabbed for the field glasses. Before he could get them to his eyes, the face behind the window curtain disappeared. Cole had not gotten a good look at who had moved the curtain, but at least he now knew that someone was in his apartment.

Who was it? Zachary? Christina? Perhaps more gunmen, laying an ambush, waiting for him to return?

The questions facing Cole continued to mount, and answers seemed further and further from his grasp.

The sun was almost down when Cole saw something that made his heart pound in his chest. He spotted the rented carriage coming down the street. When Loretta Pembrook stepped out of the carriage, Cole leaned with his elbows on the window ledge, peering through the field glasses. The gunman with Mr. Kjellgaard tipped his hat to Loretta, and Cole felt a chill start in the pit of his stomach.

What in God's name was Loretta doing there? And why did Zachary's thugs know her?

More than an hour passed, each second ticking by with agonizing slowness for Cole. He never took the field glasses from his eyes. His former lover, the love of his life, and his childhood friend, might all be in the apartment — his apartment — together.

Cole tried to keep scenarios from forming in his mind. It would do no good to think about what *might* be happening. But his intellectual willpower was not equal to his mental agitation.

Cole could picture Zachary, Loretta, and Christina sitting together, drinking his wine, plotting how they would divide the reward they'd get for capturing him.

Another scenario had Loretta and Christina, both feeling abandoned by Cole, working together, believing that sooner or later Cole would return to one of them. When that happened, they would need Zachary to confirm the capture, or perhaps he was to be the paymaster for their five-thousand-dollar reward.

And they might also be . . .

Cole shook his head, forcing himself to concentrate only on events he could influence. He rubbed his eyes and tried to ignore the headache he'd gotten from staring through the field glasses at window curtains that never moved.

What are they doing in there? Is Christina in there? Angelina was right, Cole thought bitterly. *Thinking too much is going to drive me crazy.*

For the hundredth time since he left Angelina in her little one-room shack of a house, Cole wanted to just shrug his shoulders of his doubts and fears and self-imposed duties. He wanted to forget that he loved Christina more than he dreamed he could ever love any woman. He thought of walking away from Colton Jurrell and John Colter and everyone else. He could create a new identity for himself in New York. He could start his life all over again.

Cole knew that he could walk away from everything else . . . but never his love for Christina. Not until he found out that she did not love him and never really had. And he couldn't walk away from his duty to see the murderer of his father punished. Until that time, Cole had to carry the weight of responsibilities that had been thrust upon him. He simply had no other choice.

Loretta stayed in the apartment for almost two hours. Cole's active imagination and restless mind came up with a thousand different things that could be accomplished in two hours, and he didn't like any of his ideas.

He noticed the gunmen all gave Loretta a polite nod when she entered the carriage to leave, but none of them left with her. Obviously, their job was to stick with the apartment.

Are they protecting whoever is inside the apartment, or waiting for me to return? Cole wondered.

It wouldn't have been difficult for Cole to stop the carriage and abduct Loretta. She was essentially weak, Cole figured. For all of her misanthropy and contempt for the world, Loretta was a coward in the core of her soul. It wouldn't take much of a threat to get her to tell Cole everything she knew, and maybe a little more than that.

It was a few minutes after eight when activity resumed at the front doors of the apartment. A heavyset gunman who looked uncomfortable in the new suit he wore hailed an open carriage. As the carriage rolled to a stop, more gunmen appeared from inside the building.

Cole now counted a total of seven hired guns . . . and those were only the men he had seen. Like cockroaches and rats, he thought, you only need to see a few to know there's a whole bunch more just out of sight.

The gunmen looked up and down the street. At least one stared directly at the third-floor window, but Cole knew he was safe in the darkness behind the curtains.

A slender man, in his middle thirties and having the bearing of a military officer, stepped out of the apartment and into the street. He made a motion with his hand, then Zachary Webb and Christina Sands stepped through the double doors.

For a moment, Cole thought his heart had actually stopped beating. The doubts that Angelina had planted in his mind came immediately to the fore. All Cole's confusion and fear jumbled together in his mind. But there really was no cause for confusion because it was all so plain—the woman he loved above life itself was with the man he hated with every fiber in his body.

Christina had her hand inside Zachary's arm as he led the way down to the carriage. Though they were visible to Cole for only a few seconds, it was long enough for him to realize that Zachary Webb absolutely loved having Christina at his side and that Webb had serious concerns about Cole returning to St. Paul. Cole could almost taste Zachary's paranoia in the air, even from a third-floor apartment across the street.

But there was something wrong with the scene, though Cole could not say exactly what it was. He only knew something was wrong. He hoped he was listening to his outlaw instincts rather than his heart. Cole's heart wanted nothing more than to be near Christina again, to feel the velvety length of her voluptuous body pressed close to his own, to smell the freshness of her skin and hair and look into the clear, blue, sapphire depths of her eyes.

243

Seven men followed closely behind Zachary and Christina in a second carriage. Cole watched the cadre of mercenaries follow Zachary and Christina at a discreet distance.

By the time the carriages had disappeared around the corner, Cole had a loosely designed plan of attack worked out. He checked his Colt, his hideaway derringer, and his knife to make sure all were within speedy reach and wouldn't bind in his clothing if he had to get them into action.

Cole Jurrell left the apartment he had broken into, leaving no trace at all of his presence there.

Christina sat in angry silence beside Zachary. The ritual was continuing tonight, just as it had almost every night since Zachary had forced himself into her world.

She glanced sideways at Zachary and wondered if he would ever tire of this charade. Part of Christina wanted nothing more than for the game to end. Another part of her knew that when the charade ended, when the game had run its course, Marcus's life would come to an abrupt end.

Christina closed her eyes against the thought of Marcus's death. Her lips pressed into a thin line, giving her usually soft and delicate facial features a hard cast.

"What's bothering you now?" Zachary asked crossly, eyeing Christina.

"Nothing."

"Nothing, nothing, nothing! That's all you ever say to me. How am I to know how to make you happy if you won't talk to me?"

The words stung Christina. Hadn't Cole said almost the same thing to her? It was strange how two very different men could say virtually the same words and draw two entirely different reactions from Christina.

"Don't worry about it," Christina said, turning her face away from Zachary. "It's nothing you can do anything about."

Christina could feel Zachary's gaze upon her. She had learned during her time as a prisoner that it was usually best for her to keep her opinions to herself. If she said anything to offend Zachary, he invariably made her pay for her temerity in one way or another.

At least he hasn't touched me yet, Christina thought.

In her heart, Christina knew that Zachary would eventually force himself upon her. She did not know why he had kept his distance from her so far, but she was certain that he wouldn't stay away from her forever. Christina couldn't believe that Loretta was so satisfying in the bedroom that Zachary wouldn't want anyone else. Christina had seen the lustful look in Zachary's eyes many times.

"Where are we going tonight?" Christina asked quietly, not really caring if she got an answer.

"The MacMillan House. Heard of it?"

Christina said she had. She did not say that Cole had taken her to the fine restaurant, which was quickly gaining the reputation of being an office away from the office for many of the powerful flour mill businessmen. It was the kind of place where rumors could start and grow with incredible speed, just the kind of place Zachary loved to be seen with Christina. There would be plenty of the powerful businessmen at the MacMillan House for Zachary to meet, and they would all want to be introduced to Christina. He was certain that if enough businessmen in Minneapolis and St. Paul saw Christina with him, sooner or later Cole would find out about it. When Cole came looking, Zachary would be waiting for him with a small army of killers.

Too many days and nights of inactivity had made Zachary's hired gunmen complacent. Cole had almost no trouble making it past the roving security man to get onto the roof of his own apartment building.

The sniper was there, sitting near the edge of the building with his back to Cole. A long-barreled Winchester was propped against the ledge near his feet, within easy reach.

Cole studied the gunman for a moment. Though Zachary had hired a lot of men to handle his security, he had chosen quantity over quality.

Cole never made a sound as he moved up behind the amateur mercenary. The man, in fact, never realized he wasn't alone until the muzzle of Cole's .44 touched his skull just behind the ear.

"Move away from the edge," Cole whispered. His voice was cold yet carried a promise of deadly rage should the gunman not do everything he was told.

The gunman took a step backward. He raised his hands until they were level with his shoulders. His hands were trembling visibly.

"Don't shoot, mister."

"Another step back, then get down on your stomach."

The gunman did as he was instructed. Cole frisked him quickly, removing a pistol and knife. He pocketed both weapons, holstered his Colt, then drew his knife from the sheath at the small of his back. He touched the razor-sharp blade against the man's neck. The gunman's body tensed as he waited for death to take him.

"Please, mister," the man said in a whining voice. "I ain't done nothin' to you."

"Don't talk unless I tell you to." Cole added an ounce of pressure behind the knife, adding authority to his words. "Do you know who I am?"

"Mister, you got the jump on me clean. I ain't even heard you let alone seen your face." The man's eyes were squeezed tightly shut. Cole hated him for his cowardice. "Please, God, mister, don't kill me."

"My name is Colton Jurrell. I'm the man you're looking for." The words made the gunman's body quiver. Cole began to feel more confident that his hastily concocted plan would work. "What are your orders?"

"To stay up here an' look for you. Anybody sees you is supposed to shoot first an' ask questions later." The gunman licked his lips nervously. "Mr. Webb's got men all over the place."

"I know. But if you're thinking your friends can help you, you'll be dead wrong." The gunman's whole body was shaking with fear. Cole kept the point of his lethal knife against the man's neck. "Start talking. What have Zachary and those women been up to?"

In a voice that trembled with the fear of death, the gunman told his story. Cole listened carefully, never interrupting the man even when he got off the subject. It was best, Cole thought, to just let him ramble on.

He called the women "Miss Loretta" and "Miss Christina," which confirmed Cole's presumption that the man did not know the whole story of who the women were.

"Where did Zachary and Christina go tonight?"

"They go a different place every night. I don't know 'zactly where they went."

Cole added pressure behind the knife, very nearly drawing blood. Cole knew this pathetic excuse for a man would have gunned him down without the slightest hesitation. It was not an easy thing for Cole to restrain himself, especially now, when he knew the man was lying.

"That's a lie!" Cole spat. "What good are bodyguards if they don't know where the boss man is? That's the last lie you'll ever tell unless I get the answer real quick!"

"The MacMillan House! It's over on—"

"Shut up. I know where it is." Cole bent over the man, keeping the knife in place against his neck. "If Zachary finds out you talked to me, he'll kill you. He likes killing people. He kills them just for the fun of it. Just think of what he would do to a *traitor.*"

"Mister, you didn't leave me no choice!" The gunman's voice had gotten high-pitched as panic gripped him like a vise. "You said you'd kill me if I didn't tell ya everything!"

"Zachary Webb won't look at it that way. He'll look at you as a hired gun who sold him out." Cole leaned close enough to the man to whisper menacingly into his ear. "If I were you, I'd get off this roof without letting a soul know

247

about it. Then I'd find a new city to live in for a couple of years. Now, you're thinking that I'm going to let you live, and how much you'd like that big fat reward the Webbs have put on my head, aren't you? But what happens if I get to Zachary before you do? What happens if I let *him* live, too."

"Mister, if you let me live, I'll leave this city tonight and I swear I ain't never comin' back!"

Cole knew the gunman was telling the truth. He was too frightened to do anything else.

Chapter 24

Cole was banking on several things *not* happening. Consequently, this was precisely the type of operation he hated the most. It was never good to hope for negatives, and Cole disliked having so little control over the odds of his success. His plans hinged, in part, on the bodyguards being hesitant to use their guns in a public restaurant, where innocent victims — and witnesses — made the situation more complicated.

The MacMillan House was doing a brisk business. Cole's inspection of the restaurant and hotel had convinced him that Zachary was not expecting any trouble in a public place. Cole knew there were bodyguards with Zachary and Christina, but none of them had been stationed outside the MacMillan House.

Amateurs, Cole thought.

He cautioned himself against overconfidence. The problem with amateurs is that they were quick to overreact, and therefore unpredictable.

And this time, Cole had Christina's safety to deal with.

The lavishness and opulence the MacMillan House showed its customers was only a partial picture. In back, where the refuse bins were, where only the bums, alcoholics, and low-level employees ever went, the MacMillan House looked and smelled no different than any other low-class eating establishment. Cole wrinkled his nose at the smell.

A drunk was rummaging through the garbage, sucking out the last few drops from the empty liquor bottles he found. Cole gave the man a dollar and told him to leave. Cole didn't want the old drunk in the line of gunfire.

What if Christina doesn't want to be freed?

Cole shook the thought away. If he could just talk to her alone for a little while, he would know the truth. Would he be glad if she was being forced against her will? Should he be less selfish about getting things his way? Should he attempt a rescue—if a rescue it was—at all?

"I must really love her," Cole said under his breath. "Thinking about her has turned my mind to oatmeal."

Through a greasy window, Cole surveyed the kitchen of the MacMillan House. He counted three cooks, one very young dishwasher, and four waiters who scuttled back and forth through the batwing doors that separated the restaurant from the kitchen.

Cole saw no maître d' checking in on the kitchen staff; there was no one around who looked like management of the MacMillan House.

Luck, so far, was with Cole.

Cole stepped through the rear door, striding boldly into the kitchen. The head chef began to complain, then the words got caught in his throat. Seeing the tall, blond man dressed all in black, with knee-high moccasins and a tied-down holster low on his thigh for speed, stopped his words. When he looked into Cole's cold, steel-gray eyes, the head chef shivered and dropped the ladle he had.

"I don't see nothin' an' I don't say nothin'," the head chef said quietly with a thick Scandinavian accent.

Cole, with his right hand resting on the butt of his Colt, took the time to meet the gaze of each man in the kitchen. He would receive no opposition here.

"Smart man," Cole said. He smiled a little with his mouth but not his eyes, indicating he did not *want* to hurt anyone. Whether he would hurt any of them if it was necessary was left in doubt . . . and that was the thought

250

Cole wanted uppermost on the minds of the MacMillan House staff.

Cole peered over the batwing doors, looking into the restaurant. He found the hired guns first. The three men sat in silence, their suit coats bulging with badly hidden pistols. All Cole had to do was follow their gaze to find Christina. Zachary sat beside her.

Cole looked at Christina and felt his pulse quicken at her beauty. He had to tear his eyes away from her. He twisted away from the batwings, fearful of drawing the attention of restaurant customers or the armed bodyguards. His chest felt tight, as if a hand around his heart had suddenly clenched into a fist.

Christina! She was so close that Cole couldn't wait to touch her, to wrap his arms around her and hug her tenderly. He hungered for the scent of her honey hair, the touch of her silken skin.

Cole held his hands in front of himself, fingers outstretched. His hands were steady as a surgeon's. The cooks and dishwashers looked at Cole silently. No one knew who Cole was, but they suspected *what* he was. They would do nothing to make Cole angry. He was trouble, but someone else's trouble.

Cole looked over the batwing doors again. There were times he was living with Christina in the apartment when Cole questioned himself, wondering if it was possible for her to look more lovely. Tonight, in a black gown, she was more beautiful than ever. He realized it was only the time he had spent away from Christina that made her so lovely, but that knowledge did not take anything away from her.

She looks thin, Cole thought after a moment.

He spun away from the doorway again as a waiter entered the kitchen. Cole put a finger to his lips. The waiter nodded his head, his eyes wide and frightened.

"I'm no hero," the waiter whispered after a moment.

"Sit," Cole whispered.

The waiter sat on the floor. Cole frowned. He had not intended the waiter to sit there. Cole did not, by nature,

251

enjoy inspiring fear in people. Sometimes fear was a necessary tool that Cole used, but he never enjoyed it and he tried to never abuse the power.

The third time Cole looked at Christina, he was able to see her objectively. She had lost weight, and there was a darkness under her eyes. Rage boiled inside Cole's veins and he immediately blamed Zachary Webb for Christina's condition.

What sealed Cole's decision that Christina needed rescuing was her expression. Cole had seen that exact look on Christina's face when she was on the run from the posse and she knew she had no choice but to be with Cole.

Cole drew his Colt and derringer and pushed through the doors.

"Take it easy," Cole said sharply to the heavyset bodyguard. He pointed the Colt at the man's nose. He thumbed the hammer of the derringer back and pointed it at Zachary's open mouth. "Christina, get up. We're getting out of here."

"No."

"What?" Cole exclaimed, shocked at her succinct refusal. "Christina, this isn't the time to argue with me."

The hired guns were to Cole's right; Zachary and Christina to his left. Cole had to keep glancing back and forth. To make matters worse, Zachary was looking more confident by the second, and the three hired thugs were looking more bold. Christina was holding on to the arms of her chair with white-knuckled tension. It would take dynamite to get her out of that chair.

"Take him," Zachary hissed to his men. "Goddamn it! What do I pay you for?"

Cole pointed his pistol at the wiry, anxious-looking bodyguard, aiming it at the tip of his nose. "You'll never clear leather," Cole said.

"Kill him! Kill that sonofabitch!" Zachary shouted.

"Shut up, Webb, or I'll gun you down where you sit!"

Zachary took the lapels of his jacket between the tips of his fingers and thumbs. He slowly opened his coat, showing Cole and the stunned patrons of the MacMillan House that he was unarmed.

"I thought you didn't kill unarmed men, Jurrell," he said with smug defiance. The double-barreled derringer pointed at his face did not frighten him. He knew his adversary well. "Huh, Cole? Can you kill an unarmed man?"

No matter how great Cole's desire for revenge was, no matter how much the world needed to be free of Zachary Webb, Cole could not become the man the Webbs said he was. He could kill. He could not murder.

"Christina, we're getting out of here. Now, damn it! Get on your feet!"

"I can't! I want to, but I can't!" Christina cried out, pulled at the arms of the chair as though she was tied to it.

"Get up!"

Zachary's countenance glowed, his eyes were brilliant, glistening with the power he felt he had. "She's mine now, Cole! Face it! This time I've won!"

"Christina, we've got to leave *now!*"

"I can't! I want to, but I can't!?" Christina cried out, her face ashen. She was half standing, but her hands were locked onto the chair as though frozen there. "Get out! Save yourself!"

Cole moved to within arm's reach of Christina. He would drag her out of the MacMillan House kicking and screaming if necessary.

"I'm not leaving without you," Cole said. His eyes, like those of a hunted animal being surrounded by a pack of hungry wolves, flashed back and forth from the bodyguards to Zachary and Christina. He touched the twin muzzles of the derringer to Zachary's chest. "Don't even breathe!"

Zachary's smile was tight. A few ounces of pressure on the trigger would put an end to him. But Cole was a predictable man in some ways. Zachary knew he would not kill an unarmed man, no matter how great his hatred was.

Zachary looked to his men and said in a voice of icy calm, "Kill this man."

It was over in seconds. The wiry man moved first, leaping sideways out of his chair and reaching inside his jacket. Cole shot him as he dove for the floor. The other two gunmen stood up, clawing for their weapons. Spinning, moving away from Christina so that she would not accidently be shot, Cole leveled the derringer and the Colt and fired both weapons almost simultaneously.

The roaring guns were deafening in the confined space. Cole had counted on the gunmen being unwilling to risk the lives of innocent restaurant patrons, and he had gambled poorly.

A bullet whizzed past his ear. Cole thumbed back the hammer and fired one last time. The third hired gun crumpled to the floor. The smell of burned gunpowder mingled with that of expertly prepared meals. Two dozen patrons, some of them diving for the safety of the floor, looked at Cole with stunned horror.

Cole stuffed the derringer into his coat pocket. He grabbed Christina's wrist and hauled her to her feet. His eyes never left Zachary's.

"Someday it's just going to be you and me," Cole said to Zachary, loud enough for all to hear. "I won't have my back for you to shoot, either. Someday you won't be able to hide behind your stolen money." He knew he only had a moment to make his case in the court of public opinion.

Zachary's smile was gone. He had been given a lesson in Cole's skill with handguns. When they were in their teens, Cole had always been the faster and more accurate marksman. Zachary hoped that the years of practice he had put in would make up for that difference. It hadn't. Cole was the fastest, most accurate shot Zachary had ever seen.

"The law . . ." Zachary managed to say. His eyes went from Cole to the three men who only moments earlier been paid to protect him. Zachary had thought the three men—the best of the lot that he had hired—would be enough protection against one man. He was wrong. He croaked, "The law will be here soon . . ."

Cole, pulling Christina along, ran through the kitchen and out the rear door of the MacMillan House.

St. Paul, his safe haven, had been taken away from him. Cole could only guess what story Zachary would tell the law officers who would soon be at the restaurant.

Everything had been taken from Cole . . . but he had Christina with him now. He had Christina back. That was all that mattered.

This sort of thing was no longer new to Christina. She had been on the run in Enderton, in Fargo, and now in St. Paul. After initially pulling against Cole, Christina had followed him, not knowing where they were headed. He kept his large, powerful arm wrapped around her wrist, and Christina, in something of a daze after the gunplay and bloodshed, felt pain at Cole's strong grip but said nothing.

"Cole, wait," Christina panted as they ran down an alleyway that emptied out onto a wide, cobblestone street. Carriages rumbled past them. "Wait, please. I've got to talk to you."

Cole looked over his shoulder at Christina. He allowed her only a glance. Now was not the time, his frozen, gray eyes told her, for an argument. He would make the decisions and she would obey them.

"I've got to go back," Christina whispered.

Cole stopped. He looked straight out, then his chin dropped to his chest. He released Christina's wrist, expelling his breath in a defeated sigh.

"I don't want to go back to Zachary, but I have to."

"Why?" Cole did not look at Christina.

"He's having Marcus Kensington watched. Unless Zachary's men get a telegram from him every night, Marcus will be killed."

Cole turned toward Christina. There was a look of utter disdain on his handsome, unshaven face.

255

"Am I supposed to believe that?"

"It's the truth." Christina reached for Cole, but he took a step away from her, moving out of reach. "You've got to believe me. I have no choice. I hate Zachary and I hate being near him . . . but I can't leave him."

"To hell with it," Cole whispered. Cole turned away from Christina. Walking down the street, wearing his gun for the whole world to see, he drew the curious gaze of onlookers. "Live your lies, Christina," he said over his shoulder. "I just don't care anymore."

Tears streamed down Christina's cheeks, though she did not know that she was crying. She ran after Cole, oblivious to the attention she was drawing, wanting nothing more than his understanding.

I don't want to lose him again, she thought, then said, "Get away from here, Cole. We can't win. We can't fight Nicholas and Zachary on our own."

"We can fight them if we want to." Cole allowed Christina to take his arm and stop him. "It's a lie, Christina. I talked with Marcus a couple days ago. He's fine. He's just goddamned fine, and so are you!" Cole spit the words out, shaking his head with disgust. "Go back to Zachary, if that's who you want. He's got lots of money. He can keep you in fine style. And when you're done with him, you can move right on up the ladder to Nicholas. Now there's where the *real* money is."

Christina couldn't believe the words she was hearing. They cut her soul almost as deeply as the hatred she saw in Cole's eyes.

Marcus safe? It was absurd to even think such a thing. Christina had lived every minute of every day with Marcus's safety always on her mind. Every night she thought of how easy it would be to run out of the apartment while Zachary slept. Each time such thoughts entered her head, Christina chased them away as though they were something evil, knowing—or at least *believing*—that to run away from Zachary would mean signing away Marcus Kensington's life.

"I'm telling you the truth," Christina said. Tears rolled unheeded down her pale cheeks. "With God as my witness, I'm telling you the truth."

In the distance, from the direction of the MacMillan House, a shrill whistle blew. It was a policeman's whistle. Christina flinched at the sound of it. It was only a matter of minutes before law officers everywhere would have Cole's description and whatever story Zachary had given them of the shooting in the restaurant.

Christina looked into Cole's eyes and whispered, "I am telling you the truth."

"Right," Cole replied without the slightest bit of understanding in his tone.

He reached for Christina's hand. Together they moved away from the busy street, into the shadows and the alleyways that had become so much a part of Christina's life.

The small rowboat drifted with the current. The two occupants sat in silence, eyes scanning the banks of the Mississippi River for anyone or anything that looked suspicious.

Christina guessed they had floated several miles downstream from St. Paul by this time in the stolen rowboat. Though they had seen nothing that warranted the continued vigilance of their search, neither of them was willing to break the empty silence that separated them.

Cole used the oars only to keep the rowboat in the middle of the narrow, winding Mississippi River. Sound, he had told Christina, travels extraordinarily well over water. Though she knew this was the truth, Christina suspected Cole used this as an excuse from having to talk to her.

What is he thinking about? Christina wondered.

She was certain Cole believed her story of Zachary's threat to kill Marcus. The fact that it was a lie, that Marcus's life was not actually in danger, was only proof of Zachary's cunning and treachery. But what else separated

257

Cole from Christina?

He thinks I had sex with Zachary, Christina concluded sadly. *That's what he believes, and he can never love me thinking I've slept with another man.*

"He never touched me," Christina whispered. She could not see Cole's face in the moonlight. His hat was pulled low over his eyes. "He threatened to rape me, but he never did."

"You don't have to talk about it," Cole replied quietly. "It's not your fault."

From his tone, Christina knew that Cole didn't believe her. She got off her seat and knelt in front of Cole.

"I'm telling you the truth. I never slept with him."

"Okay. I believe you. We don't have to talk about it."

Christina touched Cole's face with her fingertips. Where had all his warmth gone? Why couldn't he just understand that she needed him now, needed his compassion and strength, more than she ever had before?

"I love you," Christina whispered. She tasted the saltiness of her own tears. It seemed as though she had cried constantly for weeks. "You are the only man ever to touch me, Cole. Only you. Please believe me."

Cole didn't believe her, and Christina didn't need to look into his eyes to know it.

She went back to her seat. Christina wrapped her arms around her legs, then placed her head upon her knees. After several minutes, Christina sat upright again. Her eyes were dry. She would shed no more tears. She had cried herself out. She had been hurt as much as she could possibly be hurt and she had survived. But now Cole's love had been stolen from her. He believed she had slept with Zachary. That was all that mattered to him, or so it seemed.

Christina had lost the only man she could ever love and now that his heart no longer belonged to her, she no longer had anything worth crying for.

Chapter 25

"You imbecile! You bloody, damn fool!" Nicholas Webb was red-faced with rage. He stepped closer to his son, pointing a thick, well-manicured finger in Zachary's face. "You had her and you let her escape? I can't believe you'd let such a thing happen!"

The tongue-lashing Zachary was receiving had, at first, made him feel guilty. He had, after all, botched the assignment his father had given him. But enough was enough. After five minutes of being told he was a fool, Zachary was annoyed. After thirty minutes more of verbal abuse, Zachary began wondering how he would kill his father when the time came. Murder with style, perhaps? Poison in a glass of vintage wine? Or maybe something less subtle and more sure-fire? A bullet in the ear while dear ol' Daddy slept dreamily?

"What was going through your mind?" Nicholas asked in a booming voice that echoed off the study walls. "Were you using your mind at all?"

"I've told you already. I was trying to lure Cole out of hiding. I wanted to get both Christina *and* Cole."

"Well, at least you accomplished something. Jurrell came right out of hiding. *He took her from you!*" Nicholas turned away from his son. He took giant strides toward the liquor cabinet. "The only reason you're alive right now is because you didn't have a gun on you. Otherwise, you'd be just as dead as those three clowns you hired to protect you."

"He had the jump on you before, too, or don't you remember that little fiasco on the train?" Zachary's tone was thick and oily with sarcasm. "Seems to me Cole played you for a fool then. Not only did he take the payroll, but he kept one of his men from blowing your brains from here to kingdom come."

Zachary saw the muscles in his father's shoulders tighten beneath his velvet smoking jacket. After thirty minutes of having his back to the wall, Zachary had finally landed a telling blow. Now he was coming out swinging.

"Sure, I underestimated Cole," Zachary continued. "So did you. But when I was in St. Paul, I was living in *his* apartment, spending *his* money. You, on the other hand, couldn't keep Cole out of your *own home.*"

Zachary sensed he was close to the edge with his father. He wanted to put an end to the argument while he still had the upper hand.

"Look—he won the battle, but the war isn't over. I've failed . . . *we've* failed to lasso him for the past two years. But Cole's running out of tricks. He can't go back to St. Paul. That's something. How long can he last now?"

Nicholas placed his hands on the brightly polished walnut table. The rage going through him fizzled. It had burned itself out and now there was nothing left for Nicholas to do but wait.

"You had her," Nicholas whispered. His tone was uncharacteristically soft with the defeat and loss that he felt. "She could have been here with me. Christina . . . here now, where Cole could never have reached her, where I could have had her all to myself."

Nicholas poured himself a large Scotch. He had not offered one to Zachary. "So close . . ." He opened and closed a hand, as though he could get a stranglehold on Cole, or perhaps trying to clutch onto the dream of Christina Sands.

Nicholas turned abruptly. His eyes narrowed in concentration and anger as he glared at Zachary.

"You didn't . . . ?"

Zachary shook his head. On this particular subject, he wouldn't twist the knife in his father's back. Nicholas was too volatile, his emotions too unpredictable.

"No. I've told you before and I'll tell you again. I never laid a finger on her. I admit I thought about it often enough—it's hard not to think about things like that with Christina—but I found someone else to give me what I need."

"Cole will come back sooner or later," Zachary said to his father's back. "He's disappeared before, then he shows up out of the blue to make our lives miserable. This time we'll be waiting for him. And if he hasn't got Christina with him, we'll catch him and make Cole tell us where she is. Then I'll kill him myself and bring his head to you on a silver platter."

Zachary pushed his hat back from his forehead. He rubbed his face and sighed with exhaustion.

"I'm dog tired. I'm going to bed. Try to not think about Christina too much."

Nicholas cleared his throat. When he spoke, there was an unusual tone of pride in his tone.

"The trick . . . telling Christina you had Marcus being watched . . . that was absolutely brilliant. I wish I had thought of it."

Nicholas raised his face, turning halfway around. For the first time in several minutes he actually met gazes with his son. Zachary gave Nicholas a smile. "Thanks," he said.

Before Zachary had left Nicholas's study, he had decided the bullet-while-father-sleeps was probably the best method of patricide. He had so many enemies already, Zachary could probably sell tickets to the execution.

"I want to help."

"No," Cole said without a second's hesitation.

He glanced up and gave Christina a curious look. Then

261

he made a huffing sound and shook his head, knowing the gesture would irk her. Her audacity never failed to amaze him. Suddenly, the dirty line shack seemed to have shrunk, closing in around Cole and Christina, forcing them to be too close to each other.

"Why not? It's my fight, too. I've earned the right to see him brought down."

"You'd only get in the way. I've got enough to worry about without babysitting you."

Christina stood with her hands on her hips. There was a defiant set to her jaw and a fire in her eyes that declared she would not be easily put off. She was not going to be denied her chance to taste revenge and work for justice. Cole wouldn't just shrug her off since he freed her from the invisible bars of Zachary Webb's prison.

"You need help. Don't deny that," Christina continued. She tried to keep her voice level and calm. "You had a gang once, men who could back you up. They're all in jail now."

"Or dead," Cole added under his breath, thinking about Bobby. He hoped, fleetingly, that Bobby's bloody demise would discourage her misdirected bravado.

Christina felt her anger rising, though she knew that if she showed it, she'd only draw a similar reaction from Cole. She had to control her temper, to stay calm and level-headed. Once she got Cole angry, she knew she'd never be able to reason with him.

"We're all we've got left for each other, you and me," Christina said. "Bobby, Hans, and Jackie . . . they're gone. It's just you and me, whether you want to admit it or not."

Cole thumbed another cartridge into the leather loop in his holster. He could feel Christina's nearness, but he did not look up. Whenever he looked at her, Cole felt all those strange and sad things inside, and this was not the time for such feelings. She was beautiful, scared, tattered from the difficult and dangerous trip from St. Paul. Her dress was soiled and torn. The stockings Cole had given her when they shared their happiness in St. Paul were ruined. Her slippers, all the rage among fashionable women, were manifestly ill-suited for the range.

Whenever Cole looked at Christina, he felt apologetic and vaguely guilty for how dramatically her life had changed. He wanted to hold her in his arms and tell her that everything would be okay. He wanted to do more than that with her, but whenever he looked into her sapphire-blue eyes, he thought of Zachary and wondered what lengths Christina had gone to protect Marcus Kensington. Such thoughts and unspoken questions left Cole with a cold, empty feeling inside.

"I want to go with you on the next raid," Christina said tautly.

"I already told you the answer was no."

"It wasn't a question."

"No, it wasn't a question, it was a joke. Only it's not very funny, is it?"

Christina made a soft, laughing sound that came from her throat. "Not this time," she said. "Not this time."

Cole had no idea what Christina meant, and he wasn't going to ask her. He wanted to tell her that they weren't invincible, that they'd been incredibly lucky so far, that her anger and desire for revenge were a profound liability. He also wanted to hurt her by telling her that he had to trust her to fight with her at his side, but he told himself he didn't have the energy to finish that argument.

Going with him on a raid of the Webb payroll? It was laughably absurd. But Cole wasn't laughing . . . and neither was Christina.

"I do all right on my own," Cole said, turning his concentration back to cleaning his pistol. He refused to look up at Christina. "In fact, I probably do *better* on my own."

"You told me yourself there were times when you needed someone to watch your back. That's why you had Hans and the others with you." Christina stepped closer to Cole, close enough so that he could not help but see her raggedy slippers as he cleaned his gun. "Or were you lying about that, too?" She took a deep breath. "Your words aren't enough anymore, Cole. You lost my blind loyalty. We've grown beyond that. I see you for who you are, and who you aren't."

"You distrust everything I say now. If I told you the sun was going to rise in the east tomorrow and set in the west, you'd say I was lying."

"Well, I haven't exactly got a monopoly on suspicion, have I?"

Cole raised his face. He looked into Christina's eyes. Despite his best intentions, his gaze drifted down to her full bosom. The dress was one of his favorites, though it was torn and dirty. The black décolletage made Christina's full breast appear even more creamy and inviting.

He lowered his face, ashamed of himself for his thoughts, angry that Christina could ignite his masculine senses under any and all circumstances. He just couldn't look at Christina and not be affected by her beauty, not remember the times they had shared in and out of the bedroom, not think about their teasing little games and how they made loving each other a spiritual experience at times and almost giddy, childlike fun at other times. They had been able to make loving a game they both always won. But now the game they were playing had the rules set by Zachary.

"You've never even shot a gun," Cole said, breaking the silence, wishing Christina would go to the other side of the room so that he couldn't feel her enticing, sensuous closeness.

"You could teach me." Christina smiled, but there was a slightly malicious quality to it. "You've taught me many things. Why not add shooting to it?"

Sitting cross-legged on the floor of the line shack, Cole set his holster aside and looked around the room. This was one of several hideouts he had scattered around the perimeter of Enderton in the Dakota Territory where he had hidden clothes, guns, ammunition, and money. It was his insurance against getting caught completely defenseless.

"It's going to be dangerous, Christina. Haven't you seen enough danger and bloodshed already?"

"I have the right to fight against the Webbs, too," she repeated.

Very slowly, looking up at Christina, Cole reached into the breast pocket of his black shirt. What he had to show her, if his suspicions were correct, would prove to Christina once and for all how deadly this particular game was. It wasn't a game to be dabbled in by amateurs. Maybe it would prove to Christina that she should leave the fighting to men.

"Recognize this?" Cole asked, opening his palm to show Christina the pipe tool. "I found it in Zachary's bedroom."

The blood drained from Christina's face. Her lips trembled softly. Cole waited for the tears to come, but they never did.

"I thought as much. It was your father's, right?"

Christina nodded her head. She cleared her throat and said softly, "May I have it, please?"

Cole handed the pipe tool to Christina. He hated himself for hurting her, even though he knew it was best for her. Now she had to realize that goodness and kindness didn't count for anything against the Webbs. Kind-hearted people were killed off early. The only way to fight viciousness was with matching viciousness.

"We're about fifty miles south and west of Fargo," Cole explained quietly. "About fifty miles south and east of Enderton. I can ride with you to Lamoure, if you want. I haven't got much money, but you can have it all. We'll put you on a train and get you out of here. It'll be best for everyone."

Christina walked away from Cole. She stared at the pipe tool in her hands, remembering the countless times she'd watched her father use it. She raised it to her nose and could still smell, very faintly, tobacco on it. She felt the tears begin to form.

"No, I'm not running away," Christina said, her back to Cole."If you don't help me, I'll do it alone." She turned slowly. Cole had never seen such an expression on her face. "This isn't a choice for you to make. The choice is mine, Cole. Now *I've* got my duty, too. I won't let anyone take that away from me . . . not even you." She paused and took a breath. "Especially you. Don't you think I loved my father as much as you loved yours?"

Cole closed his eyes and nodded his head. His plan had backfired. Now Christina would never leave. A part of Cole was overjoyed that she would stay with him, but he was also afraid for her safety.

Still . . . just maybe, with time . . . Cole would forget about what Christina had had to do when she spent her days and nights with Zachary Webb. The thought of Zachary and Christina together brought physical pain to Cole. And maybe, on some fine day, Christina would look at Cole and not wonder if he had been with another woman.

"Okay," Cole replied in a whisper that rasped through the darkened shack. "If that's the way it's got to be, I'll accept it."

"Good. We'd better get some sleep. It's going to be a long day tomorrow."

Christina went to the thin mattress and stretched out on her stomach. She turned her face away from Cole, who sat on his own threadbare mattress on the other side of the room.

Cole shifted to his back and stared at the dark roof above them. The last time he had left Christina alone, she ended up Zachary Webb's captive. Perhaps it was best that she stay with him, he thought.

Or, more likely, I'm just being weak and selfish because I want her close to me.

There were times when Cole wished he could just stop thinking.

Cole rolled onto his side so that he could look at Christina as she slept. He saw, in profile, the swell of her breasts, rising and falling as she breathed. He felt guilty for allowing Christina to stay with him, but he didn't care.

He knew he'd pay any price to keep her at his side.

Christina felt she should be sad, but, strangely enough, she wasn't. Cole had left early in the morning, saying he wanted to check the area surrounding the line shack. He'd had enough surprises. He didn't want any more.

During her time alone, Christina had tidied up the shack, bathed, and washed her undergarments. She had thought of washing her gown, then decided against it. The gown was ruined, its delicate fabric not made to withstand the trauma that Christina had put it through in the last four days. Washing could only make it worse.

It pleased Christina that she had learned to think like Cole had always said she should. Her father had been murdered by Zachary Webb. It was, therefore, her duty to see that the guilty man was punished. She would not go off after Zachary in a flurry of rage—that would accomplish nothing of lasting significance and might likely cause her to be under Zachary Webb's control once again.

This time, Christina would write the rules of the game and dictate how it was to be played. She would choose when and where she would strike out against Zachary and Nicholas. She would cut the tentacles of their criminal enterprise. And when they had been weakened, and she was strong, she would deliver the telling blow, thrusting a knife into the very heart of their evil empire.

To Christina, it was all just as simple as that.

She snapped her camisole in the breeze, removing as much water from it as possible before hanging it on a tree limb. The sun was warm against her bare legs.

It's like I'm setting up house with Cole again, Christina thought. *Only this time it's not in an expensive apartment but in an abandoned shack.*

Only a few months earlier, the very thought of Christina even setting foot in a house that had a dirt floor would have disgusted her. Though she had never had great wealth, Christina had always lived a financially comfortable life, and whenever she was without the accoutrements of creature comforts, she had gotten angry. But that was a different Christina. Now, the dirt-floor shack was just fine. It felt safe. It was a feeling she had not known much of in the past weeks.

The drumming sound of hooves beating against thick grass drew Christina's attention. She turned quickly toward the sound, raising a hand to shield her eyes from the sun. The rider was dressed all in black, and Christina breathed a sigh of relief.

Cole rode his horse between the trees, winding his way through the thick foliage. When he spied Christina, he reined his mount to a stop. For several weighty seconds, he looked at Christina, gazing at her as though she must surely be a beautiful mirage for his thirsty eyes and hungry heart.

His red-and-black-checked flannel shirt was all she wore. Raising a hand to block the sun from her eyes caused the shirttails to ride high on the left side, exposing more of her firm, creamy, tapered thigh.

Christina could practically feel the heat of Cole's desire, even from twenty yards. Her first thought was that she should go immediately to the shack and put on her dress, but it was dirty and soiled and she was fresh from her bath.

What difference does it make? Christina thought angrily. *He's seen me before. And Cole may want me, but he considers me damaged goods, so he won't touch me.*

Cole walked his horse closer to Christina, and she felt a small amount of satisfaction in knowing that she was disturbing him with her scant attire. She had a strong sense of modesty, but she would fight against the natural inclinations if it would draw a response—*any* response—from Cole.

"I must say, you look much better in my shirt than I do." Cole swung a long, lean leg over the back of the tired old mare and dismounted beside Christina. "Much better, in fact."

268

"Uncharacteristic modesty, coming from you."

Cole ignored the bait. Despite the comment, Christina's disposition seemed as sunny as the day. And though it was nice to see her attitude had improved, it wasn't that making his pulse throb powerfully and his mouth feel dry.

"Is everything all right?" Christina walked beside Cole, heading for the shack. With the grass beneath her bare feet, she felt like a child again . . . almost.

"Yes." Cole cleared his throat and tried to keep from looking at Christina. He might just as well have tried to keep the sun from shining. "I made a complete circle. There's no one around for a couple miles."

Cole saw the pantalets and camisole hanging from the tree limb. His chest felt tight and it took all his strength of will to keep from taking Christina into his arms right then and there.

He had gone too long without a woman. Chastity was not something Cole accepted gladly or willingly. Refusing Loretta was easy; ignoring his desire for the vivacious, voluptuous woman beside him was impossible.

Don't rush her, an inner voice warned. *After being with Zachary, the thought of being touched by a man would probably disgust her. And I can't really blame her for thinking that way, either. If anyone has the right and reason to hate men, she does.*

"Do you have any ideas of when we'll begin?" Christina waited until Cole tied the mare's reins to the T-post beside the shack before she opened the rickety door and stepped inside.

Cole watched the tails of his shirt flick inward, slapping against the backs of Christina's smooth thighs with every step. He watched with hungry eyes the sway of her hips and the undulation of her buttocks. She seemed utterly oblivious of the way she was dressed, and Cole was determined to act as though nothing was unusual in it.

He had won Christina's love once, and if he was ever to have it back, he would have to go slow. He would have to wait until the horror of Zachary Webb's vile touch had left

269

Christina's soul . . . if it ever would. Cole felt certain that if he even allowed Christina to see that he still desired her, still hungered for her caresses, she would be repulsed by him. She had to learn to trust Cole all over again, and he wanted to make that as easy as possible.

"Well?" Christina asked again when Cole didn't answer. "Leave the door open, please. It's so dank and dark in here with the door closed."

Cole walked over to his mattress and sat down on it, folding his long legs beneath him. When Christina crossed the room, he watched the firm rise and fall of her breasts beneath the shirt. Cole felt his body reacting to what his eyes caressed. He turned his gaze away from her. Being this close to her, dressed the way she was, was torture to him. Almost a month of celibacy had put his nerves on edge and strung him tight as a bowstring. With the single most provocative woman he'd ever known so close to him, looking so painfully erotic, Cole felt as nervous as a teenager.

"Well?" Christina repeated, demanding an answer.

"I thought we might start with a free herd payroll. It's not a big one, but it'll give us some money to work with, and it shouldn't be too heavily guarded." Cole fidgeted on the floor. He inspected his fingernails, fighting against his body as the hunger he had for Christina burned through him. "Webb's got a herd of prime Herefords not too far from here. It takes five men or so to keep the herd in order. Once a month the payroll comes in. I figured we'd hit that, hide low for a couple days until Webb sends a replacement payroll, then take that one, too."

Christina issued a throaty chuckle. The sound of it, of her good humor and high spirits, was music to Cole's ears, more pleasing than any symphony or opera he'd taken Christina to in St. Paul.

"That should rile Nicholas. Stealing the same payroll twice?" Christina's voice became slightly deeper, concern showing for innocent cowpunchers, as she asked, "You're sure they'll send a second payroll?"

"Nicholas will have to. If he doesn't, he has no guarantee the men won't up and leave. He's got a lot invested in that herd. By comparison, the payroll is nothing."

"You're sure?"

"Positive."

Christina could see the tension in Cole. She allowed herself a small smile, but only because he wasn't looking at her and wouldn't see it.

"Are you always so positive of yourself, Mr. Jurrell?"

Cole looked up. It was a mistake. When he saw Christina — wearing nothing more than the shirt and a family heirloom locket — his senses began a riotous assault on his self-control.

"Not always," he replied tensely, feeling himself falling under Christina's allure. He got to his feet, keeping his gaze away from Christina. "I've got to leave for a little while. You'll find a spare pair of denim trousers in my bedroll. Try them on. They'll be better suited for what you need than your dress."

Cole untied his mare and leaped onto her back. He wheeled the horse around and kicked her with his moccasin-shod heels. He couldn't be close to Christina a moment longer. Not if he was going to keep his hands to himself, not if he was going to keep what little was left of his sanity.

Chapter 26

If Cole had his druthers, he would have changed just about everything. He would have Christina tucked away in a safe spot where he knew she wouldn't get hurt. He would have someone like Jackie or Hans riding with him—a man he knew he could trust, and who had plenty of experience with guns. He would have spent a day, or perhaps two, checking the comings and goings of the intended victims. And he would have planned at least three escape routes. Also, the booty for the raid would be more than the hundred or so dollars he'd net on this payroll heist.

But Cole didn't have his druthers. Christina was sitting behind him on the mare, pretending that she wasn't scared. She had only fired the rusted Spencer less than twenty times, for the gun was corroded beyond repair, and Cole didn't trust it. And he didn't have time to check the area out because the payroll was coming in now and he had less than three dollars cash in his pocket. Poverty takes away a man's alternatives.

They were looking down on a shallow valley of wild grass. Here in the Red River Valley, the grass grew thick and high. Perfect for fattening cattle and virtually free for the taking. Nicholas Webb had control of the land, and he wasn't about to relinquish it to anyone.

"There it is," Cole said, reining in the mare.

Christina looked over Cole's shoulder at a line shack,

not unlike the one they had left that morning. It wasn't much — an unpainted wooden structure with a slanted roof, made as cheaply as possible and probably drafty.

Smoke from a cooking stove drifted from the chimney in a lazy spiral. Tied to the hitching post outside the shack were three horses. The shack had the aura of dissoluteness and neglect.

"You're sure the payroll will be coming?" Christina asked quietly.

"Yes."

Cole looked at the shack, some four hundred yards off, but his mind was not concentrating on what problems lay ahead of him. What sat behind him toyed and teased with Cole's male senses. He felt the fullness of Christina's breasts against his back, and the warmth and firmness of their touch conjured up memories that hit him forcefully.

"Want to get down?" Cole asked, needing to put distance between himself and Christina if he was ever going to put all his intellectual energies on the raid. Cole twisted in the saddle, taking Christina's arm just above the elbow to help her down. "We'll give the ol' girl a breather."

Christina's blue eyes twinkled mischievously. "I hope you're talking about the horse," she said, laughter in her tone.

Cole chuckled softly and replied, "I am."

This is all wrong, Cole thought. *This isn't a time for making jokes. It isn't a time for romantic fantasies.*

In all the raids he'd masterminded and participated in, he had never once felt anything other than anxious prior to the theft. It used to be Bobby who Cole had to keep in line. Now it was Christina who was making light of the situation, failing to see the potential dangers involved in even the simplest operation. And, worst of all, Cole was smiling right along with her. He couldn't see her dazzling, joyous smile without being strongly and happily affected by it.

He helped Christina to the ground, then dismounted. The mare, a sorry replacement for his beloved Black Jack, was as much horse as Cole had been able to afford. If they were chased after the raid, Cole and Christina would be caught for sure. The old mare was just biding her time. She'd run as much as she was going to in her life, and she did not like having to carry the weight of two riders, even if one of them weighed barely over a hundred pounds.

"Let's go over it one more time," Cole said, taking a couple of steps deeper into the trees on the leeward side of the ridge. "What's your first move going to be?"

A soft breeze blew directly into Cole's face. The cowboy's horses would catch no scent of approaching riders. In the background, he heard Christina's voice as she recited her well-rehearsed moves.

Cole knew Christina had memorized her role in the robbery. He liked hearing her voice, and keeping her talking about what they were about to do prevented any chance of dealing with the secondary problem—the chasm of doubt and guilt that now kept them distanced emotionally.

"Beautiful," Cole said when Christina stopped speaking. "Do it just like that and we should still be alive tomorrow morning."

Christina hadn't complained that Cole had made her recite the same thing many times. In fact, she hadn't complained about anything—not even about her monumentally inappropriate shoes. Cole was certain Christina's feet were hurting. What had changed inside Christina that now made her smile through pain? What kept her from complaining when she had every right in the world to?

Christina sat at the base of a tree. Cole looked at her out of the corner of his eyes. How could any woman, wearing man's denim trousers that were tight in the rump and loose at the waist and a flannel shirt that was several sizes too large for her, look so ravishing?

Cole tried to neuter his feeling for Christina by telling himself that no woman could possibly look sexy wearing men's clothing. Wearing trousers!

The only thing impossible for Christina, though, was

her inability to hide her opulent curves. Cole almost laughed at his own frivolity. Christina would be sexy in a flour sack.

A free herd is separated from the main herd to fatten the cattle up before selling them at the stockyards. A grassy area, where the cattle can eat without competition for food, is found. Then men are assigned to watch over the herd.

The men who lord over free herds live for only two things: payday, which comes once a month and the chance to go to the nearest saloon, which happens shortly after payday.

It is a hard, miserable existence. The cowboys work seven days a week, with time off only for eating and sleeping. Since a free herd is almost always located in some godforsaken, out of the way place, there isn't any entertainment to be found. There are few distractions to the work.

Whatever a man's moral character prior to riding over a free herd, it degenerates quickly to base-level existence. Personal grooming is forgotten, for there isn't anyone worth gussying up for. Eating is what a man does when he's hungry, not out of any great pleasure for the food, since it consists of canned beans, whatever game happens to get shot during the day, and beef.

So the men live for their thirty dollars a month. As payday approaches, they plan for their trip to the closest saloon where the working girls are friendly, willing, and not too expensive for the cowboy's budgets.

The men, as payday approaches, begin telling stories about this bargirl and that one. The stories have all been told before, and it doesn't matter that they are complete fabrications. None of the other cowboys believe the stories anyway. What matters is that the men know they will soon have money, and working girls will be available to spend that money on.

After a week of talking about women, and having seen nothing but men for a month, the free herd cattlemen—unwashed, unshaven, and unwholesome in body and spirit—are primed and ready for fun. When they saw the blond woman, dressed in man's clothes and carrying a rifle, they opened the door to the line shack and let her in. For anyone else, guns would have been drawn and the intruder chased away or buried in an unmarked grave.

Christina had unbuttoned the shirt enough to show a glimpse of her cleavage, giving an enticing hint of what lay beneath the faded flannel. She could have waved a red flag and drawn a similar reaction from a three-year-old bull as from the three cattlemen in the shack.

The lust flashed in their eyes, foul and lethal. It took only a glance for Christina to know that the men would never let her out of the shack of their own free will.

The old and rusted Spencer in Christina's hands came up, as if by its own accord. Christina's soft blue eyes took on a hard-edged quality that a few months earlier they never could have had.

"Nobody moves and nobody'll get hurt!" Christina snapped. She waved the rifle about, letting the three men know she meant business. "You haven't got anything worth dying for."

Cole entered the shack a moment later, gun in hand. He almost smiled when he saw Christina's stance and the look on her face. The Spencer, he knew, was barely operational. And Christina was just as likely to shoot him as anyone else in the shack. But the cowboys didn't know that, and that's what Cole had been counting on.

"Where's the payroll?" Cole demanded, pointing his revolver at the nearest man.

"There ain't one," the cattleman replied. His eyes went from Cole down to the revolver pointed at his chest, then over to Christina. "It ain't come yet. Honest."

"The rider got here an hour ago!" Christina said like a shot, her voice brittle with tension. "We just want the money, nothing else!"

276

"The others will be comin' in soon, comin' at sundown," the cowboy said, his courage still holding up. "If I were you two, I'd hightail it outta here whilst I could."

Cole stepped closer to the man. He pointed his Colt at the tip of the man's nose. "Don't lie to me. You're working for Webb and we both know how the system works. The other men won't be back until tomorrow morning. That's when you divvy up the money. Now where is the payroll?"

Christina saw the man's throat bob. When he looked at her, the anger that burned from his eyes was undisguised and vile. Given half a chance, he would force himself upon her, and she knew it. That knowledge made it easier for Christina to steal from these men who she believed hadn't done anything to her.

"His name is Cole Jurrell," Christina said, quietly but with authority. "I'm Christina Sands. If you've heard of us, you know what we've done."

"Lord A'mighty!" exclaimed the cowboy. He looked at Christina with fear now showing in his eyes instead of anger. "You're the filly that back-shot Mr. Webb's legal man!"

Christina looked at the man. With her eyes she let him think that she had, in fact, murdered Richard O'Banion.

"It's in the strongbox under the floorboards," the cowboy said, his quivering voice betraying the emotions going through him.

"Get it!" Christina barked, keeping the rusted Spencer trained on the man's colleagues.

Several of the floorboards were loose. The man quickly withdrew the strongbox. To Cole's surprise, the box was not locked. Inside was ninety dollars. Cole pocketed the money.

"Now let's have your shares," Cole said. He turned eyes as cold and deathly as hell itself on the cowboys. "Don't hold out. You know who I am and what I've done."

The cowboy looked at the man sitting beside him. He shrugged his shoulders. "Better give it to him," he said. "I heard Cole Jurrell shot his pappy. Any man mean enough to kill his pappy is mean enough to kill fer money."

Another ninety dollars was produced. Cole stuffed the paper bills into his pocket. Christina's quick thinking worked. By telling these degenerates who she was, she had ensured total cooperation.

"Anybody tries to follow us finds the end of the trail," Cole warned, using the age-old adage for the death of a cowboy.

The men were made to kneel on the floor, with Christina standing watch over them. Cole saddled a gelding in record time, freed the other horses, then returned for Christina. Before leaving, he took all the firearms he could find.

"Hey, mister!"

Cole stopped at the door and looked at the cowboy.

"Nicholas Webb's gonna kill you fer sure fer this," the cowboy said.

"Maybe . . . and maybe I'll kill Webb," Cole replied.

Chapter 27

"Did you see that?" shouted Christina, prancing and leaping around Cole with childlike joy. "Those creeps! They never would have let me out of there! And then I put the gun on them and not a one had anything to say!"

Cole wanted to tell Christina to settle down, but he didn't. He remembered vividly his own tingling excitement after his first raid against Nicholas Webb's men. The thrill of having walked on the edge, of having accomplished something daring and worthwhile without hurting any innocent people, was a thrill that boggled the senses.

Besides, Christina was happy now. And he wasn't going to be the one to push her pleasure away.

"We stole Nicholas's money, we stole his horses, we even stole guns from him! He's going to go right out of his mind!"

Christina pranced around as Cole began building a campfire. The excitement flowing through her made her feel carefree and light-headed, like she had the evening Cole introduced her to a full-bodied Italian burgundy wine that had gone straight to her head.

"Did you see me, Cole?"

Cole scratched a match and put it to the dried twigs he'd assembled. "Yes," he said, smiling at Christina, his attention diverted between what had to be done and the young woman whose obvious happiness gave him a personal sense of satisfaction. "I saw everything you did. You were perfect."

"Didn't I tell you I would be a good student?" Christina did a little pirouette with her head tilted back, letting her long blond hair cascade around her shoulders. "And the best part of it all is that I fought back! *I . . . fought . . . back!*"

Christina moved over to Cole. She got down on one knee so that she could look into his face as the campfire between them slowly came to life. Shadows and light highlighted the handsome planes of Cole's face.

"I fought back, Cole. For the first time in my life, I fought back." Her tone was now quietly serious. Though her exuberance had vanished, it was replaced with a deep, personal sense of accomplishment that Cole did not miss. "After all the things that have been done to me, all the things I've been put through, I finally fought back. Can you see what that means to me?"

Christina was smiling as she looked into Cole's eyes. She watched his gaze move downward, drifting, as it had in happier days, to her bosom. She had unfastened two buttons of the shirt prior to stepping into the line shack, and somewhere during the wild ride through the night after the raid, another button had come unfastened. The lacy trim of the camisole he had bought for her was visible, peeking between the coarse material of the man-cut shirt.

Cole turned his face away from Christina. She watched as he squeezed his eyes tightly shut for a moment.

"Does it bother you that much to look at me? Am I that ugly to you now? Zachary never touched me."

Christina looked down at her bosom, then up to Cole's face. She remembered the times in Cole's apartment when she'd seen desire in his eyes as he looked at her. But that was before she had been kidnapped by Zachary. Apparently, she was a different woman now in Cole's judgment. Perhaps she *was* different, but not in the way he thought. Suddenly angry, Christina buttoned the shirt up to her throat.

"Better?" she asked quietly. She felt like something inside her was slowly dying, being choked to death by forces that were heartless and beyond her control.

Cole took his hat off. He pushed his fingers through his hair.

"It's not like that, Christina. It's not like that at all." Cole felt the tightness in his chest, and the proximity of Christina. He was not a man comfortable with words that came from the heart. "You must know how beautiful you are—"

"How will I know if you won't tell me?" Christina bit her lip, instantly regretting her words.

"Christina, never in my life have I wanted a woman as much as . . . no woman has ever made me so crazy as you do."

As Cole spoke, Christina got to her feet. She walked several steps and turned slowly to face Cole again.

"Those aren't exactly the smooth lovewords I heard form you before," she said drily. "Crazy? That's hardly the emotion a woman wants to inspire."

Yes it is! Christina thought. *I don't want Cole to think about anyone or anything but me! I want him crazy about me.*

Cole poked at the fire with a stick, adding larger branches to the flames. He couldn't look at Christina. It was impossible to look at her and still say the things that she had the right to hear.

"I love looking at you," Cole said, barely above a whisper. "I just didn't want to hurt you, that's all. I thought that after—" he didn't have to say "Zachary" for Christina to know what he meant "—that you wouldn't want to . . . that the thought of being touched by a man, any man, would make you feel so . . . ."

"You wonderful idiot," Christina whispered. Warm tears of happiness glistened on her lashes. "Even if Zachary had raped me, do you really think that would change the way I feel about you? Don't you understand? He has no power over you and me. Our love for each other

281

is the one thing we have that nobody—not Nicholas or Zachary or anybody else— can steal from us." In a trembling whisper, Christina said, "You're not Zachary."

Cole stared at the flames that licked up from the campfire into the night sky. Christina looked at Cole and thought, *He hurt me by trying to protect me. Such a foolish man to fall in love with . . . but I love him for his foolishness.*

Christina pulled the overlong flannel shirttails out of the denim slacks. Working from the bottom to the top, she began to unbutton the shirt. Her eyes never left Cole, and he never looked away from the flames that seemed to have mesmerized him.

"Cole . . . Cole, I want you to look at me."

Cole raised his face. Shock registered in his gray eyes at first, then Christina saw a fire in them that put the campfire to shame.

She unbottoned the shirt slowly. When she was finished, she shrugged her shoulders and the garment filtered down her arms, falling to the ground behind her.

"I like the way I feel inside . . . when you look at me like that," Christina whispered. "Haven't we been apart too long?" She leaned forward to take off her slippers. Her breast tumbled forward, straining inside the lacy bodice of her light camisole. When her shoes were removed, Christina straightened. "It's different when you look at me," she continued, pulling loose the rope that served as a belt. "When Zachary looked at me . . . or those men in the line shack . . . I felt dirty because I knew men like that wanted me. But when you look at me . . . when I see how much you want me just by looking in your eyes, it makes me feel pretty. I feel desired and loved, not just lusted after."

Christina's fingers slowly flicked open the buttons of the denim slacks. Cole's eyes never left the slender-fingered hands as the brass buttons came undone.

"Do you see the difference, Cole? Do you understand?"

Christina doubted that Cole did fully understand. Perhaps he would someday, perhaps not. Maybe it was impossible for a man to truly understand such a thing. But Christina knew the difference, and that was the important thing.

She pushed the slacks past the rounded curves of her hips, working the fabric down her legs. Christina was well aware of the fact that by bending directly forward, she allowed Cole to see into her camisole. She could feel the heat of his gaze caressing her responsive flesh covetously, possessively. When she stepped out of the slacks, dressed now only in pantalets and camisole, the internal turmoil she saw on Cole's face made her shiver with pleasure and anticipation.

"I'm the same woman, Cole. The same woman I've always been."

"No, you're not," Cole said, his voice rasping, the timbre hoarse with tension. "You're more than the woman you were." His eyes sought all the delicious curves of the scantily clad woman. His gaze upon her was physical, tactile in its force. "You're not the frightened, naive girl I first met. You're strong now, Christina. Stronger that I ever imagined you could be."

Christina was both thrilled at Cole's obvious approval of her and a bit self-conscious at her own boldness. Did Cole like a woman to be as forward as she was being now? Was it the kind of thing he liked in a woman he would spend the rest of his life with, or just in a woman that he hungered for sexually?

Christina crossed an arm over the bosom, hiding her breasts from Cole's heated gaze. She turned her face aside, her courage slipping through her fingers like water.

"Don't hide yourself," Cole said.

He took a step toward Christina, then stopped. His next step, he knew, would put him over the edge. His strength of will—the power to control himself and his own emotions—was what Cole took the most personal pride in. He took another step toward Christina, and that strength left him in a rush of emotions so fiery he felt as though his skin would burn the clothes from his body.

283

"I need you!" Cole gasped, rushing to Christina, wrapping her in the tight circle of his arms. "I need you so much!"

Christina clung to Cole, tilting her head back to receive his kiss. The kiss was fiercely passionate, all the fiery hunger of their month-long separation exploding in a crescendo of need and desire that washed over them in a floodtide of ache and want.

"I need you," Christina whispered.

Her legs were weak as she kissed Cole, nibbling at this lips. It wasn't until she felt the grass, cool and prickly, against her bare knees that she realized she had knelt together with Cole.

Their bodies, one hard and lean, the other softly feminine and voluptuous, were pressed together from knees to mouth. Christina shivered, feasting on Cole's lips, when his hand moved from the small of her back to cup the swell of her buttocks. He pulled her tighter against his body. Christina felt the hardness of his passion pressing against her. She sighed, knowing the love and pleasure this man could give her, secure at last that whatever doubts Cole had of his feelings for her had been cast aside.

"Every night I dreamed of you," Cole whispered, his breath warm against Christina's ear. His strong hands squeezed Christina while her hand explored the leonine muscles in his arms, back, and shoulders. "Every night away from you was agony!"

"You're with me now, Cole." Christina held his face between her palms, looking into his eyes. "Be with me tonight," she said quietly. "Be with me every night."

There, beneath the stars with the campfire warm against their naked bodies, they made love slowly, gently. They made love with their hearts as much as their bodies. And when at last ecstasy claimed them, it gave them a passion and pleasure that neither had experienced before.

Christina could not sleep. Her head was spinning and

an excitement—like that of a child on Christmas Eve—kept her from any serious consideration of sleep.

Christina tilted her head far back on her shoulders as she sat cross-legged and naked on the blanket. She had Cole's jacket draped over her shoulders. She looked at the stars and they winked slyly at her, co-conspirators in her plot to regain her happiness.

Her body tingled all over in the delicious afterglow of lovemaking. Cole and Christina had made love tenderly the first time. The second time they were very nearly savage. Even after Cole had curled up on the blanket and fallen soundly asleep, Christina felt her whole system charging with renewed vitality.

She had Cole back! In her arms and in her life! Making beautiful love to her!

After a moment of thought, Christina realized that she had more than just Cole back in her life. She had, in fact, something that she'd never had before. For the first time in her entire life, Christina had *herself.* She felt in control of her own destiny. She was taking an active role in the struggle against the men who had killed her father and destroyed the way of life she had known and loved.

She was stronger now, more resilient and confident than ever before in her life. To no small extent, Christina owed a debt to Cole Jurrell for the woman she had become. She also owed Nicholas and Zachary Webb, and if she was lucky and they were very *un*lucky, the father and son would get what they deserved.

Closing her eyes, Christina felt a breeze playing over her naked body, fluffing the golden hair about her shoulders. *Cole loves my hair,* Christina thought. *He tells me so when we make love.*

She looked over at Cole. He was sleeping on his back, one knee raised, a forearm beneath his head. His right hand was curled around the butt of his Colt, disturbing the idyllic image. Christina frowned and wondered if their love would be as intense, as fulfilling and exciting, if they had the chance to lead a normal life together.

Of course it would! Our life was normal when we lived together in Cole's apartment, she thought.

But just as quickly she concluded, *No, that wasn't a normal life. His friends called him John Colter, and he only introduced me as Christina. Nobody asked for a last name. Nobody asks many questions of the mistress. That's not a normal life.*

Christina pushed such thoughts from her mind. Now was not the time to ponder what-might-have-been's or even what-will-be's. She was with Cole, the man who loved her even if he couldn't say so, and she was fighting back against the Webbs. She was her own woman, and she was choosing to share herself, her heart, and her life with Cole. That was enough for Christina.

She began to feel a little chilled and crawled over until she was beside Cole. He tensed for a second, then relaxed when he realized it was Christina.

"Someday you won't have to sleep with one eye open," whispered Christina.

She pulled the blanket over herself as Cole's arm looped comfortably around her shoulders. Christina issued a soft, satisfied sigh as her flesh, cooled in the evening air, was warmed by Cole's.

"Let me sleep late in the morning," Christina murmured, a smile toying with her sensuous mouth.

Someday we will *have a normal life together!*

For Christina, it was a vow, not just a dream.

"Christina Sands, you are positively the most immoral young woman I have ever met in my entire life," Cole said, shaking his head.

"I'm just the student," Christina taunted, keeping her distance from Cole. She did not have a stitch of clothing on. Christina was smiling. Cole was flustered, holding her flannel shirt in one hand, her denim slacks in the other. "If I am immoral, the blame belongs at the feet of the teacher, not the student!"

Cole made a growling sound of frustration and tossed the clothes to the ground. He was trying very hard to look angry with Christina, but was not succeeding. Anger was not the emotion uppermost in his mind when he could watch Christina's breasts sway, could see the fluidity and athletic grace of her unrehearsed dance, was witness to the lean, tapered length of her legs, the firm roundness of her behind, the sun-catching spray of her golden hair.

"Listen to me now," Cole said through clenched teeth, struggling to ignore the unsettling image that Christina presented him, trying to sound authoritative. He was having an impossible time making Christina see the obvious. "Last night we stole a payroll from six very violent men. We've made them very angry. When Nicholas Webb finds out what we've done, he's going to be very angry, too. Wouldn't it be best if we stayed on the move? Doesn't that make just a wee bit of sense to you?"

Christina stopped her dancing for a moment, putting on a face of stern concentration. She crossed her left arm over her breasts, cupping her right elbow in the upturned palm. She placed her chin in the cup of her right hand, looking at Cole with blue eyes that, had she been dressed, indicated she was mulling over some vital business advice.

"You know, that does make a great deal of sense," Christina said, nodding her head approvingly. Her tone was solemn as a judge. "However, we also have the opportunity here, I believe, to find out whether the magic that occurred last night was a one-time phenomenon, like a shooting star, or whether we are capable of sustaining such prolonged pleasure-making."

Cole's eyebrows raised for a moment, a sly smile pulling at the right side of his mouth. "Pleasure-making? Christina, I've heard it called a lot of different things before, but never pleasure-making."

"Well, that's what I want to call it." Christina put her hands on the curve of her hips. She had gone so long without being able to draw any kind of reaction from Cole that she now took great delight in showing him what his

287

ridiculous pride and wrongly placed concern had kept him from. "Besides, you promised to show me how to shoot one of those pistols. I won't go anywhere until you show me. A promise is a promise." Christina pouted, and though Cole wanted to kiss that pout from her lips, he just rolled his eyes toward the sky.

Christina, taking exquisite delight in taunting, teasing, and tormenting Cole, followed him to where they had piled the weapons they'd stolen from Webb's cowhands.

"You can use this one," Cole said, grabbing one of the holsters with a pistol in it. "It's got the longest barrel. You just might be able to hit something with it. Now when you fire it, the first thing you've got to do is—"

"Let me put it on."

Cole clenched his teeth. Christina doubted he was really getting angry with her, but he was trying hard to. When he turned toward her, she gave him her most innocent look. Cole's eyes, however, could not help but stray downward to linger appreciatively on the peaked mounds of her breasts.

Christina felt little tingles go through her, but she was determined to ignore them. At least for a while longer. She was enjoying herself too much now to change the rules of the game.

"If you're going to wear the holster, I suggest you put your pants on first," Cole said, holding only tenuous control over himself and none over Christina.

It pleased Christina to see Cole's aloofness, that self-control he was so damnably proud of, get shredded to bits right before her eyes.

"If I have to." Christina sounded like a child who had just been told by her parents that it was past her bedtime and she absolutely had to go to bed. "But they're your pants, not mine."

"I don't give a damn whose pants you put on! Just put somebody's pants on, *please!*"

Christina put on the denim slacks and returned to Cole in a slow walk, but she had not, as Cole had undoubtedly wanted, put on the camisole and shirt. No matter how hard Cole tried, he couldn't keep from looking at Christina or keep his amorous thoughts from showing in his angry gray eyes.

She took the revolver and holster from Cole. When she put the holster around her hips, the weight of the weapon tugged the holster down low on the right side.

"The belt's too big. You'll have to put a hole in it so I can cinch it tighter," Christina said.

Cole's eyes narrowed. He pulled the knife from its sheath at the small of his back. Christina wondered how long Cole could continue to put business above pleasure.

"Where do you want the hole?"

"Measure it for me . . . so that it'll have the right fit and everything."

Cole got down on his knees in front of Christina. He concentrated very hard *only* on the holster belt and the task at hand.

"Does this feel about right?" Cole asked, freeing the belt and pulling it further through the brass buckle. The holster simply was not made for a woman's narrow waist.

"That's about right," Christina whispered. "But first, would you look up at me?"

Cole raised his eyes slowly, over Christina's flat stomach and the white mounds of her breasts. He looked at her beautiful face and impish expression through the pale valley of her breasts and whispered, "Damn!"

Christina was laughing throatily when Cole pulled her to the ground. She never did get her first lesson in shooting before she rode off with Cole.

"What do we steal next?"

Cole sighed with exasperation. "Let's just concentrate on one thing at a time, shall we? Now hold the gun steady, with your left hand over your right."

Cole stepped up behind Christina. She had fired a dozen times so far. Judging from what she'd hit—which did not include the empty can of peaches he'd set up for her at the base of an oak tree—his only hope was that the sound of her shooting the revolver would scare away the enemy.

"Now keep both eyes open, just like I told you, concentrate on your target, then squeeze the trigger."

Cole watched as Christina fired the pistol again. Wood splinters flew a foot from the can. If she didn't have such a disappointed look on her face, and if she wasn't taking this with such dead seriousness, he would have said she couldn't hit the proverbial side of a barn when shooting from the inside.

"Damn," Christina hissed.

Cole inched up closer behind her, sliding his arms around to help her aim.

"Swearing like I do isn't going to make you shoot like I do," Cole chided. He felt the warmth of her body against his, felt her hair tickling his cheek. He thumbed back the hammer of the revolver. "Let me help you this time. Concentrate now. Point the gun like you'd point your finger, hold your breath for a second, then squeeze the trigger when you're ready."

This time Christina missed the can by only a couple of inches. She glowed with happiness. Looking over her shoulder, Cole peeked inside the red-and-black flannel shirt and saw the upper swells of her breasts, which he so loved to kiss and caress.

"Okay . . . concentrate," Cole said, his tone different now, his attention divided. "Think only about your target. Don't think about anything but the target."

She likes to tease, Cole thought. *It's my turn to do a little teasing!*

Christina fired again, coming even closer this time. Cole's hands slipped from Christina's, running up her forearms, then let his fingertips graze lightly over her breast, circling the nipples.

"Cole . . ."

"Concentrate," Cole replied. "You'll never learn to shoot until you can concentrate. Pull back the hammer and try again."

Christina's head rested back against Cole's shoulder for a moment. Then she righted herself and aimed down the barrel of the pistol. Cole's fingertips circled the taut crests briefly before he cupped the mounds and squeezed them firmly, drawing a sigh from Christina.

"Continue, Christina. It's the only way you'll ever learn."

"But, Cole . . . I can't . . ."

"Yes, you can. Now aim and shoot."

The pistol roared, but neither of them paid much attention to where the bullet went. Christina cocked the weapon one more time, trying desperately to ignore the fact that her shirt was being slowly and artfully unbottoned.

The gun bucked in Christina's hands, but her eyes were closed by this time. Strong fingers, gentle and knowing, slipped inside the bodice of her chemise.

"You are terrible," Christina whispered.

Chapter 28

"Three weeks! *Three weeks!*" Nicholas fumed. "For the last three weeks those two have stolen from me almost every day!" The thefts were a personal affront to Nicholas. Townspeople were saying Cole would never get caught. Nicholas waved a finger, taking in Zachary, Sheriff Bellows, and Deputy Miller. "I want it stopped, and I want it stopped now! Do you hear me? Now!"

"Try to take it easy," Zachary said, enjoying his father's fury, but also a little worried by it. "It's not going to do any good to lose your head."

Nicholas rushed around his desk. He stepped up to his seated son, jabbing a finger into Zachary's chest.

"You'll be the one losing your head if these raids don't stop," Nicholas hissed.

If they hadn't fully known of Nicholas's contempt for Zachary, Bellows and Miller knew at that moment that there wasn't a glimmer of love between father and son. They hated each other, and all a person had to do was see them glaring at each other to know the hatred was deep, intense, and lethal.

The air was heavy with unspoken insults and threats. Bellows and Miller wanted desperately to leave, but neither was willing to attract attention to himself by making the first move. The sheriff and deputy realized, better than anyone else in Enderton, that Nicholas Webb was above the law.

After long moments of silence, Nicholas's intense glare locked with his son's, the elder Webb turned away. He went to the window to survey his domain, as he often did in times of serenity or turmoil.

"Tell me everything they've done so far," Nicholas said, in control of himself once again.

Bellows and Miller looked at each other in a flurry of confusion. Zachary, seeing their fear, cleared his throat, then began speaking.

"They raided three different free herd line houses, and they took the payroll that was headed north."

"North?"

"For the men we've got watching the sheep up north. It's on that property near Canada you picked up late last year." Zachary was exaggerating the proximity to Canada.

"Yes, of course. I forgot about that."

"You shouldn't. The wool has proven very valuable."

"Yes, yes, of course. Go on."

Zachary spoke slowly, in an even tone that sounded eerily like Nicholas. But his mind was not on the words that passed between his lips. Nicholas forgetting about one of his businesses? Never in all the years that Zachary had helped his father run the family's various enterprises and interests had he ever known Nicholas to forget anything, least of all a company that had been picked up for a song and a dance, with just a little extralegal maneuvering.

He's losing control, thought Zachary with zealous delight. *Christina's made him completely forget what's important. I should have raped her when I had the chance. I have nothing to fear from this pathetic old man. He's searching for his youth in Christina, but he'll never find it. All he's going to find is a bullet from my gun!*

"You two, get out of here," Nicholas said suddenly, pointing a finger at Bellows and Miller.

Nicholas looked at Zachary, a feral glow in his eyes. Zachary sat quietly, cautious of a trap. Nicholas waited until he was alone in his study with his son before he spoke again.

"I've got an idea that I think just might bring Christina to me . . ."

Christina found it odd that she could, once she really put her mind to it, adopt an outlaw's ways. She now slept during the day to avoid being seen, and traveled only at night. She could eat cold food straight from a can. She could sleep on the ground with Cole at her side, and awoke to the slightest sound. She even learned to keep her Colt nearby, within easy reach.

But for some reason—some damnably inexplicable reason—Christina still couldn't shoot straight. She cussed and practiced and did everything the way Cole told her to. But she couldn't hit what she was aiming at if her life depended upon it . . . and Christina had a justifiable fear that her life *just might* depend on how well she used a six-shooter.

A cool breeze fluffed Christina's shimmering hair, which was combed straight back and held with a strip of cloth. She no longer wore her hair up in a delicate coiffure, as she had when she was a shopkeeper's daughter. An outlaw didn't have time for such finery. All the expensive, pretty dresses that Cole had bought for her were still in St. Paul. Now her sartorial splendor began and ended with three changes of underclothing, two shirts, and two pairs of denim slacks. The slacks, not tailored for a woman's figure, were snug in the hips and loose at the waist. Christina would have complained about the fit had it not drawn such a positive response from Cole the first time he saw her in the new clothes.

"I still don't understand why we want to be in there before the payroll money gets in," Christina whispered. She was belly-down on the ground beside Cole. It was a couple of hours before sunup. They were surveying the site of their next raid.

"We've been hitting Webb pretty hard lately," Cole explained. "We're no longer just a nuisance to him. We've got to be causing him a serious pain in the finances. Also, with so many men having to wait extra days for the money that is due them, morale among the men has got to be low."

"I understand all that. But why not take the money *before* they get it inside?"

"Because that's the way you and I have always done it. It's what they're expecting by now. We've never once touched the money after it arrives, except on that first free herd payroll. And that really wasn't enough to draw much — that kind of money is hardly going to draw Nicholas's attention." Cole glanced sideways at Christina. He had that serious look to him that he took on before they went into a dangerous situation. "As soon as they get inside, they're going to think it's all clear. You've seen how the security guards have doubled in number recently."

Actually, Christina had not noticed. She had no experience to draw on, except what she'd gotten in the past month raiding Webb payrolls with Cole.

"I see," Christina murmured, though she still was unsure of Cole's theory. She kept her reservations to herself. Cole was not a man who made mistakes — at least not when it came to stealing money from Nicholas Webb — and she doubted he was making one now.

They left their horses — Black Jack, having been retrieved from the livery in Fargo, and Daisy, a heavily muscled, nimble-footed mare Cole had purchased at the same time — deep in the trees where they would not be spotted.

The collection of buildings along the single street gave the appearance of a town that had sprung to life, then died without decaying. There were six buildings, three on either side of the single, rutted street. All were newly built and freshly painted. But this was not a small, friendly town where outsiders were welcome. This was Nicholas Webb's encampment, and he owned everything and everyone in it.

It was from here that Nicholas managed two large herds

of prime holstein stock, as well as a flock of sheep rumored to be the largest in the upper half of the United States. Not only were the sheep used for feed, but the wool, which was extremely thick in the cold climes, added additional income to the operation.

The six buildings constituted three bunkhouses, one building for management of the operations, and one for a general goods store. The last building gave the outward appearance of being a hotel, but an outsider could not rent a room for the evening. Nicholas Webb, fully aware of the weaknesses of men and not at all beyond exploiting them, used the sixth building only when he brought prostitutes for his men. Though the women visited the settlement only for a week or so every other month, the reputation Nicholas gained by bringing the prostitutes to his men kept a steady stream of cowpunchers wanting to work for him.

Christina followed Cole into the shadows of the encampment, keeping three or four steps behind him. She held the pistol in both hands and kept a wary eye behind her. It was her responsibility to protect the rear. Christina accepted that responsibility with something akin to a sacred oath. Cole had not wanted her working with him, but now that she was, she wasn't going to do anything to suggest his decision had been in error.

They slipped between two buildings, moving on silent feet. At this time of the morning, there wasn't even the sound of raucous laughter coming from the bunkhouses to let Cole and Christina know the place wasn't deserted. The men were sleeping the deep slumber of alcohol. They would not awaken easily.

Cole, in a half-crouch, turned so that he could look at Christina. He pointed up at the porch roof, and she nodded in understanding. During the past month, they had perfected a limited sign language.

Christina holstered her pistol. Cole put his back to the operations building, bending over at the waist. He laced his fingers together, forming a stirrup for Christina.

The building, a two-story structure, had a porch at the

front and rear doors. Nicholas Webb never intended the porch roof to be used to get into the second-story windows, where the foremen had their office and where the payroll safe was kept. That idea came straight from Cole Jurrell.

Christina was just about to put her foot in Cole's hands so he could boost her up to the porch roof when an idea struck her. Though Cole was shaking his head in negation, Christina quickly removed the boots that she had bought several weeks earlier, the first thing she had ever purchased with stolen money.

Christina put her bare foot in Cole's hand. He lifted her, and she was able to get a solid handhold on the drain pipe and the side of the porch roof. From there, she was able to shimmy onto the roof.

Turning around, Christina held her hand out. Cole tossed her boots up one at a time. She was certain she saw respect for her foresightedness in his eyes, for realizing the boots would have been noisy against the roof.

Cole climbed to the porch roof by using the drain pipe. His moccasins were silent against the porch's slat-shingled roof.

A thin-bladed knife was inserted between two sections of the second-floor window, then Cole and Christina entered without a sound.

Once inside, when Cole was certain that he and Christina had entered unobserved, he knelt near the window and withdrew his watch. It was three-thirty. The money wouldn't arrive until at least six-thirty or seven. Shortly after that, the men would be lining up for their pay.

"We'd better get in position," Cole whispered.

Christina nodded, her gleaming smile shining brilliant white in the dim light. She was enjoying this more than she wanted Cole to know, but wasn't doing a good job of hiding her pleasure. He had explained to her that they would make the raids he had already planned but had deemed not lucrative enough for top priority status. The small jobs were Christina's training ground. This time, the payroll wouldn't be the few hundred dollars intended for a half dozen or so men. By Cole's rough estimate, it would take at least seventy men to keep control of the operation Webb had going here in the northern part of the Dakota Territory.

The room was lined with straight-backed wooden chairs. At one end of the room was a large desk with a single leather-covered chair behind it. Near that was a massive steel safe with three dials on it, similar to ones used by banks. Once the money was inside the safe, it was impossible to get to.

"Here's where the men get their money," Cole whispered, squinting his eyes to pick out objects in the shadowy room. "Just like I suspected."

Cole was smiling, and Christina felt love blossom in her breast. He still hadn't truly confessed that he loved her. Sometimes he said loving things, occasionally going so far as to say he loved this or that about Christina, especially when they were making love. But he had never straightforwardly confessed his love. Still, when Christina saw such joy on Cole's face—Christina knew that she loved him with all her heart and soul. She loved him more than everything she held true and dear in this world, and all she wanted was to experience the time when Cole felt confident enough in his love for her that he could let his heart speak the words she knew he felt.

"Where are we going to hide?" Christina asked after a moment, trying to push pleasant thoughts of last night's activities to the back of her mind. She had more important things to think about than daydreaming about amorous adventures.

Cole did not answer. He walked slowly, careful not to bump into anything, to the large desk and opened the wide, shallow middle drawer. From his shirt pocket he took a match and lit it, keeping the flame low so that it wouldn't reflect off the windows.

The drawer was almost empty. A couple of different ledgers indicated how much each man was to receive on a monthly basis. One ledger indicated the money that had been given in advance—at a usurious interest rate—to certain men. There were several pens and a spare bottle of ink.

"Webb's got grand plans," Cole said softly. He shook out the match before it burned his fingers. Cole waited until the match was cool, then put it back in his pocket. This was not the time to get careless with an errant match.

"How so?"

"This whole compound isn't set up to handle seventy or a hundred men, it's for three or four or five hundred men. It looks unused now, or at least underused. But you can just bet Nicholas plans to someday have as much control in this part of the territory as he does in Enderton."

A shudder went through Christina. She now hated hearing the name of that town. There was a time when Enderton meant home to her. Now she considered it the most dangerous place in the world for her, and she despised Nicholas Webb and his despicable son for making her afraid of her home.

Cole used a final match to check the contents of the desk. He returned everything to the exact place it had been in, then crossed the room again. Christina followed him, holding her boots in her left hand so the heels would not click against the wooden floor.

"Let's get in position," Cole whispered. "You can bet there's going to be at least one paymaster and a foreman on the job long before the money arrives."

There were two doors at the back of the room. One door led to an unused office, which confirmed Cole's suspicion of Nicholas's "grand plan." The other door led to a small closet, which held only a broom and a dust pan.

Cole said, "Not good. Once inside, we won't be able to see what's going on."

Christina felt the doorplace. She gave Cole a smile. Even in the dim light, it was a dazzling smile that pulled at Cole.

"Sometimes, it pays to be the daughter of a merchant,"

Christina whispered. She was standing close enough to Cole to feel the masculine force of him. "The lock is a Jaymes and Mitchell. Give me a match and I'll show you something."

Cole was curious and wary, but he fished out a match from his shirt pocket and handed it to Christina.

"Watch this." Christina scratched the match on the inside of the closet door. She waited until the sulfur had burned away, leaving an even flame, then placed the match just below the doorknob. She put her hand on the opposite side of the door and, in her palm and in the outline of the lock, Cole saw light. "See? We can look through the lock. Nicholas probably bought all the locks at the same time to save money. That explains why there's a lock on a closet door."

"Smart girl," Cole murmured, speaking the words with pride and honesty. "I knew there was a reason I brought you along."

Christina laughed lightly, her eyes shining like rare blue jewels in the soft light.

"You brought me along because you didn't have a choice in the matter," she purred. "Besides, you won't admit it, but we both know you're lost without me."

"Sure, sure," Cole replied, pretending there was no truth to what Christina said. "Let's do a little investigating, as long as we've got the place to ourselves for a couple hours."

The "investigating" didn't last very long. Cole and Christina found a man snoring away on a sofa in the neighboring room. Cole guessed he was a foreman who had drank too much the previous night and had decided to sleep it off where he had to work. At least that way he would be on the job when the money arrived.

As Cole and Christina made their way quietly to the closet Cole checked his watch one last time. It was fifteen minutes to four in the morning. They had hours to wait together in the closed, cramped janitor's closet.

Christina put on her boots, then stepped in behind Cole

and closed the door. She had to stand so close to Cole her body was lightly touching his.

Doesn't this feeling ever end when I'm with Cole? Christina asked herself, amused that her desire for Cole, and, apparently, his desire for her, was undiminished in all the weeks they had spent together.

"How long do you think we'll have to wait?" Christina asked. Out of habit and desire, she raised her hands, placing them lightly on Cole's shoulders.

"I would guess two and a half to three hours. That's when the money will get here. If we're not long gone by the time the men arrive for their pay, we're as good as . . ."

Christina felt a chill grip her insides. She didn't like to think about what *might* happen. There were so many uncertainties to the life she was living now. She knew that there might come a time when her luck would run out and she and Cole would be captured. On two separate occasions, Cole had been insistent that she understand this undeniable fact of life as an outlaw. But she didn't want to dwell on such things, and had settled into a truce with Cole: she would take their robberies with dead seriousness as long as he never talked about the two of them dying.

"Why didn't we ever make love at the theater?" Christina asked suddenly.

It was so dark in the closet, Christina could not see the change on Cole's face. But in her mind, her vision of his quizzical expression was so clear it brought a smile to her lips. She felt his body tense. Cole Jurrell did not like talking about personal matters.

"Why ask that now? We're a long way from the theater."

"Because I need to know. It's important to me."

She felt the warmth of Cole's breath when he sighed in a slightly exaggerated manner. She had him trapped and he couldn't walk away from her questions.

"Come on," Christina prodded. Her hands had moved up Cole's chest until they were at the base of his neck. She began to knead the sinewy muscles atop his shoulders. "Tell me."

301

"I just didn't think that you . . . would like doing something like that. That's why. Can we drop it now?"

"Did you make . . ." Christina stopped herself; Cole had not, in her mind, made *love* to anyone but her in his entire licentious life. "Did you sleep with any women at the theater before?"

"I thought you didn't want me to talk about women I've slept with."

"I'm bringing the subject up this time, so you're forgiven. Now give me an answer." Christina moved closer to Cole. Just enough so that her breasts, full and round, pressed warmly against Cole's shirtfront. Feeling the strength in his body, she pressed herself against him harder still.

"We shouldn't talk."

"We're whispering. Nobody can hear us. Now give me the answer. The honest answer."

She felt Cole's chest expand as he inhaled deeply. A tingling began where Christina's body touched Cole's. The sensation worked its way slowly through her body.

"Okay, you win," Cole hissed. He knew that once Christina made her mind up on something, she didn't quit until she got her way. "I didn't try anything because I didn't think you'd want to . . . when we might get caught."

"Oh . . . so you'd do that with another woman, but you wouldn't with me. Is that it?"

"That's not what I said."

"You didn't have to."

Christina felt Cole sigh again and looked up to where she imagined his face was. Her hands slipped slowly down from the arch of Cole's neck to his chest.

"Why the sudden interest?" Cole asked. "Why all the questions now? Here? You didn't seem interested before."

Christina was glad that Cole could not see her blush with embarrassment. She was glad, too, that he couldn't see the passion she knew must be showing on her face and in her eyes. She felt impish. She also felt, at that moment, young, daring, alive.

302

"I've heard other girls talk," Christina started. She hesitated, searching for just the right words. "And they always say that when they first became a bride, the husband was very . . . loving. But as time went on, that . . . loving nature . . . became less frequent."

"What's your point?"

When she placed her hands a little lower on Cole's chest, Christina could feel the beating of his heart. And his heart was not pumping like *that* because he was worried about the raid. He was just as aware of Christina's intimate yet possibly innocent body contact as she was.

"I was just wondering when I should expect our . . . your loving nature to become less frequent." Christina paused briefly, then, to prevent any misunderstanding, added, "It's not something that I look forward to, Mr. Jurrell."

"Is that so, Miss Sands?"

"Am I as pleasing as the others?" Christina's, fingers, even in total darkness, found the top button of Cole's shirt. Through practiced ease, she unfastened it. "Hmmm? Am I as daring and exciting as"—Christina stopped herself before the name "Loretta" passed between her lips—"those other women?"

"Darling, there has never, ever been a woman who excited me as much as you do. I take one look at you and I go crazy inside."

"But what about now? You can't see me in here. What makes me exciting to you now?" Three more buttons came unfastened under Christina's slender fingers. She was almost to Cole's belt. "What's going to happen when I get old? Will you go looking for a young woman because I'm not as pretty anymore?"

She heard Cole swallow. He was having trouble speaking. When he did manage to force words through dry lips, his voice sounded strained, as though he was in the midst of some tumultuous inner struggle.

"This is not the time for this," Cole whispered hoarsely.

"This is a *beautiful* time for this," Christina responded.

She kissed Cole's chest. Her hands worked free the last of the shirt's buttons, then moved lower, past his belt buckle, over his holster to the buttons of his slacks.

Cole issued a strangled curse. Christina's lips found his nipple. She tugged at his slacks and Cole's manhood sprang out, fiercely aroused, exciting and yet frightening her. She touched him tentatively with her fingertips. Then, finding courage from where she had thought there was no more, took him in both hands.

"A beautiful time . . . for the beautiful man," Christina purred, her words coming out muffled against the solid surface of Cole's stomach, rippled with knotted muscles.

She felt Cole's fingers pull at the ribbon she used to keep her silky blond hair in a pony tail. When her hair was free, Christina gave her head a little shake, sending her hair spraying over her shoulders the way she knew Cole liked it.

Christina was hesitant. This was something she had never done for Cole, but had sensed that he wanted. In total darkness, unable to see the object of her desire, she kissed him. Cole sighed.

That sigh was all the encouragement Christina needed to continue. Cole had told her many times that she was the most beautiful woman he'd ever seen. But Christina wanted to be more than that. She wanted to be the most daring, exciting, erotic woman he'd ever known.

Emboldened by Cole's obvious pleasure, Christina took him deeply. She heard, seemingly from high above her, a single word spoken with a hissing sigh.

Cole had said, "Beautiful!"

Chapter 29

Several hours later, Christina pressed her face tighter against the door plate, peering through the keyhole into the room. Two kerosene lanterns had been lit by the man who had entered the room. Christina had yet to see his face, but she knew that he was the paymaster.

She dared not speak to Cole, not unless she could put her lips to his ear to issue the softest of whispers. And she was afraid that if she stood she would make some sound that would draw the paymaster's attention. When the paymaster went to his desk, Christina was finally able to see his face.

He was a fat man with a thick red moustache. His head seemed planted on his shoulders without the benefit of a neck. His cheek was swelled out with an enormous wad of chewing tobacco. From inside the desk, he withdrew a large ledger and opened it.

With her hands lightly touching the door, Christina rose and stood beside Cole. She reached up in the darkness, her fingers curling around Cole's neck, sliding under his tawny hair. She pulled his head down so their cheeks touched and her lips were close to his ear.

"He's sitting at the desk. He just took out that big ledger you looked at," Christina whispered in a voice so soft it could not possibly carry through the closet door.

"What do we do?"

"Everything is working fine," Cole replied. "Now we wait until the money arrives—which shouldn't be long—and then we get the hell out of here."

Despite the seriousness of the situation and the task they were about to undertake, and even though her legs were weary from standing in one place for several hours, Christina smiled in the midnight black closet.

"Is it all that bad, Mr. Jurrell, to be cooped up with me in such cramped quarters?"

She felt Cole's cheek against hers as he grinned. Christina trembled softly, still shocked at her own boldness. When she was with Cole, she had the courage to be daring.

They had to wait almost another hour. Cole and Christina stood together, facing each other, neither saying a word. The sound of boots against the wood slat floor, and then the muffled greeting of two men who rarely saw each other, sent Christina's heart tripping against her ribs once again.

"Check it out," Cole whispered. He privately damned himself for not being the one near the door. "If it's right, make your move. I'll be right behind you. Just make sure you stay down."

Christina looked through the keyhole again. The paymaster was shaking hands with a younger man who wore the clothes of the range. His holster was tied down low on his thigh gunfighter-fashion, the same way Cole wore his gun. Other men moved in the periphery of Christina's vision.

Her right hand was curled around the smooth handle of the revolver strapped to her own hip. Once again, as she always did just prior to a raid, Christina asked herself whether she could use the gun. *Yes, but only if I have to save Cole,* she answered herself immediately.

Christina threw the door open. She leaped out and moved to her right, drawing the Colt in the same move, extending the big, heavy-caliber weapon in both hands.

"Don't move!" she hissed.

Cole twisted around the doorframe, drawing his own weapon. The paymaster was seated at his desk. When he saw the guns pointed at him, he squeezed his beady eyes shut. Was he cursing himself, or praying he wouldn't get shot? Cole wondered as he moved into the room.

Four men were gathered around the pot-bellied stove, pouring themselves steaming cups of coffee. Cole panned the group, moving his barrel ever so slightly from one to another. The four riders, all heavily armed, had leaned their rifles and shotguns against the wall, grateful to relax after the long ride. All four, upon seeing Cole and Christina leap from the closet, took a half-step toward the rifles or began reaching for their revolvers.

"You'll never make it," Cole said in an icy tone. He advanced quickly, his cold gray eyes darting around the room. "Quickly now, do exactly as I tell you and nobody will get hurt. With your left hands, drop you holsters. Anybody gets cute and everybody dies."

Christina knew her role. She went for the squat, rectangular, heavy box on the edge of the paymaster's desk. The strongbox was locked.

"Open it," Christina said to the paymaster. When she looked into the fat man's eyes, she was a bit surprised that she didn't see even the slightest trace of fear.

The paymaster waited a second, just looking at Christina as the other four men dropped their holsters. Slowly, so that Christina had no doubts that he was only going for a key, he reached into the breast pocket of his shirt. He offered the key to Christina.

"You do it," Christina hissed, still holding her gun in both hands to keep it as steady as possible.

The paymaster hesitated again, his eyes staying on Christina's face. A smile, small at first but becoming larger, appeared on his face. When the paymaster smiled, his eyes narrowed to slits, and Christina wondered if he could even see.

"I'm not paid to get myself killed," the paymaster said

after a moment. "That's not my job at all." He unlocked the strongbox, pocketed the key, then leaned back in his chair. "Have it all, Miss Sands . . . but you'll never get the chance to spend it."

Cole, casting a sideways glance at the paymaster, said icily, "Shut up! Don't talk unless I ask you a question."

Christina pulled the small, folded canvas bag from her holster belt at the small of her back. The money inside the strongbox—all neatly stacked and tied in bundles—took her breath away. She'd never seen so much money in one place at one time in her life. Christina had to consciously keep from saying something about the fortune to Cole. He had warned her they shouldn't talk any more than necessary. Christina shook open the canvas bag and began filling it with the strongbox money.

The paymaster chuckled softly, watching Christina pushing money into the canvas bag, using only her left hand.

"Take it," the paymaster said, a vicious amusement showing in his tone. "Take it all, But you'll never spend it, little lady. I can promise you that."

Cole's voice was edged with danger when he said, "I told you to shut up!"

The paymaster raised his hands, holding his palms toward Cole to show they were empty. "Word's out on you, Jurrell. You don't kill unarmed men. As you can see, I ain't got a gun."

Christina had a feeling. She couldn't say exactly what it was. But a tiny voice inside her whispered that something was wrong. Something . . . but what? Why did she have this fear, when everything was going exactly as Cole had planned? She continued stuffing the money into the bag and tried to push her fears away, but her apprehension stubbornly remained.

"Your time's running out, Miss Sands," the paymaster said, and now he sounded absolutely delighted by the proceedings.

"Cole told you to be quiet! Now be quiet!" The words

308

shot from Christina's mouth. She felt terror pooling inside her bosom, welling up like floodwater against the leaky walls of an unstable dam. Her hands were shaking. The small voice inside her was whispering louder now. Very soon it would be shrieking in terror.

"Does the name Marcus Kensington mean anything to you?" the paymaster asked. Christina's head snapped up and she looked straight into the paymaster's heavily lidded eyes. "Thought so. You see, Mr. Webb's put the word out. He said that when you came for the money, we were to give you a message."

"Don't push your luck, old man! You know what I've done!" Cole said.

The paymaster just chuckled, and even though Cole briefly turned the weapon on him, the smile never left his fleshy face.

"I'm not a stupid man, Mr. Jurrell. I never once believed you killed your papa. If I was a betting man, and I am, I'd say Mr. Webb had his boy gun your papa down." The paymaster was grinning. Christina could tell that he was a man who had killed before. There was a cruelty to him that showed in every move he made, in the tone of his voice, and in his contemptible self-assurance. "That's the way Mr. Webb does business. When he sees a problem, he gets rid of it permanently."

Christina could hear her pulse pounding in her ears. The canvas bag was stuffed with paper money, and still there were many stacks of currency left in the strongbox.

Cole had the four gunmen who'd brought the money leaning with their hands against the wall. He stepped toward the paymaster. "If I find out you had anything to do with my father's murder, there won't be a rock flat enough for you to hide under. I'll kill you . . . and being unarmed won't save your life."

"Me? I didn't have anything to do with that, Jurrell." He spoke as though to a friend. The paymaster watched Christina struggling to cram more money into the canvas bag. "Would you like a hand with that, miss?"

Cole took notice of Christina's trembling hands. "Forget it," he said to her. "We've got enough. Leave the rest. We've got to get out of here."

"But there's more money there, Jurrell," the paymaster said. He was grinning evilly. He kept his hands where Cole could see them. "But if you've got to rush off, I suppose I can't blame you. Just the same, I think you should hear what Mr. Webb has to say to you."

Christina jerked at the heavy twine drawstring, pulling it around the top of the canvas bag. The bag, overfilled with money, couldn't close completely.

"Mr. Webb has got Marcus Kensington at his place," the paymaster continued, hurrying his words now, afraid his audience would make a hasty exit before he could finish what he'd only hinted at so far. "Mr. Webb said that unless you go to him right away, Miss Sands, he's going to cut old Marcus Kensington into tiny little pieces and feed him to the hogs." Christina's gaze met the paymaster's. Her eyes were filled with terror. "He says that the first time his boy was only fooling you, but he's not fooling this time. No, ma'am, I do believe he's telling the truth."

"He's lying." Cole, holding four holsters in his left hand and the rifles in the crook of his arm, stepped between Christina and the paymaster. "It's just another trick. Come on, we've got to get out of here *now*."

"It was a lie. Nothing more than a lie," Cole said. He sat cross-legged on the ground before a small campfire, his hands filled with crisp paper money. He counted out what they'd stolen. "Don't let it worry you, Christina."

Christina was pacing around the campfire. She didn't care that Cole had already counted out nearly a thousand dollars, and that he had more money to go. All she could think about was Marcus Kensington and what a living hell he was going through if Nicholas Webb had kidnapped him.

"What if he's not lying, Cole? You know he's capable of anything!"

Cole looked up from the money. "Yes, I know that. But I also know that Marcus Kensington is one of the most respected men in Enderton. Nicholas Webb isn't going to do something against Marcus that will draw outside attention to himself. That's the last thing in the world he wants."

Christina frowned at Cole. "You don't believe that, Cole, and neither do I. If that was the case, your father and my father would both be alive today." Christina shook her head negatively, her blond hair reflecting light from the campfire. "You don't understand what Marcus means to me. He's more than just a friend. He's really all the family I have left. After Daddy died, Marcus was always there for me. He gave me strength. He helped me get by." Very softly, she said, "He's all that I have left of my old life, Cole." Christina cleared her throat, straightening her shoulders, forcing herself to be strong. "He's got Marcus this time, Cole. He does. And unless I give myself up to Nicholas, Marcus is going to be killed."

"You know what kind of liar Webb is." Cole had resumed counting the money in his hands. "It's just one more of his tricks. It worked before, so he figures it'll work again."

"But Cole . . ."

Cole looked up again, and this time Christina saw that there was honest concern showing in his eyes.

"I can't let you go to him, Christina," he said softly, sincerely. "If he does have Marcus, it may already be all over. There's nothing to be gained by giving yourself up to Nicholas. Do you think he'd let Marcus live even if you did go to him?" Cole closed his eyes briefly as unsettling memories crowded his thoughts. "I lost you to Zachary once. I can't lose you to Nicholas now. Can't you see that, Christina? Can't you see what it would do to . . ."

Cole's words caught in his throat. He was being selfish, he knew, to want—to *need*—Christina at his side. Work-

311

ing with Christina, sleeping with her, fighting with her against a common enemy—it had strengthened Cole's love for Christina and made him respect her as he'd never before respected any person, man or woman. She was strong, mentally and emotionally. She could endure hardships silently. And this woman, this strong, special woman, was his.

If she left, would his life be worth living? What would he do? After Christina, could he ever again be satisfied?

"I can't let you go, Christina. I'm sorry, but that's just the way it is, the way it has to be." Cole was squeezing the money tightly in his hands, crumpling the crisp new bills. "We'll work together, just like we have, to get Marcus freed . . . *if* Nicholas really does have him. But you can't just give yourself up to Nicholas. You just can't, Christina. That won't solve anything."

For a long moment, Cole and Christina looked into each other's eyes.

"We can talk about it later," Christina whispered. "We're both tired. Neither of us is thinking clearly."

"Yes, sleep," Cole said, his voice barely above a whisper. "Tomorrow we can figure out what must be done." Christina knelt next to Cole. He cupped her chin in his palm, forcing her to look into his gray eyes. "If I thought it would save Marcus, I'd give myself up to Nicholas rather than let you ride in there. But it wouldn't do any good. You've got to see that. If we're to save Marcus's life, we must rescue him. It's the only way."

Cole's arm went around her shoulders. He lay back in the grass, pulling Christina with him so that her head rested on his chest and the full length of her body was pressed against him.

"We need rest," Cole whispered, stroking Christina's honey hair. "Tonight, we'll know what must be done. Tonight . . . tonight."

It went against everything Cole had learned to fight Nicholas directly. Cole's sense of self-preservation told him that an assault on Nicholas was suicide. But what he

312

also knew was that if he did not help Christina, she would attempt to free Marcus herself. And that surely would be suicidal, or worse.

He had no choice. The woman he loved had too gentle a heart, too loving a nature, for her to allow Marcus Kensington to be punished because of her. And Cole loved Christina too much to do what his instincts told him.

Cole kissed Christina's hair. Her willful ways prevented Cole from stopping Christina. All he could do was help her . . . and hope that they both lived through it.

Chapter 30

Nicholas was smiling, but his lips were tight across the straight line of his white teeth. He looked at Zachary. *Soon enough, I'll have to kill you, son,* he thought. *You're thinking I've gone soft because of Christina, and that's making you brave. You've underestimated me, Zachary, but I haven't underestimated you.*

"They took it late last night or early this morning," Zachary said, tossing his slender body into a chair in his father's study. "A man rode straight through, getting here to say they needed another payroll." Zachary looked at Nicholas through squinting eyes. He was paying now for last night's heavy drinking. "If we don't get money up to those boys quick, you can bet we're going to lose men in droves."

Nicholas shrugged his shoulders. "Of course. I expect as much. Make sure we send some women up there, and have a man ride ahead of the strongbox. Knowing the women are coming will hold the men." Nicholas made a small smile. "Isn't it amazing what lust will make a man do?"

"You're that sure Christina is going to walk right here and give herself to you? Why isn't she here yet? Our man made it. Why shouldn't she be here?"

"Our man's alacrity was motivated by greed. He took a

314

straight track here, and he rode through the night. We can't count on Christina doing the same thing." Nicholas opened a cherrywood humidor and selected a cigar. As he moistened the tip, he kept his eyes on his son. "Christina will walk right through those doors and give herself to me. And Cole will be right behind her. Know your enemy, son — know him better than he knows himself."

Zachary wasn't as convinced as his father and it showed in the way he looked at Nicholas. "Whatever you say. I'm going to get a little sleep now, if that's okay with you."

"Fine . . ."

Nicholas kept his excitement to himself. Very soon, he would have Christina under his control. And the young man who vexed his life — Cole Jurrell — would be dead. It was the best of all possible worlds. Nicholas thought of Zachary and felt a pang of regret. Sometimes he wished he had a normal father-son relationship with the boy. But it was too late to mend whatever affection they had had for each other. The barriers that separated them were too high and too wide.

He has to die, Nicholas thought, looking at Zachary. A smile crossed his lips now that he had made a final decision. His only concern now was whether he would pull the trigger on Zachary himself, or if he would assign the assassination to one of his men. He knew there were plenty of men who would be more than willing to murder his son. Nicholas wouldn't even have to pay to have the job done.

Zachary was at the door when Nicholas stopped him. "Is Kensington still alive?"

Zachary nodded, then grimaced from the hangover. "Yeah, more or less. The boys and I have given him a pretty good going-over. He never knew where Christina and Cole have been hiding. If he did know, he'd have spilled his guts by now."

"Keep him alive," Nicholas replied quietly, not looking at his son. "At least until after I've got Christina. Then

315

you can do with him whatever you want."

"Sure," Zachary said, then left the room.

When Nicholas was alone in his study, he savored his cigar and let his mind wander to the pleasingly amorous images that flashed in his brain. Christina Sands . . . the pursuit had made her more desirable. Nicholas had always been able to buy whatever he wanted, whoever he wanted. But Christina was different. She wasn't for sale at any price. That wouldn't keep Nicholas from having Christina. Nothing would stand in his way.

Memories of what her kisses tasted like came back to him. He could almost feel her body wriggling as she struggled against him. Nicholas shuddered softly. *Why her?* he asked himself. *Why was she so enticing that he absolutely had to possess her?*

"She's here!"

Nicholas bolted upright in bed. He fumbled for a match at his nightstand, then lit a lamp. He blinked against the light, his eyes not yet accustomed to it.

"What?" he asked, but he knew what Zachary was talking about.

"She's here! Christina!"

Nicholas gave his son a smile and said, "Didn't I tell you she'd come right to me? Didn't I?" Nicholas tossed the blankets aside and strode across the room, pushing Zachary out of the way as he headed for his robe. "I want to see her in the library first. And tell the servants that I'm not to be disturbed tonight. They are all to stay in their rooms."

When Zachary didn't move quickly enough, Nicholas shooed him away, unaware that it was exactly as he had done to his son when Zachary was an attention-hungry small boy.

Had his time finally come? Nicholas had always believed that sooner or later he would own Christina's body. Once he possessed that, her heart would inevitably

316

follow. The prospect of possessing her within minutes, to control however he wanted, was an intoxicating stimulant that made the surface of his flesh tingle.

Nicholas forced himself to maintain some semblance of calm. He ached for the feel of Christina beneath him, but it wouldn't do to have Christina see him as another love-starved suitor. Stepping over to the full-length mirror in the corner of his bedroom, Nicholas inspected himself. He looked dashing and prosperous enough, he thought, and a woman of Christina's modest means would surely be impressed. His pajamas were hand-sewn, made of Chinese silk, as was the matching black robe he wore. He stepped into a pair of soft buffalo-hide slippers, ran a brush through his salt-and-pepper hair, then left his bedroom to meet the object of his dreams and fantasies.

Christina was waiting for him in the library, sitting stiffly in a large wine-colored leather chair. She did not look wild-eyed frightened, as Nicholas had thought she would. And though Christina was stunningly beautiful, she did not look like the Christina Sands of Nicholas's nightly dreams. She wore men's clothes, not a bejeweled evening gown, and her face was smudged with dirt. Her golden hair was tied back with a blue ribbon that looked strikingly out of place with the denim slacks and flannel shirt with the sleeves rolled up past her elbows.

"Good evening," Nicholas said, stepping into the library. "It's good to see you again, Christina."

Christina's blue eyes were bright and alert as she turned them on Nicholas. She had prepared herself for this moment, but her heart hammered against her ribs at finally seeing her nemesis.

Silk pajamas, she thought sardonically. *This man knows nothing but comfort. How well would he fare living his life on the run, eating cold food and sleeping on the ground?*

Nicholas walked past Christina, his nonchalant attitude bothering her. He went to the small, wheeled cart where crystal decanters held aged Scotch and brandy.

317

"Would you care for anything?"

"Brandy, if you have it."

Nicholas's eyebrows raised for a moment. He seemed surprised that Christina would want a drink so strong. "Of course," he said after a beat.

Christina noticed that Nicholas's hands trembled slightly as he poured brandy into a glass. *He's not as calm as he wants me to think he is,* she decided.

Nicholas walked once again past Christina, this time sitting on the long leather sofa. He held the glasses in his hands, extending one to Christina.

"Why don't you join me on the sofa? We're not exactly strangers, after all." Nicholas smiled, a powerful man in control of his world.

Christina pushed herself out of the chair, feigning exhaustion. She was thankful she'd slept before walking to Nicholas's compound. The rest had rejuvenated her. She sat on the opposite side of the sofa, as far away from Nicholas as possible.

"Over here," Nicholas said, his tone carrying a slight undercurrent of violence in it. He was enjoying telling Christina what she had to do.

Christina slid over on the sofa until she was beside Nicholas. His arm went around her shoulders. Christina closed her eyes for only a moment as a shudder of revulsion went through her. She took the brandy and sipped it. Memories of sipping brandy with Cole came back with a vengeance, happy memories that she could not dwell on now.

"Much better." Nicholas squeezed Christina's shoulder, smiling at her. When she looked into his eyes, she was not at all surprised to see that his soul was still an empty void. "You gave me quite a run for the money. I was beginning to wonder if you would ever be mine."

Nicholas leaned over to kiss Christina, but she pulled away. "Marcus," she said softly but sternly. "Before we . . . I want to see Marcus. I've got to know he's all right."

318

Anger flashed in Nicholas's eyes. Christina forced herself to smile. It was a demure smile, telling Nicholas he had total power over her. She had to manipulate Nicholas if her plan to rescue Marcus was to be successful. But what was the right approach? Defiance, so her capitulation would be the ultimate spoil of war? Or should she be docile and obedient, pampering Nicholas's inflated sense of dominance?

"He's alive," Nicholas said. Though he smiled, there was anger simmering in his eyes. Christina tried to keep looking at him, but that was almost impossible. "He's just fine. And he'll stay that way . . . but only if you make me a very happy man, Christina. Do you understand me?"

Christina took another sip of the brandy, then put the glass aside. She could not allow her senses to get clouded. She shrugged her shoulders and the rise and fall of her breasts drew and held Nicholas's gaze. Christina saw his eyes widen visibly with carnality. She turned her face away from him, hiding her contempt and shame.

Christina answered in a whisper. "Yes . . . I understand." She had to force words from her throat that her heart did not feel. "I understand many things, Mr. Webb. I've changed since the last time we talked. You see, I now know how powerful you are. I've felt your power, and I'm tired of fighting it."

Christina was not looking at Nicholas, but she could hear his breathing become more rapid. These were the words that he had wanted to hear and however foul they tasted on her tongue, Christina knew she had to continue them if Marcus's life was to be spared.

"I can be good to you," Christina said softly, trying hard to ignore Nicholas's hand on her shoulder. "I can make you happy. I know I can. In return, all I want from you are two things."

"Oh? And what might those two things be?" There was rich amusement in Nicholas's tone. Christina's subservience made Nicholas feel strong, manly.

"I need to know that Marcus will be safe . . . that nothing bad will happen to him as long as I'm with you."

"And . . . ?"

"And I want to be with *you*. I can make you happy, Nicholas, I know I can. I'm tired of being on the losing side all the time. Now I want to be with a winner."

Nicholas chuckled softly, genuinely pleased with Christina. "My dearest child, I do believe you and I are going to be better for each other than even I thought possible." His hand slipped from her shoulder, roaming down the front of Christina's body almost to the ripe swell of her breast. "I need someone at my side. Zachary is . . . well, let's say that I doubt Zachary and I will be together for very much longer."

This man is planning to murder his own son! thought Christina.

"I can teach you many things," Nicholas whispered.

Christina smelled the liquor on his breath. Everything in her screamed that she should knock his hand from her body, but she knew she mustn't do anything to offend him. She prayed silently that he wouldn't touch her more intimately. Nicholas's words droned on, and Christina had to force herself to concentrate on the words so that she wouldn't miss anything that might help Marcus.

"You would be my prodigy," Nicholas continued. "You would have to prove your value to me, of course. And I don't just mean your value to me in the bedroom. But if you listen carefully to everything I can teach you, you will have power, Christina. Real power. When you give orders, men will follow those orders without hesitation, without question. You'll have riches, jewelry . . . anything you want." Nicholas leaned closer to Christina. "But first . . . you must make me happy, Christina. You must make me very, *very* happy."

Nicholas tried again to kiss Christina. She smiled at him but leaned away so that her lips would not be defiled by his. Once before, Nicholas had kissed her, and the memory of that disgusting experience was still sharp

320

and abhorrent to Christina.

"Wait . . . wait, please," Christina whispered. She placed her fingertips to Nicholas's lips and he kissed them. Christina gave him as much of a smile as she could manage. "We're not in any hurry, are we?"

Christina tried to keep smiling. She saw lust and anger glitter maniacally in Nicholas's eyes. His jaw was clamped tightly shut. She saw a muscle flicker in his cheek. His fingers were squeezed tight around the crystal brandy snifter.

"I could make you," Nicholas threatened, low and menacing.

"Of course you could. We both know that." Christina felt panic bubbling up inside her. She couldn't hold her façade in place much longer. Being with Nicholas was just too repulsive for her to pretend it was anything other than horrifying. "But wouldn't you enjoy it more if I willingly gave you . . . what you want? After I got cleaned up? Had a hot bath and put something nice on? Wouldn't you enjoy that more, Mr. Webb?"

Nicholas's face cracked into a lustful grin. "Yes," he said, drawling the word out, hissing the *s*. "You're absolutely right, my dear. I've waited so long for this evening that I'm afraid I've become rather impatient."

"This is an evening we'll never forget," Christina heard herself say, repeating words she had rehearsed. "Let's savor this evening together, not devour it greedily." Her voice was warm and sultry as Christina purred, "And believe me when I tell you, Mr. Webb, that you won't be disappointed with me. This is going to be a night you'll remember for the rest of your life."

Christina prayed that Nicholas would, in fact, never forget this evening. She prayed it would be a nightmare that would haunt Nicholas for all the years that he would spend in jail.

The room looked like it might have been a small wine

cellar, but it was really a jail cell. When Zachary opened the door, Christina's breath caught in her throat at the sight of Marcus Kensington.

"Marcus! Oh, Marcus!" Christina cried, rushing to take the silver-haired gentleman into her arms. Christina held Marcus tenderly. He had been brutally beaten. When Christina turned her eyes to Zachary, blue flames shot from them. Her unveiled hatred drew a throaty chuckle of amusement from Zachary.

"He's alive, just like Pa said." Zachary sneered at Marcus, then turned his gaze to Christina, defiling her with his eyes. "I should have taken you when I had the chance."

"You were too busy with Loretta Pembrook, or have you forgotten about her already?" Christina snapped, then turned away from Zachary, cradling Marcus's head in her arms. "Can I please have a few moments alone with him?"

The door closed, and Christina cringed when she heard the tumblers of the lock click into place. She looked at the once-handsome face of Marcus Kensington and tears seeped from her eyes. Marcus's lips were cracked and swollen. One eye had been blackened, and it was swollen shut. His shirt was ripped. Christina saw swelling and bruises over Marcus's ribs.

"I'm sorry . . . I'm so sorry," Christina whispered, tears falling from her cheeks. "This wouldn't have happened to you if not for me."

Marcus's eye blinked as he struggled to free himself from semi-consciousness. At first he looked at Christina with confusion, as though he did not trust his own vision. Then, sure that it really was his beloved Christina with him, a deep sadness spread across Marcus's abused and battered features.

"I had hoped—"

"No, Marcus, don't try to talk."

"I had hoped and prayed that the Webbs would never catch you." He coughed, then groaned and held on to his chest. Christina was certain at least one of Marcus's ribs was broken.

"You're going to be all right now, Marcus, " Christina whispered, tasting tears on her lips as she spoke. She stroked Marcus's silver hair, smoothing it away from his swollen-shut eye. "I'm going to doctor you up just as good as new."

"Don't worry about me. Get away . . . if you can." Marcus had to force the words from his throat, but with each passing second he was getting stronger. He seemed to take strength from Christina. He tried to push himself into a more erect sitting position, but Christina held him secure. "Those men are a plague. Save yourself. Escape while you can. I'm an old man. A better place waits for me."

"Shhh!" Christina put a finger to Marcus's lips. "Be quiet now. Save your strength. I've come here to get you out." Christina looked into Marcus's eye, hoping that his mind was still lucid enough through the pain to understand the importance of what she had to say. "We're going to get you out of here. Rest now, but be ready for anything."

"We?"

"Cole and me," Christina answered. She saw the change in Marcus's eyes — a twinkle, a glimmer of hope. His hope rekindled hers. Marcus obviously believed that Cole had a chance to free him. If he was willing to believe after all he'd suffered, she would believe in Cole, and in herself, one more time.

The door opened and Zachary stepped partially into the room. He shook his head disdainfully when he looked at Marcus and Christina. "Don't you two make just the loveliest couple? Come on, Christina, my dear father is getting impatient. There's a bath upstairs, all hot, soapy, and ready for you."

Anguish overtook Marcus's face. "No, no, Christina! You can't! You . . ." His voice cracked in despair.

Christina whispered to Marcus, "Be ready to run.

323

Don't worry about a thing."

Christina followed Zachary. Walking up the dark stairway leading to the main floor of the mansion, Christina put her hand lightly on Zachary's forearm. He stopped, twisting his upper body to give her a quizzical look.

"You should know that your father is planning to kill you," Christina said. She glanced to the door at the top of the stairs, as though afraid someone would hear her.

Zachary's mouth twisted in a scowl. "I know that."

Christina, her hand still lightly touching Zachary's arm, leaned closer to him. She looked up into his face. Zachary was wary, and it showed. Christina had no expression at all.

"I know that whatever happened to Marcus happened because Nicholas ordered it. If you were the one who beat him up, I know you were only following orders."

Zachary smiled, nodding his head. He liked Christina's version of the beating and interrogation. "Yeah. That's right. I was only following orders."

"I've been running for a long time, Zachary. I'm tired of running. When I was in St. Paul—first with Cole and then with you—I got used to having certain things. Other women have things—now it's my turn. I want everything. Beautiful dresses, jewelry . . ."

"And a man in your bed?"

Christina swallowed, fighting desperately to say the words that Zachary wanted to hear. "Yes," she said after several seconds. "I don't like sleeping alone anymore."

"Pa can give you dresses. And he may be an old man, but he is a man." Zachary's eyes traveled down to her bosom, then went back to her face. Her hints of intimacy made him suspicious, but the potential of being with her was a powerful inducement, making him weak against his better judgment.

"Of course Nicholas can give me nice clothes, and he can be a warm body beside me at night. But I need more than just a warm body beside me. He's an old man . . . and I don't want to have to start over with someone new

324

to get what I want, if you know what I mean."

After a moment, Zachary smiled. "Yes, I believe I do," he said. "But why the sudden change of heart? In St. Paul you didn't exactly warm up to me. And just a moment ago, if looks could kill, you'd have dropped me dead."

Christina huffed indignantly, as though Zachary couldn't understand the obvious. She hated the feel of her hand on his chest. "I'm tired of hitching my wagon to a horse that isn't going anywhere. Nicholas is rich, but he's old. You'll have all the money when he's gone. Even if I choose Nicholas, eventually the two of you are going to have it out. When that happens, I think you'll be the only one alive. Why waste my time with Nicholas when I know he's not going to be living much longer?"

Zachary touched Christina's face. For a second, she was afraid he was going to kiss her. "What about Cole? I thought you were all-fire in love with him?"

"Cole is my past. What concerns me now is the future. For the last month I've been sleeping on the ground and eating out of tin cans. You can offer me much more than that."

"You can forget him?"

Christina smiled softly and let her eyelashes flutter a bit. "I can . . . if I have someone else to help me."

Zachary pushed his fingers into Christina's hair. He was about to kiss her, but she pushed him away.

"We haven't got time now," Christina said quickly, glancing toward the door. "Soon, Zachary, we can both get what we want. I'll meet you in your bedroom later tonight." Christina headed up the stairs, not allowing Zachary time to taste the pleasure of her kisses. At the door she turned and said, "Later tonight . . . I'll come to you."

Chapter 31

Cole Jurrell knew what it was to exercise patience. On many occasions, it was patience that was key to making the successful robbery of a Webb payroll. But never had keeping his patience been so difficult for him as when Christina walked off toward Nicholas Webb's massive ranch house.

He was shrouded in almost total darkness. Crouching at the unfinished boulder wall, Cole squinted into the black night. The sentries, he noted, were not the same ones who had been on duty the last time he slipped into Nicholas's home. Cole could only wonder what Nicholas had done to punish the alcoholic fellow with the bushy moustache.

Both sentries on this side of the mansion appeared relaxed. Cole could hear them talking to each other and occasionally laughing. One time he heard Christina's name spoken, followed by low mumbling, then raucous laughter. Guessing that the sentries were making lewd comments about Christina set Cole's teeth on edge.

Cole felt cold inside, but warm on the surface of his skin. A thousand times he cursed himself for allowing Christina to try such a foolish plan. But as headstrong as she was, Cole's only real options were to help her or not help her. She would try to free Marcus with or without him. At least with his help, the chances for success were better.

He tried to stay crouched behind the three-foot wall as much as possible, or as much as curiosity allowed him. Every ten or fifteen seconds, he checked the windows on the west wall of the ranch house. All of them were dark, with the shades drawn.

I can't wait any longer, thought Cole. *I've got to get inside. At least then I might be able to protect Christina.*

It was then, just as Cole was about to vault over the boulder wall, that a shade was raised on the second floor, near the middle of the ranch house. A lamp inside the room made the window glow. A moment later, a candle appeared in the window. Cole unconsciously held his breath, peering just over the wall, staring at the candle, waiting . . . waiting to be sure.

The candle held steady for several seconds, then moved right and left. It stopped, repeated the action, then was extinguished.

She made it! So far, so good!

Cole had thirty minutes to wait. Knowing exactly how long he had to remain immobile, away from the action, was infinitely easier than having no end in sight. He bent his head down, hiding himself completely.

Thirty minutes. Just a half hour more and he would be with Christina.

Christina rubbed her long blond hair vigorously with the towel, removing as much water from the thick tresses as possible. Her pale skin had a pinkish hue from the hot water. Christina's usual good mood after bathing was not with her now, though, as she frowned at herself in the mirror.

Had Cole seen the signal? Would he make it past the first set of guards?

Forcibly pushing such doubts from her mind, Christina concentrated on the things she could influence. *I have seen Cole in action many times,* she thought with rising confidence, *and he has always proven himself superior to other men. He will make it through. Everything will go just as we planned.*

A soft knock at the door startled Christina. Her nerves were frayed at the edges, though she was still in control of herself. She couldn't allow herself to fall apart.

"Christina . . . are you finished, sweetheart?" Nicholas asked quietly through the door.

Christina wrapped a thick towel tightly around herself, padding barefooted to the door. "It's going to take me a little while," Christina replied.

"Christina . . ."

The hard edge to Nicholas's tone worried her. Christina's power over him was such a tenuous thing! Steeling her courage, she opened the door a little, stepping to her right so that Nicholas could look at her.

"Please, Nicholas, try to be patient," Christina said with a pleasant though false smile. "You want me to look my best, don't you?"

Nicholas's gaze swept boldly up and down over Christina. She stifled the contempt she felt rising in herself.

"You look pretty damn good right now."

Christina gave Nicholas a scolding look, then chuckled softly to dampen the effect. "My hair is still wet. It's not even brushed. Please, now . . . this is going to be an evening we're going to remember for the rest of our lives. We've got no reason to rush." She held the towel with her right hand, and with her left reached out to gently brush her fingertips against the silvery hair at Nicholas's temple. "Honestly . . . I'm worth the wait."

For a moment, she thought that Nicholas was actually going to salivate. His breathing became deep and rapid, and she saw his pupils dilate. He looked into her eyes for long, breathless seconds. Then his gaze, heated with a primitive lust, roamed over her body once again. Christina shivered with disgust, but managed to keep the smile plastered tautly over her mouth.

"You make me tremble when you look at me that way,"

Christina said teasingly. "You'd better leave now, or this evening is never going to get underway. Shoo, now. I'll be with you soon."

Christina closed the door on Nicholas and she leaned against it murmuring a prayer. For the time being, she had put him off. She knew she couldn't delay him forever.

In a hurry now, Christina pulled a brush through her hair, ignoring the tangles and the tugging against her scalp. She brushed her hair straight back, and the wet strands held tightly to her skull. She tied her hair in a queue with the small piece of ribbon she'd used before.

At the door, Christina stopped and looked around the bedroom again. She had used one towel to dry her body and one for her hair. On impulse, Christina crossed the room quickly and snatched up the remaining three unused towels.

Christina opened the door slowly and glanced into the hallway. To her left she saw light emanating from the stairway. Nicholas was waiting for her downstairs. To her right, the hallway was dark. When Christina stepped into the hallway, a shadow moved and again she let out a soft gasp of shock.

"Relax, it's just me," Zachary said. He stepped out of the shadows, walking with a swagger in his step. "I was thinking that maybe . . ." he grinned lewdly at Christina. "Before you and Pa . . . we might . . ."

"You thought wrong!" Christina hissed. She felt vulnerable with just the towel around her. "He's old, but not a fool. He would know. Do you want to get both of us killed? Get away from here before Nicholas catches you. You're going to ruin everything!"

Zachary moved closer. Christina backed up until she felt the wall against her naked shoulders. She couldn't give up any more ground to Zachary even if she wanted to.

"You're awful jumpy for a lady who seems to have decided I'm not such a bad fellow." Zachary stepped directly in front of Christina. She could only see one side of his face in the dim light. Though logic told her otherwise, she thought it was an ugly face. "You're not just teasing me now, are you, Christina? You wouldn't try something like that on me, would you?"

"I'm not teasing," Christina replied, but there wasn't much conviction in her tone. "I just don't want you to spoil it now."

Very softly, Zachary said, " 'Cause if you're teasing me, Christina, you'll be very sorry. Nobody makes fun of me. Certainly not a *woman*." He drawled the word out as though the gender was offensive in some way to him, or, at least, inferior. "I'll cut you up, Christina. I'll cut you real bad, but I won't kill you."

Christina looked at Zachary, and she knew that he was telling the truth. Forcing the words from her constricted throat, she said, "Go to your bedroom and wait for me. He's old. He'll be asleep before long."

Zachary made a look of disgust. "I don't accept seconds, not even with someone like you."

Christina did her best to smile flirtatiously. "The first one is an obligation. It's just to buy us time. The second one is for pleasure. Trust me, Zachary, I know how to make you happy. I'll be worth the wait."

"Cole teach you some tricks?"

For only a moment, Christina closed her eyes. This whole conversation was unbearably disgusting to her, and now Zachary had to defile her intimate memories of Cole.

"Yes," she said woodenly. "He taught me many things. He said I was a . . . a natural."

Zachary chuckled, turning away from Christina. "I'll be waiting," he said over his shoulder. He took several steps, stopped, then turned so he again faced Christina. With the light behind Zachary, all she could see was the outline of him. "If I wake up tomorrow morning and you haven't been in my bed . . ."

He never finished the sentence. He didn't need to. The threat was there, and Christina could not misunderstand

330

it.

Christina waited until Zachary disappeared down the hall before she stepped into the bedroom she was to use as her dressing room. Near the bed, a lamp was turned low, putting a glow over the bed, illuminating the dress that had been placed there for her. Christina could guess what character of woman it was designed for. Near the window was the candle she'd used to signal Cole.

Christina pulled the dress over her head and buttoned it as quickly as her nervous fingers allowed. Then she pulled the sheets and blankets from the bed and began tying the ends together. She also added the towels that she'd taken from the other room.

The makeshift rope did not seem long enough to reach to the ground from the second floor window. Frantically, Christina searched for something more to add to the rope. The time seemed to race by and Christina felt the rising panic that had never been far from the surface since she walked up to the sentry and surrendered to Nicholas Webb, the murderer of her father.

Christina abandoned the search. It would have to do. No more time could be spent on that particular problem when she had so many more to solve. What was she going to tie the rope to?

The only thing that looked sturdy enough to support Cole's weight was the four-poster bed, but that was not near the window. Christina guessed she was strong enough to move the bed, but with Nicholas and probably Zachary downstairs, one of them would surely hear the bedposts scraping against the floor and come to investigate. But if not the bed, what?

She made her decision and acted upon it quickly. There was no time to second-guess herself. Wrapping one end of the bedding-rope around her fist, she pushed against the window glass just below the wooden middle cross section. The glass cracked. She lifted one piece out of the frame, but another dropped and shattered on the floor. She raised the window frame a few inches, tied the rope around the bottom crosspiece, and pushed the knot to the side of the window, where the frame would be the strongest. She tossed the rest of the rope out the window and prayed that Cole would be able to reach it.

"Good luck, darling," she murmured.

Small fragments of broken glass were on the floor. Christina felt a splinter bury itself in her toe and she grimaced. She didn't dare take the time now to remove the glass.

Christina met Nicholas in the hallway on the way to her room. "I dropped the hand mirror. A bit nervous, I guess," Christina explained without being asked. She continued down the hallway, away from the room that Cole would soon be entering. "I'm sorry."

"I'll buy you a thousand mirrors—but none can capture your loveliness."

Nicholas looked at Christina. The dress had been purchased by Zachary as a gift to one of the sporting ladies he frequented. Why Zachary had never delivered the present, Nicholas didn't know and hadn't asked. But the dress reflected the intended wearer's occupation and Zachary's taste in women. With Christina wearing it, with its low décolletage straining against her full bosom, she looked provocative and slightly flashy. Whatever suspicions Nicholas had when he first heard the sound of glass breaking he forgot when he let his gaze linger on Christina.

"Are you all right?"

"I've got a sliver of glass in my foot, I think." Christina hobbled a bit for effect, keeping the weight on her heel. "Will you help me get it out?"

They went downstairs and into the dining area. Christina was surprised to see plates of cheese and various cold meats of sausage on engraved silver trays. She would have guessed that Nicholas had one of the servants do the work if the sliced cheeses and meats had been more neatly arranged. There was a bottle of wine, already opened, and two glasses.

"Very nice," Christina said, sitting down at the table in one of the twelve chairs. She made a vague wave of her hand toward the food and wine. "This is what I was hoping for."

"There's no reason we can't act civilized," Nicholas replied, pleased with himself. He got down on one knee in front of Christina. She put her naked foot in his hand. "Such small feet. I prize that in a woman. Japanese women bind their feet to keep them small." He held the foot caressingly, his left hand sliding up beneath the dress to glide lightly over Christina's calf.

"The glass," Christina said softly. "It feels like a small piece, in my toe."

Nicholas took his time, passing his fingertips very softly along the sole of her foot. Christina hated his touch, but she was willing to endure it without complaint. The longer Nicholas busied himself with such pursuits, the less time Christina had to defend herself against more serious offenses to her body, soul, and spirit.

Nicholas found the sliver of glass and carefully plucked it from Christina's foot.

"Thank you," Christina said. Nicholas bent to kiss her. Christina offered her cheek and was relieved when he accepted it.

"Better?"

"Yes. I know I should put some shoes on, but all I have are my boots."

"I'll buy you a dozen pairs of slippers," Nicholas said expansively as he took a chair next to Christina. "You'll be the most stylishly dressed woman in the territory." He poured wine, handing Christina a glass. "To you, my dear . . . the most beautiful woman ever to grace my home."

Christina looked straight into Nicholas's soulless eyes and said in a husky, sensual purr, "Our home, Nicholas. *Our* home."

They talked for twenty minutes. Nicholas didn't seem to indicate anything was at all strange in Christina being with him. It bothered Christina that even now Nicholas

333

had to pretend, at least to himself, that she was with him willingly. He could not accept that no woman who really knew him would ever willingly be with him.

"I think it's time, don't you?" Nicholas placed his hand over Christina's, curling his fingers into her palm.

Christina looked at Nicholas's hand covering her own. "Yes," she whispered. "It's time."

Hand in hand, they walked through the mansion in silence, going up the stairway and past Zachary's room to Nicholas's bedroom. He opened the door and stepped aside for Christina to enter first.

It was the bedroom of a man who saw himself as king. Everything—from the bed to the full-length mirror to the hand-carved bureau—was oversized and one of a kind. Christina looked around the room, stunned by the opulence. She hardly felt Nicholas squeezing her hand. She knew she should respond to him, but her willpower was not strong enough to overcome her revulsion.

"Do you like your new bedroom? Does it meet with your approval?" Nicholas boasted. He was certain there could be only one answer.

"It's beautiful."

Nicholas walked to the bed, still holding Christina's hand in his. He sat down at the edge of the mattress and for a moment just looked up at Christina. "Sit next to me," he whispered. "I've waited so long to have you here with me."

She could hear her pulse throbbing in her ears. This was it. Christina had played for as much time as she possibly could. Now she either had to make good her promises to Nicholas or suffer the consequences of lying to a self-appointed, deranged king.

"Before we start, there's something I have to do first," Christina whispered. Nicholas shot her a cold glare. Christina answered it with a warm smile. "Don't worry. I'm not going to run away. I haven't even got shoes on."

"Then why leave?"

Christina let her eyes dip down. "I want to be ready for

334

you. We don't want to stop part way, do we?" Nicholas looked challengingly at Christina. He had waited months for this moment. She added, "Nicholas . . . the wine. You understand, don't you?"

She wouldn't have believed Nicholas could blush unless she saw it herself. In his strange, self-serving code of honor, he was allowed to do most anything—lie, cheat, steal, murder, rape—but not inquire about a woman's toilet.

"I'll be right back." Christina bent quickly and kissed the top of Nicholas's head, once again avoiding having to put her lips against his. "Why don't you get in bed?" She gave Nicholas her most appealing smile and added, "I hate crawling between cold sheets."

Nicholas pulled loose the sash of his robe. Christina turned away from him, repulsed by the thought of what she might see. She heard him say, "Tomorrow I'll buy you some new dresses. The one you're wearing doesn't suit you. You're much too lovely for that one. Zachary bought it for one of his—"

"I would like that," Christina said. She opened the door and, with her back to Nicholas, whispered. "I'll be back in just a minute."

The moment the door was closed, Christina rushed down the hall to the bedroom where, if luck and the Fates were with her, Cole would be waiting. She stepped into the room and looked down the barrel of Cole's deadly .44.

"They believe me so far," Christina whispered. When Cole stepped up to her, Christina pulled his head down and kissed him quickly and firmly on the mouth. "Marcus is downstairs in the wine cellar. Do you know where it is?"

"Yes. Zachary and I used to hide down there whenever Nicholas was angry with us."

"You get Marcus. Then meet me at the front door in ten minutes."

"Why not come with me?"

335

Christina gave Cole a confident smile. "My work's not finished yet . . . we need a bit more time. Don't ask me to explain. Everything is under control." She kissed him furtively. "Be careful, darling. I love you."

Cole asked, "Do you know what you're doing?" Christina shook her head but smiled bravely. "Let's hope you haven't run out of luck yet."

Christina was almost out the door when Cole's hand squeezed her shoulder. She turned and was surprised when Cole pulled her into his tight embrace, his mouth slanting down to claim hers. He kissed her hard, forcing her body to mold against his own.

"I love you," Cole said, his lips still caressing Christina's even as he spoke. "I love you more than I ever thought possible. Please, please be careful."

Christina pushed herself gently out of Cole's grasp, blinking away a tear that somehow appeared from nowhere. "I will. I'm pretty tough, though, remember?"

"And brave. That's what scares me. The more I love you, the more afraid I am of losing you."

"You could never lose my love, Cole. Never." Christina raised up on her tiptoes to kiss Cole again. "Zachary and Nicholas are both in their bedrooms. The servants have been ordered to stay in their rooms. You shouldn't have any trouble."

Christina stepped into the hallway with Cole close behind her. She watched him move like a stalking cougar — all grace and stealth — down the hall and down the stairs without making a sound. *Everything will be all right,* she thought. *Cole loves me. That's going to make everything all right.*

Christina followed Cole downstairs, but went straight to Nicholas's study. Alone in the room, she had the eerie sensation of evil closing in around her, of being surrounded by something unconscionably wicked. It was here, she knew, that Nicholas planned his unholy deeds. Christina felt as though she had just stepped into hell, that she was trespassing in the devil's own lair.

336

She lit a lantern on Nicholas's desk, turning the wick up high. The desktop was cluttered with reports and personal notes scrawled on bits of paper. Christina studied each scrap of paper for a second before dropping them to the floor.

She had no facts to go on, only intuition. That intuition told Christina that Nicholas's notebook was the key to his undoing, his personal *bête noire*. From the time that Nicholas took Christina to Fargo and secretly manipulated her contract with the help of Richard O'Banion, he had told Christina to keep copious notes on everything she did, on the people she saw, and who she did business with. If Nicholas followed his own advice, then his notebook had to be in his sanctum sanctorum.

Christina's hands felt clammy with fear. She searched through the desk drawers, and though she found two different notebooks that had information in them, they were only facts and figures on cattle production.

She looked at the walls of the study and shivered. The cases were filled with books. What she was looking for—and she didn't know for sure, even, if she wasn't searching for an illusion created in her own troubled mind—could be any one of these several hundred books.

Think! she admonished herself. *Think faster!*

Christina forced herself to sit in the kingly, overstuffed leather chair behind the desk. She wheeled the chair around, sitting in the position Nicholas would usually assume at the desk.

If I was Nicholas, where would I hide my most important information? Where would I put something that I wouldn't want anyone to see—even my son? Zachary must know the combination to the safe, so he wouldn't put it there . . .

Her mind was blank. Christina tried to think like Nicholas, but nothing came to mind. She tried to think like Cole, and still ideas eluded her.

Christina sighed. She looked through the desk again. She had tried, but the odds had been too long. She pushed herself out of the chair slowly, rising to her feet.

But something was wrong. What, exactly, Christina couldn't say. She sat in Nicholas's chair once again and looked around the room. It looked just the same as it always had. When she stood up a second time, she was aware of what had drawn her attention. The feeling was so vague, she hadn't been able to identify it at first.

A smile creased Christina's mouth as she spun around and lifted the thick leather seat cushion of Nicholas's royal throne. There, with a well-worn leather cover, was the ledger. Nicholas left it under his chair, which only he was allowed to sit in.

Christina placed the notebook on the desk and opened it. The first entry she saw read: "June 2—Paid John $1,000 to overrule land deed to the Proctor property in the NW corner of territory."

She'd found it!

"I've got you now, you bastard!" Christina hissed under her breath. The foul language tasted good on her tongue when she thought of Nicholas, knowing that he was in bed waiting for her.

She reached over the desk to put out the lantern and, almost as an afterthought, picked it up by the base. She shook three stick matches from the crystal holder and stuck them in the corner of her mouth. Carrying the ledger and lantern, Christina left the study, and went to the top of the stairway. She set the lamp and ledger down and blew out the flame. She touched the glass shade lightly. It was too hot to touch. Licking her fingertips, Christina picked up the shade and set it down on the floor. Next, she unscrewed the filler cap for the kerosene.

Christina started with the rug at the stairway landing. She let the kerosene trickle out slowly. She did not have enough to waste. When the rug was damp, she worked her way down the steps. Each step had at least enough kerosene on it to dampen the wood. She took the last few drops out of the lamp, disappointed she hadn't made it to the main-floor landing.

After retrieving the ledger from the top of the stairs, Christina raced back to the bottom, took a match from her mouth, and scratched it against the wall. The match fizzled for a moment, then there was a soft *whoosh!* as the kerosene caught.

The flames spread quickly, moving up one step of the stairs at a time. Christina watched the flames as they reached the top landing. The woven wool rug, doused with kerosene, accepted the fire without delay. Three-foot flames leaped from the rug. Smoke began rolling up the walls and along the ceiling.

It had taken slightly more than a minute for the stairway to become completely engulfed in flames. Nicholas and Zachary were trapped upstairs. The servants, living on the main floor, would escape easily.

Christina heard a sound behind her. She wheeled about, afraid the flames had attracted a servant. It was Cole and Marcus. Cole had his left arm around Marcus's waist, helping to support his weight. In his right hand was the Colt.

"Thank God you made it!" Christina whispered excitedly, rushing over to them. She held the leather-bound ledger up. "I found it!"

Cole was smiling. Christina thought he had chosen the oddest time possible to find humor. He watched, a beaming, proud grin on his face and in his eyes, as the stairway railing accepted the flames.

"You thought of that?" he asked, nodding to the burning stairway.

"Yes."

"They're up there?" He was nearly shouting as the fire grew hotter and louder.

"Yes! Cole, we've got to go!"

Cole looked at Christina, shaking his head in amazement. "Nice work! Damn nice work!"

The railing was crackling with yellow flames. Where the wool rug had been, the flames now reached the ceiling. Zachary and Nicholas rushed into the hallway at the head of the stairs, moving to the edge of the railing to look down at Cole, Christina, and Marcus.

Nicholas's eyes locked on Christina with a hatred straight from hell. She stared back, unwavering and smiling slightly. Slowly, like an athlete raising a trophy, she lifted the ledger above her head. Recognition flashed across Nicholas's face.

"You bitch!" Nicholas shouted, pointing a finger at Christina. He instinctively started for the stairway, but the heat quickly forced him back.

In that single second, Nicholas turned all the hate in the world against Zachary and Christina. He realized then how Christina had manipulated him. And all he had to do was look at Zachary—dressed in a silk robe and laughing sheepishly—to know that his son had intended to sleep with Christina, too. And one look at Christina—her face flushed with triumph and holding his precious ledger—convinced Nicholas that she had played him for a fool again.

"Cole, we've got to get out of here now!" Christina shouted, grabbing him by the wrist, tugging him toward the front door of the mansion.

As Cole, Christina, and Marcus stepped into the cool darkness of the night, they could hear Nicholas screaming, "You bitch! I'll kill you for this! I'll kill all of you!"

Chapter 32

Nicholas stared at the flames that rose a hundred feet and more into the night sky. The mansion, completely enveloped by fire, was burning so hot that Nicholas had to back farther away from it.

But it was not his home burning that most bothered Nicholas. His home was the castle of his kingdom. He had apparently lost that . . . but if he didn't stop Cole and Christina from getting to Fargo with his ledger, he would lose his kingdom, too, and probably his life.

He watched as men hurried about, searching for water buckets. *Bunglers and fools,* Nicholas thought. Zachary, still in his silk housecoat, was shouting orders for the men to form a bucket brigade.

"Zachary, come here!" Nicholas shouted. He had to repeat the order several more times before he finally got his son's attention.

"Yeah?"

"Forget the house—"

"What?" Zachary exclaimed. He looked at his father as if Nicholas had lost his mind.

"It's not important right now. We have bigger problems." Zachary made a move to turn away. Nicholas grabbed him by the arm, squeezing hard. "Don't argue with me, boy. This isn't the time. We have to stop them."

While the flames grew hotter and licked higher into the sky, Nicholas explained, as quickly as possible, what information he had kept in the ledger. Zachary didn't have to be told what would happen to the Webb fortune if such information got into the hands of an honest official of the territorial court.

Zachary hissed an obscentiy. "Why? Why did you write everything down?"

"If they get to Fargo, and that book gets in the wrong hands, we'll both hang," Nicholas shouted. "Get the men—all of them, and send somebody after the sheriff and deputy— and tell them it's shoot on sight. Put ten thousand dollars on Cole and Christina. Ten thousand a piece. And add another ten thousand for the return of that ledger."

"You're an old fool!"

"Probably, but it doesn't matter now. It only matters that Christina had that ledger with her when she left with Cole and Kensington. And Zachary, believe me when I say that you're a dead man if that ledger gets into the wrong hands. I wrote down everything . . . including how you killed Cole's father, and Christina's."

If he'd had a gun with him, Zachary would have shot his father then and there. But he didn't; instead, he just felt his father's fear take root deep inside him.

The men were gathered quickly, and with the promise of ten thousand dollars to the man who killed Cole or Christina, any reservations against murder were quickly forgotten. Zachary borrowed clothes from the men for himself and for Nicholas while the horses were saddled and weapons prepared.

Thirty-four men, led by Zachary and Nicholas, rode away from the burning mansion.

Though Black Jack had no problem carrying Marcus's additional weight, Cole took it slow and easy. Three of

Marcus's ribs were broken. Being jostled on a horse could easily put one of those broken ribs through a lung. From there, as badly beaten as Marcus was, death could not be far behind.

"Just a little bit farther," Cole said. Against his shoulder, he felt Marcus nod his head weakly. "You're a trooper, Marcus. You are one hell of a man, and all I can tell you is that I wish I'd known you better before this."

Christina reined Daisy in, getting the mare in step with Black Jack. "How is he?" Christina asked Cole.

"Still conscious, but just barely. He needs bed rest, laudanum for the pain, and food."

To Marcus, Christina said, "Hang on. Just hang on. It'll be over soon." She bit her lip, cursing herself silently for her bad choice of words. The look she received from Cole would have been humorous had the situation not been so grave.

At Angelina's, Cole jumped off Black Jack, then helped Marcus to the ground. Christina tied the horses and moved so that she could put Marcus's free arm over her shoulders. The door to the small home opened on creaky hinges and a young woman with Mexican features stepped out.

"Bring him in. Put him in my bed," the woman said calmly.

They nearly had to drag Marcus to the small bed. He drifted in and out of consciousness. The ride from Nicholas Webb's burning mansion had sapped the last of his strength.

Angelina held the door open. "He's Mr. Kensington, isn't he?"

"Yes," Christina answered. She straightened and for the first time took a good look at Angelina. Cole hadn't told her much of the woman who had saved his life. Christina wondered what Cole had said about her to Angelina. "Will you help him?"

Christina received a cross look from Angelina for her

question. Angelina said nothing. When she looked at Cole, who was busy unbuttoning Marcus's torn shirt, Christina saw undisguised admiration in Angelina's eyes.

"I'll heat water and get the bandages," Angelina said to Cole. "What else will I need?"

"He's got some busted ribs. Other than that, it seems to be just bruises. He's been badly beaten, but he'd already be dead if there was anything more serious." Christina wondered who Cole spoke to. Cole opened the shirt. The bruised chest area brought a soft gasp from Angelina. "Zachary's work," he explained.

"Once again," Angelina replied softly.

Christina saw the two of them exchange another look. Though she fought against the feeling, Christina felt anguish at the fact that someone else—a very attractive young woman—shared special memories with Cole. Even if they were painful memories, they were memories that did not include her. And though Cole had said he and Angelina were not lovers and never had been, jealousy was not far from the surface of Christina's emotions.

Angelina and Cole worked together as a well-rehearsed team. They bandaged Marcus's ribs. They bathed his face and wrapped his ankle, which Christina now saw was thick and swollen. As they nursed the semi-conscious man, Christina saw how well Cole and Angelina worked together. They did not have to say what they expected of each other. Such needs remained unspoken but were always fulfilled. Christina felt excluded, but felt guilty for her emotions. She wanted to be the woman who knew Cole better than any other, and until this time, she had believed that she was. Especially after Cole's vow of love in Nicholas's mansion. But in this time of crisis, it was Angelina who was at his side.

Stop being so insecure! thought Christina, berating herself for resenting Cole's emotional closeness to Angelina. *It's you he loves, not Angelina. You've no right to resent Angelina just because she met Cole first. Remem-*

ber, if it wasn't for her, Cole wouldn't be alive today. He'd have died before you ever had the chance to meet him.

Without even being aware of what she was doing, Christina took the heirloom locket in her hand and rubbed its surface with her thumb. It was the locket, stolen by Bobby, that had allowed Christina to meet Cole.

Christina sat at the kitchen table and watched Cole and Angelina finish doctoring Marcus's wounds. When Marcus was stretched out on the small bed, Christina looked around the small house. There was only the one bed in the one-room home. She wondered where Angelina would sleep now that Marcus was in her bed . . . and where Angelina had slept while she had nursed Cole back to health.

"He'll sleep now," Angelina said quietly, looking down at Marcus. "It will take time, but he will get better. I am sure of it."

Cole looked down at Angelina and smiled, and Christina felt pangs of an emotion she tried to pretend did not exist in her heart. Cole and Angelina moved over to the area of the house where Christina sat.

"I'm going to take a look around," Cole said. His eyes met with Christina's. Sensing she needed reassurance, he bent down, touched her chin with his fingers to raise her face, and kissed her lightly on the lips. "I'll be back in a couple of minutes. That should give you and Angelina time to find out whether you're going to be friends or enemies."

"Cole!" Christina shrieked, shocked that he'd put to words what had been in her mind, and probably, she guessed, in Angelina's, too.

Cole's deep, throaty chuckle left with him as he made a quick exit out of the small house. Alone with Angelina, Christina felt guilty for the bad thoughts that had been haunting her.

"I think I owe you an apology," Christina said. Her

345

gaze met Angelina's briefly. It did not help Christina's jealousy that Angelina was a very attractive woman.

"You don't owe me an apology. Your reactions are quite natural. They are what is to be expected from a woman in love." Angelina sat at the table across from Christina. Their eyes made contact again. "If there must be apologies, then I should give mine, too."

Christina frowned, cocking her head slightly to one side. Christina wasn't certain she wanted to know what the lovely young woman with raven hair and doe eyes had done wrong.

Angelina cleared her throat, then told her story of how she had been the one to explain to Cole that Christina was in St. Paul with Zachary Webb. Angelina left nothing out. She told the unvarnished truth, right down to how she had tried desperately to convince Cole that the best thing he could do for himself was to completely forget about Christina.

When she was finished, Angelina leaned back in her chair. Christina got the feeling she was being sized up. Angelina loved Cole, and she was concerned that Christina would hurt him.

"I love him," Christina said softly. She smiled, and felt herself blush. "I've never confessed that to anyone but Cole."

"And he loves you."

"He's the only man I've ever loved."

"Then you are a lucky woman, Christina. Perhaps if we had met differently, Cole and I, we, too, could have been lovers. But it was not to be. We became friends instead. That is enough for me."

Christina looked straight into Angelina's eyes as she said, "You love him, too, don't you?"

Angelina nodded. She pushed a thick strand of ebony hair behind her ear. "Yes. I love him, but not as you love him. Cole and I love each other, but we are like family to each other. We are . . . you've got to understand, I am of

346

mixed blood. Most people in this territory will not associate with anyone of Mexican blood."

Christina replied, "That doesn't matter to Cole. He doesn't think that way."

Christina found herself warming to Angelina as the conversation continued. The young woman had shown the courage to tell her the truth, and Christina respected that. Also, Angelina had Cole's safety and happiness in mind. Though it worried Christina that there was a history between the man she loved and Angelina, she also believed that Angelina only wanted what was best for Cole.

"The kiss . . . just before Cole went outside . . that was to reassure you that you're the one he loves," Angelina said in a soft voice. "He understands women."

Christina laughed lightly and said, "Not all the time."

"He loves you very much. You are a lucky woman."

"Yes," Christina replied. Secure that she did not have to worry about Angelina trying to steal Cole's heart, the topic of her love for Cole became uncomfortable. "You live so far from Enderton by yourself? How do you manage?"

"I find it easier living alone. There is no one here to insult me. The land doesn't care that I am the daughter of a white woman and a Mexican man. The land only cares that I show it respect. It needs only the rain and the sun and me." Angelina looked over at Marcus, who breathed slowly, shallowly. "He will live," she said, not looking at Christina. "I will nurse him back to health."

"Then you will have saved the life of the two men in this world that I love. I owe you a lot. I don't know how I can ever repay you."

"You can repay me by taking good care of Cole. He needs someone to look after him." Angelina rose rorm her chair. "Would you like some brandy? It's Napoleon. A gift from Cole."

"I'm afraid we haven't got time. Cole and I need to get

347

to Fargo."

"I understand," Angelina replied.

Does she? wondered Christina. She did not know how much information she could give Angelina about the ledger. It seemed that Cole trusted her, but hadn't Cole also said that no one, under any circumstances, should be trusted? Christina wondered if she was just being petty and jealous.

Angelina sat down in the chair again. When she looked at Christina, she made a little smile. "Perhaps you would like a different dress? You can have one of mine, if you want."

Christina blushed furiously. With everything else that had been happening, she had forgotten about the lurid dress she had on.

"I'm afraid I haven't made a very good first impression with you," Christina said, stumbling for words, not knowing what to say, or what Angelina must be thinking. "This isn't my dress. It was—"

"You don't have to explain. From what Cole had told me about you, I could guess that the dress was not yours." Angelina patted the back of Christina's hand. "If the dress really was yours, I doubt that Cole would have fallen in love with you. When he was with me the last time, and I tried to convince him to forget about you, I saw the depth of his love. I knew then that you were not a common woman. Cole is not a man who makes many mistakes. Certainly not when the heart is concerned. He protects his heart."

"I hope that someday . . . when all of this is over and our lives can be at peace, you and I can become good friends," Christina said. Her voice was so soft Angelina could barely hear it. "I need friends. I never did have many, and now I've lost the ones I had."

"I, too, can use a friend. It gets lonely out here alone. But I won't be alone now. At least not for a while. Having Mr. Kensington here will give me a reason for being. Like I had before, with Cole."

"What happened to Cole? I've seen the scars, and he's told me that you saved his life. But he hasn't told me what really happened."

Christina followed Angelina to a corner of the home, where Angelina's gray dress hung from a peg. She glanced at Marcus. He was still sleeping. While Christina stripped out of the provocative dress and into the gray one, Angelina began her story.

"Cole had suspicions that it was Zachary who had killed Mr. Jurrell. Cole was very close to his father. But he made a mistake. He challenged Zachary with what he believed. There was a fight, I guess. I don't know all the facts. As Cole was riding away, Zachary shot him with a shotgun. In the back. The slugs did not go in deep, but there were so many of them. Zachary left him for dead. I found Cole and brought him home and bandaged the wounds." Angelina looked away. Dreadful memories of that fateful night made her shiver. "The bullets had to be cut out of his back."

"You did that?"

Angelina nodded. "I wanted to get a doctor, but that was too dangerous. If anyone knew that Cole was with me, Mr. Webb and his men would have come and taken him away. One by one I took the slugs out with Cole's own knife. I thought he would die, but he didn't. Cole is strong. His soul is powerful. He wanted to live, so he did."

Images flashed in Christina's mind of what Angelina must have gone through. Seeing, in her mind's eye, Cole wounded and helpless made Christina realize the full extent of her love for him.

"You're a very brave woman, Angelina. You risked your life to save a man you didn't even know."

Angelina looked at Christina's toes peeking out beneath the hem of the dress. "I have winter boots. Maybe they will fit."

Angelina wanted to change the subject, but Christina persisted. "And while Cole was getting better, you got to know him? That's when you became friends?"

"Yes. Every day I expected the men to come here, to take Cole away from me, but they never did. People don't come near a Mexican woman in the Dakota Territory unless they have to. They want nothing to do with us."

"You saved Cole's life. That's the truth of it." Christina placed her hands lightly on Angelina's shoulders. "I hope that someday you will find the love that I have found. I want you to be happy, and I want you to always consider me your friend. It is . . . an honor for me to have met you."

They looked at each other. Each woman loved Cole in her own way, neither threatened by the other's love for him. Christina knew now why Cole had such a deep respect for Angelina. She was strong and independent. But did he see the lonely woman behind that strength and independence? Did he understand that Angelina hungered for the kind of love that she had found with Cole?

Christina hugged Angelina softly, the two young women rocking slowly from side to side. They had shared their lives with Cole, and now they could share their friendship with each other.

When Cole stepped into the house, he saw Angelina and Christina hugging. He cleared his throat and the women parted, Angelina quickly wiping away crystal tears from her long, dark lashes.

"Am I missing something?" Cole asked, the side of his mouth pulling up in a half-smile.

"That," Christina said, looking sternly at Cole, "is none of your business." She wasn't going to tolerate Cole making fun of her and Angelina.

Cole went to the kitchen table and placed a thick stack of money down.

"I don't need that. You don't have to pay me to help Mr. Kensington," Angelina said quickly, embarrassed and hurt.

"It's not payment," Cole replied. "I tried to hide our tracks coming here, but I can't be sure Webb's men haven't followed it. If they come, tell them I forced you to take care of Marcus. Tell them I threatened you, I said that if Marcus died, you would die. Tell them I gave you the money." Cole tapped the stack of bills. "I've put you in danger again, Angelina. This money is to protect you. If you give it to Webb or his men, maybe that'll save you. It's an alibi, not a payment."

Angelina took the money, tucking it behind a sack of flour on her counter. "When you come back, it will be here."

The winter boots were a little too big for Christina, but they were infinitely better than going barefooted. She and Angelina kissed cheeks, then she rode east to Fargo with Cole, as the sun was just coming up in the eastern sky.

Chapter 33

It had been years since Nicholas had pushed himself so hard. Sweat dribbled down his neck and into the coarse work shirt he had borrowed from one of his men. He untied the red bandanna and wiped his neck, then dried his forehead. He didn't have a hat and the sun was beating down on him, baking his brain inside his skull. His head throbbed brutally.

"We must have passed them by now," Nicholas said to Zachary. "We passed them somewhere. They couldn't have ridden this hard with Kensington beaten up like that."

"Maybe," Zachary said, riding loose in the saddle. Younger and stronger than his father, he wasn't nearly so fatigued. "Maybe not. You're certain they're going to Fargo?"

"Yes. They've got the ledger. The only power around that would dare challenge me is at the district court-house."

"I thought you bought the judges."

"I bought some of the judges. I didn't buy all of them."

Nicholas looked at his son, wondering whether Zachary was playing dumb or if he really had no understanding of the things that needed to be done — and the people who had to be paid off — in order to attain wealth and then keep it. It seemed that each day heightened Nicholas's

352

contempt for his son.

"If you're sure they're headed for Fargo, then we've got to keep going." When Christina and Cole were dead, it would be time for Nicholas to die. Zachary figured he had allowed his father to live too long already. That ledger, the one that was supposed to contain so much damaging information on the things that he and Nicholas had done, was a sign of his father's loss of control. Zachary would never have been so foolish as to chronicle his own dirty deeds.

They rode on weary horses toward Fargo, thirty-six men armed to the teeth, hungry and tired, thirsting for blood and money.

"They're ahead of us."

Christina looked over at Cole and frowned. "You're sure?"

He nodded. "Look at the tracks. Too many horses there for it to be anything but Nicholas and his men. Who else would be riding this range? Twenty-five or thirty men, I'd guess. Riding hard. No cattle, either. This is cattle country, Christina. Any time you've got that many men together, there had better be cattle around or you've got yourself an army." He shook his head sadly. "Nothing good can come of this."

Christina unconsciously glanced to Cole's saddlebag. Inside was the ledger. "Can I look at it again? Maybe I'll find something new."

Cole opened the saddle bag and handed her the private ledger. As Daisy walked on, Christina turned the pages.

"Some of these entries are more than ten years old," Christina said, talking as much to herself as to Cole. "I can't believe how many people he's given money to."

"Believe it. That's how business works. Even my father did it." Cole grinned at Christina when she gave him a stunned look. "We needed a variance to reroute water in

353

Griswold County. The mayor of Griswold was a greedy little man. He had the power to stop us, even though it wouldn't have hurt anyone or anything. Some money changed hands—under the table, of course—and we got what we needed."

"Of course," Christina said softly, clearly disappointed.

"It's just the way things are sometimes done, Christina. I didn't make the rules, and neither did my father. We just learned to play by them better than most people, that's all. Nothing we ever did hurt anybody. That's the difference between us and the Webbs."

Christina looked at Cole's profile, wondering how much she really knew about this man. He openly admitted to bribing officials to get what he wanted. He even approved of such practices. What else did he approve of?

"It seems like a lot of self-justification," Christina said under her breath. She closed the ledger, twisting on Daisy to look directly at Cole. "If you are so sure that Nicholas and his men are ahead of us, why are we still going to Fargo? Why not go somewhere else?"

Cole smiled at Christina, giving her the grin he used whenever he treated her like a naive child who could not see the world around her for what it really was. Christina hated the look.

"Until now, we were a nuisance to Nicholas. Stealing the payrolls and that sort of thing hurt him financially, but it was never enough to cripple him, never enough to put an end to him. That ledger—which, incidentally, we never would have gotten if you weren't so damn clever—is the key to Nicholas's demise. With that, everything he's stolen, everybody he's killed or had killed, is going to come back to haunt him. This time he's got the possibility of losing everything. That means that he's going to throw all he's got at us. We lost our advantage dropping Marcus off with Angelina. That's how Nicholas got ahead of us."

"And so . . . ?" Christina knew, but she liked to hear Cole's explanations. She liked being treated like his

354

partner.

"The longer it takes us to get to the territorial governor in Fargo or to a judge, the less likely our chances are of making it. Right now, Nicholas is disorganized. He's on the run, just like we are. But soon he'll be able to marshal his forces. He'll have all his money, all his power, all his men out to stop us."

Christina felt cold fear in the pit of her stomach. The fight against Nicholas had been thrilling to Christina so far. She had never once had to fire the pistol at anyone, and so far, no one had tried to shoot her.

"You make it sound so . . . final."

Cole chuckled softly. It was a hollow, deathly sound, like something that should come from a killer, not from the man she loved.

"It *is* final, Christina." Cole had a look in his eyes that was different from anything Christina had seen before. "This time, we've gone too far. Now Nicholas has to kill us. If he doesn't, he's finished and he knows it. There's no turning back for us, or for him. Now he's got to kill us, or die trying."

Christina realized then how she had, like Cole, gotten caught up in the excitement of living outside the law. Living outside civilized society was glamorous and never dull as long as she never got hurt or hurt anyone else. But the excitement of her life as an outlaw was based on Cole's ability to keep them out of any real danger. Christina was suddenly and ominously aware of her own mortality.

She looked over at Cole and saw that he still had that strange, undefinable expression on his face. She knew now why she had never seen him look this way before. He, too, was coming to terms with what they had done, and what dangers were ahead of them.

"There's no turning back," Christina heard herself say. "My God, Cole, this time we really *have* gone too far."

Cole looked into Christina's eyes. He smiled and nod-

355

ded his head . . . and Christina wondered if he was looking forward with pleasure to the final, bloody confrontation that awaited them in Fargo, or if he was just relieved that soon his days as a fugitive would be over with . . . one way or another.

"This looks familiar," Cole said, peering around the corner of the redbrick building at the majestic, territorial courthouse across the street.

"Why?" Christina was standing behind Cole, looking under his arm at the courthouse. The last time she had been to the courthouse, she was escorted by Nicholas, who had said he was just helping her arrange all the legal matters to ensure the smooth transfer of ownership of the dry goods from her father's name to her own.

"When I went back to St. Paul for you," Cole explained quietly, "I broke into the apartments across the street. Zachary had his men in the street, just like they are now." He nodded his head toward two scruffy-looking men leaning against the courthouse. "Those two ride with the Webbs."

Christina looked at the men. They looked like all the other cowboys, their hats, stained with sweat and dirt, pulled low over their eyes, their clothes faded. Each man had his arms crossed over his chest. They watched the people walking by with hawkish eyes.

"How can you tell?"

"I can smell 'em," Cole said. He stepped back, hiding himself behind the surveyor's office again. "After a while, it's something you just sense. I can't explain it any better than that."

"Can we get in?" Christina followed Cole back down the alleyway to where Daisy and Black Jack stood. "The men who work for Webb are killers. I know that much. But they wouldn't kill us in plain sight, would they? Not even Nicholas Webb has that much power."

356

"You think those men are worried about a murder trial? Don't bet your life on it. Webb's got enough lawyers to tie any trial up for months. His men know that. By the time it finally got to court — if it ever did — whoever killed us would be long gone. And he'd have enough money in his saddlebag to live comfortably for the rest of his life." Cole pulled a long-barreled revolver from the boot of Black Jack's saddle. "Either that, or Webb would have whoever killed us killed before it came to trial."

"How can you be so sure?"

"Because if I was in Nicholas's boots, that's what I'd do."

"I wish you wouldn't talk that way. It makes you sound like . . ."

Cole checked the revolver's cylinders. He did not respond to Christina's comment. He knew what kind of man he sounded like.

This is what I've finally come to, thought Cole. *I think like Nicholas. I've become like the man I hate. Maybe, with Christina's love, I'll become a decent man when all this is over.*

"Here," he said, handing the weapon to Christina. "Keep it hidden in your arms as much as possible." When Christina took the gun, Cole touched her chin lightly, forcing her to look up into his eyes. "This time you'd better be prepared to use that. We haven't got the element of surprise working for us. He knows what we've got to do." Cole stroked Christina's cheek with the back of his hand. "I can do this alone, you know. Maybe you should step away from this one."

"No. We've got to do this together. We need each other."

Cole knew better than to argue with Christina. He didn't even try to convince her to stay out of this final battle with Nicholas Webb.

"Let's go," he said. "You know what to do."

They circled the courthouse with a casual gait, Cole

keeping well ahead of Christina. Nicholas's men were looking for a man and woman together. There were men along all four sides of the courthouse. Cole counted nine of them and he knew there were many more combing the streets of Fargo. When the gunplay started, as he was certain it would, those men would come running with guns drawn.

As he looked out the corner of his eye at a pair of sentries Webb had posted, Cole wondered how big the bounty on his head was. Five thousand dollars? Seven thousand? Maybe even ten? He found a perverse fascination in the price on his head, valuing himself by his worth as a corpse. He found he understood the power of money over these men and took no offense. He also hoped he would not make anyone a rich man today.

Cole stopped, turning his back to the courthouse. He looked into a bakery and studied the reflection of hired gunmen in the baker's window. It was time. He tugged on his right earlobe, giving the signal, then turned and headed for the courthouse, every nerve in his body tingling with excitement, his reflexes taut and ready for action.

Christina held the revolver against her stomach, holding tightly onto the handle with her finger curled around the trigger. She kept the weapon hidden with Nicholas's ledger. She walked quickly, but not so fast as to draw attention to herself. Rounding the corner, she walked parallel to the courthouse. There were two gunmen ahead of her, but their eyes were trained on the street, not the sidewalk.

The bark of a handgun made Christina jump. First one shot, then two more following so rapidly the explosions almost came out as one. Christina could not tell how many guns were firing. She knew that Cole could fire a gun very fast and with extreme accuracy — but was he good enough to go against such terrible odds, against so many guns?

Calm. Stay calm, she heard Cole say in her mind.

"The other door!" the gunman ahead of Christina shouted to his colleague.

The men ran past Christina without giving her notice. She silently thanked Angelina again for the nondescript dress. Christina squeezed the handle of the Colt tighter. She continued walking, moving away from the gunfight around the corner of the courthouse. All around her, men and women were running to protect themselves. A small group of teenage boys, spurred on by curiosity, ran toward the gunshots. Christina wanted to stop the youngsters, to keep them away from danger, but they were too fast and too determined.

She went up the marble steps of the courthouse. On the main floor, men were running toward the side entrance. It was from that direction that more gunshots rang out. And, if Christina's guess was correct, Cole would soon be rushing through the entranceway.

Christina couldn't keep her feet from running. Cole had told her to remain calm, but Christina could not be calm. All around her, men were scurrying about, some of them rushing for the protection of their offices, others trying to see exactly what was happening.

Christina turned left and headed for the stairway leading to the second floor. That's where the judge's chambers were, she remembered. The territorial governor's office was on the third floor. Behind and below her, she heard the sharp reports of weapons being fired.

Please, Cole, don't die!

Christina noticed several men running down the stairway on the opposite side of the courthouse. Their guns were drawn, and they wore range clothes. Christina knew they were Webb's men. *There are so many of them!* she thought. The odds appeared even worse than Cole had guessed they'd be.

Christina was almost to the second floor landing when, out of an office on the far side of the courthouse, she saw

Zachary step out into the walkway. She ducked, hiding behind the thick marble railing, as Zachary headed in the direction of the gunfire . . . and in the direction of Cole.

Another gun against Cole. He'll never make it. Please. God, don't let him die.

Shots rang out, echoing through the courthouse. It seemed as though there were dozens of guns all going off at the same time. Christina watched Zachary disappear through the side door. She started down the hallway in search of the judge's chambers. Christina had hardly taken a step before Zachary reappeared. He kicked the heavy side door shut and leaned against the wall, holding tightly on to his pistol. The distance that separated Christina from Zachary was not enough to mask the unbound fear that gripped Cole's childhood friend.

Cole is alive! Christina thought joyously, looking down at Zachary. She remained crouched behind the marble railing. *Only Cole could make Zachary that frightened.*

Christina watched, looking between the thick pedestals of the railing, as Sheriff Bellows pushed open the door. He staggered into the foyer of the building. As he turned toward Zachary his revolver fell from bloody fingers, thumping against the floor. Bellows appeared to say something, but Christina was too far away to hear what words—if any—were spoken. Sheriff Bellows fell facedown on the floor and did not move.

"Come on, you bastard! Let's get it over with now!" It was Cole's voice. Christina looked but could not see him. He was still outside, but near the doorway. "Let's do this like men, face to face!"

Zachary scrambled farther away from the door. Christina watched as he checked the ammunition in the cylinder of his handgun. He had apparently seen Cole the moment he stepped outside. That's why he had returned to the courthouse foyer in such a hurry, with fear plainly etched across his face.

Zachary moved into position where he could see Cole

as soon as he entered. He was set for an ambush.

Christina stuck her head above the marble railing and shouted, "Look out, Cole! It's a trick!"

There was a moment, less than a second, where Zachary's head snapped about on his shoulders and he looked up at Christina. Their eyes met, and Christina saw that Zachary was a frightened animal, reduced to his basest instincts, willing to kill anything and everyone to save his own life. He fired at Christina. His bullet took a chip out of the marble railing, then richocheted with a whining sound.

"Christina, are you okay?"

"I'm fine! Zachary's trying to ambush you!" In the brief lull in gunfire, Christina's voice echoed through the large antechamber.

Zachary sent another shot at Christina. This time the bullet would have hit Christina had it not been for the railing. Christina pressed her cheek against the marble, her eyes squeezed tightly shut. Fear—raw, blinding, heart-stopping fear—exploded in her breast. She was being shot at!

Snap out of it, Christina! her mind screamed. *Fight back! Don't give up now! Cole needs your help!*

Christina raised her weapon above the railing and sent a bullet in Zachary's direction. Though she didn't come very close to hitting him, she sent him diving for cover.

Zachary turned over a table, sending the carved marble bust of some political canon toppling to the floor where it shattered to bits.

"Christina! Christina!" Cole shouted, still outside the courthouse. She could hear the panic in his voice.

"I'm okay, Cole. We've got him between us!" Christina felt bolder now that she had fired at Zachary. Her concern was for Cole.

"Cole, come on in," Zachary shouted.

Christina could tell that Zachary was frightened. There was a high-pitched whine to his voice. It was shrill,

361

almost falsetto. The vengeful side of her still remembered with savage clarity the torturous days and nights that she had been forced to be near Zachary, to watch and listen to his immoral conduct with the equally abhorrent Mrs. Loretta Pembrook and took delight in seeing his cowardice coming to the fore.

Christina sent another shot at Zachary who was hunched behind the overturned table when Cole bolted into the room. His lightning reflexes sent a bullet into the table, nearly hitting Zachary.

"You're a dead man, Cole! You'll never get out of here alive! I've got men everywhere!"

Cole emitted a sharp, cruel laugh. "You've got men outside, Zachary. And not nearly as many as you started with. It's safer for them to stay outside. Did you really think they would die for you? You don't inspire that kind of loyalty."

Between the heavy, protective pedestals, Christina smiled at Cole and she raised the ledger just high enough for him to see it. The book was ripped from her hands when Zachary's bullet punched through the worn leather covers.

"Stay down, Christina!" Cole shouted, staying hidden behind a marble pillar that supported the second-floor balcony.

"She can't move, Cole! Give it up or I swear I'll kill her!"

Christina crawled over to the ledger. After retrieving it she returned to the safety of the marble railing and inspected it. She saw the hole was neat and round, where the bullet had entered, about the diameter of her finger, but where it had exited, was a jagged, huge hole. The mental image of what that bullet would have done to her had she been hit made her quiver.

"Just stay where you are," Cole said to Christina. "Don't move. He can't hurt you unless you move."

Along the row of offices on the second floor, near

362

Christina, a handful of people were peering out of doorways, keeping themselves protected yet curious enough to see what was happening below them. She let her revolver be visible to several men and they slipped back into their offices, closing the doors behind them.

When Cole spoke again, his voice was low and even, the sound carrying through the silent, tomblike courthouse foyer. "The whole world is going to be rushing in here soon, Zachary. What'll it be? You want to talk with the law or me? Christina got your father's records and you are mentioned by name. What's it going to be, Zachary? I'll turn my back again, if that's what you need. Shooting people in the back is your style, isn't it?"

"Shut up, damn you! My men will be here in thirty seconds! They're going to fill you with lead, Cole! They're going to fill you full of lead!"

"You killed my father! Gunned him down in the back! That's what a yellow belly like you does, Zachary! How does it feel to know in your soul that you're a coward? What's that make you feel like inside?" Cole glanced quickly around the pillar. He saw the top of Zachary's hat above the heavy tabletop. Even if he hit what he could see, the bullet wouldn't strike Zachary. Time was running out. He had to make a final move very soon. "What about it? A Mexican stand-off? Once and for all? Just you and me, face to face, one last time?"

Two of Webb's gunmen burst into the foyer, kicking the door open, rushing in with guns ready. Both men died without firing a shot. Christina was stunned at Cole's awesome, deadly skills.

Cole heard men moving restlessly around outside the courthouse. The two corpses on the floor verified that Zachary and Nicholas had upped the ante on his head, for only the possibility of great wealth would make the men commit such a dangerous and foolhardy act. In a way, Cole almost pitied the men.

There was more movement outside the courthouse.

Cole had no way of knowing if the men were more hired guns, or courthouse employees, or the local militia coming to put an end to the gunplay once and for all. Whoever they were, Cole doubted he'd have the chance to give his side of the story before a dozen guns opened up on him. He'd left enough corpses outside to make men think twice about rushing into the courthouse, enough dead men behind to make others shoot first and ask questions later.

Cole felt perspiration trickle down his spine. If Christina didn't make it to the judge's chambers with that ledger, everything he had been fighting for would be lost. Everything . . . including Christina. Cole had to make his move, whether Zachary was willing to act manly or not.

"I'm stepping out now, Zachary. Can you do the same? Can you draw on a man who's looking you in the eye?" Cole kept the pace of his words slow and taunting so Zachary could feel the effect of them and so that the people in the surrounding office could hear him. Perhaps he could shame Zachary into a draw. It was a long shot, but Cole, with time trickling through his fingers, was running out of options.

"It's time to see if you can measure up as a man, Zachary," Cole continued, stepping away from the pillar. "Can you? Have you got a backbone, Zachary?"

Cole stepped away from the pillar, holding the gun at his side. Christina saw for the first time the long red stain of blood that started just below Cole's left arm and went down his shirt to the waistband of his slacks.

Cole's hurt! So much blood!

"Don't, Cole! You're hurt!" Christina cried out without thinking, half rising from her hiding spot. She ducked a moment before Zachary's bullet cut through the air where her head had been. Her heart was hammering, the blood pulsing in her temples.

"I'm coming out, Cole. You want a fair draw, and that's what you'll get!" Zachary shouted, speaking much louder than he had before.

Christina cursed herself. She'd let Zachary know that Cole was hurt. If she'd only kept her mouth shut, maybe this wouldn't be happening. Part of her wanted to pray and part of her wanted to shoot Zachary. And Christina knew in her heart of hearts that if she had been certain she could hit Zachary, she *would* gun him down without a word of warning. He deserved no better.

The two men, who years earlier had been friends, who had grown up together and then grown apart, faced each other one final time. Each man stood with his gun at his side, his holster empty. Christina, above them and at a right angle, saw how Cole's shirt stuck wetly to his side.

"You're hurt," Zachary said, his voice just loud enough to carry to Cole and Christina but not into the closed offices where the frightened masses huddled in horror. He did not want the audience to hear what he had to say to Cole. "Is that going to slow you down? It's not going to kill you, is it? Seems a hell of a shame if you'd die by some stranger's bullet. No, Cole, you should die by a good friend's bullet. Mine, for instance."

Cole looked into Zachary's eyes. He wondered if the pain shooting through his senses showed in his eyes. He himself did not know how bad the wound was. There was blood. A lot of it.

"Huh?" Zachary taunted. "You still want to draw?"

"It might slow me a little, Zachary, but not so much that I can't beat you." Cole looked straight into Zachary's dark, angry, confident eyes. It was the eyes, he knew, where a man makes his first move. Watching the hands can fool a man, but the eyes never lie. Cole slowly placed his gun in the well-oiled holster strapped to his right hip. "Shall we do this properly?"

Zachary's smile was an ugly, twisted thing. Like a cat that plays with a mouse before he kills it, he was enjoying his advantage over Cole.

Quietly, out of the corner of his mouth, Zachary said

to Christina, "Thanks for the help. I've always been just about a half a step behind Cole." He kept his voice down. He didn't want anyone but Christina to hear what he had to say. "All my life it's been that way. With women. With guns. In school. Cole's always been a hop ahead of me. But not this time." Zachary's lips pulled back to show his teeth. It might have been a smile or a grimace. "You're a dead man, Cole, " he said, then went for his gun.

Chapter 34

The two explosions sounded as one. Cole went down, his left leg jerked from beneath him as though by a powerful, unseen hand. Zachary's body was tossed straight backward, arms and legs outstretched, the gun flying from his hand. He landed on his back, his eyes still open, staring at the ornately painted ceiling of the Fargo courthouse with eyes that could no longer see.

Christina ran down the marble stairway, taking three steps at a time, her feet suddenly feeling awkward inside the ill-fitting boots.

"Cole! Cole!" she shouted.

She tried to take Cole into her arms, but he pushed her away. A bullet had ripped into Cole's thigh and blood flowed freely from the wound. It spilled out, puddling on the floor, starkly red against the smooth, polished surface.

"The judge," Cole said through gritted teeth, trying to get to his feet. He squeezed the wound, but blood flooded through the fingers of his left had. "The ledger. You've got to see the judge."

So much blood! He'll bleed to death if I don't stop the bleeding! Christina thought frantically.

A gunshot exploded and Cole was again tossed across the floor. He rolled onto his stomach and fired a shot a heartbeat later. Deputy Silas Miller spun as he fell. He tried to fire one last time at Cole, but his life was slipping out of his body.

"Hurry, Christina," Cole gasped, trying with failing strength to push her away. On the floor beside him, sticky with his own blood, was Nicholas's ledger. Cole kicked it toward her. "Take it and go, damn it!"

"I won't leave you."

Christina's face was ghastly white, her eyes frightened and startlingly blue, beloved eyes Cole wondered if he'd ever gaze into again. The pain in his side had lessened to a steady burning sensation and his leg no longer hurt. Cole knew what that meant. First the pain stops, then the heart. Christina was pulling at him, trying to get him to his feet. Cole looked down, wondering where Miller's bullet had hit him. He was surprised to feel blood trickling from his calf, for he never even felt the bullet hit him.

"Help me, Cole!" Christina shouted. She pushed her head under Cole's right arm and with all her might picked him up. She staggered to the side, carrying nearly all his weight. When she looked at him, he had a faintly satisfied look on his face, which panicked Christina. He was, it seemed, accepting his fate, accepting his death. "You've got to help me, Cole, or we'll both die!"

Cole shook his head, not in negation of what Christina had said but to clear his vision. Cole had lived on the edge of sudden and violent death long enough to accept the end as inevitable. He could accept death calmly and bravely. His death . . . not Christina's.

He tried to put weight on his left leg. Pain raced up his body and exploded in his brain. With the pain came full consciousness.

"Help me," Cole hissed, his teeth clamped shut. A shadow appeared at the doorway. Cole pointed his weapon and fired without looking. He thumbed back the

368

hammer again, and this time when he squeezed the trigger, all he heard was the dull click of the firing pin striking against an empty chamber.

"Upstairs, Cole," Christina whispered, dragging Cole to the stairway. "We can't give up now!"

"The gun . . . I need your gun." Christina had left it on the floor.

"Come on, Cole. Help me!"

"The ledger."

"I've got it! Damn it, Cole, help me!"

Each step was a tortuous excursion into a world of pain that Cole had never known before. Not even when he had felt Angelina cutting the shotgun slugs out of his back had he known such insane, redhot pain. In a way Cole welcomed the pain, for it kept him away from the warm, comfortable delirium that was a half-step away from death.

They took the steps slowly, Cole forcing his body to respond to the tortured urgings of his brain, Christina taking as much of his weight as she could. Twice she begged for courthouse employees to help her. Doors were shut quickly. The courthouse square was littered with the bodies of people who had gotten too close to Cole and Christina.

When they made the second-floor landing, Christina heard an elderly man say. "Lord in heaven, isn't that Nicholas Webb's boy down there? He killed Zachary Webb!" The door was slammed shut as Christina and Cole went past it.

"The end of the hall," Christina said, pulling along. She felt the blood from his side wound moistening her fingers. Unless something was done very soon to stop the bleeding, not even Cole's great will would keep him alive.

They took each step together down the hall. It was the longest walk of their lives, one foot forced in front of the other, again and again, until at last they stood in front of the door with gold lettering on it that read: JUDGE J. T. KAMISKY.

Christina had both arms around Cole to support him, squeezing the ledger against his side wound in hopes of stopping the flow of blood. Cole turned the knob and together they fell into the office.

Judge John Thomas Kamisky sat behind his desk in his flowing black robe. What hair he had left on his head, a slender strip of curly white, circled from ear to ear. His nose was slender, hooked, and had veins close to the surface of the skin from habitual alcohol abuse. His eyes, as dark as his hair was light, were very round and oddly unsurprised at the sight of Cole and Christina entering his office.

Christina dropped the ledger and helped Cole push himself against the wall as he slumped to the floor. "Squeeze as tightly as you can," she instructed, taking Cole's hands and placing them over the wounds on his thigh.

She picked up the ledger, rose unsteadily to her feet, and said, "This is for you."

But it was not the judge who replied to Christina. "I believe that's mine. Thank you for returning it to me, Christina," Nicholas Webb, standing in a corner of the office, said softly. He stepped forward to take the ledger. Before he could take it from Christina, Judge Kamisky pulled it from her grasp.

Nicholas smiled benevolently at Christina, then looked at Judge Kamisky and nodded his head, indicating everything had worked out exactly as he had said it would.

"You . . . dear God . . . it can't be you . . . here." As though in a daze, Christina stepped backward until she was near Cole. She sat on the floor beside him.

Though Nicholas wore the cheap clothes of a cowboy, the look in his eyes and on his face—vicious, confident, deadly — was the same as it always had been.

"Christina, I'd like to introduce you to an old friend of mine, Judge J. T. Kamisky. I've know John for twenty years. You might say that I've contributed generously to his election campaigns," Nicholas said softly.

He looked down at Cole. One side of his mouth pulled up in a smile that didn't quite become full. "Did you kill Zachary? If so, you've saved me the trouble. Almost worth having you for a pest these past two years. My son was much more dangerous to me than you could ever hope to be."

Cole turned his eyes that were glassy with pain and loss of blood to Judge Kamisky. "He . . . bought you." The judge said nothing.

Nicholas held the ledger gingerly in his hands, avoiding the blood that was on the leather cover, and said, "I don't like to look at it that way, Cole. I don't buy people, I just ensure their continued friendship and support by helping them when they're in a time of financial need." Nicholas nodded his head toward Judge Kamisky. "I believe that John here is the right man for the territorial judge. He's a man who knows how business should be done." Nicholas smiled again. "John might even be territorial governor someday."

Christina pressed her hand against Cole's side wound. The bullet apparently had followed his ribs, making a long and bloody tear in his skin without damaging internal organs.

"You're the John in the ledger," Christina said in a voice tinged with contempt and confusion. "I saw the heading. He's given you hundreds over the years."

"Not hundreds, Christina, *thousands!*" Nicholas interrupted. He began to pace the office. "That's how I know that John is going to find your hero here guilty of murder." He kicked Cole's leg. "It would almost be a crime if he didn't hang, wouldn't it, John? Bleeding to death is too good for Cole after all the trouble he's

371

caused me these past two years."

Nicholas, feeling victory close at hand, was talkative, jubilant. He had thought his own defeat was almost assured after Christina had stolen the ledger. Now he had Cole and Christina with him, and the ledger. He felt invincible. He would win again.

"You gave up so much, Christina," Nicholas continued, moving over to lean against the judge's desk. "You could have had me—money, power, and luxuries galore. But instead you had to choose him." Nicholas looked at Cole and shook his head sadly. "Looking at you now, I can't understand why I didn't catch you earlier. There's nothing special about you. Nothing at all."

From the hallway a male voice called out, "Judge Kamisky, you all right in there?"

"Better close the door," Kamisky said to Nicholas quietly. When the door to the office was closed, Kamisky shouted, "I've got everything under control in here. Just stay away until I tell you otherwise. Understand?" There was a pause. "Understand?"

"Yes, sir," the voice said.

Kamisky opened the ledger and said quietly, "These matters are best handled in private, I believe. Don't you agree, Mr. Webb?"

Nicholas smiled. "Precisely."

"What do you intend to do with the girl?"

Nicholas let his eyes caress Christina. He chuckled softly. "I'm not sure yet. Prison doesn't really seem the place for her. All that lovely flesh going to waste. But I don't trust her. And looking the way she does, she's hardly someone I would invite to the bedroom. Of course, I've seen her looking like this before. A bath would do her a world of good."

"I'd rather rot in prison than let you touch me," Christina spat.

The insult drew a short laugh from Nicholas. "What

about it, Christina? Can't we start up again where we left off? We've got . . . unfinished business. I always like to finish what I start. That's why I've always gotten whatever I wanted." He jerked a thumb over his shoulder at Judge Kamisky. "Unless you'd like to find out what my friend here can sentence you with." Nicholas bent over at the waist to put his face closer to Christina's. His eyes were dark, menacing, glittering triumphantly. "And *I* can do *whatever* I want with you, too."

Judge Kamisky found his page in Nicholas's ledger. Each entry was dated, and across from the date was the amount he'd received from Nicholas Webb. There were several entries that included brief notes on men who Judge Kamisky had freed on Nicholas's behalf, other entries on those he had sent to prison. Judge Kamisky opened a drawer of his desk. He pulled a small revolver out, pointed it at Nicholas's back, and thumbed back the hammer.

"Move away from the desk, Mr. Webb," Judge Kamisky said quietly.

Nicholas looked over his shoulder. He saw the gun, frowned, then smiled and moved away. "I hadn't really planned on you finishing Cole off this way, but I do appreciate it, John."

Nicholas took another step to the side, moving so that he was no longer between Judge Kamisky and Cole. The muzzle of the revolver was still pointed at his stomach. Realization dawned on his face.

"John, have you forgotten who your friends are? I've been more than generous to you for the past twenty years and I've never asked for much in return." The confidence was slipping from Nicholas's eyes. He looked from the gun to Judge Kamisky's face, then back to the gun. "Damn it, John, this isn't funny at all."

Cole, with his head resting against the wall, squeezed his leg with what little strength he had left. The bleeding had slowed down. Cole wondered if the blood was clotting or if he was simply running out of blood. There was barely enough strength for him to move his head. He opened and closed his eyes several times before they focused clearly. He smiled at what he saw.

"So there is no honor among thieves," Cole whispered. "I always suspected as much."

"Shut up, Cole, or I'll strangle you right goddam now!" Nicholas snapped. An artery throbbed visibly in his neck. He turned to Judge Kamisky, his hands outstretched, almost pleading. "Come on, John, let's be reasonable. What's going on here? I don't understand. Why? Just tell me what you want and it's yours. Haven't I always been generous with you? Haven't I always been a good friend? You want to be territorial governor? Fine! The job's yours."

Nicholas took a step toward Judge Kamisky. The gun was raised until it was pointed squarely between Nicholas's eyes.

"I'll kill you," Judge Kamisky said softly. "I swear to God, I'll kill you if you open your mouth one more time."

Judge Kamisky, continuing to hold the revolver on Nicholas, ripped the page of personal entries from the ledger and crumpled it. He took a stick match, scratched it against the top of his desk, then lit a corner of the paper. It didn't take long for the single sheet of paper to burn to ashes on the judge's desktop.

"What the hell are you doing, John? If it's a matter of money, all you have to do is ask. You know that. We're friends, aren't we?" Nicholas licked his lips nervously. His lips moved as though he wanted to speak.

"Friends? Dear God, Nicholas, I've cursed the day I ever met you. Money? Sure, you were always right there when I needed money. But when it started out, I thought it was just a contribution. I didn't realize you were actually buying me until it was too late. I'd already sold my soul, so I figured I'd sell it for as much as I could." Judge Kamisky looked like he could spit on Nicholas at that moment. "I should have taken your stinking money and thrown it right back in your face!" The judge looked at Cole, then at Christina, then back again at Cole. There was an expression of intense sadness in his eyes. "Cole, I don't know if you're going to live or not, but just in case you do, I want to make you a proposition. Can you hear me, son?"

Cole nodded his head.

"The deal is this: if I put Nicholas in prison for the rest of his life, then quit the bench, will you forget about me? I know all about you. I don't want to live the rest of my life waiting for you to step out of a shadow. If you give me your word—"

"What are you talking about?" Nicholas cut in. He couldn't believe the words he was hearing. "Damn it, John, I put you on the bench! If it wasn't for me, you'd just be another two bit country lawyer. You'd be nothing at all! I bought you the judgeship. I paid for you!"

Judge Kamisky's lips curled in a foul sneer. "You sicken me," he said to Nicholas. "Yes, I took your money, but it was a mistake. A terrible mistake. I used to be an honest man, then I met you and made my pact with the devil. Funny thing about being a judge—seems a person comes to respect and love the law the more he understands it." With his left hand, Judge Kamisky crushed the ashes on his desk. "This is all the evidence you had on me, isn't it? I've been sitting on the bench long enough to know when a man's hiding something from me, when a man's lying to me."

"You've lost your mind," Nicholas whispered. There wasn't anger in Nicholas's tone. It was shock. He could not believe that his victory would be lost by betrayal.

"More like I've finally found where my guts are,

Webb. Now you stand there and stay quiet, or so help me God I'll gun you clean through." Judge Kamisky looked at Cole again. He shook his head slowly. "It's a damn miracle you're not dead already. Never seen anybody lose that much blood and still be alive. Just the same, I want your word on it, son. I'll put this scoundrel in jail for the rest of his life, then I retire. In return, you forget my name was ever in this here book." He tapped the bloody ledger on his desk.

"It's a deal. I give you my word." Cole whispered hoarsely.

Cole looked up into Christina's eyes. "We've done it. I love you. I want you to be—"

"Shhh! Cole, save your strength. Don't say anything now." To Judge Kamisky she said, "Get a doctor in here *now!*"

Cole coughed, then smiled. "Judge . . . when was the last time you officiated a marriage?"

Chapter 35

"What are you thinking about?" Christina asked, snuggling in beneath Cole's arm. "Work?"

"A little," Cole replied, his eyes just slightly open.

"More like a lot." Christina scratched her husband's chest lightly with her fingernails, studying his profile. "Come on, we're on our honeymoon. You're not to think about anything or anyone but me." Christina purred. "I've become terribly selfish since we got married, haven't I?"

Cole gave a half-smile to the ceiling. "I really was only thinking a little bit about work. Mostly, I was thinking about Angelina and Marcus. Think they'll find anything in common?"

Christina was pleased. She didn't want to have Cole's attention diverted with work, but she liked having him thinking about the happiness of others. "Cole Jurrell, are you telling me you're secretly a matchmaker?"

Cole sighed exaggeratedly, glancing briefly at Christina. "That's not what I'm saying, and that's not what I'm doing. I was just wondering, you know, since they've spent so much time together lately, if they'll . . . well . . . you know."

Christina raised her knee, sliding her smooth thigh over Cole's muscular one. It was always lovely for her to wake up at her husband's side, with the bed and their bodies all warm and cozy. She kissed his chest, moving just a little closer.

"Is that why you asked them to stay at the house while we're on our honeymoon?" Christina was grinning now, seeing the plan beyond Cole's actions. "It is, isn't it?"

"That's not true," Cole said, matching his wife's grin. "It doesn't even come close to being true. I needed someone to oversee the operation of the ranch, and Marcus has plenty of experience in such matters. And since Marcus is still pretty beat up, I thought it would be good if Angelina stayed with him at the ranch. It's a big house—nine bedrooms, remember? There's plenty of room for them to be away from each other. They won't be crowded."

"And plenty of bedrooms for them to spend time alone together," Christina amended.

They were silent for a moment. Christina had not thought it possible to love Cole more than she had on that day a week earlier when she became Mrs. Jurrell, but she loved him even more now. The more Christina thought about Angelina and Marcus, the more plausible it seemed. Marcus was still, in many ways, a vigorous young man. He had been desperately lonely since the death of his wife. And Angelina, living out in the country away from Enderton and the small minds of many of its inhabitants, had also been lonely. Together, perhaps, Marcus and Angelina could chase away their private demons and find the happiness that had eluded them.

"You beautiful matchmaker, you," Christina whispered. She wriggled up on the bed high enough to give Cole a quick, happy kiss on the cheek. "I never thought you had such a soft spot."

"I'm not a matchmaker, and I don't have a soft spot."

"Oh?"

"No. I simply thought it would be in my best interests if I had Marcus managing my—*our*—business interests and the ranch while we're away. And he still does need Angelina to look after him."

"Of course," Christina injected, trying not to smile too broadly.

"That's right. And if Angelina and Marcus should, in the two months or so that we'll be away, discover that the ranch can either be a big and lonely place if they stay far apart from each other or a cozy and warm home where they can find love if they're together, that's not my fault and none of my doing. You can't hold me responsible for what they do. They're both adults."

Christina purred softly, placing her cheek against Cole's naked chest. His fingertips were tracing circles on her shoulder, and the touch was sending tingles through her.

"I've never been to New York City," Christina whispered. "What's it like?"

"Big. Crowded. Noisy. Exciting. It's a thousand different things. I like New York for a little while, then I've got to escape from it. There are no open spaces. You can't see a thing because the buildings are all built so high."

"What if I don't like it?"

"Then we'll keep right on going. There's still Boston, and Niagara Falls."

"You're going to spoil me," Christina said, her breath soft and warm against Cole's chest.

"Didn't I say that was what I was going to do?" Cole turned his head just enough to lightly plant a kiss on Christina's head. He inhaled, smelling the freshness of the young woman next to him. Her hair against his naked chest was a disquieting, silken caress. "It's a husband's inalienable right to spoil his wife. Especially on the honeymoon. Seriously, it's a law. It's in the Constitution somewhere. Usually overlooked—"

"Too often overlooked," Christina cut in. "But not by my husband." She shifted on the bed, pressing closer to Cole on the spacious hotel bed. "So you're really determined to spoil me?"

"Absolutely."

Christina rolled so that she could look down into Cole's eyes. Her hair tickled his face and she blew the offending strands away, then grinned at him. "And not just during our honeymoon?"

"Always," Cole said, his eyes alive with amusement. With a tone of absolute sincerity, he said, "I, Cole Jurrell, do solemnly swear to love, honor, cherish, and spoil silly, my lovely bride, Christina Jurrell, from this day forth to the ends of our life. And maybe even beyond that, though I can't really promise about the hereafter."

"In that case, Mr. Jurrell," Christina whispered, kissing the tip of Cole's nose, then his cheek, then his mouth. "Please allow Mrs. Jurrell to spoil you once in a while, too."

Cole chuckled softly, his arms tightening around Christina's middle. He felt the plush, firm weight of her breasts against his chest, the warmth of her body against his.

"Mrs. Jurrell, I will always be in love with you," Cole whispered, then trembled as Christina kissed him firmly on the mouth, shifting her body against his. "Always, Christina . . . always!"

TURN TO CATHERINE CREEL—THE REAL THING—FOR THE FINEST IN HEART-SOARING ROMANCE!

CAPTIVE FLAME   (2401, $3.95)

Meghan Kearney was grateful to American Devlin Montague for rescuing her from the gang of Bahamian cutthroats. But soon the handsome yet arrogant island planter insisted she serve his baser needs—and Meghan wondered if she'd merely traded one kind of imprisonment for another!

TEXAS SPITFIRE   (2225, $3.95)

If fiery Dallas Brown failed to marry overbearing Ross Kincaid, she would lose her family inheritance. But though Dallas saw Kincaid as a low-down, shifty opportunist, the strong-willed beauty could not deny that he made her pulse race with an inexplicable flaming desire!

SCOUNDREL'S BRIDE   (2062, $3.95)

Though filled with disgust for the seamen overrunning her island home, innocent Hillary Reynolds was overwhelmed by the tanned, masculine physique of dashing Ryan Gallagher. Until, in a moment of wild abandon, she offered herself like a purring tiger to his passionate, insistent caress!

SURRENDER TO THE
PASSION OF RENÉ J. GARROD!

WILD CONQUEST   (2132, $3.75)
Lovely Rausey Bauer never expected her first trip to the big
city to include being kidnapped by a handsome stranger
claiming to be her husband. But one look at her abductor
and Rausey's heart began to beat faster. And soon she found
herself desiring nothing more than to feel the touch of his
lips on her own.

ECSTASY'S BRIDE   (2082, $3.75)
Irate Elizabeth Dickerson wasn't about to let Seth Branting
wriggle out of his promise to marry her. Though she despised the handsome Wyoming rancher, Elizabeth would
not go home to St. Louis without teaching Seth a lesson
about toying with a young lady's affections—a lesson in love
he would never forget!

AND DON'T MISS OUT ON THIS OTHER
HEARTFIRE SIZZLERS FROM ZEBRA BOOKS!

LOVING CHALLENGE   (2243, $3.75)
by Carol King
When the notorious Captain Dominic Warbrooke burst into
Laurette's Harker's eighteenth birthday ball, the accom-
plished beauty challenged the arrogant scoundrel to a duel.
But when the captain named her innocence as his stakes,
Laurette was terrified she'd not only lose the fight, but her
heart as well!

*Available wherever paperbacks are sold, or order direct from the
Publisher. Send cover price plus 50¢ per copy for mailing and handling to Zebra Books, Dept. 2638, 475 Park Avenue South, New
York, N.Y. 10016. Residents of New York, New Jersey and Penn-
sylvania must include sales tax. DO NOT SEND CASH.*

ROMANCE REIGNS
WITH ZEBRA BOOKS!

SILVER ROSE   (2275, $3.95)
by Penelope Neri

Fleeing her lecherous boss, Silver Dupres disguised herself as a boy
and joined an expedition to chart the wild Colorado River. But
with one glance at Jesse Wilder, the explorers' rugged, towering
scout, Silver knew she'd have to abandon her protective masquer-
ade or else be consumed by her raging unfulfilled desire!

STARLIT ECSTASY   (2134, $3.95)
by Phoebe Conn

Cold-hearted heiress Alicia Caldwell swore that Rafael Ramirez,
San Francisco's most successful attorney, would never win her
money . . . or her love. But before she could refuse him, she was
shamelessly clasped against Rafael's muscular chest and hungrily
matching his relentless ardor!

LOVING LIES   (2034, $3.95)
by Penelope Neri

When she agreed to wed Joel McCaleb, Seraphina wanted nothing
more than to gain her best friend's inheritance. But then she saw
the virile stranger . . . and the green-eyed beauty knew she'd never
be able to escape the rapture of his kiss and the sweet agony of his
caress.

EMERALD FIRE   (1963, $3.95)
by Phoebe Conn

When his brother died for loving gorgeous Bianca Antonelli, Evan
Sinclair swore to find the killer by seducing the tempress who lured
him to his death. But once the blond witch willingly surrendered all
he sought, Evan's lust for revenge gave way to the desire for unre-
strained rapture.

SEA JEWEL   (1888, $3.95)
by Penelope Neri

Hot-tempered Alaric had long planned the humiliation of Freya,
the daughter of the most hated foe. He'd make the wench from
across the ocean his lowly bedchamber slave—but he never suspected she would become the mistress of his heart, his treasured
SEA JEWEL.